CONTENTS

INTRODUCTION

For years, Willa Cather and her work have been obscured by a cloud of misconceptions and oversimplifications. Often regarded as essentially uncomplicated, Cather's narratives are both sophisticated and intricate, comparable in many ways to the work of Faulkner (who occasionally appropriated both her insights and her literary strategies). Her novels and short stories are filled with subtle allusions, double meanings, sly (even bawdy) humor, dry irony, and sometimes bitter social satire. The structure of these narratives, always designed with great care and more complex than they appear, is often tantalizingly enigmatic. Cather subverted certainty and renounced reliable resolutions in her major works, eliminating the comfortable closures that had become conventional; thus her readers are often frustrated when they attempt to evaluate fictional characters or to assess the problems they have been invited to consider. Art best imitates life, Willa Cather seems to argue, when it refuses to provide perfect, happy endings or confident conclusions.

To some extent, the misperception of Cather as a simple, readily accessible author has been reinforced by popular notions of her personality and life. Because she wrote four important novels that were set in Nebraska, Cather has become intrinsically associated with that state; many readers have assumed that she was born on the Great Prairies, even that she spent most of her life there, and they have integrated her personality into a composed, positive stereotype of sturdy Midwestern farm life in America. Moreover, the usual photographs do little to dispel this stereotype: they show a substantial, reliable-looking woman who might be a favorite high school teacher or someone's "Aunt Willa." Little wonder, then, that generations of readers have missed the genius of her work and the complexity of her life.

Surprisingly, Cather's life began not in Nebraska, nor even the Midwest, but in the little village of Back Creek, just a few miles northwest of Winchester, Virginia, a city that had suffered unusual hardship and pain throughout the Civil War. While it is true that by the time Willa Cather was born (on December 7, 1873), the Civil War had been over for almost ten years, bitter memories of this conflict were still very much alive. There had been three major "Battles of Winchester"; the town had changed hands more than *seventy* times during the war; when the strife was finally over, more than two hundred buildings in Winchester had been destroyed, and most of them were not restored even by the 1890s. Most humiliating of all, this proud Virginia town was forced to submit to an occupation government of Union soldiers until the spring of 1870. Thus the region that Cather would have called "home" did not forget the Civil War for many, many decades; and because Willa Cather was born so soon after the Union government had been withdrawn, the atmosphere of her childhood was indelibly colored by the aftermath of war.

Resentment against Union sympathizers was tenacious. Those who had refused to fight for the Confederacy were held in contempt; and if their choice seemed the result of cowardice, violence might erupt. Thus the emotional turbulence of conflict lingered; sometimes, it festered; occasionally, it became brutal. The deep valley of Back Creek, hard by the West Virginia border, may have been even more bitter and more resistant to reconciliation than its cosmopolitan neighbour, Winchester. Stripped bare by the war, thinly settled afterwards, and profoundly impoverished, it was certainly a more violent place than Winchester: for if there were prosperous, well-educated gentleman-farmers like Willa's grandfather, William Cather, in Back Creek, there were also unlettered, hard-drinking hill families whose notions of "negotiation" and "justice" could be executed in surprisingly primitive ways. For example, memoirs of this little region report murders with an easy, informal, matter-of-fact tone: murder was just one of the things that happened in Back Creek—as unremarkable as hunting squirrels or trapping rabbits.

The Cathers had a hired girl named Margie Anderson, a simple, uneducated woman who had come from a hill family on nearby Timber Ridge. Whenever Margie went home to see her mother, she would take Willa along, and Mrs. Anderson would tell stories to the little girl. Mary Ann Anderson knew the contorted history of the hills—tales of families with their complex, often turbulent relationships, and tales of The War—and she told them in the soft cadences of western Virginia. Her daughter, Margie, continued with the Charles Cather family as a much valued hired girl, and she even went with them when they moved to Nebraska; Willa Cather had a lifelong love for Margie, and she continued to treasure the tales of Margie's mother; in 1896 (a grown-up young woman of twenty-two), Willa Cather visited Mrs. Anderson yet one more time to hear her engrossing tales of "real people." Years later, a famous author, Willa Cather would trace the roots of her storytelling to this humble beginning. Addressing a conference at the Bread Loaf School of English in 1922, she told her students that she had learned to tell stories from an illiterate Virginia hill woman: a woman who understood the life of the mountains and who remembered the folk phrases that no one had recorded or even *could* write down—a woman who knew all the local family secrets and used a regional language that was the product of many generations.

Today, even with a state highway cutting through, Timber Ridge and Back Creek are filled with nature's enchantment; during Willa Cather's childhood, they must have seemed a rustic paradise. But if they seemed an attractive paradise, they could be a dangerous one as well. Not all of Mary Ann Anderson's stories were happy or serene.

Cather's educated and refined parents seem somewhat out of place in postwar Back Creek. Although their home, Willow Shade, was a farmhouse and not a plantation, nonetheless it was an extraordinarily elegant farmhouse—brick in a valley of clapboard houses, spacious and graceful and finished with tasteful architectural details. Everything about Willow Shade bespoke money and success, and just the possession of such a house might make a man the object of his neighbors' envy. Willa Cather's parents, Charles and Virginia Cather, were fourth-generation Virginians, members of a highly revered "aristocracy." Moreover, before the Civil War, ancestors from both sides had served in the Virginia Legislature.

Together, they even represented both Virginian attitudes toward the recent Civil War, and these separate loyalties persisted throughout their lives: mother, Virginia Boak Cather, had come from a distinguished Confederate family; father, Charles Cather, belonged to a family whose members were outspoken Union sympathizers. "Blue against gray" continued in the Cather household even after the war, and spirited debates formed an intrinsic part of Willa Cather's girlhood. Even the family's move to Nebraska was to some extent influenced by the post–Civil War currents of hostility and conflict.

Willa Cather's grandfather, William Cather, and his sons George and Charles had played what seemed to their neighbors a dubious—if not despicable—role during the years of battle. Charles Cather and his older brother George had slipped across the nearby border to West Virginia, removing themselves from the Confederacy to escape conscription into the Secessionist army. Nothing but draft dodgers, so a great many of their neighbors thought. During the conflict, William Cather was rumored to be a Union spy; after the war he held an exceptional number of profitable offices under the Government of the Occupation, thereby reaping sizable gains from a sympathetic Union army. At a time when his neighbors had worthless Confederate bills, he was earning good hard Union cash. Small wonder, then, that many thought him little more than a "profiteer."

In 1873, Willa's Uncle George moved out to Nebraska—the first of the family to go. Perhaps he was distressed by the family's awkward position in the postwar world of Virginia; however, the principal attraction for George Cather was money. Nebraska, along with other sparsely populated Western states, had mounted a campaign to lure settlers: it promised cheap land, fertile soil, and quick prosperity to those who would come and settle with their family. Once in Nebraska, George and his new wife wrote glowing letters back to Virginia, urging the rest of the Cathers to follow. They emphasized the prospect of quick money, to be sure. However, they cited another advantage, and one particularly appealing to Willa's grandparents, William and Caroline Cather—Nebraska's unusually crisp, dry, "healthy" air. William and Caroline had lost all of their sons except Charles and George to consumption; and they had two adult daughters at home who were sick with the same disease. They visited George and his wife in 1873; and in 1875 they joined them, leaving Charles and his family to work the sheep farm at Willow Shade.

Charles and Virginia Cather were reluctant to make the move that had taken the rest of the family to Nebraska: Virginia's widowed mother lived within easy walking distance; Charles enjoyed the life of a sheep farmer; and unlike William Cather's family, their own family had no consumption and thus no compelling reason to leave the Back Creek valley. And all were deeply attached to the graceful beauty of Willow Shade.

However, the valley folk had long memories. Many saw the beauty of Willow Shade as a galling, daily reminder of "draft dodgers" and "war profiteers." Finally, in a characteristically emphatic way, they expressed their desire to rid themselves of Willow Shade's owners: they set the home's immense barn on fire, and it burned to the ground in a colossal conflagration. The message was emphatic and clear. William Cather, at least, grasped it immediately. As soon as he got the news, he wrote from Nebraska observing that Charles had better leave Back Creek before the *house* caught fire too; and he urgently insisted that they join their kin in the Midwest. So it was that in February of 1883 Charles sold Willow Shade, auctioned off the farm equipment, and took his wife and children to Nebraska. They joined Willa's grandparents and Uncle George in a brand-new town that had been named with characteristic modesty: Catherton, Nebraska.

Willa Cather was nine years old when she was thus abruptly uprooted—old enough to have been imprinted with the conflicts and complexities of those Virginia years. Perhaps her deepest realization was that although a conflict is over, it may still be far from resolved: the long shadow of a war that had ended before she had been born taught her this lesson; and the disputes, however good-natured, between her Confederate mother and her Unionist father affirmed it at dinner almost every night. In the fictions, then, her habit of eschewing closure—of denying the reader a "happy ending," or indeed, often *any* definitive resolution—is in part a legacy of these early Virginia lessons. Almost as deep is the recognition that violence, often unanticipated and inexplicable violence, is an inescapable part of life. Servants by the kitchen fireplace at Willow Shade and the care-worn hill woman from Timber Ridge told the little girl tales about the kind of violence that was often such a casual part of Back Creek life—violence of the sort that had burned the great barn to the ground. Finally, Willa Cather could not ignore the acquisitive drive that was especially apparent in Grandfather and Uncle George. Her own father, whose gentleness she treasured, never had much success in business; but she preferred his amiable nature (with all its deficiencies) to the sort of success that focuses on money and the world of commodities.

Yet the Virginia heritage also imparted an element of self-esteem to the girl: there was a sense of being "different," perhaps even "better" than the usual run of folk. Successor to the "first families of Virginia," Willa Cather had been an aristocrat during her early years. In her later years, this sentiment was translated into a conviction that she was meant to achieve something extraordinary. It gave her great drive and ambition, not for monetary success, but for the something "special" that could be affirmed by some unusual accomplishment. Eventually it both gave her the discipline to become an artist and defined the essence of that vocation. "Artist" was fully as distinguished an inheritance as "Virginian."

There had been enough in the last Virginia days to frighten any child; but the prospect of the vast Nebraskan prairies—unmarked by trees, uncultivated by farms, uncivilized by homes, with a merciless, relentless wind—terrified the child even more.

Cather had two brothers and a sister by the time the family moved to Nebraska (eventually, her mother had three more children), and Willa treasured their company—all the more so because the prairies' isolation was so frightening. Much later, after she had become a distinguished author, Willa Cather remembered her bleak reaction to the new home.

> The roads were mostly faint trails over the bunch grass in those days. The land was open range and there was almost no fencing. As we drove further and further out into the country, I felt a good deal as if we had come to the end of everything—it was a kind of erasure of personality.

During that first summer, Willa Cather had a pony; she rode it every day—widely, sometimes frantically over the prairie—and she began to know her neighbors. Neither educated aristocrats nor bourgeoisie living a genteel middle-class life, these people were hard-working farmers, many living in humble, dug-out dirt homes. Germans and Czechs and Poles and Russians and Bohemians: a polyglot people who had come from Europe to start over in Nebraska. Once she got to know them, Willa began to solicit their stories, especially the narratives that the grandmothers told—tales from across the seas and colorful accounts of family life. Although these stories were told not in the musical rhythms of Virginia, but in a halting, immigrant tongue, the old women of the Divide did much to continue the work that Mary Ann Anderson had begun; and the themes of the Nebraskan stories were often remarkably similar to those of Virginia.

After about a year, the Charles Cathers moved from Catherton into the little town of Red Cloud. Although it had only about 1,200 residents when the Cathers moved there, it did have one immense advantage: the town was on the railroad line. It had a roundhouse and railroad shops and a hotel, eventually even an "opera house" (that is, a large room over the hardware store where performances could take place). These were links with the larger world, the world of culture and ideas; and so were the various townsfolk who became Willa Cather's friends. In Red Cloud, the girl encountered an extraordinary mixture of people, many with backgrounds of learning and cultivation that exceeded even what she might have encountered in Virginia. Mrs. Miner, the mother of Willa's best friend, was the daughter of the oboe soloist in the Royal Norwegian Orchestra; she had attended a school founded by the Dowager Queen and was, herself, an accomplished and knowledgeable musician. "Uncle" William Drucker began to teach Willa Cather Latin in 1884 when she was not yet twelve; and Mr. and Mrs. Charles Wiener, who spoke both French and German and taught her how to read French novels, were the original source for her exhaustive knowledge of French literature.

It had been a long journey and a difficult one—from post–Civil War Virginia to rural Nebraska, from Catherton to the small town of Red Cloud. However, Cather had begun to accumulate a rich store of experience as foundation for her later work.

During her adolescence and throughout her college years at the University of Nebraska (1890–95) Willa Cather began to formulate her beliefs about art: that art could render incomparable (sometimes dangerously alluring) beauty; that it could explore and disclose the complex, timeless realities of human existence; that art could organize and contain the unavoidable dangers of life, the violence and uncertainty, thus robbing them of their terror. However, by the same token, art could become a kind of trap, presenting an idealized world that cannot withstand the cold light of reality. And at length, the mature writer Willa Cather learned one more sobering lesson: that a creative life is an essentially lonely one.

From the moment performers began to come into Red Cloud and put on plays in the opera house, Willa Cather was infatuated with the stage. She enjoyed organising amateur plays with her family and friends; off the stage she cultivated a series of personae, wearing male costumes and calling herself William Cather, M.D.; she read everything she could find about the theater; and when she went to college in Lincoln, she became a devoted theatergoer (even hanging around backstage after the show to chat with the players). She was ambitious and apparently filled with self-confidence; and in her junior year of college (still one month short of being twenty) she began to sell columns to the *Nebraska State Journal*, eventually becoming their regular theater reviewer. Her commentaries were blunt, uncompromising, often scathing. As Will Owen Jones, the managing editor of the *Journal*, observed:

> Many an actor of national reputation wondered on coming to Lincoln what would appear next morning from the pen of the meat-ax young girl of whom all of them had heard. Miss Cather did not stand in awe of the greatest actors, but set each one in his place with all the authority of a veteran metropolitan critic.

Willa Cather wrote more than a hundred reviews in Lincoln, and all have this singular stamp of severity. However, the sternness of her criticism was balanced by her many kindnesses to actual people. She lent money to actresses who were "down on their luck"; she became a sympathetic ear for the women whose unfaithful or unscrupulous husbands and lovers had robbed them or deserted them for another woman. And this intimate, complex involvement with the theater did much to enlarge Cather's understanding of artists and the creative process.

Surprisingly, although Willa Cather had an extraordinarily precocious intellectual beginning, she did not begin her career as a novelist until she was almost forty. Instead, she began to earn her living as a newspaper woman. By the time she had finished college, Cather was an experienced and skillful journalist; and although she never wavered in her desire to write fiction, until 1910 she had to make her living principally as a newspaper writer. Her first job was editor of the *Home Monthly* in Pittsburgh; next, she interrupted her newspaper work for about two years to become a high school teacher; then she began working for the *Pittsburgh Leader* and *The Pittsburgh Gazette*. Finally she moved to New York to work with the staff of *McClure's* magazine from 1906 until about 1911, eventually becoming its managing editor; and she made New York her more or less permanent home. Although Cather published two books before 1910—*April Twilights* (1903), a volume of poetry, and *The Troll Garden* (1905), a superb collection of short stories —so much of her time had been committed to editing the work of others that she could not undertake a long piece of fiction. Thus at the conclusion of her stint with *McClure's*, she gave up journalistic work for good.

In one way, then, Cather lost more than a decade of her creative life; in another way, however, she gained something positive from having pursued the rigorous discipline required to rework other people's prose. The tone of Willa Cather's earliest writing, especially the essays written while she was still in college, is florid and melodramatic; it was, by her own later admission, embarrassingly overwrought. More important, it was vastly different from the supple, subtle use of language that characterises her mature work. Today we might call Willa Cather a minimalist. She revised her fictions with painstaking care, and her revisions always took the form of removing excess verbiage to make a complex work of fiction as concentrated as possible—brief and apparently simple. Just as she expanded her notions of art and the artist during her years as theater critic and friend of travelling actresses, so she honed her skills as a writer throughout the dreary years of editing and teaching writing. It is true that Willa Cather published her first novel later than most major novelists; however, the quality of her work reveals the emotional and technical complexity she had gained from this long apprenticeship.

The stories in this volume display a wide range of Cather's work. The earliest, "Peter," written while she was still an undergraduate, was the first story to be published; it appeared first in a Boston magazine, *The Mahogany*, and later in *The Hesperian*, the University of Nebraska literary magazine. In some ways this is a primitive piece of fiction; however, it gathers together many of the themes that would run through her later work. Nature's ruthlessness, the lust for commodities that debases human nature, mankind's potential for brutality, and a passion for the beauty of art that is both tenacious and tenuous. "Peter" is significant in another way. A Bohemian farmhand named Frank Sadelek committed suicide; Cather heard an account of it from the immigrant grandmothers shortly after she arrived in Red Cloud, and the tale haunted her memory for many years. Ultimately it was transformed into fiction, becoming "Peter." Cather often worked in this manner—finding inspiration in one or more actual events or people, transforming them, and creating fictions that bore an uncanny (but entirely ambiguous) resemblance to the original source of inspiration. She employed this technique so frequently and so subtly that readers were often inclined to mistake her fictions for realistic accounts. It's always a combination—she would exclaim emphatically—*never* a literal portrait. The most striking use of this same material clearly supports her protestations: the core elements of Francis Sadelek's suicide lingered so persistently that more than twenty years later, it was reworked again, now to become an episode in her great novel, *My Ántonia*, where "Peter" became Ántonia's father.

A fuller and more tantalizing treatment of the themes of hardship and brutality can be found in "The Profile," a story whose imperfections are outweighed by its significance in Cather's development. If the adversity of the Nebraskan tale was a spur to Cather's imagination, "The Profile" makes it clear that such difficulties were not limited to the Midwestern frontier. Here, the artist Dunlap in the story is almost entirely motivated by the need to recompense the anguish of a specifically Virginia past. In part it is his pain, the mutilation inflicted by his ignorant, uncaring grandfather; to an even greater extent, however, it is the pain that has been endured by the women he has known:

> Dunlap had come from a country where women are hardly used. He had grown up on a farm in the remote mountains of West Virginia, and his mother had died of pneumonia contracted from taking her place at the washtub too soon after the birth of a child. When a boy, he had been apprenticed to his grandfather, a country cobbler, who, in his drunken rages, used to beat his wife with odd strips of shoe leather. The painter's hands still bore the mark of that apprenticeship, and the suffering of the mountain women he had seen about him in his childhood had left him almost morbidly sensitive.

Dunlap's response to his harrowing ordeal has been to reward every woman he paints with some essential core of beauty. In short, his art becomes compensation or atonement for the suffering of all women; and in serving this end, the aesthetic and emotional power of his portraiture has been compromised. His renderings are merely pretty, never great. And his encounter with Virginia, the disfigured woman he marries, becomes a tragic test of this artistic decision. In this tale, Cather clearly intends her reader to have the work of other writers in mind, especially Hawthorne, whose stories "The Birthmark" and "The Artist of the Beautiful" raise many of the same issues.

Cather was knowledgeable about the visual arts, and her fictions are replete with references to them. Thus a reader should not overlook the painting *Circe's Swine* that opens this narrative, nor dismiss the various reactions to it. It is a "freakish" image of mankind, just as Virginia's scar is a freak of nature. What, Cather asks, *is* the scar? the freakishness? Indeed, are we justified in seeing such things as "freaks" or deviations from nature? Is it ever wise so casually to turn away from whatever these blemishes represent? In the end, what are we to make of the series of decisions that Dunlap has made?

"The Joy of Nelly Deane," which treats the tragic destiny of women more directly, also reveals Cather's abiding interest in mythology. It opens with a scene explicitly designed to suggest the Three Fates, here personified by Mrs. Dow, Mrs. Freeze, and Mrs. Spinny. Guy Franklin's mercenary marriage suggests one source for the tragedy of Nelly's life. The character of Scott Spinny suggests another. With a "grim and saturnine" body, a "bearded face," and "strong, cold hands," his image recalls the god of the Underworld, and Nelly's marriage to him is surely like some voyage into Hades. However, unlike Persephone, Nelly has no Demeter to rescue her. Indeed, wherein, one might ask, *is* her "joy"?

Surely, one is inclined to protest, the radiant vitality and beauty of a Nelly Deane ought not to have perished so soon and so needlessly. The introduction of *Queen Esther* suggests the possibility of an alternative fate, a prospect of regal strength and powerful influence. Yet insofar as Nelly is "fated" to such a short and sorrowful life, can we find a cause for the tragedy? Who or what is to blame? (Or is it simply futile to raise the question of "blame"?) Cather refuses to resolve the various forces she has presented or to provide an answer to the questions a reader might ask. Much later in her career, Willa Cather returned to the essential material of this short story and reworked it into a full-length novel, *Lucy Gayheart*. In the novel, the issues are more complex; however, there is still no "reason" given for the ultimate fate of the characters.

"Behind the Singer Tower" is uncharacteristic of Cather's work because it seems to partake of the "muck-raking" school of writing (for which *McClure's* had been famous) and to focus narrowly and rather specifically on the need for social reform; it may even have been inspired by a disastrous fire in New York's Triangle Shirt Waist Company in 1911, for it was written while *McClure's Magazine* was running a series of articles on the crucial need for fire escapes in New York City's multistoried buildings. Nonetheless, this narrative has a number of elements that mark it as distinctively Catherian. Perhaps most obvious is Cather's mistrust of engineers, a dislike for their arrogance and their indifference to the needs of humanity. In this respect, "Behind the Singer Tower" anticipates Cather's first novel, *Alexander's Bridge*; even more, perhaps, it looks forward to the complex character of Louis Marcellus in *The Professor's House*. Next, there is the bleak vision of a money-hungry society, infatuated with commodities and accelerating into tragedy. Finally, and perhaps most important, there is the deflation of the phallic imagery; this symbol, embodied not merely in the Singer Tower but in the entire skyline of New York, reflects the engineer's overweaning pride and the businessman's lust for money and power. Later, in novels like *O Pioneers!* and *My Ántonia*, Cather would elaborate a semiotic system of female complexity and power that became the creative alternative to the cold, cruel dominance of the phallic ambition represented here.

"The Enchanted Bluff" is perhaps the most appealing of the "Uncollected Stories" here (and readers who are familiar with *The Professor's House* will recognize the tale as a prelude to that novel). It may remind us of *Tom Sawyer* or *Huckleberry Finn*; nor is this association inappropriate, for Willa Cather was both an acquaintance of Mark Twain's and a great admirer of his work. Here, as in "The Joy of Nelly Deane," we can see youthful dreams that remain unfulfilled; and in this story, it is perhaps the touching innocence of the Sandtown boys that makes the compromises of their adult lives seem so poignant. And yet it is a "bluff" they are seeking, and an "enchanted" one at that. Are we to infer, then, that all such dreams are, by their very nature, elusive—forever beyond our grasp?

The publication history of *Youth and the Bright Medusa* is interesting. During the Christmas season of 1919, Willa Cather wrote a story just to please herself—that is, not one that had been commissioned by a magazine—and the result was "Coming, Aphrodite!" One of her very best short tales, this little narrative seems to have pleased her a great deal, and she decided to fashion a collection of stories that would put "Coming, Aphrodite!" into a congenial setting. Alfred Knopf, who had just become her publisher, had been urging her to reissue her first collection of short stories, *The Troll Garden*. Instead, she suggested, why not excerpt several stories from the earlier collection and combine them with more recent work to make a volume that dealt entirely with art and the artist. Mr. Knopf was delighted with her idea, and the result was *Youth and the Bright Medusa*.

Before discussing the stories, we might pause to think about the title. Medusa, in Greek mythology, was one of the Gorgons, three once-beautiful sisters whose hair had been turned into snakes and whose eyes would turn an onlooker into stone. The Gorgons represented both great danger and the opportunity for great heroism. Ultimately, Perseus, a son of Zeus, slew Medusa by looking not at the creature herself but at her reflection in the burnished back of his shield. Later, he presented the head of Medusa to Athena, the goddess of wisdom, fertility, handicrafts, and judicious warfare. We might wonder what it tells the reader about *art* (the organising "subject" of this collection) that Cather has introduced this figure of Medusa. Why is she "Bright"? Why does Cather stipulate her connection with "Youth"? (And in connection with these queries, we might remember that Cather's first collection of short stories—also largely about art and the artist—had also been given a tantalizingly ambiguous title, *The Troll Garden*.)

In this collection, the last four stories are drawn from *The Troll Garden*, and to some extent they reflect Cather's earliest concerns as a serious author, the anxieties of a gifted woman who had only recently left the harsh plains and come to the city to write (for although the collection was published in 1905, all the stories in it were written between 1901 and 1903). Willa Cather's genius had been her salvation, a passport from nowhere to a world of art and music and serious thought. Yet at the beginning of her career, Cather's letters reveal her uneasiness about the fact that the very success that had brought happiness to her life had also fundamentally separated her from the rest of her family. "I have less and less in common with the folks at Red Cloud," she had written to a friend. And until she devised some way to bridge this gap (as she did in her later years), she would continue to feel the pain of this separation.

Her uneasiness is announced even on the volume's opening page: Cather cites two quotations that amplify the title. The first is from a poem, "Goblin Market," by Christina Rossetti: "We must not look at Goblin men, / We must not buy their fruits; / Who knows upon what soil they fed / Their hungry, thirsty roots?" The second is from a lecture entitled "The Roman and the Teuton," by Charles Kingsley: "A fairy palace, with a fairy garden: . . . Inside the trolls dwell . . . working at their magic forges, making and making always things rare and strange." The quotation from Kingsley's lecture suggests both Cather's own sense of isolation and, more broadly, the unavoidable division between an artist and those who cannot understand the creative act. Kingsley's lectures told of the invasion of Rome by the barbarians: the Romans are the artisans of civilization while the forest people, those outside the garden, are both wonderstruck and envious at the artisans' creations. Eventually, they break in and overrun the garden, only to find that they cannot rebuild what they have demolished. Rossetti suggests a different perspective. The poem as a whole deals with two sisters, one of whom is lured out of their cottage into a sinister glen where animalistic goblins sell their luscious but forbidden fruit; eventually, she succumbs and tastes the fruit. Immediately, she falls into physical decline and grows prematurely old; far from being satisfied, once having tasted the fruit, she longs for more, and only the love of her sister can save her. The implications of these introductory quotations are various, and they have been the subject of a good deal of critical investigation; but we might make a few brief observations.

The quotation from Kingsley has to do with the progress of civilization; it suggests that although separation from others is an inevitable component of the creative process, art and creativity are intrinsically good; they contribute to the progress of mankind. However, it also indicates that the artist and her work will be the object of the others' malignant envy. Such is the burden of genius. By contrast, one might very well read Rossetti's work in sexual terms; it suggests that if a woman accepts a man's "fruit" by engaging sexually with him, only disaster can follow; she will grow old and ill before her time (worn down from bearing children perhaps), and only the love of a sister can save her. In many ways, the story recounted by Rossetti recalls the myth of Persephone and Demeter, a tale that Cather used in many of her works.

Taken together, these two quotations seem to describe the precarious situation of an emergent female artist: she will become foreign to those who cannot understand her vocation and subject to the envy of others; moreover, she cannot rely on the conventional supports of husband and children, for the cares of a family will drain her vitality. Cather herself had at least one offer of marriage while she was in Pittsburgh; it was from a doctor, a man whom she considered appropriate in every way. She considered the proposal seriously, even consulted several trusted friends for their opinion, but ultimately she turned it down because she feared that marriage would hinder her career.

In one respect, however, these quotations make a unified statement: there is something "strange" and magical about art; and if it has beauty and the power to elevate our lives, it also has a potentially destructive component. One might tumble into art's compelling illusions—and drown.

All four of the stories from *The Troll Garden* are among Cather's best. "The Sculptor's Funeral" is perhaps the most accessible narrative: it portrays the disparity between an acclaimed artist and the "barbarians" among whom he grew up, the townspeople who know that the casket contains a man who has become, in some incomprehensible way, "great" by the world's standards. The style of the tale is brilliantly controlled, so restrained that the tale becomes a kind of anti-pastoral. Quiet, subdued realism becomes graphic indictment, for *this* country village is but a "desert of newness and ugliness and sordidness," without sensitivity or soul.

"A Wagner Matinée" is somewhat complementary to the previous story; it presents a vivid contrast between the harsh, culturally barren world of Midwestern farm life and a world where great art and music are so readily available that one can find a concert in the afternoon, and even at the last minute. However, this is a city; and here, the situation is more emotionally complex. The narrator's tone is severe and consistently condescending, despite the fact that he acknowledges a great emotional debt to his unwelcome Aunt Georgiana. Thus we are invited to compare the narrator's judgment throughout with our own perhaps more balanced assessment; and in reaching an evaluation, we might recollect that like the sister who succumbed to the Goblin men's "fruit," Aunt Georgiana has married a farmer and left New England, voluntarily putting the narrator's world behind her. The narrator is appalled at her decision. Might Cather's thoughts be more complex? Perhaps entirely different?

If the first two stories present the emptiness of life without the luminous presence of art, " 'A Death in the Desert' " and "Paul's Case" examine the potentially unwholesome side of art, its capacity to delude, engulf, and even destroy. " 'A Death in the Desert' " deals with many variations on the theme of delusion: the man who is consistently mistaken for his brother, the room in Wyoming that resembles a New York studio, the woman who sacrifices everything, even her own career, to worship the genius who has deserted her. Cather invites us to compare this story with "A Wagner Matinée." Have both women made a tragic mistake? Only one? If so, which woman is more essentially unhappy?

"Paul's Case" is the most famous of these four tales, and by far the most often reproduced. To some extent it was inspired by a young man whom Cather met while teaching high school in Pittsburgh; and to some extent (as Cather later confessed) it was based upon some of the author's own yearnings in her earliest years. It has become a classic study of a morbid personality disorder; of the beckoning, seductive power of art; of the plight of a poor boy in a world where the seductive commodities of wealth and luxury are everywhere displayed. Above all, of course, it is an agonizing account of the power of illusion.

Cather so often portrays the harshness of farm life that it is rare to see her portraying poverty within the city. Yet during her early years in Pittsburgh, Willa Cather grew to know the city very well: for amusement, she would ride the streetcars out to the end of the line and back; and she had a bicycle that she rode everywhere up and down the steep hills of this vast river city, a metropolis whose air was so blackened by soot from the factories that prosperous businessmen would bring an extra shirt to work and change in the middle of the day. Pittsburgh was the repository of great wealth, the home of Fiske and Carnegie; and the "Carnegie Hall" in which Paul works is not New York's, but Pittsburgh's. Willa Cather eagerly attended concerts and plays there; however, she also found ample opportunity to observe the grimy zinc tubs, cracked mirrors, dripping spigots, and Sunday afternoons on the front stoop in Pittsburgh. And in a world that "always wore the guise of ugliness," is it not, perhaps, a reasonable alternative to feel, as Paul does, that "a certain element of artificiality [is] necessary in beauty"? We might ask, then, to what extent Paul's escape is a failure. What are the causes for his behavior? And if we do judge him to have failed, how might he have done things differently?

Several of the later stories here continue to develop the notion of art as potentially destructive; however, in her more mature years, Cather was less preoccupied with the danger of losing oneself in an alluring illusion than with her disgust at watching prosaic parasites feeding upon the careers of successful artists.

"The Diamond Mine," "A Gold Slipper," and "Scandal" all recall Willa Cather's experiences backstage—chatting with actresses about their money problems or the scourge of unfaithful husbands and lovers. Often Cather seems to equate the problems of an actress's situation with those of women in general; and consistently, she proposes that all women can be secure only when they are in charge of their own lives. Her mother had given birth to seven live children and had miscarried several more; Virginia Cather's life had been cannibalised by marriage and child-bearing, and her oldest daughter had been indelibly affected by the sight of a mother thus burdened. Early in her life, while writing theater reviews in college, Willa Cather could see that many married actresses were little more than bank accounts for indigent husbands, and that married actresses seldom succeeded. Cather herself made the decision not to marry lest it interfere with her career. And in *The Song of the Lark*, the diva heroine Thea Kronborg wrestles painfully with the conflict between romantic love and her operatic career—choosing to marry only when she has become powerful enough to control her own money and to refuse to bear children.

Of these stories, "The Diamond Mine" is the most bitterly bleak about the possibilities for unselfish actresses. Cressida "more than any other woman . . . appealed to the acquisitive instinct in men." She has married one abusive, dishonest husband after another; she continues to be generous to a jealous and rapacious family; and yet after her death, even her will becomes the object of greedy contention. Like "A Diamond Mine," "Scandal" also touches upon an actress's vulnerability to rapacious men; however, principally it plays with the notion of various levels of illusion—on the stage, in the actual world, and in every person's vision of the self. "A Gold Slipper" takes a more amused and sophisticated look at the notion of illusion and combines it with a playful refutation of men's stereotyped notions about "weak," "ignorant," "selfish," or "shallow" actresses.

Yet in all these studies of the relationship between artistic women and the men who engage their emotions, none is more graceful, complex, and compelling than the tale that Cather wrote just for herself. "Coming, Aphrodite!" was something of a personal exercise: Willa Cather lived in New York's Greenwich Village for nearly two decades, and the studio apartments of Don Hedger and Eden Bower are modeled on Cather's own accommodations during the first years there, her own season of vitality and art and innocence.

The story printed here is the version Cather herself wished to publish; however, virtually alone among Cather's work, this tale was bowdlerized before initial publication so that it wouldn't offend public taste. Although Anthony Comstock had died in 1915, The Society for the Suppression of Vice that he had founded was still active and powerful in 1920. Tons of printed material had been sacrificed to the prudish notions of propriety that were embodied in the laws The Society had supported, and publishers were not yet willing to test the prevailing legal system. Although any number of small changes were made in this narrative, only several are worth noting. First, the title of the story was changed to "Coming, Eden Bower!" lest the title character be confused with the singer Mary Garden, who had just performed as Aphrodite with the Chicago Opera Company. Second, Eden Bower does her exercises clad in chiffon (and not entirely and beautifully naked, as Cather would have had it). Finally, the Aztec slave who couples with the Princess is not "gelded," but merely "maimed." These changes may seem merely foolish today, but they do call attention to one feature of the story that will affect all readers: this story is deeply sensuous, perhaps the most sexually explicit story Cather ever wrote.

Although both the male and the female in this erotic tale are artists, their temperaments are vastly different: as his name suggests, Hedger lives a life that has been defined by denials. He has certain attributes, appurtenances, habits: his shabby clothes, his habit of exercise, his pipe, his dog, his aversion to linking art with commercial success. Yet there are many intimations that his masculine energy is stifled, tensed and waiting to be released: phallic imagery like the dog's "bony tail stuck out hard as a hickory withe"; or Hedger's instinctive, unconsciously masturbatory gesture as he watches the sensuous performance of Eden's exercises ("his fingers curved as if he were holding a crayon [and then] the charcoal seemed to explode in his hand"). Yet when we first encounter Don Hedger, the liberation of these vital elements in his nature is merely potential.

By contrast, Eden Bower is the embodiment of grace and vigor, and she is fearless—boldly, insouciantly confident. "Eden got a summer all her own. . . . She had the easy freedom of obscurity and the consciousness of power." She has beauty and talent; but she lacks sensual experience because for all her beauty, she has been utterly circumspect with her many beaux. Moreover, she has no sense of the potential dangers to which her beauty and talent and easy, open manner might expose her.

For both Hedger and Eden Bower, then, this will be a summer of erotic experimentation and aesthetic fulfillment: as man and artist, he needs the fire of her nature; as woman and artist, she requires the dark experiences intrinsic to his somber Aztec tale, an account of the tragic possibilities of erotic rapture. Most of all, as man and woman during this lovely, languid summer, they crave the fulfillment of desire itself: they need to couple with each other.

Interestingly, Cather makes it clear that while it is necessary for both the man and the woman here to gain intimate knowledge of "the other," neither of them needs or wants a permanent commitment. By the time fall is drawing near, each has procured what he or she required: a glorious sexual affair that has contributed to the artistic advancement of each—different as their aesthetic visions may be. At the end of the story, we learn that Eden Bower has gained wealth and the fame she had craved, and that Hedger has become a highly respected experimental painter who has somehow continued to elude monetary success.

"Old Mrs. Harris" was written long after the other stories in this volume, at a time when Cather's father had recently died and her mother was near death; and to some extent it is a tribute to them —to the life that young Willa Cather had led in the home of the transplanted, overburdened Southern belle and her genial, unsuccessful husband. In fact, superficially many of the characters in the tale resemble the people who lived in Willa Cather's girlhood home. Grandmother Boak, Virginia Cather's mother, had come west to Nebraska with her daughter's family; and when Virginia and Charles Cather moved to Red Cloud, Grandma Boak had moved with them. She helped with the children, took her place in the kitchen, tried to relieve her still-beautiful daughter of cares—in short, played a role very similar to that of old Mrs. Harris. Vickie, with her impatient, self-centered ambition, is a rough, rather harsh characterization of the young Willa Cather, selfish as only the young can be selfish. And Mr. Templeton's affable absences echo the business patterns of Charles Cather. In short, the sheer number of apparently personal elements from the author's life is so strong that readers may be tempted to read this story as autobiography. And that would be a considerable mistake.

What Cather offers here is a generational array of feminine consciousness, the woman as she moves through the life cycle; and if her own persona is anywhere in the story, it is not with Vickie (who seems to resemble her younger self so much), but with old Mrs. Harris. Nor are value judgments easy to make. Even the well-intentioned Mrs. Rosen misapprehends the situation. There is no doubt that old Mrs. Harris's comforts are overlooked amidst the confusion of work and commitments that burden the other women. However, Mrs. Rosen's inclination to disapprove (which may reflect the reader's initial reaction) is very much a result of her failing to understand the culture from which the Templetons have come. In some sense, each of the women is locked not merely in her "time of life," but in her set of "expectations" as well. Vickie, in the heedless impatience of adolescence, is moving forward into a different way of life, into a future that no other woman in the story can foresee or understand; the post–Civil War belle, Mrs. Templeton, in the ripe, cluttered, overburdened years of motherhood, is drowning in her own fecundity; and Mrs. Harris, a remnant of the Old South, is living in her final years with dignity, attempting to preserve the values of her own time. Moreover, the behavior of each is oddly appropriate.

The story celebrates life itself, with all its glorious diversity and all the intractable ignorance and pain. There is something vital in the moment—of being Vickie, of being Mrs. Templeton, even of being old Mrs. Harris—something potent in the very miracle of existence. Most of all, the story urges compassion for all that we did not understand in time: for the mother who seemed not to pay us enough attention, for the grandmother we had casually neglected, and even for the young selfish person that we used to be.

At the end of the narrative, Cather introduces the voice of an omniscient narrator, an extremely rare occurrence in her fictions. This voice—perhaps the consciousness of old Mrs. Harris herself or perhaps the voice of a novelist who managed to grow wise with years—offers a perspective that transcends time. "When they are old. . . ." The reader's last task is to fathom that voice. Is it a poignant, melancholy insight that asserts, in effect, that no one *can* ever know enough in time to do things "right"? Or does it celebrate the reassuring belief that even if we don't understand now and even if we do make mistakes, someday we finally *will* understand?

SUGGESTIONS FOR FURTHER READING

BOOKS BY WILLA CATHER

April Twilights (poetry). Boston: Badger, 1903.

The Troll Garden (stories). New York: McClure, 1905.

Alexander's Bridge (novel). Boston: Houghton Mifflin, 1911.

O Pioneers! (novel). Boston: Houghton Mifflin, 1913; Edited with an Introduction by Blanche H. Gelfant. New York: Penguin Classics, 1989.

My Autobiography [S. S. McClure]. New York: Frederick A. Stokes Co., 1914.

The Song of the Lark (novel). Boston: Houghton Mifflin, 1915.

My Ántonia (novel). Boston: Houghton Mifflin, 1918; Edited with an Introduction by John J. Murphy. New York: Penguin Classics, 1994.

Youth and the Bright Medusa (stories). New York: Alfred A. Knopf, 1920.

One of Ours (novel). New York: Alfred A. Knopf, 1922.

A Lost Lady (novel). New York: Alfred A. Knopf, 1923.

The Professor's House (novel). New York: Alfred A. Knopf, 1925.

My Mortal Enemy (novel). New York: Alfred A. Knopf, 1926.

Death Comes for the Archbishop (novel). New York: Alfred A. Knopf, 1927.

Shadows on the Rock (novel). New York: Alfred A. Knopf, 1931.

Obscure Destinies (stories). New York: Alfred A. Knopf, 1932.

Lucy Gayheart (novel). New York: Alfred A. Knopf, 1935.

Not Under Forty (essays). New York: Alfred A. Knopf, 1936.

Sapphira and the Slave Girl (novel). New York: Alfred A. Knopf, 1940.

The Old Beauty and Others (stories). New York: Alfred A. Knopf, 1948.

RESOURCES ON WILLA CATHER AND HER WORK

Arnold, Marilyn. *Willa Cather's Short Fiction.* Athens: Ohio University Press, 1984.

Bennett, Mildred R., ed. *Early Stories of Willa Cather.* New York: Dodd, Mead, 1957; Apollo, 1966.

Bohlke, L. Brent, ed. *Willa Cather in Person.* Lincoln: University of Nebraska Press, 1986.

Byrne, Kathleen D., and Richard Snyder. *Chrysalis: Willa Cather in Pittsburgh, 1896–1906.* Pittsburgh: Historical Society of Western Pennsylvania, 1980.

Carlin, Deborah. "Obscuring Destinies: Threading the Narrative of 'Old Mrs. Harris,' " in Deborah Carlin, ed. *Cather, Canon, and the Politics of Reading.* Amherst: University of Massachusetts Press, 1992, pp. 89–115.

Crane, Joan. *Willa Cather: A Bibliography.* Lincoln: University of Nebraska Press, 1982.

Faulkner, Virginia, ed. *Willa Cather: Collected Short Fiction, 1892–1912.* Introduction by Mildred R. Bennett. Lincoln: University of Nebraska Press, 1965; rev. ed., 1970.

Garden, Mary, and Louis Biancolli. *Mary Garden's Story.* New York: Simon and Schuster, 1951.

Gerber, Philip. *Willa Cather.* Boston: Twayne, 1975; rev. ed., New York: Twayne, 1995.

Giannone, Richard. *Music in Willa Cather's Fiction.* Lincoln: University of Nebraska Press, 1968.

Jones, Howard Mumford. *The Bright Medusa.* Urbana: University of Illinois Press, 1952.

Kasson, John F. *Amusing the Million: Coney Island at the Turn of the Century.* New York: Hill and Wang, 1978.

Lewis, Edith. *Willa Cather Living: A Personal Record.* 1953; repr. with a foreword by Marilyn Arnold. Athens: Ohio University Press, 1989.

Lee, Hermione. *Willa Cather: Double Lives.* New York: Pantheon, 1990.

Lee, Hermione, ed. *Short Stories of Willa Cather.* London: Virago Press, 1989.

March, John. *A Reader's Companion to the Fiction of Willa Cather.* Marilyn Arnold, ed., with Debra Lynn Thornton. Westport, Conn.: Greenwood Press, 1993.

Meyering, Sheryl L. *A Reader's Guide to the Short Stories of Willa Cather*. New York: G. K. Hall, 1994.

O'Brien, Sharon. *Willa Cather: The Emerging Voice*. New York: Oxford University Press, 1987.

O'Brien, Sharon, ed. *Willa Cather: Stories, Poems, and Other Writings*. New York: Library of America, 1991.

Rosowski, Susan J. *The Voyage Perilous: Willa Cather's Romanticism*. Lincoln: University of Nebraska Press, 1986.

Ryder, Mary Ruth. *Willa Cather and Classical Myth: The Search for a New Parnassus*. Lewiston, N.Y.: Edwin Mellen Press, 1990.

Sadie, Stanley, ed. *New Grove Dictionary of Opera*, 4 vols. London: Macmillan Press, 1992.

Schroeter, James, ed. *Willa Cather and Her Critics*. Ithaca, N.Y.: Cornell University Press, 1967.

Slote, Bernice, ed. *Uncle Valentine and Other Stories: Willa Cather's Uncollected Short Fiction, 1915–1929*. Lincoln: University of Nebraska Press, 1973. (Includes "Variants in 'Coming, Eden Bower!' and 'Coming, Aphrodite!' ")

Sutherland, Donald. "Willa Cather: The Classical Voice," in Bernice Slote and Virginia Faulkner, eds. *The Art of Willa Cather*. Lincoln: University of Nebraska Press, 1974, pp. 156–79.

Thurin, Erik Ingvar. *The Humanization of Willa Cather: Classicism in an American Classic*. Lund, Sweden: Lund University Press, 1990.

Wagenknecht, Edward. "Willa Cather's Uncollected Short Stories," in *Willa Cather*. New York: Continuum, 1994, pp. 163–75.

Wasserman, Loretta. *Willa Cather: A Study of the Short Fiction*. Boston: Twayne, 1991.

Willa Cather's "Paul's Case." Videocassette. Lamont Jackson, dir. PBS American Short Story Series, Learning in Focus; distributed by Monterey Home Video through International Video Entertainment, 1980, 52 minutes.

Woodress, James. *Willa Cather: A Literary Life*. Lincoln: University of Nebraska Press, 1987.

Woodress, James, ed. *The Troll Garden: A Definitive Edition*. Lincoln: University of Nebraska Press, 1983.

A NOTE ON THE TEXT

THE EIGHT STORIES in *Youth and the Bright Medusa* in this edition were taken from the Alfred A. Knopf edition of 1920. All the stories had appeared previously in magazines, and the last four—"Paul's Case," "A Wagner Matinée," "The Sculptor's Funeral," and " 'A Death in the Desert' "—were in Willa Cather's first story collection, *The Troll Garden* (New York: McClure) of 1905. In 1937 Houghton Mifflin began publishing a twelve-volume Autograph Edition of Cather's book-length works, and *Youth and the Bright Medusa* was volume 6. " 'A Death in the Desert' " was dropped completely in this version of the collection. The greatest change in each story was the addition of a date of completion for each, and these dates are given in this edition in the Explanatory Notes. Textual variants among these versions are discussed by the editors Virginia Faulkner in *Willa Cather: Collected Short Fiction, 1892–1912*; Bernice Slote in *Uncle Valentine and Other Stories: Willa Cather's Uncollected Short Fiction, 1915–1929*; James Woodress in *The Troll Garden: A Definitive Edition*; and Joan Crane in *Willa Cather: A Bibliography*. The five uncollected stories that follow are printed here as in their magazine appearance, with occasional typographical errors or spelling inconsistencies regularized. All five also appear in *Willa Cather: Collected Short Fiction, 1892–1912.*

The final story, "Old Mrs. Harris," appeared as the central piece in the 1932 collection *Obscure Destinies* (New York: Knopf).

COMING, APHRODITE!

AND OTHER STORIES

YOUTH AND THE BRIGHT MEDUSA (1920)

We must not look at Goblin men,
We must not buy their fruits;
Who knows upon what soil they fed
Their hungry, thirsty roots?

"GOBLIN MARKET"[1]

Coming, Aphrodite![1]

I

DON HEDGER had lived for four years on the top floor of an old house on the south side of Washington Square, and nobody had ever disturbed him. He occupied one big room with no outside exposure except on the north, where he had built in a many-paned studio window that looked upon a court and upon the roofs and walls of other buildings. His room was very cheerless, since he never got a ray of direct sunlight; the south corners were always in shadow. In one of the corners was a clothes closet, built against the partition, in another a wide divan, serving as a seat by day and a bed by night. In the front corner, the one farther from the window, was a sink, and a table with two gas burners where he sometimes cooked his food. There, too, in the perpetual dusk, was the dog's bed, and often a bone or two for his comfort.

The dog was a Boston bull terrier, and Hedger explained his surly disposition by the fact that he had been bred to the point where it told on his nerves. His name was Caesar III, and he had taken prizes at very exclusive dog shows. When he and his master went out to prowl about University Place or to promenade along West Street, Caesar III was invariably fresh and shining. His pink skin showed through his mottled coat, which glistened as if it had just been rubbed with olive oil, and he wore a brass-studded collar, bought at the smartest saddler's. Hedger, as often as not, was hunched up in an old striped blanket coat, with a shapeless felt hat pulled over his bushy hair, wearing black shoes that had become grey, or brown ones that had become black, and he never put on gloves unless the day was biting cold.

Early in May, Hedger learned that he was to have a new neighbour in the rear apartment—two rooms, one large and one small, that faced the west. His studio was shut off from the larger of these rooms by double doors, which, though they were fairly tight, left him a good deal at the mercy of the occupant. The rooms had been leased, long before he came there, by a trained nurse who considered herself knowing in old furniture. She went to auction sales and bought up mahogany and dirty brass and stored it away here, where she meant to live when she retired from nursing. Meanwhile, she sub-let her rooms, with their precious furniture, to young people who came to New York to "write" or to "paint"—who proposed to live by the sweat of the brow rather than of the hand, and who desired artistic surroundings. When Hedger first moved in, these rooms were occupied by a young man who tried to write plays,—and who kept on trying until a week ago, when the nurse had put him out for unpaid rent.

A few days after the playwright left, Hedger heard an ominous murmur of voices through the bolted double doors: the lady-like intonation of the nurse—doubtless exhibiting her treasures—and another voice, also a woman's, but very different; young, fresh, unguarded, confident. All the same, it would be very annoying to have a woman in there. The only bath-room on the floor was at the top of the stairs in the front hall, and he would always be running into her as he came or went from his bath. He would have to be more careful to see that Caesar didn't leave bones about the hall, too; and she might object when he cooked steak and onions on his gas burner.

As soon as the talking ceased and the women left, he forgot them. He was absorbed in a study of paradise fish at the Aquarium, staring out at people through the glass and green water of their tank. It was a highly gratifying idea; the incommunicability of one stratum of animal life with another,—though Hedger pretended it was only an experiment in unusual lighting. When he heard trunks knocking against the sides of the narrow hall, then he realized that she was moving in at once. Toward noon, groans and deep gasps and the creaking of ropes, made him aware that a piano was arriving. After the tramp of the movers died away down the stairs, somebody touched off a few scales and chords on the instrument, and then there was peace. Presently he heard her lock her door and go down the hall humming something; going out to lunch, probably. He stuck his brushes in a can of turpentine and put on his hat, not stopping to wash his hands. Caesar was smelling along the crack under the bolted doors; his bony tail stuck out hard as a hickory withe, and the hair was standing up about his elegant collar.

Hedger encouraged him. "Come along, Caesar. You'll soon get used to a new smell."

In the hall stood an enormous trunk, behind the ladder that led to the roof, just opposite Hedger's door. The dog flew at it with a growl of hurt amazement. They went down three flights of stairs and out into the brilliant May afternoon.

Behind the Square, Hedger and his dog descended into a basement oyster house where there were no tablecloths on the tables and no handles on the coffee cups, and the floor was covered with sawdust, and Caesar was always welcome,—not that he needed any such precautionary flooring. All the carpets of Persia would have been safe for him. Hedger ordered steak and onions absentmindedly, not realizing why he had an apprehension that this dish might be less readily at hand hereafter. While he ate, Caesar sat beside his chair, gravely disturbing the sawdust with his tail.

After lunch Hedger strolled about the Square for the dog's health and watched the stages[2] pull out;—that was almost the very last summer of the old horse stages on Fifth Avenue. The fountain had but lately begun operations for the season and was throwing up a mist of rainbow water which now and then blew south and sprayed a bunch of Italian babies that were being supported on the outer rim by older, very little older, brothers and sisters. Plump robins were hopping about on the soil; the grass was newly cut and blindingly green. Looking up the Avenue through the Arch, one could see the young poplars with their bright, sticky leaves, and the Brevoort[3] glistening in its spring coat of paint, and shining horses and carriages,—occasionally an automobile, mis-shapen and sullen, like an ugly threat in a stream of things that were bright and beautiful and alive.

While Caesar and his master were standing by the fountain, a girl approached them, crossing the Square. Hedger noticed her because she wore a lavender cloth suit and carried in her arms a big bunch of fresh lilacs. He saw that she was young and handsome, —beautiful, in fact, with a splendid figure and good action. She, too, paused by the fountain and looked back through the Arch up the Avenue. She smiled rather patronizingly as she looked, and at the same time seemed delighted. Her slowly curving upper lip and half-closed eyes seemed to say: "You're gay, you're exciting, you are quite the right sort of thing; but you're none too fine for me!"

In the moment she tarried, Caesar stealthily approached her and sniffed at the hem of her lavender skirt, then, when she went south like an arrow, he ran back to his master and lifted a face full of emotion and alarm, his lower lip twitching under his sharp white teeth and his hazel eyes pointed with a very definite discovery. He stood thus, motionless, while Hedger watched the lavender girl go up the steps and through the door of the house in which he lived.

"You're right, my boy, it's she! She might be worse looking, you know."

When they mounted to the studio, the new lodger's door, at the back of the hall, was a little ajar, and Hedger caught the warm perfume of lilacs just brought in out of the sun. He was used to the musty smell of the old hall carpet. (The nurse-lessee had once knocked at his studio door and complained that Caesar must be somewhat responsible for the particular flavour of that mustiness, and Hedger had never spoken to her since.) He was used to the old smell, and he preferred it to that of the lilacs, and so did his companion, whose nose was so much more discriminating. Hedger shut his door vehemently, and fell to work.

Most young men who dwell in obscure studios in New York have had a beginning, come out of something, have somewhere a home town, a family, a paternal roof. But Don Hedger had no such background. He was a foundling, and had grown up in a school for homeless boys, where book-learning was a negligible part of the curriculum. When he was sixteen, a Catholic priest took him to Greensburg, Pennsylvania, to keep house for him. The priest did something to fill in the large gaps in the boy's education,—taught him to like "Don Quixote"[4] and "The Golden Legend,"[5] and encouraged him to mess with paints and crayons in his room up under the slope of the mansard. When Don wanted to go to New York to study at the Art League, the priest got him a night job as packer in one of the big department stores. Since then, Hedger had taken care of himself; that was his only responsibility. He was singularly unencumbered; had no family duties, no social ties, no obligations toward any one but his landlord. Since he travelled light, he had travelled rather far. He had got over a good deal of the earth's surface, in spite of the fact that he never in his life had more than three hundred dollars ahead at any one time, and he had already outlived a succession of convictions and revelations about his art.

Though he was now but twenty-six years old, he had twice been on the verge of becoming a marketable product; once through some studies of New York streets he did for a magazine, and once through a collection of pastels he brought home from New Mexico, which Remington,[6] then at the height of his popularity, happened to see, and generously tried to push. But on both occasions Hedger decided that this was something he didn't wish to carry further,—simply the old thing over again and got nowhere,—so he took enquiring dealers experiments in a "later manner," that made them put him out of the shop. When he ran short of money, he could always get any amount of commercial work; he was an expert draughtsman and worked with lightning speed. The rest of his time he spent in groping his way from one kind of painting into another, or travelling about without luggage, like a tramp, and he was chiefly occupied with getting rid of ideas he had once thought very fine.

Hedger's circumstances, since he had moved to Washington Square, were affluent compared to anything he had ever known before. He was now able to pay advance rent and turn the key on his studio when he went away for four months at a stretch. It didn't occur to him to wish to be richer than this. To be sure, he did without a great many things other people think necessary, but he didn't miss them, because he had never had them. He belonged to no clubs, visited no houses, had no studio friends, and he ate his dinner alone in some decent little restaurant, even on Christmas and New Year's. For days together he talked to nobody but his dog and the janitress and the lame oysterman.

After he shut the door and settled down to his paradise fish on that first Tuesday in May, Hedger forgot all about his new neighbour. When the light failed, he took Caesar out for a walk. On the way home he did his marketing on West Houston Street, with a one-eyed Italian woman who always cheated him. After he had cooked his beans and scallopini, and drunk half a bottle of Chianti, he put his dishes in the sink and went up on the roof to smoke. He was the only person in the house who ever went to the roof, and he had a secret understanding with the janitress about it. He was to have "the privilege of the roof," as she said, if he opened the heavy trapdoor on sunny days to air out the upper hall, and was watchful to close it when rain threatened. Mrs. Foley was fat and dirty and hated to climb stairs,—besides, the roof was reached by a perpendicular iron ladder, definitely inaccessible to a woman of her bulk, and the iron door at the top of it was too heavy for any but Hedger's strong arm to lift. Hedger was not above medium height, but he practised with weights and dumbbells, and in the shoulders he was as strong as a gorilla.

So Hedger had the roof to himself. He and Caesar often slept up there on hot nights, rolled in blankets he had brought home from Arizona. He mounted with Caesar under his left arm. The dog had never learned to climb a perpendicular ladder, and never did he feel so much his master's greatness and his own dependence upon him, as when he crept under his arm for this perilous ascent. Up there was even gravel to scratch in, and a dog could do whatever he liked, so long as he did not bark. It was a kind of Heaven, which no one was strong enough to reach but his great, paint-smelling master.

On this blue May night there was a slender, girlish looking young moon in the west, playing with a whole company of silver stars. Now and then one of them darted away from the group and shot off into the gauzy blue with a soft little trail of light, like laughter. Hedger and his dog were delighted when a star did this.

They were quite lost in watching the glittering game, when they were suddenly diverted by a sound,—not from the stars, though it was music. It was not the Prologue to Pagliacci,[7] which rose ever and anon on hot evenings from an Italian tenement on Thompson Street, with the gasps of the corpulent baritone who got behind it; nor was it the hurdy-gurdy man, who often played at the corner in the balmy twilight. No, this was a woman's voice, singing the tempestuous, over-lapping phrases of Signor Puccini,[8] then comparatively new in the world, but already so popular that even Hedger recognized his unmistakable gusts of breath. He looked about over the roofs; all was blue and still, with the well-built chimneys that were never used now standing up dark and mournful. He moved softly toward the yellow quadrangle where the gas from the hall shone up through the half-lifted trapdoor. Oh yes! It came up through the hole like a strong draught, a big, beautiful voice, and it sounded rather like a professional's. A piano had arrived in the morning, Hedger remembered. This might be a very great nuisance. It would be pleasant enough to listen to, if you could turn it on and off as you wished; but you couldn't. Caesar, with the gas light shining on his collar and his ugly but sensitive face, panted and looked up for information. Hedger put down a reassuring hand.

"I don't know. We can't tell yet. It may not be so bad."

He stayed on the roof until all was still below, and finally descended, with quite a new feeling about his neighbour. Her voice, like her figure, inspired respect,—if one did not choose to call it admiration. Her door was shut, the transom was dark; nothing remained of her but the obtrusive trunk, unrightfully taking up room in the narrow hall.

II

For two days Hedger didn't see her. He was painting eight hours a day just then, and only went out to hunt for food. He noticed that she practised scales and exercises for about an hour in the morning; then she locked her door, went humming down the hall, and left him in peace. He heard her getting her coffee ready at about the same time he got his. Earlier still, she passed his room on her way to her bath. In the evening she sometimes sang, but on the whole she didn't bother him. When he was working well he did not notice anything much. The morning paper lay before his door until he reached out for his milk bottle, then he kicked the sheet inside and it lay on the floor until evening. Sometimes he read it and sometimes he did not. He forgot there was anything of importance going on in the world outside of his third floor studio. Nobody had ever taught him that he ought to be interested in other people; in the Pittsburgh steel strike, in the Fresh Air Fund, in the scandal about the Babies' Hospital. A grey wolf, living in a Wyoming canyon, would hardly have been less concerned about these things than was Don Hedger.

One morning he was coming out of the bath-room at the front end of the hall, having just given Caesar his bath and rubbed him into a glow with a heavy towel. Before the door, lying in wait for him, as it were, stood a tall figure in a flowing blue silk dressing gown that fell away from her marble arms. In her hands she carried various accessories of the bath.

"I wish," she said distinctly, standing in his way, "I wish you wouldn't wash your dog in the tub. I never heard of such a thing! I've found his hair in the tub, and I've smelled a doggy smell, and now I've caught you at it. It's an outrage!"

Hedger was badly frightened. She was so tall and positive, and was fairly blazing with beauty and anger. He stood blinking, holding on to his sponge and dog-soap, feeling that he ought to bow very low to her. But what he actually said was:

"Nobody has ever objected before. I always wash the tub,—and, anyhow, he's cleaner than most people."

"Cleaner than me?" her eyebrows went up, her white arms and neck and her fragrant person seemed to scream at him like a band of outraged nymphs. Something flashed through his mind about a man who was turned into a dog, or was pursued by dogs, because he unwittingly intruded upon the bath of beauty.[9]

"No, I didn't mean that," he muttered, turning scarlet under the bluish stubble of his muscular jaws. "But I know he's cleaner than I am."

"That I don't doubt!" Her voice sounded like a soft shivering of crystal, and with a smile of pity she drew the folds of her voluminous blue robe close about her and allowed the wretched man to pass. Even Caesar was frightened; he darted like a streak down the hall, through the door and to his own bed in the corner among the bones.

Hedger stood still in the doorway, listening to indignant sniffs and coughs and a great swishing of water about the sides of the tub. He had washed it; but as he had washed it with Caesar's sponge, it was quite possible that a few bristles remained; the dog was shedding now. The playwright had never objected, nor had the jovial illustrator who occupied the front apartment,—but he, as he admitted, "was usually pie-eyed, when he wasn't in Buffalo." He went home to Buffalo sometimes to rest his nerves.

It had never occurred to Hedger that any one would mind using the tub after Caesar;—but then, he had never seen a beautiful girl caparisoned for the bath before. As soon as he beheld her standing there, he realized the unfitness of it. For that matter, she ought not to step into a tub that any other mortal had bathed in; the illustrator was sloppy and left cigarette ends on the moulding.

All morning as he worked he was gnawed by a spiteful desire to get back at her. It rankled that he had been so vanquished by her disdain. When he heard her locking her door to go out for lunch, he stepped quickly into the hall in his messy painting coat, and addressed her.

"I don't wish to be exigent, Miss,"—he had certain grand words that he used upon occasion—"but if this is your trunk, it's rather in the way here."

"Oh, very well!" she exclaimed carelessly, dropping her keys into her handbag. "I'll have it moved when I can get a man to do it," and she went down the hall with her free, roving stride.

Her name, Hedger discovered from her letters, which the postman left on the table in the lower hall, was Eden Bower.

III

In the closet that was built against the partition separating his room from Miss Bower's, Hedger kept all his wearing apparel, some of it on hooks and hangers, some of it on the floor. When he opened his closet door now-a-days, little dust-coloured insects flew out on downy wing, and he suspected that a brood of moths were hatching in his winter overcoat. Mrs. Foley, the janitress, told him to bring down all his heavy clothes and she would give them a beating and hang them in the court. The closet was in such disorder that he shunned the encounter, but one hot afternoon he set himself to the task. First he threw out a pile of forgotten laundry and tied it up in a sheet. The bundle stood as high as his middle when he had knotted the corners. Then he got his shoes and overshoes together. When he took his overcoat from its place against the partition, a long ray of yellow light shot across the dark enclosure,—a knot hole, evidently, in the high wainscoating of the west room. He had never noticed it before, and without realizing what he was doing, he stooped and squinted through it.

Yonder, in a pool of sunlight, stood his new neighbour, wholly unclad, doing exercises of some sort before a long gilt mirror. Hedger did not happen to think how unpardonable it was of him to watch her. Nudity was not improper to any one who had worked so much from the figure, and he continued to look, simply because he had never seen a woman's body so beautiful as this one,—positively glorious in action. As she swung her arms and changed from one pivot of motion to another, muscular energy seemed to flow through her from her toes to her finger-tips. The soft flush of exercise and the gold of afternoon sun played over her flesh together, enveloped her in a luminous mist which, as she turned and twisted, made now an arm, now a shoulder, now a thigh, dissolve in pure light and instantly recover its outline with the next gesture. Hedger's fingers curved as if he were holding a crayon; mentally he was doing the whole figure in a single running line, and the charcoal seemed to explode in his hand at the point where the energy of each gesture was discharged into the whirling disc of light, from a foot or shoulder, from the up-thrust chin or the lifted breasts.

He could not have told whether he watched her for six minutes or sixteen. When her gymnastics were over, she paused to catch up a lock of hair that had come down, and examined with solicitude a little reddish mole that grew under her left arm-pit. Then, with her hand on her hip, she walked unconcernedly across the room and disappeared through the door into her bedchamber.

Disappeared—Don Hedger was crouching on his knees, staring at the golden shower which poured in through the west windows, at the lake of gold sleeping on the faded Turkish carpet. The spot was enchanted; a vision out of Alexandria, out of the remote pagan past, had bathed itself there in Helianthine fire.[10]

When he crawled out of his closet, he stood blinking at the grey sheet stuffed with laundry, not knowing what had happened to him. He felt a little sick as he contemplated the bundle. Everything here was different; he hated the disorder of the place, the grey prison light, his old shoes and himself and all his slovenly habits. The black calico curtains that ran on wires over his big window were white with dust. There were three greasy frying pans in the sink, and the sink itself— He felt desperate. He couldn't stand this another minute. He took up an armful of winter clothes and ran down four flights into the basement.

"Mrs. Foley," he began, "I want my room cleaned this afternoon, thoroughly cleaned. Can you get a woman for me right away?"

"Is it company you're having?" the fat, dirty janitress enquired. Mrs. Foley was the widow of a useful Tammany man,[11] and she owned real estate in Flatbush. She was huge and soft as a feather bed. Her face and arms were permanently coated with dust, grained like wood where the sweat had trickled.

"Yes, company. That's it."

"Well, this is a queer time of the day to be asking for a cleaning woman. It's likely I can get you old Lizzie, if she's not drunk. I'll send Willy round to see."

Willy, the son of fourteen, roused from the stupor and stain of his fifth box of cigarettes by the gleam of a quarter, went out. In five minutes he returned with old Lizzie,—she smelling strong of spirits and wearing several jackets which she had put on one over the other, and a number of skirts, long and short, which made her resemble an animated dish-clout. She had, of course, to borrow her equipment from Mrs. Foley, and toiled up the long flights, dragging mop and pail and broom. She told Hedger to be of good cheer, for he had got the right woman for the job, and showed him a great leather strap she wore about her wrist to prevent dislocation of tendons. She swished about the place, scattering dust and splashing soapsuds, while he watched her in nervous despair. He stood over Lizzie and made her scour the sink, directing her roughly, then paid her and got rid of her. Shutting the door on his failure, he hurried off with his dog to lose himself among the stevedores and dock labourers on West Street.

A strange chapter began for Don Hedger. Day after day, at that hour in the afternoon, the hour before his neighbour dressed for dinner, he crouched down in his closet to watch her go through her mysterious exercises. It did not occur to him that his conduct was detestable; there was nothing shy or retreating about this unclad girl,—a bold body, studying itself quite coolly and evidently well pleased with itself, doing all this for a purpose. Hedger scarcely regarded his action as conduct at all; it was something that had happened to him. More than once he went out and tried to stay away for the whole afternoon, but at about five o'clock he was sure to find himself among his old shoes in the dark. The pull of that aperture was stronger than his will,—and he had always considered his will the strongest thing about him. When she threw herself upon the divan and lay resting, he still stared, holding his breath. His nerves were so on edge that a sudden noise made him start and brought out the sweat on his forehead. The dog would come and tug at his sleeve, knowing that something was wrong with his master. If he attempted a mournful whine, those strong hands closed about his throat.

When Hedger came slinking out of his closet, he sat down on the edge of the couch, sat for hours without moving. He was not painting at all now. This thing, whatever it was, drank him up as ideas had sometimes done, and he sank into a stupor of idleness as deep and dark as the stupor of work. He could not understand it; he was no boy, he had worked from models for years, and a woman's body was no mystery to him. Yet now he did nothing but sit and think about one. He slept very little, and with the first light of morning he awoke as completely possessed by this woman as if he had been with her all the night before. The unconscious operations of life went on in him only to perpetuate this excitement. His brain held but one image now—vibrated, burned with it. It was a heathenish feeling; without friendliness, almost without tenderness.

Women had come and gone in Hedger's life. Not having had a mother to begin with, his relations with them, whether amorous or friendly, had been casual. He got on well with janitresses and washwomen, with Indians and with the peasant women of foreign countries. He had friends among the silk-skirt factory girls who came to eat their lunch in Washington Square, and he sometimes took a model for a day in the country. He felt an unreasoning antipathy toward the well-dressed women he saw coming out of big shops, or driving in the Park. If, on his way to the Art Museum, he noticed a pretty girl standing on the steps of one of the houses on upper Fifth Avenue, he frowned at her and went by with his shoulders hunched up as if he were cold. He had never known such girls, or heard them talk, or seen the inside of the houses in which they lived; but he believed them all to be artificial and, in an aesthetic sense, perverted. He saw them enslaved by desire of merchandise and manufactured articles, effective only in making life complicated and insincere and in embroidering it with ugly and meaningless trivialities. They were enough, he thought, to make one almost forget woman as she existed in art, in thought, and in the universe.

He had no desire to know the woman who had, for the time at least, so broken up his life,—no curiosity about her every-day personality. He shunned any revelation of it, and he listened for Miss Bower's coming and going, not to encounter, but to avoid her. He wished that the girl who wore shirt-waists and got letters from Chicago would keep out of his way, that she did not exist. With her he had naught to make. But in a room full of sun, before an old mirror, on a little enchanted rug of sleeping colours, he had seen a woman who emerged naked through a door, and disappeared naked. He thought of that body as never having been clad, or as having worn the stuffs and dyes of all the centuries but his own. And for him she had no geographical associations; unless with Crete, or Alexandria, or Veronese's[12] Venice. She was the immortal conception, the perennial theme.

The first break in Hedger's lethargy occurred one afternoon

when two young men came to take Eden Bower out to dine. They went into her music room, laughed and talked for a few minutes, and then took her away with them. They were gone a long while, but he did not go out for food himself; he waited for them to come back. At last he heard them coming down the hall, gayer and more talkative than when they left. One of them sat down at the piano, and they all began to sing. This Hedger found absolutely unendurable. He snatched up his hat and went running down the stairs. Caesar leaped beside him, hoping that old times were coming back. They had supper in the oysterman's basement and then sat down in front of their own doorway. The moon stood full over the Square, a thing of regal glory; but Hedger did not see the moon; he was looking, murderously, for men. Presently two, wearing straw hats and white trousers and carrying canes, came down the steps from his house. He rose and dogged them across the Square. They were laughing and seemed very much elated about something. As one stopped to light a cigarette, Hedger caught from the other:

"Don't you think she has a beautiful talent?"

His companion threw away his match. "She has a beautiful figure." They both ran to catch the stage.

Hedger went back to his studio. The light was shining from her transom. For the first time he violated her privacy at night, and peered through that fatal aperture. She was sitting, fully dressed, in the window, smoking a cigarette and looking out over the housetops. He watched her until she rose, looked about her with a disdainful, crafty smile, and turned out the light.

The next morning, when Miss Bower went out, Hedger followed her. Her white skirt gleamed ahead of him as she sauntered about the Square. She sat down behind the Garibaldi statue[13] and opened a music book she carried. She turned the leaves carelessly, and several times glanced in his direction. He was on the point of going over to her, when she rose quickly and looked up at the sky. A flock of pigeons had risen from somewhere in the crowded Italian quarter to the south, and were wheeling rapidly up through the morning air, soaring and dropping, scattering and coming together, now grey, now white as silver, as they caught or intercepted the sunlight. She put up her hand to shade her eyes and followed them with a kind of defiant delight in her face.

Hedger came and stood beside her. "You've surely seen them before?"

"Oh, yes," she replied, still looking up. "I see them every day from my windows. They always come home about five o'clock. Where do they live?"

"I don't know. Probably some Italian raises them for the market. They were here long before I came, and I've been here four years."

"In that same gloomy room? Why didn't you take mine when it was vacant?"

"It isn't gloomy. That's the best light for painting."

"Oh, is it? I don't know anything about painting. I'd like to see your pictures sometime. You have such a lot in there. Don't they get dusty, piled up against the wall like that?"

"Not very. I'd be glad to show them to you. Is your name really Eden Bower? I've seen your letters on the table."

"Well, it's the name I'm going to sing under. My father's name is Bowers, but my friend Mr. Jones, a Chicago newspaper man who writes about music, told me to drop the 's.' He's crazy about my voice."

Miss Bower didn't usually tell the whole story,—about anything. Her first name, when she lived in Huntington, Illinois, was Edna, but Mr. Jones had persuaded her to change it to one which he felt would be worthy of her future. She was quick to take suggestions, though she told him she "didn't see what was the matter with 'Edna.' "

She explained to Hedger that she was going to Paris to study. She was waiting in New York for Chicago friends who were to take her over, but who had been detained. "Did you study in Paris?" she asked.

"No, I've never been in Paris. But I was in the south of France all last summer, studying with C——.[14] He's the biggest man among the moderns,—at least I think so."

Miss Bower sat down and made room for him on the bench. "Do tell me about it. I expected to be there by this time, and I can't wait to find out what it's like."

Hedger began to relate how he had seen some of this Frenchman's work in an exhibition, and deciding at once that this was the man for him, he had taken a boat for Marseilles the next week, going over steerage. He proceeded at once to the little town on the coast where his painter lived, and presented himself. The man never took pupils, but because Hedger had come so far, he let him stay. Hedger lived at the master's house and every day they went out together to paint, sometimes on the blazing rocks down by the sea. They wrapped themselves in light woollen blankets and didn't feel the heat. Being there and working with C—— was being in Paradise, Hedger concluded; he learned more in three months than in all his life before.

Eden Bower laughed. "You're a funny fellow. Didn't you do anything but work? Are the women very beautiful? Did you have awfully good things to eat and drink?"

Hedger said some of the women were fine looking, especially one girl who went about selling fish and lobsters. About the food there was nothing remarkable,—except the ripe figs, he liked those. They drank sour wine, and used goat-butter, which was strong and full of hair, as it was churned in a goat skin.

"But don't they have parties or banquets? Aren't there any fine hotels down there?"

"Yes, but they are all closed in summer, and the country people are poor. It's a beautiful country, though."

"How, beautiful?" she persisted.

"If you want to go in, I'll show you some sketches, and you'll see."

Miss Bower rose. "All right. I won't go to my fencing lesson this morning. Do you fence? Here comes your dog. You can't move but he's after you. He always makes a face at me when I meet him in the hall, and shows his nasty little teeth as if he wanted to bite me."

In the studio Hedger got out his sketches, but to Miss Bower, whose favourite pictures were Christ Before Pilate and a redhaired Magdalen of Henner,[15] these landscapes were not at all beautiful, and they gave her no idea of any country whatsoever. She was careful not to commit herself, however. Her vocal teacher had already convinced her that she had a great deal to learn about many things.

"Why don't we go out to lunch somewhere?" Hedger asked, and began to dust his fingers with a handkerchief—which he got out of sight as swiftly as possible.

"All right, the Brevoort," she said carelessly. "I think that's a good place, and they have good wine. I don't care for cocktails."

Hedger felt his chin uneasily. "I'm afraid I haven't shaved this morning. If you could wait for me in the Square? It won't take me ten minutes."

Left alone, he found a clean collar and handkerchief, brushed his coat and blacked his shoes, and last of all dug up ten dollars from the bottom of an old copper kettle he had brought from Spain. His winter hat was of such a complexion that the Brevoort hall boy winked at the porter as he took it and placed it on the rack in a row of fresh straw ones.

IV

That afternoon Eden Bower was lying on the couch in her music room, her face turned to the window, watching the pigeons. Reclining thus she could see none of the neighbouring roofs, only the sky itself and the birds that crossed and recrossed her field of vision, white as scraps of paper blowing in the wind. She was thinking that she was young and handsome and had had a good lunch, that a very easy-going, light-hearted city lay in the streets below her; and she was wondering why she found this queer painter chap, with his lean, bluish cheeks and heavy black eyebrows, more interesting than the smart young men she met at her teacher's studio.

Eden Bower was, at twenty, very much the same person that we all know her to be at forty, except that she knew a great deal less. But one thing she knew: that she was to be Eden Bower. She was like some one standing before a great show window full of beautiful and costly things, deciding which she will order. She understands that they will not all be delivered immediately, but one by one they will arrive at her door. She already knew some of the many things that were to happen to her; for instance, that the Chicago millionaire who was going to take her abroad with his sister as chaperone, would eventually press his claim in quite another manner. He was the most circumspect of bachelors, afraid of everything obvious, even of women who were too flagrantly handsome. He was a nervous collector of pictures and furniture, a nervous patron of music, and a nervous host; very cautious about his health, and about any course of conduct that might make him ridiculous. But she knew that he would at last throw all his precautions to the winds.

People like Eden Bower are inexplicable. Her father sold farming machinery in Huntington, Illinois, and she had grown up with no acquaintances or experiences outside of that prairie town. Yet from her earliest childhood she had not one conviction or opinion in common with the people about her,—the only people she knew. Before she was out of short dresses she had made up her mind that she was going to be an actress, that she would live far away in great cities, that she would be much admired by men and would have everything she wanted. When she was thirteen, and was already singing and reciting for church entertainments, she read in some illustrated magazine a long article about the late Czar of Russia, then just come to the throne or about to come to it. After that, lying in the hammock on the front porch on summer evenings, or sitting through a long sermon in the family pew, she amused herself by trying to make up her mind whether she would or would not be the Czar's mistress when she played in his Capital. Now Edna had met this fascinating word only in the novels of Ouida,[16]—her hard-worked little mother kept a long row of them in the upstairs storeroom, behind the linen chest. In Huntington, women who bore that relation to men were called by a very different name, and their lot was not an enviable one; of all the shabby and poor, they were the shabbiest. But then, Edna had never lived in Huntington, not even before she began to find books like "Sapho" and "Mademoiselle de Maupin,"[17] secretly sold in paper covers throughout Illinois. It was as if she had come into Huntington, into the Bowers family, on one of the trains that puffed over the marshes behind their back fence all day long, and was waiting for another train to take her out.

As she grew older and handsomer, she had many beaux, but these small-town boys didn't interest her. If a lad kissed her when he brought her home from a dance, she was indulgent and she rather liked it. But if he pressed her further, she slipped away from him, laughing. After she began to sing in Chicago, she was consistently discreet. She stayed as a guest in rich people's houses, and she knew that she was being watched like a rabbit in a laboratory. Covered up in bed, with the lights out, she thought her own thoughts, and laughed.

This summer in New York was her first taste of freedom. The Chicago capitalist, after all his arrangements were made for sailing, had been compelled to go to Mexico to look after oil interests. His sister knew an excellent singing master in New York. Why should not a discreet, well-balanced girl like Miss Bower spend the summer there, studying quietly? The capitalist suggested that his sister might enjoy a summer on Long Island; he would rent the Griffiths' place for her, with all the servants, and Eden could stay there. But his sister met this proposal with a cold stare. So it fell out, that between selfishness and greed, Eden got a summer all her own,—which really did a great deal toward making her an artist and whatever else she was afterward to become. She had time to look about, to watch without being watched; to select diamonds in one window and furs in another, to select shoulders and moustaches in the big hotels where she went to lunch. She had the easy freedom of obscurity and the consciousness of power. She enjoyed both. She was in no hurry.

While Eden Bower watched the pigeons, Don Hedger sat on the other side of the bolted doors, looking into a pool of dark turpentine, at his idle brushes, wondering why a woman could do this to him. He, too, was sure of his future and knew that he was a chosen man. He could not know, of course, that he was merely the first to fall under a fascination which was to be disastrous to a few men and pleasantly stimulating to many thousands. Each of these two young people sensed the future, but not completely. Don Hedger knew that nothing much would ever happen to him. Eden Bower understood that to her a great deal would happen. But she did not guess that her neighbour would have more tempestuous adventures sitting in his dark studio than she would find in all the capitals of Europe, or in all the latitude of conduct she was prepared to permit herself.

V

One Sunday morning Eden was crossing the Square with a spruce young man in a white flannel suit and a panama hat. They had been breakfasting at the Brevoort and he was coaxing her to let him come up to her rooms and sing for an hour.

"No, I've got to write letters. You must run along now. I see a friend of mine over there, and I want to ask him about something beforc I go up."

"That fellow with the dog? Where did you pick him up?" the young man glanced toward the seat under a sycamore where Hedger was reading the morning paper.

"Oh, he's an old friend from the West," said Eden easily. "I won't introduce you, because he doesn't like people. He's a recluse. Good-bye. I can't be sure about Tuesday. I'll go with you if I have time after my lesson." She nodded, left him, and went over to the seat littered with newspapers. The young man went up the Avenue without looking back.

"Well, what are you going to do today? Shampoo this animal all morning?" Eden enquired teasingly.

Hedger made room for her on the seat. "No, at twelve o'clock I'm going out to Coney Island. One of my models is going up in a balloon this afternoon. I've often promised to go and see her, and now I'm going."

Eden asked if models usually did such stunts. No, Hedger told her, but Molly Welch added to her earnings in that way. "I believe," he added, "she likes the excitement of it. She's got a good deal of spirit. That's why I like to paint her. So many models have flaccid bodies."

"And she hasn't, eh? Is she the one who comes to see you? I can't help hearing her, she talks so loud."

"Yes, she has a rough voice, but she's a fine girl. I don't suppose you'd be interested in going?"

"I don't know," Eden sat tracing patterns on the asphalt with the end of her parasol. "Is it any fun? I got up feeling I'd like to do something different today. It's the first Sunday I've not had to sing in church. I had that engagement for breakfast at the Brevoort, but it wasn't very exciting. That chap can't talk about anything but himself."

Hedger warmed a little. "If you've never been to Coney Island,[18] you ought to go. It's nice to see all the people; tailors and bartenders and prize-fighters with their best girls, and all sorts of folks taking a holiday."

Eden looked sidewise at him. So one ought to be interested in people of that kind, ought one? He was certainly a funny fellow. Yet he was never, somehow, tiresome. She had seen a good deal of him lately, but she kept wanting to know him better, to find out what made him different from men like the one she had just left—whether he really was as different as he seemed. "I'll go with you," she said at last, "if you'll leave that at home." She pointed to Caesar's flickering ears with her sunshade.

"But he's half the fun. You'd like to hear him bark at the waves when they come in."

"No, I wouldn't. He's jealous and disagreeable if he sees you talking to any one else. Look at him now."

"Of course, if you make a face at him. He knows what that means, and he makes a worse face. He likes Molly Welch, and she'll be disappointed if I don't bring him."

Eden said decidedly that he couldn't take both of them. So at twelve o'clock when she and Hedger got on the boat at Desbrosses Street, Caesar was lying on his pallet, with a bone.

Eden enjoyed the boat-ride. It was the first time she had been on the water, and she felt as if she were embarking for France. The light warm breeze and the plunge of the waves made her very wide awake, and she liked crowds of any kind. They went to the balcony of a big, noisy restaurant and had a shore dinner, with tall steins of beer. Hedger had got a big advance from his advertising firm since he first lunched with Miss Bower ten days ago, and he was ready for anything.

After dinner they went to the tent behind the bathing beach, where the tops of two balloons bulged out over the canvas. A red-faced man in a linen suit stood in front of the tent, shouting in a hoarse voice and telling the people that if the crowd was good for five dollars more, a beautiful young woman would risk her life for their entertainment. Four little boys in dirty red uniforms ran about taking contributions in their pillbox hats. One of the balloons was bobbing up and down in its tether and people were shoving forward to get nearer the tent.

"Is it dangerous, as he pretends?" Eden asked.

"Molly says it's simple enough if nothing goes wrong with the balloon. Then it would be all over, I suppose."

"Wouldn't you like to go up with her?"

"I? Of course not. I'm not fond of taking foolish risks."

Eden sniffed. "I shouldn't think sensible risks would be very much fun."

Hedger did not answer, for just then every one began to shove the other way and shout, "Look out. There she goes!" and a band of six pieces commenced playing furiously.

As the balloon rose from its tent enclosure, they saw a girl in green tights standing in the basket, holding carelessly to one of the ropes with one hand and with the other waving to the spectators. A long rope trailed behind to keep the balloon from blowing out to sea.

As it soared, the figure in green tights in the basket diminished to a mere spot, and the balloon itself, in the brilliant light, looked like a big silver-grey bat, with its wings folded. When it began to sink, the girl stepped through the hole in the basket to a trapeze that hung below, and gracefully descended through the air, holding to the rod with both hands, keeping her body taut and her feet close together. The crowd, which had grown very large by this time, cheered vociferously. The men took off their hats and waved, little boys shouted, and fat old women, shining with the heat and a beer lunch, murmured admiring comments upon the balloonist's figure. "Beautiful legs, she has!"

"That's so," Hedger whispered. "Not many girls would look well in that position." Then, for some reason, he blushed a slow, dark, painful crimson.

The balloon descended slowly, a little way from the tent, and the red-faced man in the linen suit caught Molly Welch before her feet touched the ground, and pulled her to one side. The band struck up "Blue Bell" by way of welcome, and one of the sweaty pages ran forward and presented the balloonist with a large bouquet of artificial flowers. She smiled and thanked him, and ran back across the sand to the tent.

"Can't we go inside and see her?" Eden asked. "You can explain to the door man. I want to meet her." Edging forward, she herself addressed the man in the linen suit and slipped something from her purse into his hand.

They found Molly seated before a trunk that had a mirror in the lid and a "makeup" outfit spread upon the tray. She was wiping the cold cream and powder from her neck with a discarded chemise.

"Hello, Don," she said cordially. "Brought a friend?"

Eden liked her. She had an easy, friendly manner, and there was something boyish and devil-may-care about her.

"Yes, it's fun. I'm mad about it," she said in reply to Eden's questions. "I always want to let go, when I come down on the bar. You don't feel your weight at all, as you would on a stationary trapeze."

The big drum boomed outside, and the publicity man began shouting to newly arrived boatloads. Miss Welch took a last pull at her cigarette. "Now you'll have to get out, Don. I change for the next act. This time I go up in a black evening dress, and lose the skirt in the basket before I start down."

"Yes, go along," said Eden. "Wait for me outside the door. I'll stay and help her dress."

Hedger waited and waited, while women of every build bumped into him and begged his pardon, and the red pages ran about holding out their caps for coins, and the people ate and perspired and shifted parasols against the sun. When the band began to play a two-step, all the bathers ran up out of the surf to watch the ascent. The second balloon bumped and rose, and the crowd began shouting to the girl in a black evening dress who stood leaning against the ropes and smiling. "It's a new girl," they called. "It ain't the Countess this time. You're a peach, girlie!"

The balloonist acknowledged these compliments, bowing and looking down over the sea of upturned faces,—but Hedger was determined she should not see him, and he darted behind the tent-fly. He was suddenly dripping with cold sweat, his mouth was full of the bitter taste of anger and his tongue felt stiff behind his teeth. Molly Welch, in a shirt-waist and a white tam-o'-shanter cap, slipped out from the tent under his arm and laughed up in his face. "She's a crazy one you brought along. She'll get what she wants!"

"Oh, I'll settle with you, all right!" Hedger brought out with difficulty.

"It's not my fault, Donnie. I couldn't do anything with her. She bought me off. What's the matter with you? Are you soft on her? She's safe enough. It's as easy as rolling off a log, if you keep cool." Molly Welch was rather excited herself, and she was chewing gum at a high speed as she stood beside him, looking up at the floating silver cone. "Now watch," she exclaimed suddenly. "She's coming down on the bar. I advised her to cut that out, but you see she does it first-rate. And she got rid of the skirt, too. Those black tights show off her legs very well. She keeps her feet together like I told her, and makes a good line along the back. See the light on those silver slippers,—that was a good idea I had. Come along to meet her. Don't be a grouch; she's done it fine!"

Molly tweaked his elbow, and then left him standing like a stump, while she ran down the beach with the crowd.

Though Hedger was sulking, his eye could not help seeing the low blue welter of the sea, the arrested bathers, standing in the surf, their arms and legs stained red by the dropping sun, all shading their eyes and gazing upward at the slowly falling silver star.

Molly Welch and the manager caught Eden under the arms and lifted her aside, a red page dashed up with a bouquet, and the band struck up "Blue Bell." Eden laughed and bowed, took Molly's arm, and ran up the sand in her black tights and silver slippers, dodging the friendly old women, and the gallant sports who wanted to offer their homage on the spot.

When she emerged from the tent, dressed in her own clothes, that part of the beach was almost deserted. She stepped to her companion's side and said carelessly: "Hadn't we better try to catch this boat? I hope you're not sore at me. Really, it was lots of fun."

Hedger looked at his watch. "Yes, we have fifteen minutes to get to the boat," he said politely.

As they walked toward the pier, one of the pages ran up panting. "Lady, you're carrying off the bouquet," he said, aggrievedly.

Eden stopped and looked at the bunch of spotty cotton roses in her hand. "Of course. I want them for a souvenir. You gave them to me yourself."

"I give 'em to you for looks, but you can't take 'em away. They belong to the show."

"Oh, you always use the same bunch?"

"Sure we do. There ain't too much money in this business."

She laughed and tossed them back to him. "Why are you angry?" she asked Hedger. "I wouldn't have done it if I'd been with some fellows, but I thought you were the sort who wouldn't mind. Molly didn't for a minute think you would."

"What possessed you to do such a fool thing?" he asked roughly.

"I don't know. When I saw her coming down, I wanted to try it. It looked exciting. Didn't I hold myself as well as she did?"

Hedger shrugged his shoulders, but in his heart he forgave her.

The return boat was not crowded, though the boats that passed them, going out, were packed to the rails. The sun was setting. Boys and girls sat on the long benches with their arms about each other, singing. Eden felt a strong wish to propitiate her companion, to be alone with him. She had been curiously wrought up by her balloon trip; it was a lark, but not very satisfying unless one came back to something after the flight. She wanted to be admired and adored. Though Eden said nothing, and sat with her arms limp on the rail in front of her, looking languidly at the rising silhouette of the city and the bright path of the sun, Hedger felt a strange drawing near to her. If he but brushed her white skirt with his knee, there was an instant communication between them, such as there had never been before. They did not talk at all, but when they went over the gangplank she took his arm and kept her shoulder close to his. He felt as if they were enveloped in a highly charged atmosphere, an invisible network of subtle, almost painful sensibility. They had somehow taken hold of each other.

An hour later, they were dining in the back garden of a little French hotel on Ninth Street, long since passed away. It was cool and leafy there, and the mosquitoes were not very numerous. A party of South Americans at another table were drinking champagne, and Eden murmured that she thought she would like some, if it were not too expensive. "Perhaps it will make me think I am in the balloon again. That was a very nice feeling. You've forgiven me, haven't you?"

Hedger gave her a quick straight look from under his black eyebrows, and something went over her that was like a chill, except that it was warm and feathery. She drank most of the wine; her companion was indifferent to it. He was talking more to her tonight than he had ever done before. She asked him about a new picture she had seen in his room; a queer thing full of stiff, supplicating female figures. "It's Indian, isn't it?"

"Yes. I call it Rain Spirits, or maybe, Indian Rain. In the Southwest, where I've been a good deal, the Indian traditions make women have to do with the rain-fall. They were supposed to control it, somehow, and to be able to find springs, and make moisture come out of the earth. You see I'm trying to learn to paint what people think and feel; to get away from all that photographic stuff. When I look at you, I don't see what a camera would see, do I?"

"How can I tell?"

"Well, if I should paint you, I could make you understand what I see." For the second time that day Hedger crimsoned unexpectedly, and his eyes fell and steadily contemplated a dish of little radishes. "That particular picture I got from a story a Mexican priest told me; he said he found it in an old manuscript book in a monastery down there, written by some Spanish Missionary, who got his stories from the Aztecs. This one he called 'The Forty Lovers of the Queen,' and it was more or less about rain-making."

"Aren't you going to tell it to me?" Eden asked.

Hedger fumbled among the radishes. "I don't know if it's the proper kind of story to tell a girl."

She smiled; "Oh, forget about that! I've been balloon riding today. I like to hear you talk."

Her low voice was flattering. She had seemed like clay in his hands ever since they got on the boat to come home. He leaned back in his chair, forgot his food, and, looking at her intently, began to tell his story, the theme of which he somehow felt was dangerous tonight.

The tale began, he said, somewhere in Ancient Mexico, and concerned the daughter of a king. The birth of this Princess was preceded by unusual portents. Three times her mother dreamed that she was delivered of serpents, which betokened that the child she carried would have power with the rain gods. The serpent was the symbol of water. The Princess grew up dedicated to the gods, and wise men taught her the rain-making mysteries. She was with difficulty restrained from men and was guarded at all times, for it was the law of the Thunder that she be maiden until her marriage. In the years of her adolescence, rain was abundant with her people. The oldest man could not remember such fertility. When the Princess had counted eighteen summers, her father went to drive out a war party that harried his borders on the north and troubled his prosperity. The King destroyed the invaders and brought home many prisoners. Among the prisoners was a young chief, taller than any of his captors, of such strength and ferocity that the King's people came a day's journey to look at him. When the Princess beheld his great stature, and saw that his arms and breast were covered with the figures of wild animals, bitten into the skin and coloured, she begged his life from her father. She desired that he should practise his art upon her, and prick upon her skin the signs of Rain and Lightning and Thunder, and stain the wounds with herb-juices, as they were upon his own body. For many days, upon the roof of the King's house, the Princess submitted herself to the bone needle, and the women with her marvelled at her fortitude. But the Princess was without shame before the Captive, and it came about that he threw from him his needles and his stains, and fell upon the Princess to violate her honour; and her women ran down from the roof screaming, to call the guard which stood at the gateway of the King's house, and none stayed to protect their mistress. When the guard came, the Captive was thrown into bonds, and he was gelded, and his tongue was torn out, and he was given for a slave to the Rain Princess.

The country of the Aztecs to the east was tormented by thirst, and their king, hearing much of the rain-making arts of the Princess, sent an embassy to her father, with presents and an offer of marriage. So the Princess went from her father to be the Queen of the Aztecs, and she took with her the Captive, who served her in everything with entire fidelity and slept upon a mat before her door.

The King gave his bride a fortress on the outskirts of the city, whither she retired to entreat the rain gods. This fortress was called the Queen's House, and on the night of the new moon the Queen came to it from the palace. But when the moon waxed and grew toward the round, because the god of Thunder had had his will of her, then the Queen returned to the King. Drouth abated in the country and rain fell abundantly by reason of the Queen's power with the stars.

When the Queen went to her own house she took with her no servant but the Captive, and he slept outside her door and brought her food after she had fasted. The Queen had a jewel of great value, a turquoise that had fallen from the sun, and had the image of the sun upon it. And when she desired a young man whom she had seen in the army or among the slaves, she sent the Captive to him with the jewel, for a sign that he should come to her secretly at the Queen's House upon business concerning the welfare of all. And some, after she had talked with them, she sent away with rewards; and some she took into her chamber and kept them by her for one night or two. Afterward she called the Captive and bade him conduct the youth by the secret way he had come, underneath the chambers of the fortress. But for the going away of the Queen's lovers the Captive took out the bar that was beneath a stone in the floor of the passage, and put in its stead a rush-reed, and the youth stepped upon it and fell through into a cavern that was the bed of an underground river, and whatever was thrown into it was not seen again. In this service nor in any other did the Captive fail the Queen.

But when the Queen sent for the Captain of the Archers, she detained him four days in her chamber, calling often for food and wine, and was greatly content with him. On the fourth day she went to the Captive outside her door and said: "Tomorrow take this man up by the sure way, by which the King comes, and let him live."

In the Queen's door were arrows, purple and white. When she desired the King to come to her publicly, with his guard, she sent him a white arrow; but when she sent the purple, he came secretly, and covered himself with his mantle to be hidden from the stone gods at the gate. On the fifth night that the Queen was with her lover, the Captive took a purple arrow to the King, and the King came secretly and found them together. He killed the Captain with his own hand, but the Queen he brought to public trial. The Captive, when he was put to the question, told on his fingers forty men that he had let through the underground passage into the river. The Captive and the Queen were put to death by fire, both on the same day, and afterward there was scarcity of rain.

* * *

Eden Bower sat shivering a little as she listened. Hedger was not trying to please her, she thought, but to antagonize and frighten her by his brutal story. She had often told herself that his lean, big-boned lower jaw was like his bull-dog's, but tonight his face made Caesar's most savage and determined expression seem an affectation. Now she was looking at the man he really was. Nobody's eyes had ever defied her like this. They were searching her and seeing everything; all she had concealed from Livingston, and from the millionaire and his friends, and from the newspaper men. He was testing her, trying her out, and she was more ill at ease than she wished to show.

"That's quite a thrilling story," she said at last, rising and winding her scarf about her throat. "It must be getting late. Almost every one has gone."

They walked down the Avenue like people who have quarrelled, or who wish to get rid of each other. Hedger did not take her arm at the street crossings, and they did not linger in the Square. At her door he tried none of the old devices of the Livingston boys. He stood like a post, having forgotten to take off his hat, gave her a harsh, threatening glance, muttered "goodnight," and shut his own door noisily.

There was no question of sleep for Eden Bower. Her brain was working like a machine that would never stop. After she undressed, she tried to calm her nerves by smoking a cigarette, lying on the divan by the open window. But she grew wider and wider awake, combating the challenge that had flamed all evening in Hedger's eyes. The balloon had been one kind of excitement, the wine another; but the thing that had roused her, as a blow rouses a proud man, was the doubt, the contempt, the sneering hostility with which the painter had looked at her when he told his savage story. Crowds and balloons were all very well, she reflected, but woman's chief adventure is man. With a mind over active and a sense of life over strong, she wanted to walk across the roofs in the starlight, to sail over the sea and face at once a world of which she had never been afraid.

Hedger must be asleep; his dog had stopped sniffing under the double doors. Eden put on her wrapper and slippers and stole softly down the hall over the old carpet; one loose board creaked just as she reached the ladder. The trapdoor was open, as always on hot nights. When she stepped out on the roof she drew a long breath and walked across it, looking up at the sky. Her foot touched something soft; she heard a low growl, and on the instant Caesar's sharp little teeth caught her ankle and waited. His breath was like steam on her leg. Nobody had ever intruded upon his roof before, and he panted for the movement or the word that would let him spring his jaw. Instead, Hedger's hand seized his throat.

"Wait a minute. I'll settle with him," he said grimly. He dragged the dog toward the manhole and disappeared. When he came back, he found Eden standing over by the dark chimney, looking away in an offended attitude.

"I caned him unmercifully," he panted. "Of course you didn't hear anything; he never whines when I beat him. He didn't nip you, did he?"

"I don't know whether he broke the skin or not," she answered aggrievedly, still looking off into the west.

"If I were one of your friends in white pants, I'd strike a match to find whether you were hurt, though I know you are not, and then I'd see your ankle, wouldn't I?"

"I suppose so."

He shook his head and stood with his hands in the pockets of his old painting jacket. "I'm not up to such boy-tricks. If you want the place to yourself, I'll clear out. There are plenty of places where I can spend the night, what's left of it. But if you stay here and I stay here—" He shrugged his shoulders.

Eden did not stir, and she made no reply. Her head drooped slightly, as if she were considering. But the moment he put his arms about her they began to talk, both at once, as people do in an opera. The instant avowal brought out a flood of trivial admissions. Hedger confessed his crime, was reproached and forgiven, and now Eden knew what it was in his look that she had found so disturbing of late.

Standing against the black chimney, with the sky behind and blue shadows before, they looked like one of Hedger's own paintings of that period; two figures, one white and one dark, and nothing whatever distinguishable about them but that they were male and female. The faces were lost, the contours blurred in shadow, but the figures were a man and a woman, and that was their whole concern and their mysterious beauty,—it was the rhythm in which they moved, at last, along the roof and down into the dark hole; he first, drawing her gently after him. She came down very slowly. The excitement and bravado and uncertainty of that long day and night seemed all at once to tell upon her. When his feet were on the carpet and he reached up to lift her down, she twined her arms about his neck as after a long separation, and turned her face to him, and her lips, with their perfume of youth and passion.

* * *

One Saturday afternoon Hedger was sitting in the window of Eden's music room. They had been watching the pigeons come wheeling over the roofs from their unknown feeding grounds.

"Why," said Eden suddenly, "don't we fix those big doors into your studio so they will open? Then, if I want you, I won't have to go through the hall. That illustrator is loafing about a good deal of late."

"I'll open them, if you wish. The bolt is on your side."

"Isn't there one on yours, too?"

"No. I believe a man lived there for years before I came in, and the nurse used to have these rooms herself. Naturally, the lock was on the lady's side."

Eden laughed and began to examine the bolt. "It's all stuck up with paint." Looking about, her eye lighted upon a bronze Buddah which was one of the nurse's treasures. Taking him by his head, she struck the bolt a blow with his squatting posteriors. The two doors creaked, sagged, and swung weakly inward a little way, as if they were too old for such escapades. Eden tossed the heavy idol into a stuffed chair. "That's better," she exclaimed exultantly. "So the bolts are always on the lady's side? What a lot society takes for granted!"

Hedger laughed, sprang up and caught her arms roughly. "Whoever takes you for granted— Did anybody, ever?"

"Everybody does. That's why I'm here. You are the only one who knows anything about me. Now I'll have to dress if we're going out for dinner."

He lingered, keeping his hold on her. "But I won't always be the only one, Eden Bower. I won't be the last."

"No, I suppose not," she said carelessly. "But what does that matter? You are the first."

As a long, despairing whine broke in the warm stillness, they drew apart. Caesar, lying on his bed in the dark corner, had lifted his head at this invasion of sunlight, and realized that the side of his room was broken open, and his whole world shattered by change. There stood his master and this woman, laughing at him! The woman was pulling the long black hair of this mightiest of men, who bowed his head and permitted it.

VI

In time they quarrelled, of course, and about an abstraction,—as young people often do, as mature people almost never do. Eden came in late one afternoon. She had been with some of her musical friends to lunch at Burton Ives' studio, and she began telling Hedger about its splendours. He listened a moment and then threw down his brushes. "I know exactly what it's like," he said impatiently. "A very good department-store conception of a studio. It's one of the show places."

"Well, it's gorgeous, and he said I could bring you to see him. The boys tell me he's awfully kind about giving people a lift, and you might get something out of it."

Hedger started up and pushed his canvas out of the way. "What could I possibly get from Burton Ives? He's almost the worst painter in the world; the stupidest, I mean."

Eden was annoyed. Burton Ives had been very nice to her and had begged her to sit for him. "You must admit that he's a very successful one," she said coldly.

"Of course he is! Anybody can be successful who will do that sort of thing. I wouldn't paint his pictures for all the money in New York."

"Well, I saw a lot of them, and I think they are beautiful."

Hedger bowed stiffly.

"What's the use of being a great painter if nobody knows about you?" Eden went on persuasively. "Why don't you paint the kind of pictures people can understand, and then, after you're successful, do whatever you like?"

"As I look at it," said Hedger brusquely, "I am successful."

Eden glanced about. "Well, I don't see any evidences of it," she said, biting her lip. "He has a Japanese servant and a wine cellar, and keeps a riding horse."

Hedger melted a little. "My dear, I have the most expensive luxury in the world, and I am much more extravagant than Burton Ives, for I work to please nobody but myself."

"You mean you could make money and don't? That you don't try to get a public?"

"Exactly. A public only wants what has been done over and over. I'm painting for painters,—who haven't been born."

"What would you do if I brought Mr. Ives down here to see your things?"

"Well, for God's sake, don't! Before he left I'd probably tell him what I thought of him."

Eden rose. "I give you up. You know very well there's only one kind of success that's real."

"Yes, but it's not the kind you mean. So you've been thinking me a scrub painter, who needs a helping hand from some fashionable studio man? What the devil have you had anything to do with me for, then?"

"There's no use talking to you," said Eden walking slowly toward the door. "I've been trying to pull wires for you all afternoon, and this is what it comes to." She had expected that the tidings of a prospective call from the great man would be received very differently, and had been thinking as she came home in the stage how, as with a magic wand, she might gild Hedger's future, float him out of his dark hole on a tide of prosperity, see his name in the papers and his pictures in the windows on Fifth Avenue.

Hedger mechanically snapped the midsummer leash on Caesar's collar and they ran downstairs and hurried through Sullivan Street off toward the river. He wanted to be among rough, honest people, to get down where the big drays bumped over stone paving blocks and the men wore corduroy trousers and kept their shirts open at the neck. He stopped for a drink in one of the sagging bar-rooms on the water front. He had never in his life been so deeply wounded; he did not know he could be so hurt. He had told this girl all his secrets. On the roof, in these warm, heavy summer nights, with her hands locked in his, he had been able to explain all his misty ideas about an unborn art the world was waiting for; had been able to explain them better than he had ever done to himself. And she had looked away to the chattels of this uptown studio and coveted them for him! To her he was only an unsuccessful Burton Ives.

Then why, as he had put it to her, did she take up with him? Young, beautiful, talented as she was, why had she wasted herself on a scrub? Pity? Hardly; she wasn't sentimental. There was no explaining her. But in this passion that had seemed so fearless and so fated to be, his own position now looked to him ridiculous; a poor dauber without money or fame,—it was her caprice to load him with favours. Hedger ground his teeth so loud that his dog, trotting beside him, heard him and looked up.

While they were having supper at the oysterman's, he planned his escape. Whenever he saw her again, everything he had told her, that he should never have told any one, would come back to him; ideas he had never whispered even to the painter whom he worshipped and had gone all the way to France to see. To her they must seem his apology for not having horses and a valet, or merely the puerile boastfulness of a weak man. Yet if she slipped the bolt tonight and came through the doors and said, "Oh, weak man, I belong to you!" what could he do? That was the danger. He would catch the train out to Long Beach tonight, and tomorrow he would go on to the north end of Long Island, where an old friend of his had a summer studio among the sand dunes. He would stay until things came right in his mind. And she could find a smart painter, or take her punishment.

When he went home, Eden's room was dark; she was dining out somewhere. He threw his things into a hold-all he had carried about the world with him, strapped up some colours and canvases, and ran downstairs.

VII

Five days later Hedger was a restless passenger on a dirty, crowded Sunday train, coming back to town. Of course he saw now how unreasonable he had been in expecting a Huntington girl to know anything about pictures; here was a whole continent full of people who knew nothing about pictures and he didn't hold it against them. What had such things to do with him and Eden Bower? When he lay out on the dunes, watching the moon come up out of the sea, it had seemed to him that there was no wonder in the world like the wonder of Eden Bower. He was going back to her because she was older than art, because she was the most overwhelming thing that had ever come into his life.

He had written her yesterday, begging her to be at home this evening, telling her that he was contrite, and wretched enough.

Now that he was on his way to her, his stronger feeling unaccountably changed to a mood that was playful and tender. He wanted to share everything with her, even the most trivial things. He wanted to tell her about the people on the train, coming back tired from their holiday with bunches of wilted flowers and dirty daisies; to tell her that the fish-man, to whom she had often sent him for lobsters, was among the passengers, disguised in a silk shirt and a spotted tie, and how his wife looked exactly like a fish, even to her eyes, on which cataracts were forming. He could tell her, too, that he hadn't as much as unstrapped his canvases,—that ought to convince her.

In those days passengers from Long Island came into New York by ferry. Hedger had to be quick about getting his dog out of the express car in order to catch the first boat. The East River, and the bridges, and the city to the west, were burning in the conflagration of the sunset; there was that great home-coming reach of evening in the air.

The car changes from Thirty-fourth Street were too many and too perplexing; for the first time in his life Hedger took a hansom cab for Washington Square. Caesar sat bolt upright on the worn leather cushion beside him, and they jogged off, looking down on the rest of the world.

It was twilight when they drove down lower Fifth Avenue into the Square, and through the Arch behind them were the two long rows of pale violet lights that used to bloom so beautifully against the grey stone and asphalt. Here and yonder about the Square hung globes that shed a radiance not unlike the blue mists of evening, emerging softly when daylight died, as the stars emerged in the thin blue sky. Under them the sharp shadows of the trees fell on the cracked pavement and the sleeping grass. The first stars and the first lights were growing silver against the gradual darkening, when Hedger paid his driver and went into the house,—which, thank God, was still there! On the hall table lay his letter of yesterday, unopened.

He went upstairs with every sort of fear and every sort of hope clutching at his heart; it was as if tigers were tearing him. Why was there no gas burning in the top hall? He found matches and the gas bracket. He knocked, but got no answer; nobody was there. Before his own door were exactly five bottles of milk, standing in a row. The milk-boy had taken spiteful pleasure in thus reminding him that he forgot to stop his order.

Hedger went down to the basement; it, too, was dark. The janitress was taking her evening airing on the basement steps. She sat waving a palm-leaf fan majestically, her dirty calico dress open at the neck. She told him at once that there had been "changes." Miss Bower's room was to let again, and the piano would go tomorrow. Yes, she left yesterday, she sailed for Europe with friends from Chicago. They arrived on Friday, heralded by many telegrams. Very rich people they were said to be, though the man had refused to pay the nurse a month's rent in lieu of notice,—which would have been only right, as the young lady had agreed to take the rooms until October. Mrs. Foley had observed, too, that he didn't overpay her or Willy for their trouble, and a great deal of trouble they had been put to, certainly. Yes, the young lady was very pleasant, but the nurse said there were rings on the mahogany table where she had put tumblers and wine glasses. It was just as well she was gone. The Chicago man was uppish in his ways, but not much to look at. She supposed he had poor health, for there was nothing to him inside his clothes.

Hedger went slowly up the stairs—never had they seemed so long, or his legs so heavy. The upper floor was emptiness and silence. He unlocked his room, lit the gas, and opened the windows. When he went to put his coat in the closet, he found, hanging among his clothes, a pale, flesh-tinted dressing gown he had liked to see her wear, with a perfume—oh, a perfume that was still Eden Bower! He shut the door behind him and there, in the dark, for a moment he lost his manliness. It was when he held this garment to him that he found a letter in the pocket.

The note was written with a lead pencil, in haste: She was sorry that he was angry, but she still didn't know just what she had done. She had thought Mr. Ives would be useful to him; she guessed he was too proud. She wanted awfully to see him again, but Fate came knocking at her door after he had left her. She believed in Fate. She would never forget him, and she knew he would become the greatest painter in the world. Now she must pack. She hoped he wouldn't mind her leaving the dressing gown; somehow, she could never wear it again.

After Hedger read this, standing under the gas, he went back into the closet and knelt down before the wall; the knot hole had been plugged up with a ball of wet paper,—the same blue note-paper on which her letter was written.

He was hard hit. Tonight he had to bear the loneliness of a whole lifetime. Knowing himself so well, he could hardly believe that such a thing had ever happened to him, that such a woman had lain happy and contented in his arms. And now it was over. He turned out the light and sat down on his painter's stool before the big window. Caesar, on the floor beside him, rested his head on his master's knee. We must leave Hedger thus, sitting in his tank with his dog, looking up at the stars.

* * *

COMING, APHRODITE! This legend, in electric lights over the Lexington Opera House, had long announced the return of Eden Bower to New York after years of spectacular success in Paris.[19] She came at last, under the management of an American Opera Company, but bringing her own *chef d'orchestre*.[20]

One bright December afternoon Eden Bower was going down Fifth Avenue in her car, on the way to her broker, in Williams Street. Her thoughts were entirely upon stocks,—Cerro de Pasco,[21] and how much she should buy of it,—when she suddenly looked up and realized that she was skirting Washington Square. She had not seen the place since she rolled out of it in an old-fashioned four-wheeler to seek her fortune, eighteen years ago.

"Arrêtez, Alphonse. Attendez moi,"[22] she called, and opened the door before he could reach it. The children who were streaking over the asphalt on roller skates saw a lady in a long fur coat, and short, high-heeled shoes, alight from a French car and pace slowly about the Square, holding her muff to her chin. This spot, at least, had changed very little, she reflected; the same trees, the same fountain, the white arch, and over yonder, Garibaldi, drawing the sword for freedom. There, just opposite her, was the old red brick house.

"Yes, that is the place," she was thinking. "I can smell the carpets now, and the dog,—what was his name? That grubby bathroom at the end of the hall, and that dreadful Hedger—still, there was something about him, you know—" She glanced up and blinked against the sun. From somewhere in the crowded quarter south of the Square a flock of pigeons rose, wheeling quickly upward into the brilliant blue sky. She threw back her head, pressed her muff closer to her chin, and watched them with a smile of amazement and delight. So they still rose, out of all that dirt and noise and squalor, fleet and silvery, just as they used to rise that summer when she was twenty and went up in a balloon on Coney Island!

Alphonse opened the door and tucked her robes about her. All the way down town her mind wandered from Cerro de Pasco, and she kept smiling and looking up at the sky.

When she had finished her business with the broker, she asked him to look in the telephone book for the address of M. Gaston Jules, the picture dealer, and slipped the paper on which he wrote it into her glove. It was five o'clock when she reached the French Galleries, as they were called. On entering she gave the attendant her card, asking him to take it to M. Jules. The dealer appeared very promptly and begged her to come into his private office, where he pushed a great chair toward his desk for her and signalled his secretary to leave the room.

"How good your lighting is in here," she observed, glancing about. "I met you at Simon's studio, didn't I? Oh, no! I never forget anybody who interests me." She threw her muff on his writing table and sank into the deep chair. "I have come to you for some information that's not in my line. Do you know anything about an American painter named Hedger?"

He took the seat opposite her. "Don Hedger? But, certainly! There are some very interesting things of his in an exhibition at V——'s. If you would care to—"

She held up her hand. "No, no. I've no time to go to exhibitions. Is he a man of any importance?"

"Certainly. He is one of the first men among the moderns. That is to say, among the very moderns. He is always coming up with something different. He often exhibits in Paris, you must have seen—"

"No, I tell you I don't go to exhibitions. Has he had great success? That is what I want to know."

M. Jules pulled at his short grey moustache. "But, Madame, there are many kinds of success," he began cautiously.

Madame gave a dry laugh. "Yes, so he used to say. We once quarrelled on that issue. And how would you define his particular kind?"

M. Jules grew thoughtful. "He is a great name with all the young men, and he is decidedly an influence in art. But one can't definitely place a man who is original, erratic, and who is changing all the time."

She cut him short. "Is he much talked about at home? In Paris, I mean? Thanks. That's all I want to know." She rose and began buttoning her coat. "One doesn't like to have been an utter fool, even at twenty."

"Mais, non!" M. Jules handed her her muff with a quick, sympathetic glance. He followed her out through the carpeted show-room, now closed to the public and draped in cheesecloth, and put her into her car with words appreciative of the honour she had done him in calling.

Leaning back in the cushions, Eden Bower closed her eyes, and her face, as the street lamps flashed their ugly orange light upon it, became hard and settled, like a plaster cast; so a sail, that has been filled by a strong breeze, behaves when the wind suddenly dies. Tomorrow night the wind would blow again, and this mask would be the golden face of Aphrodite. But a "big" career takes its toll, even with the best of luck.[23]

The Diamond Mine

I

I FIRST became aware that Cressida Garnet was on board when I saw young men with cameras going up to the boat deck. In that exposed spot she was good-naturedly posing for them—amid fluttering lavender scarfs—wearing a most unseaworthy hat, her broad, vigourous face wreathed in smiles. She was too much an American not to believe in publicity. All advertising was good. If it was good for breakfast foods, it was good for prime donne,—especially for a prima donna who would never be any younger and who had just announced her intention of marrying a fourth time.

Only a few days before, when I was lunching with some friends at Sherry's, I had seen Jerome Brown come in with several younger men, looking so pleased and prosperous that I exclaimed upon it.

"His affairs," some one explained, "are looking up. He's going to marry Cressida Garnet. Nobody believed it at first, but since she confirms it he's getting all sorts of credit. That woman's a diamond mine."

If there was ever a man who needed a diamond mine at hand, immediately convenient, it was Jerome Brown. But as an old friend of Cressida Garnet, I was sorry to hear that mining operations were to be begun again.

I had been away from New York and had not seen Cressida for a year; now I paused on the gangplank to note how very like herself she still was, and with what undiminished zeal she went about even the most trifling things that pertained to her profession. From that distance I could recognize her "carrying" smile, and even what, in Columbus, we used to call "the Garnet look."

At the foot of the stairway leading up to the boat deck stood two of the factors in Cressida's destiny. One of them was her sister, Miss Julia; a woman of fifty with a relaxed, mournful face, an ageing skin that browned slowly, like meerschaum,[1] and the unmistakable "look" by which one knew a Garnet. Beside her, pointedly ignoring her, smoking a cigarette while he ran over the passenger list with supercilious almond eyes, stood a youth in a pink shirt and a green plush hat, holding a French bull-dog on the leash. This was "Horace," Cressida's only son. He, at any rate, had not the Garnet look. He was rich and ruddy, indolent and insolent, with soft oval cheeks and the blooming complexion of twenty-two. There was the beginning of a silky shadow on his upper lip. He seemed like a ripe fruit grown out of a rich soil; "oriental," his mother called his peculiar lusciousness. His aunt's restless and aggrieved glance kept flecking him from the side, but the two were as motionless as the *bouledogue*, standing there on his bench legs and surveying his travelling basket with loathing. They were waiting, in constrained immobility, for Cressida to descend and reanimate them,—will them to do or to be something. Forward, by the rail, I saw the stooped, eager back for which I was unconsciously looking: Miletus Poppas, the Greek Jew, Cressida's accompanist and shadow. We were all there, I thought with a smile, except Jerome Brown.

The first member of Cressida's party with whom I had speech was Mr. Poppas. When we were two hours out I came upon him in the act of dropping overboard a steamer cushion made of American flags. Cressida never sailed, I think, that one of these vivid comforts of travel did not reach her at the dock. Poppas recognized me just as the striped object left his hand. He was standing with his arm still extended over the rail, his fingers contemptuously sprung back. "Lest we forgedt!" he said with a shrug. "Does Madame Cressida know we are to have the pleasure of your company for this voyage?" He spoke deliberate, grammatical English—he despised the American rendering of the language—but there was an indescribably foreign quality in his voice,—a something muted; and though he aspirated his "th's" with such conscientious thoroughness, there was always the thud of a "d" in them. Poppas stood before me in a short, tightly buttoned grey coat and cap, exactly the colour of his greyish skin and hair and waxed moustache; a monocle on a very wide black ribbon dangled over his chest. As to his age, I could not offer a conjecture. In the twelve years I had known his thin lupine face behind Cressida's shoulder, it had not changed. I was used to his cold, supercilious manner, to his alarming, deep-set eyes,—very close together, in colour a yellowish green, and always gleaming with something like defeated fury, as if he were actually on the point of having it out with you, or with the world, at last.

I asked him if Cressida had engagements in London.

"Quite so; the Manchester Festival, some concerts at Queen's Hall, and the Opera at Covent Garden; a rather special production of the operas of Mozart. That she can still do quite well,—which is not at all, of course, what we might have expected, and only goes to show that our Madame Cressida is now, as always, a charming exception to rules." Poppas' tone about his client was consistently patronizing, and he was always trying to draw one into a conspiracy of two, based on a mutual understanding of her shortcomings.

I approached him on the one subject I could think of which was more personal than his usefulness to Cressida, and asked him whether he still suffered from facial neuralgia[2] as much as he had done in former years, and whether he was therefore dreading London, where the climate used to be so bad for him.

"And is still," he caught me up, "And is still! For me to go to London is martyrdom, *chère Madame*. In New York it is bad enough, but in London it is the *auto da fé*,[3] nothing less. My nervous system is exotic in any country washed by the Atlantic ocean, and it shivers like a little hairless dog from Mexico. It never relaxes. I think I have told you about my favourite city in the middle of Asia, *la sainte Asie*,[4] where the rainfall is absolutely nil, and you are protected on every side by hundreds of meters of warm, dry sand. I was there when I was a child once, and it is still my intention to retire there when I have finished with all this. I would be there now, n-ow-ow," his voice rose querulously, "if Madame Cressida did not imagine that she needs me,—and her fancies, you know," he flourished his hands, "one gives in to them. In humouring her caprices you and I have already played some together."

We were approaching Cressida's deck chairs, ranged under the open windows of her stateroom. She was already recumbent, swathed in lavender scarfs and wearing purple orchids—doubtless from Jerome Brown. At her left, Horace had settled down to a French novel, and Julia Garnet, at her right, was complainingly regarding the grey horizon. On seeing me, Cressida struggled under her fur-lined robes and got to her feet,—which was more than Horace or Miss Julia managed to do. Miss Julia, as I could have foretold, was not pleased. All the Garnets had an awkward manner with me. Whether it was that I reminded them of things they wished to forget, or whether they thought I esteemed Cressida too highly and the rest of them too lightly, I do not know; but my appearance upon their scene always put them greatly on their dignity. After Horace had offered me his chair and Miss Julia had said doubtfully that she thought I was looking rather better than when she last saw me, Cressida took my arm and walked me off toward the stern.

"Do you know, Carrie, I half wondered whether I shouldn't find you here, or in London, because you always turn up at critical moments in my life." She pressed my arm confidentially, and I felt that she was once more wrought up to a new purpose. I told her that I had heard some rumour of her engagement.

"It's quite true, and it's all that it should be," she reassured me. "I'll tell you about it later, and you'll see that it's a real solution. They are against me, of course,—all except Horace. He has been such a comfort."

Horace's support, such as it was, could always be had in exchange for his mother's signature, I suspected. The pale May day had turned bleak and chilly, and we sat down by an open hatchway which emitted warm air from somewhere below. At this close range I studied Cressida's face, and felt reassured of her unabated vitality; the old force of will was still there, and with it her characteristic optimism, the old hope of a "solution."

"You have been in Columbus lately?" she was saying. "No, you needn't tell me about it," with a sigh. "Why is it, Caroline, that there is so little of my life I would be willing to live over again? So little that I can even think of without depression. Yet I've really not such a bad conscience. It may mean that I still belong to the future more than to the past, do you think?"

My assent was not warm enough to fix her attention, and she went on thoughtfully: "Of course, it was a bleak country and a bleak period. But I've sometimes wondered whether the bleakness may not have been in me, too; for it has certainly followed me. There, that is no way to talk!" she drew herself up from a momentary attitude of dejection. "Sea air always lets me down at first. That's why it's so good for me in the end."

"I think Julia always lets you down, too," I said bluntly. "But perhaps that depression works out in the same way."

Cressida laughed. "Julia is rather more depressing than Georgie, isn't she? But it was Julia's turn. I can't come alone, and they've grown to expect it. They haven't, either of them, much else to expect."

At this point the deck steward approached us with a blue envelope. "A wireless for you, Madame Garnet."

Cressida put out her hand with impatience, thanked him graciously, and with every indication of pleasure tore open the blue envelope. "It's from Jerome Brown," she said with some confusion, as she folded the paper small and tucked it between the buttons of her close-fitting gown, "Something he forgot to tell me. How long shall you be in London? Good; I want you to meet him. We shall probably be married there as soon as my engagements are over." She rose. "Now I must write some letters. Keep two places at your table, so that I can slip away from my party and dine with you sometimes."

I walked with her toward her chair, in which Mr. Poppas was now reclining. He indicated his readiness to rise, but she shook her head and entered the door of her deck suite. As she passed him, his eye went over her with assurance until it rested upon the folded bit of blue paper in her corsage. He must have seen the original rectangle in the steward's hand; having found it again, he dropped back between Horace and Miss Julia, whom I think he disliked no more than he did the rest of the world. He liked Julia quite as well as he liked me, and he liked me quite as well as he liked any of the women to whom he would be fitfully agreeable upon the voyage. Once or twice, during each crossing, he did his best and made himself very charming indeed, to keep his hand in,—for the same reason that he kept a dummy keyboard in his stateroom, somewhere down in the bowels of the boat. He practised all the small economies; paid the minimum rate, and never took a deck chair, because, as Horace was usually in the cardroom, he could sit in Horace's.

The three of them lay staring at the swell which was steadily growing heavier. Both men had covered themselves with rugs, after dutifully bundling up Miss Julia. As I walked back and forth on the deck, I was struck by their various degrees of in-expressiveness. Opaque brown eyes, almond-shaped and only half open; wolfish green eyes, close-set and always doing something, with a crooked gleam boring in this direction or in that; watery grey eyes, like the thick edges of broken skylight glass: I would have given a great deal to know what was going on behind each pair of them.

These three were sitting there in a row because they were all woven into the pattern of one large and rather splendid life. Each had a bond, and each had a grievance. If they could have their will, what would they do with the generous, credulous creature who nourished them, I wondered? How deep a humiliation would each egotism exact? They would scarcely have harmed her in fortune or in person (though I think Miss Julia looked forward to the day when Cressida would "break" and could be mourned over),—but the fire at which she warmed herself, the little secret hope,—the illusion, ridiculous or sublime, which kept her going,—that they would have stamped out on the instant, with the whole Garnet pack behind them to make extinction sure. All, except, perhaps, Miletus Poppas. He was a vulture of the vulture race, and he had the beak of one.[5] But I always felt that if ever he had her thus at his mercy,—if ever he came upon the softness that was hidden under so much hardness, the warm credulity under a life so dated and scheduled and "reported" and generally exposed,—he would hold his hand and spare.

The weather grew steadily rougher. Miss Julia at last plucked Poppas by the sleeve and indicated that she wished to be released from her wrappings. When she disappeared, there seemed to be every reason to hope that she might be off the scene for awhile. As Cressida said, if she had not brought Julia, she would have had to bring Georgie, or some other Garnet. Cressida's family was like that of the unpopular Prince of Wales, of whom, when he died, some wag wrote:

If it had been his brother,
Better him than another.
If it had been his sister,
No one would have missed her.

Miss Julia was dampening enough, but Miss Georgie was aggressive and intrusive. She was out to prove to the world, and more especially to Ohio, that all the Garnets were as like Cressida as two peas. Both sisters were club-women, social service workers, and directors in musical societies, and they were continually travelling up and down the Middle West to preside at meetings or to deliver addresses. They reminded one of two sombre, bumping electrics, rolling about with no visible means of locomotion, always running out of power and lying beached in some inconvenient spot until they received a check or a suggestion from Cressy. I was only too well acquainted with the strained, anxious expression that the sight of their handwriting brought to Cressida's face when she ran over her morning mail at breakfast. She usually put their letters by to read "when she was feeling up to it" and hastened to open others which might possibly contain something gracious or pleasant. Sometimes these family unburdenings lay about unread for several days. Any other letters would have got themselves lost, but these bulky epistles, never properly fitted to their envelopes, seemed immune to mischance and unfailingly disgorged to Cressida long explanations as to why her sisters had to do and to have certain things precisely upon her account and because she was so much a public personage.

The truth was that all the Garnets, and particularly her two sisters, were consumed by an habitual, bilious, unenterprising envy of Cressy. They never forgot that, no matter what she did for them or how far she dragged them about the world with her, she would never take one of them to live with her in her Tenth Street house in New York.[6] They thought that was the thing they most wanted. But what they wanted, in the last analysis, was to *be* Cressida. For twenty years she had been plunged in struggle; fighting for her life at first, then for a beginning, for growth, and at last for eminence and perfection; fighting in the dark, and afterward in the light,—which, with her bad preparation, and with her uninspired youth already behind her, took even more courage. During those twenty years the Garnets had been comfortable and indolent and vastly self-satisfied; and now they expected Cressida to make them equal sharers in the finer rewards of her struggle. When her brother Buchanan told me he thought Cressida ought "to make herself one of them," he stated the converse of what he meant. They coveted the qualities which had made her success, as well as the benefits which came from it. More than her furs or her fame or her fortune, they wanted her personal effectiveness, her brighter glow and stronger will to live.

"Sometimes," I have heard Cressida say, looking up from a bunch of those sloppily written letters, "sometimes I get discouraged."

For several days the rough weather kept Miss Julia cloistered in Cressida's deck suite with the maid, Luisa, who confided to me that the Signorina Garnet was *"difficile."* After dinner I usually found Cressida unencumbered, as Horace was always in the cardroom and Mr. Poppas either nursed his neuralgia or went through the exercise of making himself interesting to some one of the young women on board. One evening, the third night out, when the sea was comparatively quiet and the sky was full of broken black clouds, silvered by the moon at their ragged edges, Cressida talked to me about Jerome Brown.

I had known each of her former husbands. The first one, Charley Wilton, Horace's father, was my cousin. He was organist in a church in Columbus, and Cressida married him when she was nineteen. He died of tuberculosis two years after Horace was born. Cressida nursed him through a long illness and made the living besides. Her courage during the three years of her first marriage was fine enough to foreshadow her future to any discerning eye, and it had made me feel that she deserved any number of chances at marital happiness. There had, of course, been a particular reason for each subsequent experiment, and a sufficiently alluring promise of success. Her motives, in the case of Jerome Brown, seemed to me more vague and less convincing than those which she had explained to me on former occasions.

"It's nothing hasty," she assured me. "It's been coming on for several years. He has never pushed me, but he was always there—some one to count on. Even when I used to meet him at the Whitings, while I was still singing at the Metropolitan, I always felt that he was different from the others; that if I were in straits of any kind, I could call on him. You can't know what that feeling means to me, Carrie. If you look back, you'll see it's something I've never had."

I admitted that, in so far as I knew, she had never been much addicted to leaning on people.

"I've never had any one to lean on," she said with a short laugh. Then she went on, quite seriously: "Somehow, my relations with people always become business relations in the end. I suppose it's because,—except for a sort of professional personality, which I've had to get, just as I've had to get so many other things,—I've not very much that's personal to give people. I've had to give too much else. I've had to try too hard for people who wouldn't try at all."

"Which," I put in firmly, "has done them no good, and has robbed the people who really cared about you."

"By making me grubby, you mean?"

"By making you anxious and distracted so much of the time; empty."

She nodded mournfully. "Yes, I know. You used to warn me. Well, there's not one of my brothers and sisters who does not feel that I carried off the family success, just as I might have carried off the family silver,—if there'd been any! They take the view that there were just so many prizes in the bag; I reached in and took them, so there were none left for the others. At my age, that's a dismal truth to waken up to." Cressida reached for my hand and held it a moment, as if she needed courage to face the facts in her case. "When one remembers one's first success; how one hoped to go home like a Christmas tree full of presents— How much one learns in a life-time! That year when Horace was a baby and Charley was dying, and I was touring the West with the Williams band, it was my feeling about my own people that made me go at all. Why I didn't drop myself into one of those muddy rivers, or turn on the gas in one of those dirty hotel rooms, I don't know to this day. At twenty-two you must hope for something more than to be able to bury your husband decently, and what I hoped for was to make my family happy. It was the same afterward in Germany. A young woman must live for human people. Horace wasn't enough. I might have had lovers, of course. I suppose you will say it would have been better if I had."

Though there seemed no need for me to say anything, I murmured that I thought there were more likely to be limits to the rapacity of a lover than to that of a discontented and envious family.

"Well," Cressida gathered herself up, "once I got out from under it all, didn't I? And perhaps, in a milder way, such a release can come again. You were the first person I told when I ran away with Charley, and for a long while you were the only one who knew about Blasius Bouchalka. That time, at least, I shook the Garnets. I wasn't distracted or empty. That time I was all there!"

"Yes," I echoed her, "that time you were all there. It's the greatest possible satisfaction to remember it."

"But even that," she sighed, "was nothing but lawyers and accounts in the end—and a hurt. A hurt that has lasted. I wonder what is the matter with me?"

The matter with Cressida was, that more than any woman I have ever known, she appealed to the acquisitive instinct in men; but this was not easily said, even in the brutal frankness of a long friendship.

We would probably have gone further into the Bouchalka chapter of her life, had not Horace appeared and nervously asked us if we did not wish to take a turn before we went inside. I pleaded indolence, but Cressida rose and disappeared with him. Later I came upon them, standing at the stern above the huddled steerage deck, which was by this time bathed in moonlight, under an almost clear sky. Down there on the silvery floor, little hillocks were scattered about under quilts and shawls; family units, presumably,—

male, female, and young. Here and there a black shawl sat alone, nodding. They crouched submissively under the moonlight as if it were a spell. In one of those hillocks a baby was crying, but the sound was faint and thin, a slender protest which aroused no response. Everything was so still that I could hear snatches of the low talk between my friends. Cressida's voice was deep and entreating. She was remonstrating with Horace about his losses at bridge, begging him to keep away from the cardroom.

"But what else is there to do on a trip like this, my Lady?" he expostulated, tossing his spark of a cigarette-end overboard. "What is there, now, to do?"

"Oh, Horace!" she murmured, "how can you be so? If I were twenty-two, and a boy, with some one to back me—"

Horace drew his shoulders together and buttoned his top-coat. "Oh, I've not your energy, Mother dear. We make no secret of that. I am as I am. I didn't ask to be born into this charming world."

To this gallant speech Cressida made no answer. She stood with her hand on the rail and her head bent forward, as if she had lost herself in thought. The ends of her scarf, lifted by the breeze, fluttered upward, almost transparent in the argent light. Presently she turned away,—as if she had been alone and were leaving only the night sea behind her,—and walked slowly forward; a strong, solitary figure on the white deck, the smoke-like scarf twisting and climbing and falling back upon itself in the light over her head. She reached the door of her stateroom and disappeared. Yes, she was a Garnet, but she was also Cressida; and she had done what she had done.

II

My first recollections of Cressida Garnet have to do with the Columbus Public Schools; a little girl with sunny brown hair and eager bright eyes, looking anxiously at the teacher and reciting the names and dates of the Presidents: "James Buchanan, 1857–1861; Abraham Lincoln, 1861–1865"; etc. Her family came from North Carolina, and they had that to feel superior about before they had Cressy. The Garnet "look," indeed, though based upon a strong family resemblance, was nothing more than the restless, preoccupied expression of an inflamed sense of importance. The father was a Democrat, in the sense that other men were doctors or lawyers. He scratched up some sort of poor living for his family behind office windows inscribed with the words "Real Estate. Insurance. Investments." But it was his political faith that, in a Republican community, gave him his feeling of eminence and originality. The Garnet children were all in school then, scattered along from the first grade to the ninth. In almost any room of our school building you might chance to enter, you saw the self-conscious little face of one or another of them. They were restrained, uncomfortable children, not frankly boastful, but insinuating, and somehow forever demanding special consideration and holding grudges against teachers and classmates who did not show it them; all but Cressida, who was naturally as sunny and open as a May morning.

It was no wonder that Cressy ran away with young Charley Wilton, who hadn't a shabby thing about him except his health. He was her first music teacher, the choir-master of the church in which she sang. Charley was very handsome; the "romantic" son of an old, impoverished family. He had refused to go into a good business with his uncles and had gone abroad to study music when that was an extravagant and picturesque thing for an Ohio boy to do. His letters home were handed round among the members of his own family and of other families equally conservative. Indeed, Charley and what his mother called "his music" were the romantic expression of a considerable group of people; young cousins and old aunts and quiet-dwelling neighbours, allied by the amity of several generations. Nobody was properly married in our part of Columbus unless Charley Wilton, and no other, played the wedding march. The old ladies of the First Church used to say that he "hovered over the keys like a spirit." At nineteen Cressida was beautiful enough to turn a much harder head than the pale, ethereal one Charley Wilton bent above the organ.

That the chapter which began so gracefully ran on into such a stretch of grim, hard prose, was simply Cressida's relentless bad luck. In her undertakings, in whatever she could lay hold of with her two hands, she was successful; but whatever happened to her was almost sure to be bad. Her family, her husbands, her son, would have crushed any other woman I have ever known. Cressida lived, more than most of us, "for others"; and what she seemed to promote among her beneficiaries was indolence and envy and discord—even dishonesty and turpitude.

Her sisters were fond of saying—at club luncheons—that Cressida had remained "untouched by the breath of scandal," which was not strictly true. There were captious people who objected to her long and close association with Miletus Poppas. Her second husband, Ransome McChord, the foreign representative of the great McChord Harvester Company, whom she married in Germany, had so persistently objected to Poppas that she was eventually forced to choose between them. Any one who knew her well could easily understand why she chose Poppas.

While her actual self was the least changed, the least modified by experience that it would be possible to imagine, there had been, professionally, two Cressida Garnets; the big handsome girl, already a "popular favourite" of the concert stage, who took with her to Germany the raw material of a great voice;—and the accomplished artist who came back. The singer that returned was largely the work of Miletus Poppas. Cressida had at least known what she needed, hunted for it, found it, and held fast to it. After experimenting with a score of teachers and accompanists, she settled down to work her problem out with Poppas. Other coaches came and went—she was always trying new ones—but Poppas survived them all. Cressida was not musically intelligent; she never became so. Who does not remember the countless rehearsals which were necessary before she first sang *Isolde* in Berlin; the disgust of the conductor, the sullenness of the tenor, the rages of the blonde *Teufelin*, boiling with the impatience of youth and genius, who sang her *Brangaena*? Everything but her driving power Cressida had to get from the outside.

Poppas was, in his way, quite as incomplete as his pupil. He possessed a great many valuable things for which there is no market; intuitions, discrimination, imagination, a whole twilight world of intentions and shadowy beginnings which were dark to Cressida.

I remember that when "Trilby"[7] was published she fell into a fright and said such books ought to be prohibited by law; which gave me an intimation of what their relationship had actually become.

Poppas was indispensable to her. He was like a book in which she had written down more about herself than she could possibly remember—and it was information that she might need at any moment. He was the one person who knew her absolutely and who saw into the bottom of her grief. An artist's saddest secrets are those that have to do with his artistry. Poppas knew all the simple things that were so desperately hard for Cressida, all the difficult things in which she could count on herself; her stupidities and inconsistencies, the chiaroscuro of the voice itself and what could be expected from thc mind somewhat mismated with it. He knew where she was sound and where she was mended. With him she could share the depressing knowledge of what a wretchedly faulty thing any productive faculty is.

But if Poppas was necessary to her career, she was his career. By the time Cressida left the Metropolitan Opera Company, Poppas was a rich man. He had always received a retaining fee and a percentage of her salary,—and he was a man of simple habits. Her liberality with Poppas was one of the weapons that Horace and the Garnets used against Cressida, and it was a point in the argument by which they justified to themselves their rapacity. Whatever they didn't get, they told themselves, Poppas would. What they got, therefore, they were only saving from Poppas. The Greek ached a good deal at the general pillage, and Cressida's conciliatory methods with her family made him sarcastic and spiteful. But he had to make terms, somehow, with the Garnets and Horace, and with the husband, if there happened to be one. He sometimes reminded them, when they fell to wrangling, that they must not, after all, overturn the boat under them, and that it would be better to stop just before they drove her wild than just after. As he was the only one among them who understood the sources of her fortune,—and they knew it,—he was able, when it came to a general set-to, to proclaim sanctuary for the goose that laid the golden eggs.

That Poppas had caused the break between Cressida and

McChord was another stick her sisters held over her. They pretended to understand perfectly, and were always explaining what they termed her "separation"; but they let Cressida know that it cast a shadow over her family and took a good deal of living down.

A beautiful soundness of body, a seemingly exhaustless vitality, and a certain "squareness" of character as well as of mind, gave Cressida Garnet earning powers that were exceptional even in her lavishly rewarded profession. Managers chose her over the heads of singers much more gifted, because she was so sane, so conscientious, and above all, because she was so sure. Her efficiency was like a beacon to lightly anchored men, and in the intervals between her marriages she had as many suitors as Penelope.[8] Whatever else they saw in her at first, her competency so impressed and delighted them that they gradually lost sight of everything else. Her sterling character was the subject of her story. Once, as she said, she very nearly escaped her destiny. With Blasius Bouchalka she became almost another woman, but not quite. Her "principles," or his lack of them, drove those two apart in the end. It was of Bouchalka that we talked upon that last voyage I ever made with Cressida Garnet, and not of Jerome Brown. She remembered the Bohemian kindly, and since it was the passage in her life to which she most often reverted, it is the one I shall relate here.

III

Late one afternoon in the winter of 189–, Cressida and I were walking in Central Park after the first heavy storm of the year. The snow had been falling thickly all the night before, and all day, until about four o'clock. Then the air grew much warmer and the sky cleared. Overhead it was a soft, rainy blue, and to the west a smoky gold. All around the horizon everything became misty and silvery; even the big, brutal buildings looked like pale violet water-colours on a silver ground. Under the elm trees along the Mall the air was purple as wisterias. The sheep field, toward Broadway, was smooth and white, with a thin gold wash over it. At five o'clock the carriage came for us, but Cressida sent the driver home to the Tenth Street house with the message that she would dine uptown, and that Horace and Mr. Poppas were not to wait for her. As the horses trotted away we turned up the Mall.

"I won't go indoors this evening for any one," Cressida declared. "Not while the sky is like that. Now we will go back to the laurel wood. They are so black, over the snow, that I could cry for joy. I don't know when I've felt so care-free as I feel tonight. Country winter, country stars—they always make me think of Charley Wilton."

She was singing twice a week, sometimes oftener, at the Metropolitan that season, quite at the flood-tide of her powers, and so enmeshed in operatic routine that to be walking in the park at an unaccustomed hour, unattended by one of the men of her entourage, seemed adventurous. As we strolled along the little paths among the snow banks and the bronze laurel bushes, she kept going back to my poor young cousin, dead so long. "Things happen out of season. That's the worst of living. It was untimely for both of us, and yet," she sighed softly, "since he had to die, I'm not sorry. There was one beautifully happy year, though we were so poor, and it gave him—something! It would have been too hard if he'd had to miss everything." (I remember her simplicity, which never changed any more than winter or Ohio change.) "Yes," she went on, "I always feel very tenderly about Charley. I believe I'd do the same thing right over again, even knowing all that had to come after. If I were nineteen tonight, I'd rather go sleigh-riding with Charley Wilton than anything else I've ever done."

We walked until the procession of carriages on the driveway, getting people home to dinner, grew thin, and then we went slowly toward the Seventh Avenue gate, still talking of Charley Wilton. We decided to dine at a place not far away, where the only access from the street was a narrow door, like a hole in the wall, between a tobacconist's and a flower shop. Cressida deluded herself into believing that her incognito was more successful in such nondescript places. She was wearing a long sable coat, and a deep fur hat, hung with red cherries, which she had brought from Russia. Her walk had given her a fine colour, and she looked so much a personage that no disguise could have been wholly effective.

The dining-rooms, frescoed with conventional Italian scenes, were built round a court. The orchestra was playing as we entered and selected our table. It was not a bad orchestra, and we were no sooner seated than the first violin began to speak, to assert itself, as if it were suddenly done with mediocrity.

"We have been recognized," Cressida said complacently. "What a good tone he has, quite unusual. What does he look like?" She sat with her back to the musicians.

The violinist was standing, directing his men with his head and with the beak of his violin. He was a tall, gaunt young man, big-boned and rugged, in skin-tight clothes. His high forehead had a kind of luminous pallour, and his hair was jet black and somewhat stringy. His manner was excited and dramatic. At the end of the number he acknowledged the applause, and Cressida looked at him graciously over her shoulder. He swept her with a brilliant glance and bowed again. Then I noticed his red lips and thick black eyebrows.

"He looks as if he were poor or in trouble," Cressida said. "See how short his sleeves are, and how he mops his face as if the least thing upset him. This is a hard winter for musicians."

The violinist rummaged among some music piled on a chair, turning over the sheets with flurried rapidity, as if he were searching for a lost article of which he was in desperate need. Presently he placed some sheets upon the piano and began vehemently to explain something to the pianist. The pianist stared at the music doubtfully—he was a plump old man with a rosy, bald crown, and his shiny linen and neat tie made him look as if he were on his way to a party. The violinist bent over him, suggesting rhythms with his shoulders and running his bony finger up and down the pages. When he stepped back to his place, I noticed that the other players sat at ease, without raising their instruments.

"He is going to try something unusual," I commented. "It looks as if it might be manuscript."

It was something, at all events, that neither of us had heard before, though it was very much in the manner of the later Russian composers who were just beginning to be heard in New York. The young man made a brilliant dash of it, despite a lagging, scrambling accompaniment by the conservative pianist. This time we both applauded him vigorously and again, as he bowed, he swept us with his eye.

The usual repertory of restaurant music followed, varied by a charming bit from Massenet's "Manon,"[9] then little known in this country. After we paid our check, Cressida took out one of her visiting cards and wrote across the top of it: *"We thank you for the unusual music and the pleasure your playing has given us."* She folded the card in the middle, and asked the waiter to give it to the director of the orchestra. Pausing at the door, while the porter dashed out to call a cab, we saw, in the wall mirror, a pair of wild black eyes following us quite despairingly from behind the palms at the other end of the room. Cressida observed as we went out that the young man was probably having a hard struggle. "He never got those clothes here, surely. They were probably made by a country tailor in some little town in Austria. He seemed wild enough to grab at anything, and was trying to make himself heard above the dishes, poor fellow. There are so many like him. I wish I could help them all! I didn't quite have the courage to send him money. His smile, when he bowed to us, was not that of one who would take it, do you think?"

"No," I admitted, "it wasn't. He seemed to be pleading for recognition. I don't think it was money he wanted."

A week later I came upon some curious-looking manuscript songs on the piano in Cressida's music-room. The text was in some Slavic tongue with a French translation written underneath. Both the handwriting and the musical script were done in a manner experienced, even distinguished. I was looking at them when Cressida came in.

"Oh, yes!" she exclaimed. "I meant to ask you to try them over. Poppas thinks they are very interesting. They are from that young violinist, you remember,—the one we noticed in the restaurant that evening. He sent them with such a nice letter. His name is Blasius Bouchalka (Boú-kal-ka), a Bohemian."

I sat down at the piano and busied myself with the manuscript, while Cressida dashed off necessary notes and wrote checks in a large square checkbook, six to a page. I supposed her immersed in sumptuary preoccupations when she suddenly looked over her shoulder and said, "Yes, that legend, *Šárka*,[10] is the most interesting. Run it through a few times and I'll try it over with you."

There was another, *"Dans les ombres des fôrets tristes,"*[11] which I thought quite as beautiful. They were fine songs; very individual, and each had that spontaneity which makes a song seem inevitable and, once for all, "done." The accompaniments were difficult, but not unnecessarily so; they were free from fatuous ingenuity and fine writing.

"I wish he'd indicated his tempi a little more clearly," I remarked as I finished *Šárka* for the third time. "It matters, because he really has something to say. An orchestral accompaniment would be better, I should think."

"Yes, he sent the orchestral arrangement. Poppas has it. It works out beautifully,—so much colour in the instrumentation. The English horn comes in so effectively there," she rose and indicated the passage, "just right with the voice. I've asked him to come next Sunday, so please be here if you can. I want to know what you think of him."

Cressida was always at home to her friends on Sunday afternoon unless she was billed for the evening concert at the Opera House, in which case we were sufficiently advised by the daily press. Bouchalka must have been told to come early, for when I arrived on Sunday, at four, he and Cressida had the music-room quite to themselves and were standing by the piano in earnest conversation. In a few moments they were separated by other early comers, and I led Bouchalka across the hall to the drawing-room. The guests, as they came in, glanced at him curiously. He wore a dark blue suit, soft and rather baggy, with a short coat, and a high double-breasted vest with two rows of buttons coming up to the loops of his black tie. This costume was even more foreign-looking than his skin-tight dress clothes, but it was more becoming. He spoke hurried, elliptical English, and very good French. All his sympathies were French rather than German—the Czecks lean to the one culture or to the other. I found him a fierce, a transfixing talker. His brilliant eyes, his gaunt hands, his white, deeply-lined forehead, all entered into his speech.

I asked him whether he had not recognized Madame Garnet at once when we entered the restaurant that evening more than a week ago.

"*Mais, certainement!*[12] I hear her twice when she sings in the afternoon, and sometimes at night for the last act. I have a friend who buys a ticket for the first part, and he comes out and gives to me his passback check, and I return for the last act. That is convenient if I am broke." He explained the trick with amusement but without embarrassment, as if it were a shift that we might any of us be put to.

I told him that I admired his skill with the violin, but his songs much more.

He threw out his red under-lip and frowned. "Oh, I have no instrument! The violin I play from necessity; the flute, the piano, as it happens. For three years now I write all the time, and it spoils the hand for violin."

When the maid brought him his tea, he took both muffins and cakes and told me that he was very hungry. He had to lunch and dine at the place where he played, and he got very tired of the food. "But since," his black eyebrows nearly met in an acute angle, "but since, before, I eat at a bakery, with the slender brown roach on the pie, I guess I better let alone well enough." He paused to drink his tea; as he tasted one of the cakes his face lit with sudden animation and he gazed across the hall after the maid with the tea—she was now holding it before the aged and ossified 'cellist of the Hempfstangle Quartette. "*Des gâteaux,*" he murmured feelingly, "*ou est-ce qu'elle peut trouver de tels gâteaux ici à* New York?"[13]

I explained to him that Madame Garnet had an accomplished cook who made them,—an Austrian, I thought.

He shook his head. "*Austrichienne? Je ne pense pas.*"[14]

Cressida was approaching with the new Spanish soprano, Mme. Bartolas, who was all black velvet and long black feathers, with a lace veil over her rich pallour and even a little black patch on her chin. I beckoned them. "Tell me, Cressida, isn't Ruzenka an Austrian?"

She looked surprised. "No, a Bohemian, though I got her in Vienna." Bouchalka's expression, and the remnant of a cake in his long fingers, gave her the connection. She laughed. "You like them? Of course, they are of your own country. You shall have more of them." She nodded and went away to greet a guest who had just come in.

A few moments later, Horace, then a beautiful lad in Eaton clothes, brought another cup of tea and a plate of cakes for Bouchalka. We sat down in a corner, and talked about his songs. He was neither boastful nor deprecatory. He knew exactly in what respects they were excellent. I decided as I watched his face, that he must be under thirty. The deep lines in his forehead probably came there from his habit of frowning densely when he struggled to express himself, and suddenly elevating his coal-black eyebrows when his ideas cleared. His teeth were white, very irregular and interesting. The corrective methods of modern dentistry would have taken away half his good looks. His mouth would have been much less attractive for any re-arranging of those long, narrow, overcrowded teeth. Along with his frown and his way of thrusting out his lip, they contributed, somehow, to the engaging impetuousness of his conversation. As we talked about his songs, his manner changed. Before that he had seemed responsive and easily pleased. Now he grew abstracted, as if I had taken away his pleasant afternoon and wakened him to his miseries. He moved restlessly in his clothes. When I mentioned Puccini, he held his head in his hands.[15] "Why is it they like that always and always? A little, oh yes, very nice. But so much, always the same thing! Why?" He pierced me with the despairing glance which had followed us out of the restaurant.

I asked him whether he had sent any of his songs to the publishers and named one whom I knew to be discriminating. He shrugged his shoulders. "They not want Bohemian songs. They not want my music. Even the street cars will not stop for me here, like for other people. Every time, I wait on the corner until somebody else make a signal to the car, and then it stop,—but not for me."

Most people cannot become utterly poor; whatever happens, they can right themselves a little. But one felt that Bouchalka was the sort of person who might actually starve or blow his brains out. Something very important had been left out either of his make-up or of his education; something that we are not accustomed to miss in people.

Gradually the parlour was filled with little groups of friends, and I took Bouchalka back to the music-room where Cressida was surrounded by her guests; feathered women, with large sleeves and hats, young men of no importance, in frock coats, with shining hair, and the smile which is intended to say so many flattering things but which really expresses little more than a desire to get on. The older men were standing about waiting for a word *à deux*[16] with the hostess. To these people Bouchalka had nothing to say. He stood stiffly at the outer edge of the circle, watching Cressida with intent, impatient eyes, until, under the pretext of showing him a score, she drew him into the alcove at the back end of the long room, where she kept her musical library. The bookcases ran from the floor to the ceiling. There was a table and a reading-lamp, and a window seat looking upon the little walled garden. Two persons could be quite withdrawn there, and yet be a part of the general friendly scene. Cressida took a score from the shelf, and sat down with Bouchalka upon the window-seat, the book open between them, though neither of them looked at it again. They fell to talking with great earnestness. At last the Bohemian pulled out a large, yellowing silver watch, held it up before him, and stared at it a moment as if it were an object of horror. He sprang up, bent over Cressida's hand and murmured something, dashed into the hall and out of the front door without waiting for the maid to open it. He had worn no overcoat, apparently. It was then seven o'clock; he would surely be late at his post in the uptown restaurant. I hoped he would have wit enough to take the elevated.

After supper Cressida told me his story. His parents, both poor musicians,—the mother a singer—died while he was yet a baby, and he was left to the care of an arbitrary uncle who resolved to make a priest of him. He was put into a monastery school and kept there. The organist and choir-director, fortunately for Blasius, was an excellent musician, a man who had begun his career brilliantly, but who had met with crushing sorrows and disappointments in the world. He devoted himself to his talented pupil, and was the only teacher the young man ever had. At twenty-one, when he was ready for the novitiate, Blasius felt that the call of life was too strong for him, and he ran away out into a world of which he knew nothing. He tramped southward to Vienna, begging and playing his fiddle from town to town. In Vienna he fell in with a gipsy band which was being recruited for a Paris restaurant and went with them to Paris. He played in cafés and in cheap theatres, did transcribing for a music publisher, tried to get pupils. For four years he was the mouse, and hunger was the cat. She kept him on the jump. When he got work he did not understand why; when he lost a job he did not understand why. During the time when most of us acquire a practical sense, get a half-unconscious knowledge of hard facts and market values, he had been shut away from the world, fed like the pigeons in the bell-tower of his monastery. Bouchalka had now been in New York a year, and for all he knew about it, Cressida said, he might have landed the day before yesterday.

Several weeks went by, and as Bouchalka did not reappear on Tenth Street, Cressida and I went once more to the place where he had played, only to find another violinist leading the orchestra. We summoned the proprietor, a Swiss-Italian, polite and solicitous. He told us the gentleman was not playing there any more,—was playing somewhere else, but he had forgotten where. We insisted upon talking to the old pianist, who at last reluctantly admitted that the Bohemian had been dismissed. He had arrived very late one Sunday night three weeks ago, and had hot words with the proprietor. He had been late before, and had been warned. He was a very talented fellow, but wild and not to be depended upon. The old man gave us the address of a French boardinghouse on Seventh Avenue where Bouchalka used to room. We drove there at once, but the woman who kept the place said that he had gone away two weeks before, leaving no address, as he never got letters. Another Bohemian, who did engraving on glass, had a room with her, and when he came home perhaps he could tell where Bouchalka was, for they were friends.

It took us several days to run Bouchalka down, but when we did find him Cressida promptly busied herself in his behalf. She sang his "*Šárka*" with the Metropolitan Opera orchestra at a Sunday night concert, she got him a position with the Symphony Orchestra, and persuaded the conservative Hempfstangle Quartette to play one of his chamber compositions from manuscript. She aroused the interest of a publisher in his work, and introduced him to people who were helpful to him.

By the new year Bouchalka was fairly on his feet. He had proper clothes now, and Cressida's friends found him attractive. He was usually at her house on Sunday afternoons; so usually, indeed, that Poppas began pointedly to absent himself. When other guests arrived, the Bohemian and his patroness were always found at the critical point of discussion,—at the piano, by the fire, in the alcove at the end of the room—both of them interested and animated. He was invariably respectful and admiring, deferring to her in every tone and gesture, and she was perceptibly pleased and flattered,—as if all this were new to her and she were tasting the sweetness of a first success.

One wild day in March Cressida burst tempestuously into my apartment and threw herself down, declaring that she had just come from the most trying rehearsal she had ever lived through. When I tried to question her about it, she replied absently and continued to shiver and crouch by the fire. Suddenly she rose, walked to the window, and stood looking out over the Square, glittering with ice and rain and strewn with the wrecks of umbrellas. When she turned again, she approached me with determination.

"I shall have to ask you to go with me," she said firmly. "That crazy Bouchalka has gone and got a pleurisy or something. It may be pneumonia; there is an epidemic of it just now. I've sent Dr. Brooks to him, but I can never tell anything from what a doctor says. I've got to see Bouchalka and his nurse, and what sort of place he's in. I've been rehearsing all day and I'm singing tomorrow night; I can't have so much on my mind. Can you come with me? It will save time in the end."

I put on my furs, and we went down to Cressida's carriage, waiting below. She gave the driver a number on Seventh Avenue, and then began feeling her throat with the alarmed expression which meant that she was not going to talk. We drove in silence to the address, and by this time it was growing dark. The French landlady was a cordial, comfortable person who took Cressida in at a glance and seemed much impressed. Cressida's incognito was never successful. Her black gown was inconspicuous enough, but over it she wore a dark purple velvet carriage coat, lined with fur and furred at the cuffs and collar. The Frenchwoman's eye ran over it delightedly and scrutinized the veil which only half concealed the well-known face behind it. She insisted upon conducting us up to the fourth floor herself, running ahead of us and turning up the gas jets in the dark, musty-smelling halls. I suspect that she tarried outside the door after we sent the nurse for her walk.

We found the sick man in a great walnut bed, a relic of the better days which this lodging house must have seen. The grimy red plush carpet, the red velvet chairs with broken springs, the double gilt-framed mirror above the mantel, had all been respectable, substantial contributions to comfort in their time. The fireplace was now empty and grateless, and an ill-smelling gas stove burned in its sooty recess under the cracked marble. The huge arched windows were hung with heavy red curtains, pinned together and lightly stirred by the wind which rattled the loose frames.

I was examining these things while Cressida bent over Bouchalka. Her carriage cloak she threw over the foot of his bed, either from a protective impulse, or because there was no place else to put it. After she had greeted him and seated herself, the sick man reached down and drew the cloak up over him, looking at it with weak, childish pleasure and stroking the velvet with his long fingers. *"Couleur de gloire, couleur des reines!"*[17] I heard him murmur. He thrust the sleeve under his chin and closed his eyes. His loud, rapid breathing was the only sound in the room. If Cressida brushed back his hair or touched his hand, he looked up long enough to give her a smile of utter adoration, naïve and uninquiring, as if he were smiling at a dream or a miracle.

The nurse was gone for an hour, and we sat quietly, Cressida with her eyes fixed on Bouchalka, and I absorbed in the strange atmosphere of the house, which seemed to seep in under the door and through the walls. Occasionally we heard a call for *"de l'eau chaude!"*[18] and the heavy trot of a serving woman on the stairs. On the floor below somebody was struggling with Schubert's Marche Militaire on a coarse-toned upright piano. Sometimes, when a door was opened, one could hear a parrot screaming, *"Voilà, voilà, tonnerre!"*[19] The house was built before 1870, as one could tell from windows and mouldings, and the walls were thick. The sounds were not disturbing and Bouchalka was probably used to them.

When the nurse returned and we rose to go, Bouchalka still lay with his cheek on her cloak, and Cressida left it. "It seems to please him," she murmured as we went down the stairs. "I can go home without a wrap. It's not far." I had, of course, to give her my furs, as I was not singing *Donna Anna*[20] tomorrow evening and she was.

After this I was not surprised by any devout attitude in which I happened to find the Bohemian when I entered Cressida's music-room unannounced, or by any radiance on her face when she rose from the window-seat in the alcove and came down the room to greet me.

Bouchalka was, of course, very often at the Opera now. On almost any night when Cressida sang, one could see his narrow black head—high above the temples and rather constrained behind the ears—peering from some part of the house. I used to wonder what he thought of Cressida as an artist, but probably he did not think seriously at all. A great voice, a handsome woman, a great prestige, all added together made a "great artist," the common synonym for success. Her success, and the material evidences of it, quite blinded him. I could never draw from him anything adequate about Anna Straka, Cressida's Slavic rival, and this perhaps meant that he considered comparison disloyal. All the while that Cressida was singing reliably, and satisfying the management, Straka was singing uncertainly and making history. Her voice was primarily defective, and her immediate vocal method was bad. Cressida was always living up to her contract, delivering the whole order in good condition; while the Slav was sometimes almost voiceless, sometimes inspired. She put you off with a hope, a promise, time after time. But she was quite as likely to put you off with a revelation, —with an interpretation that was inimitable, unrepeatable.

Bouchalka was not a reflective person. He had his own idea of what a great prima donna should be like, and he took it for granted that Mme. Garnet corresponded to his conception. The curious thing was that he managed to impress his idea upon Cressida herself. She began to see herself as he saw her, to try to be like the notion of her that he carried somewhere in that pointed head of his. She was exalted quite beyond herself. Things that had been chilled under the grind came to life in her that winter, with the breath of Bouchalka's adoration. Then, if ever in her life, she heard the bird sing on the branch outside her window; and she wished she were younger, lovelier, freer. She wished there were no Poppas, no Horace, no Garnets. She longed to be only the bewitching creature Bouchalka imagined her.

One April day when we were driving in the Park, Cressida, superb in a green-and-primrose costume hurried over from Paris, turned to me smiling and said: "Do you know, this is the first spring I haven't dreaded. It's the first one I've ever really had. Perhaps people never have more than one, whether it comes early or late." She told me that she was overwhelmingly in love.

Our visit to Bouchalka when he was ill had, of course, been reported, and the men about the Opera House had made of it the only story they have the wit to invent. They could no more change the pattern of that story than the spider could change the design of its web. But being, as she said, "in love" suggested to Cressida only one plan of action; to have the Tenth Street house done over, to put more money into her brothers' business, send Horace to school, raise Poppas' percentage, and then with a clear conscience be married in the Church of the Ascension. She went through this program with her usual thoroughness. She was married in June and sailed immediately with her husband. Poppas was to join them in Vienna in August, when she would begin to work again. From her letters I gathered that all was going well, even beyond her hopes.

When they returned in October, both Cressida and Blasius seemed changed for the better. She was perceptibly freshened and renewed. She attacked her work at once with more vigour and more ease; did not drive herself so relentlessly. A little carelessness became her wonderfully. Bouchalka was less gaunt, and much less flighty and perverse. His frank pleasure in the comfort and order of his wife's establishment was ingratiating, even if it was a little amusing. Cressida had the sewing-room at the top of the house made over into a study for him. When I went up there to see him,

I usually found him sitting before the fire or walking about with his hands in his coat pockets, admiring his new possessions. He explained the ingenious arrangement of his study to me a dozen times.

With Cressida's friends and guests, Bouchalka assumed nothing for himself. His deportment amounted to a quiet, unobtrusive appreciation of her and of his good fortune. He was proud to owe his wife so much. Cressida's Sunday afternoons were more popular than ever, since she herself had so much more heart for them. Bouchalka's picturesque presence stimulated her graciousness and charm. One still found them conversing together as eagerly as in the days when they saw each other but seldom. Consequently their guests were never bored. We felt as if the Tenth Street house had a pleasant climate quite its own. In the spring, when the Metropolitan company went on tour, Cressida's husband accompanied her, and afterward they again sailed for Genoa.

During the second winter people began to say that Bouchalka was becoming too thoroughly domesticated, and that since he was growing heavier in body he was less attractive. I noticed his increasing reluctance to stir abroad. Nobody could say that he was "wild" now. He seemed to dread leaving the house, even for an evening. Why should he go out, he said, when he had everything he wanted at home? He published very little. One was given to understand that he was writing an opera. He lived in the Tenth Street house like a tropical plant under glass. Nowhere in New York could he get such cookery as Ruzenka's. Ruzenka ("little Rose") had, like her mistress, bloomed afresh, now that she had a man and a compatriot to cook for. Her invention was tireless, and she took things with a high hand in the kitchen, confident of a perfect appreciation. She was a plump, fair, blue-eyed girl, giggly and easily flattered, with teeth like cream. She was passionately domestic, and her mind was full of homely stories and proverbs and superstitions which she somehow worked into her cookery. She and Bouchalka had between them a whole literature of traditions about sauces and fish and pastry. The cellar was full of the wines he liked, and Ruzenka always knew what wines to serve with the dinner. Blasius' monastery had been famous for good living.

That winter was a very cold one, and I think the even temperature of the house enslaved Bouchalka. "Imagine it," he once said to me when I dropped in during a blinding snowstorm and found him reading before the fire. "To be warm all the time, every day! It is like Aladdin. In Paris I have had weeks together when I was not warm once, when I did not have a bath once, like the cats in the street. The nights were a misery. People have terrible dreams when they are so cold. Here I waken up in the night so warm I do not know what it means. Her door is open, and I turn on my light. I cannot believe in myself until I see that she is there."

I began to think that Bouchalka's wildness had been the desperation which the tamest animals exhibit when they are tortured or terrorized. Naturally luxurious, he had suffered more than most men under the pinch of penury. Those first beautiful compositions, full of the folk-music of his own country, had been wrung out of him by homesickness and heart-ache. I wondered whether he could compose only under the spur of hunger and loneliness, and whether his talent might not subside with his despair. Some such apprehension must have troubled Cressida, though his gratitude would have been propitiatory to a more exacting task-master. She had always liked to make people happy, and he was the first one who had accepted her bounty without sourness. When he did not accompany her upon her spring tour, Cressida said it was because travelling interfered with composition; but I felt that she was deeply disappointed. Blasius, or Blažej, as his wife had with difficulty learned to call him, was not showy or extravagant. He hated hotels, even the best of them. Cressida had always fought for the hearthstone and the fireside, and the humour of Destiny is sometimes to give us too much of what we desire. I believe she would have preferred even enthusiasm about other women to his utter *oisiveté*.[21] It was his old fire, not his docility, that had won her.

During the third season after her marriage Cressida had only twenty-five performances at the Metropolitan, and she was singing out of town a great deal. Her husband did not bestir himself to accompany her, but he attended, very faithfully, to her correspondence and to her business at home. He had no ambitious schemes to increase her fortune, and he carried out her directions exactly.

Nevertheless, Cressida faced her concert tours somewhat grimly, and she seldom talked now about their plans for the future.

The crisis in this growing estrangement came about by accident,—one of those chance occurrences that affect our lives more than years of ordered effort,—and it came in an inverted form of a situation old to comedy. Cressida had been on the road for several weeks; singing in Minneapolis, Cleveland, St. Paul, then up into Canada and back to Boston. From Boston she was to go directly to Chicago, coming down on the five o'clock train and taking the eleven, over the Lake Shore, for the West. By her schedule she would have time to change cars comfortably at the Grand Central station.

On the journey down from Boston she was seized with a great desire to see Blasius. She decided, against her custom, one might say against her principles, to risk a performance with the Chicago orchestra without rehearsal, to stay the night in New York and go west by the afternoon train the next day. She telegraphed Chicago, but she did not telegraph Blasius, because she wished—the old fallacy of affection!—to "surprise" him. She could take it for granted that, at eleven on a cold winter night, he would be in the Tenth Street house and nowhere else in New York. She sent Poppas—paler than usual with accusing scorn—and her trunks on to Chicago, and with only her travelling bag and a sense of being very audacious in her behaviour and still very much in love, she took a cab for Tenth Street.

Since it was her intention to disturb Blasius as little as possible and to delight him as much as possible, she let herself in with her latch-key and went directly to his room. She did not find him there. Indeed, she found him where he should not have been at all. There must have been a trying scene.

Ruzenka was sent away in the morning, and the other two maids as well. By eight o'clock Cressida and Bouchalka had the house to themselves. Nobody had any breakfast. Cressida took the afternoon train to keep her engagement with Theodore Thomas, and to think over the situation. Blasius was left in the Tenth Street house with only the furnace man's wife to look after him. His explanation of his conduct was that he had been drinking too much. His digression, he swore, was casual. It had never occurred before, and he could only appeal to his wife's magnanimity. But it was, on the whole, easier for Cressida to be firm than to be yielding, and she knew herself too well to attempt a readjustment. She had never made shabby compromises, and it was too late for her to begin. When she returned to New York she went to a hotel, and she never saw Bouchalka alone again. Since he admitted her charge, the legal formalities were conducted so quietly that the granting of her divorce was announced in the morning papers before her friends knew that there was the least likelihood of one. Cressida's concert tours had interrupted the hospitalities of the house.

While the lawyers were arranging matters, Bouchalka came to see me. He was remorseful and miserable enough, and I think his perplexity was quite sincere. If there had been an intrigue with a woman of her own class, an infatuation, an affair, he said, he could understand. But anything so venial and accidental— He shook his head slowly back and forth. He assured me that he was not at all himself on that fateful evening, and that when he recovered himself he would have sent Ruzenka away, making proper provision for her, of course. It was an ugly thing, but ugly things sometimes happened in one's life, and one had to put them away and forget them. He could have overlooked any accident that might have occurred when his wife was on the road, with Poppas, for example. I cut him short, and he bent his head to my reproof.

"I know," he said, "such things are different with her. But when have I said that I am noble as she is? Never. But I have appreciated and I have adored. About me, say what you like. But if you say that in this there was any *méprise*[22] to my wife, that is not true. I have lost all my place here. I came in from the streets; but I understand her, and all the fine things in her, better than any of you here. If that accident had not been, she would have lived happy with me for years. As for me, I have never believed in this happiness. I was not born under a good star. How did it come? By accident. It goes by accident. She tried to give good fortune to an unfortunate man, *un miserable*; that was her mistake. It cannot be done in this world. The lucky should marry the lucky." Bouchalka stopped and lit a cigarette. He sat sunk in my chair as if he never meant to get up again. His large hands, now so much plumper than when I first knew him, hung limp. When he had consumed his cigarette he turned to me again.

"I, too, have tried. Have I so much as written one note to a lady since she first put out her hand to help me? Some of the artists who sing my compositions have been quite willing to plague my wife a little if I make the least sign. With the Española, for instance, I have had to be very stern, *farouche*,[23] she is so very playful. I have never given my wife the slightest annoyance of this kind. Since I married her, I have not kissed the cheek of one lady! Then one night I am bored and drink too much champagne and I become a fool. What does it matter? Did my wife marry the fool of me? No, she married me, with my mind and my feelings all here, as I am today. But she is getting a divorce from the fool of me, which she would never see *anyhow*! The stupidity which, excuse me, is the thing she will not overlook. Even in her memory of me she will be harsh."

His view of his conduct and its consequences was fatalistic: he was meant to have just so much misery every day of his life; for three years it had been withheld, had been piling up somewhere, underground, overhead; now the accumulation burst over him. He had come to pay his respects to me, he said, to declare his undying gratitude to Madame Garnet, and to bid me farewell. He took up his hat and cane and kissed my hand. I have never seen him since. Cressida made a settlement upon him, but even Poppas, tortured by envy and curiosity, never discovered how much it was. It was very little, she told me. *"Pour des gâteaux,"*[24] she added with a smile that was not unforgiving. She could not bear to think of his being in want when so little could make him comfortable.

He went back to his own village in Bohemia. He wrote her that the old monk, his teacher, was still alive, and that from the windows of his room in the town he could see the pigeons flying forth from and back to the monastery bell-tower all day long. He sent her a song, with his own words, about those pigeons,—quite a lovely thing. He was the bell-tower, and *les colombes*[25] were his memories of her.

IV

Jerome Brown proved, on the whole, the worst of Cressida's husbands, and, with the possible exception of her eldest brother, Buchanan Garnet, he was the most rapacious of the men with whom she had had to do. It was one thing to gratify every wish of a cake-loving fellow like Bouchalka, but quite another to stand behind a financier. And Brown would be a financier or nothing. After her marriage with him, Cressida grew rapidly older. For the first time in her life she wanted to go abroad and live—to get Jerome Brown away from the scene of his unsuccessful but undiscouraged activities. But Brown was not a man who could be amused and kept out of mischief in Continental hotels. He had to be a figure, if only a "mark," in Wall Street. Nothing else would gratify his peculiar vanity. The deeper he went in, the more affectionately he told Cressida that now all her cares and anxieties were over. To try to get related facts out of his optimism was like trying to find framework in a feather bed. All Cressida knew was that she was perpetually "investing" to save investments. When she told me she had put a mortgage on the Tenth Street house, her eyes filled with tears. "Why is it? I have never cared about money, except to make people happy with it, and it has been the curse of my life. It has spoiled all my relations with people. Fortunately," she added irrelevantly, drying her eyes, "Jerome and Poppas get along well." Jerome could have got along with anybody; that is a promoter's business. His warm hand, his flushed face, his bright eye, and his newest funny story, —Poppas had no weapons that could do execution with a man like that.

Though Brown's ventures never came home, there was nothing openly disastrous until the outbreak of the revolution in Mexico jeopardized his interests there. Then Cressida went to England—where she could always raise money from a faithful public—for a winter concert tour. When she sailed, her friends knew that her husband's affairs were in a bad way; but we did not know how bad until after Cressida's death.

Cressida Garnet, as all the world knows, was lost on the *Ti-*

tanic.[26] Poppas and Horace, who had been travelling with her, were sent on a week earlier and came as safely to port as if they had never stepped out of their London hotel. But Cressida had waited for the first trip of the sea monster—she still believed that all advertising was good—and she went down on the road between the old world and the new. She had been ill, and when the collision occurred she was in her stateroom, a modest one somewhere down in the boat, for she was travelling economically. Apparently she never left her cabin. She was not seen on the decks, and none of the survivors brought any word of her.

On Monday, when the wireless messages were coming from the *Carpathia* with the names of the passengers who had been saved, I went, with so many hundred others, down to the White Star offices. There I saw Cressida's motor, her redoubtable initials on the door, with four men sitting in the limousine. Jerome Brown, stripped of the promoter's joviality and looking flabby and old, sat behind with Buchanan Garnet, who had come on from Ohio. I had not seen him for years. He was now an old man, but he was still conscious of being in the public eye, and sat turning a cigar about in his face with that foolish look of importance which Cressida's achievement had stamped upon all the Garnets. Poppas was in front, with Horace. He was gnawing the finger of his chamois glove as it rested on the top of his cane. His head was sunk, his shoulders drawn together; he looked as old as Jewry. I watched them, wondering whether Cressida would come back to them if she could. After the last names were posted, the four men settled back into the powerful car—one of the best made—and the chauffeur backed off. I saw him dash away the tears from his face with the back of his driving glove. He was an Irish boy, and had been devoted to Cressida.

When the will was read, Henry Gilbert, the lawyer, an old friend of her early youth, and I, were named executors. A nice job we had of it. Most of her large fortune had been converted into stocks that were almost worthless. The marketable property realized only a hundred and fifty thousand dollars. To defeat the bequest of fifty thousand dollars to Poppas, Jerome Brown and her family contested the will. They brought Cressida's letters into court to prove that the will did not represent her intentions, often expressed in writing through many years, to "provide well" for them.

Such letters they were! The writing of a tired, overdriven woman; promising money, sending money herewith, asking for an acknowledgment of the draft sent last month, etc. In the letters to Jerome Brown she begged for information about his affairs and entreated him to go with her to some foreign city where they could live quietly and where she could rest; if they were careful, there would "be enough for all." Neither Brown nor her brothers and sisters had any sense of shame about these letters. It seemed never to occur to them that this golden stream, whether it rushed or whether it trickled, came out of the industry, out of the mortal body of a woman. They regarded her as a natural source of wealth; a copper vein, a diamond mine.

Henry Gilbert is a good lawyer himself, and he employed an able man to defend the will. We determined that in this crisis we would stand by Poppas, believing it would be Cressida's wish. Out of the lot of them, he was the only one who had helped her to make one penny of the money that had brought her so much misery. He was at least more deserving than the others. We saw to it that Poppas got his fifty thousand, and he actually departed, at last, for his city in *la sainte Asie*, where it never rains and where he will never again have to hold a hot water bottle to his face.

The rest of the property was fought for to a finish. Poppas out of the way, Horace and Brown and the Garnets quarrelled over her personal effects. They went from floor to floor of the Tenth Street house. The will provided that Cressida's jewels and furs and gowns were to go to her sisters. Georgie and Julia wrangled over them down to the last moleskin. They were deeply disappointed that some of the muffs and stoles which they remembered as very large, proved, when exhumed from storage and exhibited beside furs of a modern cut, to be ridiculously scant. A year ago the sisters were still reasoning with each other about pearls and opals and emeralds.

I wrote Poppas some account of these horrors, as during the court proceedings we had become rather better friends than of old.

His reply arrived only a few days ago; a photograph of himself upon a camel, under which is written:

Traulich und Treu
ist's nur in der Tiefe:
falsch und feig
ist was dort oben sich freut![27]

His reply, and the memories it awakens—memories which have followed Poppas into the middle of Asia, seemingly,—prompted this informal narration.[28]

A Gold Slipper

MARSHALL MCKANN followed his wife and her friend Mrs. Post down the aisle and up the steps to the stage of the Carnegie Music Hall with an ill-concealed feeling of grievance. Heaven knew he never went to concerts, and to be mounted upon the stage in this fashion, as if he were a "highbrow" from Sewickley, or some unfortunate with a musical wife, was ludicrous. A man went to concerts when he was courting, while he was a junior partner. When he became a person of substance he stopped that sort of nonsense. His wife, too, was a sensible person, the daughter of an old Pittsburgh family as solid and well rooted as the McKanns. She would never have bothered him about this concert had not the meddlesome Mrs. Post arrived to pay her a visit. Mrs. Post was an old school friend of Mrs. McKann, and because she lived in Cincinnati she was always keeping up with the world and talking about things in which no one else was interested, music among them. She was an aggressive lady, with weighty opinions, and a deep voice like a jovial bassoon. She had arrived only last night, and at dinner she brought it out that she could on no account miss Kitty Ayrshire's recital; it was, she said, the sort of thing no one could afford to miss.

When McKann went into town in the morning he found that every seat in the music-hall was sold. He telephoned his wife to that effect, and, thinking he had settled the matter, made his reservation on the 11.25 train for New York. He was unable to get a drawing-room because this same Kitty Ayrshire had taken the last one. He had not intended going to New York until the following week, but he preferred to be absent during Mrs. Post's incumbency.

In the middle of the morning, when he was deep in his correspondence, his wife called him up to say the enterprising Mrs. Post had telephoned some musical friends in Sewickley and had found that two hundred folding-chairs were to be placed on the stage of the concert-hall, behind the piano, and that they would be on sale at noon. Would he please get seats in the front row? McKann asked if they would not excuse him, since he was going over to New York on the late train, would be tired, and would not have time to dress, etc. No, not at all. It would be foolish for two women to trail up to the stage unattended. Mrs. Post's husband always accompanied her to concerts, and she expected that much attention from her host. He needn't dress, and he could take a taxi from the concert-hall to the East Liberty station.

The outcome of it all was that, though his bag was at the station, here was McKann, in the worst possible humour, facing the large audience to which he was well known, and sitting among a lot of music students and excitable old maids. Only the desperately zealous or the morbidly curious would endure two hours in those wooden chairs, and he sat in the front row of this hectic body, somehow made a party to a transaction for which he had the utmost contempt.

When McKann had been in Paris, Kitty Ayrshire was singing at the Comique, and he wouldn't go to hear her—even there, where one found so little that was better to do. She was too much talked about, too much advertised; always being thrust in an American's face as if she were something to be proud of. Perfumes and petticoats and cutlets were named for her. Some one had pointed Kitty out to him one afternoon when she was driving in the Bois with a French composer—old enough, he judged, to be her father—who was said to be infatuated, carried away by her. McKann was told that this was one of the historic passions of old age. He had looked at her on that occasion, but she was so befrilled and befeathered that he caught nothing but a graceful outline and a small, dark head above a white ostrich boa. He had noted with disgust, however, the stooped shoulders and white imperial of the silk-hatted man beside her, and the senescent[1] line of his back. McKann described to his wife this unpleasing picture only last night, while he was undressing, when he was making every possible effort to avert this concert party. But Bessie only looked superior and said she wished to hear Kitty Ayrshire sing, and that her "private life" was something in which she had no interest.

Well, here he was; hot and uncomfortable, in a chair much too small for him, with a row of blinding footlights glaring in his eyes. Suddenly the door at his right elbow opened. Their seats were at one end of the front row; he had thought they would be less conspicuous there than in the centre, and he had not foreseen that the singer would walk over him every time she came upon the stage. Her velvet train brushed against his trousers as she passed him. The applause which greeted her was neither overwhelming nor prolonged. Her conservative audience did not know exactly how to accept her toilette. They were accustomed to dignified concert gowns, like those which Pittsburgh matrons (in those days!) wore at their daughters' coming-out teas.

Kitty's gown that evening was really quite outrageous—the repartée of a conscienceless Parisian designer who took her hint that she wished something that would be entirely novel in the States. Today, after we have all of us, even in the uttermost provinces, been educated by Bakst and the various Ballets Russes, we would accept such a gown without distrust; but then it was a little disconcerting, even to the well disposed. It was constructed of a yard or two of green velvet—a reviling, shrieking green which would have made a fright of any woman who had not inextinguishable beauty—and it was made without armholes, a device to which we were then so unaccustomed that it was nothing less than alarming. The velvet skirt split back from a transparent gold-lace petticoat, gold stockings, gold slippers. The narrow train was, apparently, looped to both ankles, and it kept curling about her feet like a serpent's tail, turning up its gold lining as if it were squirming over on its back. It was not, we felt, a costume in which to sing Mozart and Handel and Beethoven.

Kitty sensed the chill in the air, and it amused her. She liked to be thought a brilliant artist by other artists, but by the world at large she liked to be thought a daring creature. She had every reason to believe, from experience and from example, that to shock the great crowd was the surest way to get its money and to make her name a household word. Nobody ever became a household word of being an artist, surely; and you were not a thoroughly paying proposition until your name meant something on the sidewalk and in the barber-shop. Kitty studied her audience with an appraising eye. She liked the stimulus of this disapprobation. As she faced this hard-shelled public she felt keen and interested; she knew that she would give such a recital as cannot often be heard for money. She nodded gaily to the young man at the piano, fell into an attitude of seriousness, and began the group of Beethoven and Mozart songs.

Though McKann would not have admitted it, there were really a great many people in the concert-hall who knew what the prodigal daughter of their country was singing, and how well she was doing it. They thawed gradually under the beauty of her voice and the subtlety of her interpretation. She had sung seldom in concert then, and they had supposed her very dependent upon the accessories of the opera. Clean singing, finished artistry, were not what they expected from her. They began to feel, even, the wayward charm of her personality.

McKann, who stared coldly up at the balconies during her first song, during the second glanced cautiously at the green apparition before him. He was vexed with her for having retained a débutante figure. He comfortably classed all singers—especially operatic singers—as "fat Dutchwomen" or "shifty Sadies," and Kitty would not fit into his clever generalization. She displayed, under his nose, the only kind of figure he considered worth looking at—that of a very young girl, supple and sinuous and quicksilverish; thin, eager shoulders, polished white arms that were nowhere too fat and nowhere too thin. McKann found it agreeable to look at Kitty, but when he saw that the authoritative Mrs. Post, red as a turkey-cock with opinions she was bursting to impart, was studying and appraising the singer through her lorgnette, he gazed indifferently out into the house again. He felt for his watch, but his wife touched him warningly with her elbow—which, he noticed, was not at all like Kitty's.

When Miss Ayrshire finished her first group of songs, her audience expressed its approval positively, but guardedly. She smiled bewitchingly upon the people in front, glanced up at the balconies, and then turned to the company huddled on the stage behind her. After her gay and careless bows, she retreated toward the stage door. As she passed McKann, she again brushed lightly against him, and this time she paused long enough to glance down at him and murmur, "Pardon!"

In the moment her bright, curious eyes rested upon him, McKann seemed to see himself as if she were holding a mirror up before him. He beheld himself a heavy, solid figure, unsuitably clad for the time and place, with a florid, square face, well-visored with good living and sane opinions—an inexpressive countenance. Not a rock face, exactly, but a kind of pressed-brick-and-cement face, a "business" face upon which years and feelings had made no mark—in which cocktails might eventually blast out a few hollows. He had never seen himself so distinctly in his shaving-glass as he did in that instant when Kitty Ayrshire's liquid eye held him, when her bright, inquiring glance roamed over his person. After her prehensile train curled over his boot and she was gone, his wife turned to him and said in the tone of approbation one uses when an infant manifests its groping intelligence, "Very gracious of her, I'm sure!" Mrs. Post nodded oracularly. McKann grunted.

Kitty began her second number, a group of romantic German songs which were altogether more her affair than her first number. When she turned once to acknowledge the applause behind her, she caught McKann in the act of yawning behind his hand—he of course wore no gloves—and he thought she frowned a little. This did not embarrass him; it somehow made him feel important. When she retired after the second part of the program, she again looked him over curiously as she passed, and she took marked precaution that her dress did not touch him. Mrs. Post and his wife again commented upon her consideration.

The final number was made up of modern French songs which Kitty sang enchantingly, and at last her frigid public was thoroughly aroused. While she was coming back again and again to smile and curtsy, McKann whispered to his wife that if there were to be encores he had better make a dash for his train.

"Not at all," put in Mrs. Post. "Kitty is going on the same train. She sings in *Faust* at the opera tomorrow night, so she'll take no chances."

McKann once more told himself how sorry he felt for Post. At last Miss Ayrshire returned, escorted by her accompanist, and gave the people what she of course knew they wanted: the most popular aria from the French opera of which the title-rôle had become synonymous with her name—an opera written for her and to her and round about her, by the veteran French composer who adored her,—the last and not the palest flash of his creative fire. This brought her audience all the way. They clamoured for more of it, but she was not to be coerced. She had been unyielding through storms to which this was a summer breeze. She came on once more, shrugged her shoulders, blew them a kiss, and was gone. Her last smile was for that uncomfortable part of her audience seated behind her, and she looked with recognition at McKann and his ladies as she nodded good night to the wooden chairs.

McKann hurried his charges into the foyer by the nearest exit and put them into his motor. Then he went over to the Schenley to have a glass of beer and a rarebit before train-time. He had not, he admitted to himself, been so much bored as he pretended. The minx herself was well enough, but it was absurd in his fellow-townsmen to look owlish and uplifted about her. He had no rooted dislike for pretty women; he even didn't deny that gay girls had their place in the world, but they ought to be kept in their place. He was born a Presbyterian; just as he was born a McKann. He sat in his pew in the First Church every Sunday, and he never missed a presbytery meeting when he was in town. His religion was not very spiritual, certainly, but it was substantial and concrete, made up of good, hard convictions and opinions. It had something to do with citizenship, with whom one ought to marry, with the coal business (in which his own name was powerful), with the Republican party, and with all majorities and established precedents. He was hostile to fads, to enthusiasms, to individualism, to all changes except in mining machinery and in methods of transportation.

His equanimity restored by his lunch at the Schenley, McKann lit a big cigar, got into his taxi, and bowled off through the sleet.

There was not a sound to be heard or a light to be seen. The ice glittered on the pavement and on the naked trees. No restless feet were abroad. At eleven o'clock the rows of small, comfortable houses looked as empty of the troublesome bubble of life as the Allegheny cemetery itself. Suddenly the cab stopped, and McKann thrust his head out of the window. A woman was standing in the middle of the street addressing his driver in a tone of excitement. Over against the curb a lone electric stood despondent in the storm. The young woman, her cloak blowing about her, turned from the driver to McKann himself, speaking rapidly and somewhat incoherently.

"Could you not be so kind as to help us? It is Mees Ayrshire, the singer. The juice is gone out and we cannot move. We must get to the station. Mademoiselle cannot miss the train; she sings tomorrow night in New York. It is very important. Could you not take us to the station at East Liberty?"

McKann opened the door. "That's all right, but you'll have to hurry. It's eleven-ten now. You've only got fifteen minutes to make the train. Tell her to come along."

The maid drew back and looked up at him in amazement. "But, the hand-luggage to carry, and Mademoiselle to walk! The street is like glass!"

McKann threw away his cigar and followed her. He stood silent by the door of the derelict, while the maid explained that she had found help. The driver had gone off somewhere to telephone for a car. Miss Ayrshire seemed not at all apprehensive; she had not doubted that a rescuer would be forthcoming. She moved deliberately; out of a whirl of skirts she thrust one fur-topped shoe—McKann saw the flash of the gold stocking above it—and alighted.

"So kind of you! So fortunate for us!" she murmured. One hand she placed upon his sleeve, and in the other she carried an armful of roses that had been sent up to the concert stage. The petals showered upon the sooty, sleety pavement as she picked her way along. They would be lying there tomorrow morning, and the children in those houses would wonder if there had been a funeral. The maid followed with two leather bags. As soon as he had lifted Kitty into his cab she exclaimed:

"My jewel-case! I have forgotten it. It is on the back seat, please. I am so careless!"

He dashed back, ran his hand along the cushions, and discovered a small leather bag. When he returned he found the maid and the luggage bestowed on the front seat, and a place left for him on the back seat beside Kitty and her flowers.

"Shall we be taking you far out of your way?" she asked sweetly. "I haven't an idea where the station is. I'm not even sure about the name. Céline thinks it is East Liberty, but I think it is West Liberty. An odd name, anyway. It is a Bohemian quarter, perhaps? A district where the law relaxes a trifle?"

McKann replied grimly that he didn't think the name referred to that kind of liberty.

"So much the better," sighed Kitty. "I am a Californian; that's the only part of America I know very well, and out there, when we called a place Liberty Hill or Liberty Hollow—well, we meant it. You will excuse me if I'm uncommunicative, won't you? I must not talk in this raw air. My throat is sensitive after a long program." She lay back in her corner and closed her eyes.

When the cab rolled down the incline at East Liberty station, the New York express was whistling in. A porter opened the door. McKann sprang out, gave him a claim check and his Pullman ticket, and told him to get his bag at the check-stand and rush it on that train.

Miss Ayrshire, having gathered up her flowers, put out her hand to take his arm. "Why, it's you!" she exclaimed, as she saw his face in the light. "What a coincidence!" She made no further move to alight, but sat smiling as if she had just seated herself in a drawing-room and were ready for talk and a cup of tea.

McKann caught her arm. "You must hurry, Miss Ayrshire, if you mean to catch that train. It stops here only a moment. Can you run?"

"Can I run!" she laughed. "Try me!"

As they raced through the tunnel and up the inside stairway, McKann admitted that he had never before made a dash with feet so quick and sure stepping out beside him. The white-furred boots chased each other like lambs at play, the gold stockings flashed like the spokes of a bicycle wheel in the sun. They reached the door of Miss Ayrshire's state-room just as the train began to pull out. McKann was ashamed of the way he was panting, for Kitty's breathing was as soft and regular as when she was reclining on the back seat of his taxi. It had somehow run in his head that all these stage women were a poor lot physically—unsound, overfed creatures, like canaries that are kept in a cage and stuffed with song-restorer. He retreated to escape her thanks. "Good night! Pleasant journey! Pleasant dreams!" With a friendly nod in Kitty's direction he closed the door behind him.

He was somewhat surprised to find his own bag, his Pullman ticket in the strap, on the seat just outside Kitty's door. But there was nothing strange about it. He had got the last section left on the train, No. 13, next the drawing-room. Every other berth in the car was made up. He was just starting to look for the porter when the door of the state-room opened and Kitty Ayrshire came out. She seated herself carelessly in the front seat beside his bag.

"Please talk to me a little," she said coaxingly. "I'm always wakeful after I sing, and I have to hunt some one to talk to. Céline and I get so tired of each other. We can speak very low, and we shall not disturb any one." She crossed her feet and rested her elbow on his Gladstone. Though she still wore her gold slippers and stockings, she did not, he thanked Heaven, have on her concert gown, but a very demure black velvet with some sort of pearl trimming about the neck. "Wasn't it funny," she proceeded, "that it happened to be you who picked me up? I wanted a word with you, anyway."

McKann smiled in a way that meant he wasn't being taken in. "Did you? We are not very old acquaintances."

"No, perhaps not. But you disapproved tonight, and I thought I was singing very well. You are very critical in such matters?"

He had been standing, but now he sat down. "My dear young lady, I am not critical at all. I know nothing about 'such matters.'"

"And care less?" she said for him. "Well, then we know where we are, in so far as that is concerned. What did displease you? My gown, perhaps? It may seem a little *outré* here, but it's the sort of thing all the imaginative designers abroad are doing. You like the English sort of concert gown better?"

"About gowns," said McKann, "I know even less than about music. If I looked uncomfortable, it was probably because I was uncomfortable. The seats were bad and the lights were annoying."

Kitty looked up with solicitude. "I was sorry they sold those seats. I don't like to make people uncomfortable in any way. Did the lights give you a headache? They are very trying. They burn one's eyes out in the end, I believe." She paused and waved the porter away with a smile as he came toward them. Half-clad Pittsburghers were tramping up and down the aisle, casting sidelong glances at McKann and his companion. "How much better they look with all their clothes on," she murmured. Then, turning directly to McKann again: "I saw you were not well seated, but I felt something quite hostile and personal. You were displeased with me. Doubtless many people are, but I seldom get an opportunity to question them. It would be nice if you took the trouble to tell me why you were displeased."

She spoke frankly, pleasantly, without a shadow of challenge or hauteur. She did not seem to be angling for compliments. McKann settled himself in his seat. He thought he would try her out. She had come for it, and he would let her have it. He found, however, that it was harder to formulate the grounds of his disapproval than he would have supposed. Now that he sat face to face with her, now that she was leaning against his bag, he had no wish to hurt her.

"I'm a hard-headed business man," he said evasively, "and I don't much believe in any of you fluffy-ruffles people. I have a sort of natural distrust of them all, the men more than the women."

She looked thoughtful. "Artists, you mean?" drawing her words slowly. "What is your business?"

"Coal."

"I don't feel any natural distrust of business men, and I know ever so many. I don't know any coal-men, but I think I could become very much interested in coal. Am I larger-minded than you?"

McKann laughed. "I don't think you know when you are interested or when you are not. I don't believe you know what it feels like to be really interested. There is so much fake about your profession. It's an affectation on both sides. I know a great many of the people who went to hear you tonight, and I know that most of them neither know nor care anything about music. They imagine they do, because it's supposed to be the proper thing."

Kitty sat upright and looked interested. She was certainly a lovely creature—the only one of her tribe he had ever seen that he would cross the street to see again. Those were remarkable eyes she had—curious, penetrating, restless, somewhat impudent, but not at all dulled by self-conceit.

"But isn't that so in everything?" she cried. "How many of your clerks are honest because of a fine, individual sense of honour? They are honest because it is the accepted rule of good conduct in business. Do you know"—she looked at him squarely—"I thought you would have something quite definite to say to me; but this is funny-paper stuff, the sort of objection I'd expect from your office-boy."

"Then you don't think it silly for a lot of people to get together and pretend to enjoy something they know nothing about?"

"Of course I think it silly, but that's the way God made audiences. Don't people go to church in exactly the same way? If there were a spiritual-pressure test-machine at the door, I suspect not many of you would get to your pews."

"How do you know I go to church?"

She shrugged her shoulders. "Oh, people with these old, ready-made opinions usually go to church. But you can't evade me like that." She tapped the edge of his seat with the toe of her gold slipper. "You sat there all evening, glaring at me as if you could eat me alive. Now I give you a chance to state your objections, and you merely criticize my audience. What is it? Is it merely that you happen to dislike my personality? In that case, of course, I won't press you."

"No," McKann frowned, "I perhaps dislike your professional personality. As I told you, I have a natural distrust of your variety."

"Natural, I wonder?" Kitty murmured. "I don't see why you should naturally dislike singers any more than I naturally dislike coal-men. I don't classify people by their occupations. Doubtless I should find some coal-men repulsive, and you may find some singers so. But I have reason to believe that, at least, I'm one of the less repellent."

"I don't doubt it," McKann laughed, "and you're a shrewd woman to boot. But you are, all of you, according to my standards, light people. You're brilliant, some of you, but you've no depth."

Kitty seemed to assent, with a dive of her girlish head. "Well, it's a merit in some things to be heavy, and in others to be light. Some things are meant to go deep, and others to go high. Do you want all the women in the world to be profound?"

"You are all," he went on steadily, watching her with indulgence, "fed on hectic emotions. You are pampered. You don't help to carry the burdens of the world. You are self-indulgent and appetent."[2]

"Yes, I am," she assented, with a candour which he did not expect. "Not all artists are, but I am. Why not? If I could once get a convincing statement as to why I should not be self-indulgent, I might change my ways. As for the burdens of the world—" Kitty rested her chin on her clasped hands and looked thoughtful. "One should give pleasure to others. My dear sir, granting that the great majority of people can't enjoy anything very keenly, you'll admit that I give pleasure to many more people than you do. One should help others who are less fortunate; at present I am supporting just eight people, besides those I hire. There was never another family in California that had so many cripples and hard-luckers as that into which I had the honour to be born. The only ones who could take care of themselves were ruined by the San Francisco earthquake some time ago. One should make personal sacrifices. I do; I give money and time and effort to talented students. Oh, I give something much more than that! something that you probably have never given to any one. I give, to the really gifted ones, my *wish*, my desire, my light, if I have any; and that, Mr. Worldly Wiseman,[3] is like giving one's blood! It's the kind of thing you prudent people never give. That is what was in the box of precious ointment." Kitty threw off her fervour with a slight gesture, as if it were a scarf, and leaned back, tucking her slipper up on the edge of his seat. "If you saw the houses I keep up," she sighed, "and the people I employ, and the motor-cars I run— And, after all, I've only this to do it with." She indicated her slender person, which Marshall could almost have broken in two with his bare hands.

She was, he thought, very much like any other charming woman, except that she was more so. Her familiarity was natural and simple. She was at ease because she was not afraid of him or of herself, or of certain half-clad acquaintances of his who had been wandering up and down the car oftener than was necessary. Well, he was not afraid, either.

Kitty put her arms over her head and sighed again, feeling the smooth part in her black hair. Her head was small—capable of great agitation, like a bird's; or of great resignation, like a nun's. "I can't see why I shouldn't be self-indulgent, when I indulge others. I can't understand your equivocal scheme of ethics. Now I can understand Count Tolstoy's, perfectly. I had a long talk with him once, about his book 'What is Art?'[4] As nearly as I could get it, he believes that we are a race who can exist only by gratifying appetites; the appetites are evil, and the existence they carry on is evil. We were always sad, he says, without knowing why; even in the Stone Age. In some miraculous way a divine ideal was disclosed to us, directly at variance with our appetites. It gave us a new craving, which we could only satisfy by starving all the other hungers in us. Happiness lies in ceasing to be and to cause being, because the thing revealed to us is dearer than any existence our appetites can ever get for us. I can understand that. It's something one often feels in art. It is even the subject of the greatest of all operas, which, because I can never hope to sing it, I love more than all the others." Kitty pulled herself up. "Perhaps you agree with Tolstoy?" she added languidly.

"No; I think he's a crank," said McKann, cheerfully.

"What do you mean by a crank?"

"I mean an extremist."

Kitty laughed. "Weighty word! You'll always have a world full of people who keep to the golden mean. Why bother yourself about me and Tolstoy?"

"I don't, except when you bother me."

"Poor man! It's true this isn't your fault. Still, you did provoke it by glaring at me. Why did you go to the concert?"

"I was dragged."

"I might have known!" she chuckled, and shook her head. "No, you don't give me any good reasons. Your morality seems to me the compromise of cowardice, apologetic and sneaking. When righteousness becomes alive and burning, you hate it as much as you do beauty. You want a little of each in your life, perhaps—adulterated, sterilized, with the sting taken out. It's true enough they are both fearsome things when they get loose in the world; they don't, often."

McKann hated tall talk. "My views on women," he said slowly, "are simple."

"Doubtless," Kitty responded dryly, "but are they consistent? Do you apply them to your stenographers as well as to me? I take it for granted you have unmarried stenographers. Their position, economically, is the same as mine."

McKann studied the toe of her shoe. "With a woman, everything comes back to one thing." His manner was judicial.

She laughed indulgently. "So we are getting down to brass tacks, eh? I have beaten you in argument, and now you are leading trumps." She put her hands behind her head and her lips parted in a half-yawn. "Does everything come back to one thing? I wish I knew! It's more than likely that, under the same conditions, I should have been very like your stenographers—if they are good ones. Whatever I was, I would have been a good one. I think people are very much alike. You are more different than any one I have met for some time, but I know that there are a great many more at home like you. And even you—I believe there is a real creature down under these custom-made prejudices that save you the trouble of thinking. If you and I were shipwrecked on a desert island, I have no doubt that we would come to a simple and natural understanding. I'm neither a coward nor a shirk. You would find, if you had to undertake any enterprise of danger or difficulty with a woman, that there are several qualifications quite as important as the one to which you doubtless refer."

McKann felt nervously for his watch-chain. "Of course," he brought out, "I am not laying down any generalizations—" His brows wrinkled.

"Oh, aren't you?" murmured Kitty. "Then I totally misunderstood. But remember"—holding up a finger—"it is you, not I, who are afraid to pursue this subject further. Now, I'll tell you something." She leaned forward and clasped her slim, white hands about her velvet knee. "I am as much a victim of these ineradicable prejudices as you. Your stenographer seems to you a better sort. Well, she does to me. Just because her life is, presumably, greyer than mine, she seems better. My mind tells me that dulness, and a mediocre order of ability, and poverty, are not in themselves admirable things. Yet in my heart I always feel that the sales-women in shops and the working girls in factories are more meritorious than I. Many of them, with my opportunities, would be more selfish than I am. Some of them, with their own opportunities, are more selfish. Yet I make this sentimental genuflection before the nun and the charwoman. Tell me, haven't you any weakness? Isn't there any foolish natural thing that unbends you a trifle and makes you feel gay?"

"I like to go fishing."

"To see how many fish you can catch?"

"No, I like the woods and the weather. I like to play a fish and work hard for him. I like the pussy-willows and the cold; and the sky, whether it's blue or grey—night coming on, every thing about it."

He spoke devoutly, and Kitty watched him through half-closed eyes. "And you like to feel that there are light-minded girls like me, who only care about the inside of shops and theatres and hotels, eh? You amuse me, you and your fish! But I mustn't keep you any longer. Haven't I given you every opportunity to state your case against me? I thought you would have more to say for yourself. Do you know, I believe it's not a case you have at all, but a grudge. I believe you are envious; that you'd like to be a tenor, and a perfect lady-killer!" She rose, smiling, and paused with her hand on the door of her state-room. "Anyhow, thank you for a pleasant evening. And, by the way, dream of me tonight, and not of either of those ladies who sat beside you. It does not matter much whom we live with in this world, but it matters a great deal whom we dream of." She noticed his bricky flush. "You are very naïf, after all, but, oh, so cautious! You are naturally afraid of everything new, just as I naturally want to try everything: new people, new religions—new miseries, even. If only there were more new things— If only you were really new! I might learn something. I'm like the Queen of Sheba—I'm not above learning.[5] But you, my friend, would be afraid to try a new shaving soap. It isn't gravitation that holds the world in place; it's the lazy, obese cowardice of the people on it. All the same"—taking his hand and smiling encouragingly—"I'm going to haunt you a little. *Adios!*"

When Kitty entered her state-room, Céline, in her dressing-gown, was nodding by the window.

"Mademoiselle found the fat gentleman interesting?" she asked. "It is nearly one."

"Negatively interesting. His kind always say the same thing. If I could find one really intelligent man who held his views, I should adopt them."

"Monsieur did not look like an original," murmured Céline, as she began to take down her lady's hair.

* * *

McKann slept heavily, as usual, and the porter had to shake him in the morning. He sat up in his berth, and, after composing his hair with his fingers, began to hunt about for his clothes. As he put up the window-blind some bright object in the little hammock over his bed caught the sunlight and glittered. He stared and picked up a delicately turned gold slipper.

"Minx! hussy!" he ejaculated. "All that tall talk—! Probably got it from some man who hangs about; learned it off like a parrot. Did she poke this in here herself last night, or did she send that sneak-faced Frenchwoman? I like her nerve!" He wondered whether he might have been breathing audibly when the intruder thrust her head between his curtains. He was conscious that he did not look a Prince Charming in his sleep. He dressed as fast as he could, and, when he was ready to go to the wash-room, glared at the slipper. If the porter should start to make up his berth in his absence— He caught the slipper, wrapped it in his pajama jacket, and thrust it into his bag. He escaped from the train without seeing his tormentor again.

Later McKann threw the slipper into the wastebasket in his room at the Knickerbocker, but the chambermaid, seeing that it was new and mateless, thought there must be a mistake, and placed it in his clothes-closet. He found it there when he returned from the theatre that evening. Considerably mellowed by food and drink and cheerful company, he took the slipper in his hand and decided to keep it as a reminder that absurd things could happen to people of the most clocklike deportment. When he got back to Pittsburgh, he stuck it in a lock-box in his vault, safe from prying clerks.

* * *

McKann has been ill for five years now, poor fellow! He still goes to the office, because it is the only place that interests him, but his partners do most of the work, and his clerks find him sadly changed—"morbid," they call his state of mind. He has had the pine-trees in his yard cut down because they remind him of cemeteries. On Sundays or holidays, when the office is empty, and he takes his will or his insurance-policies out of his lock-box, he often puts the tarnished gold slipper on his desk and looks at it. Somehow it suggests life to his tired mind, as his pine-trees suggested death—life and youth. When he drops over some day, his executors will be puzzled by the slipper.

As for Kitty Ayrshire, she has played so many jokes, practical and impractical, since then, that she has long ago forgotten the night when she threw away a slipper to be a thorn in the side of a just man.[6]

Scandal

Kitty Ayrshire had a cold, a persistent inflammation of the vocal cords which defied the throat specialist. Week after week her name was posted at the Opera, and week after week it was canceled, and the name of one of her rivals was substituted. For nearly two months she had been deprived of everything she liked, even of the people she liked, and had been shut up until she had come to hate the glass windows between her and the world, and the wintry stretch of the Park they looked out upon. She was losing a great deal of money, and, what was worse, she was losing life; days of which she wanted to make the utmost were slipping by, and nights which were to have crowned the days, nights of incalculable possibilities, were being stolen from her by women for whom she had no great affection. At first she had been courageous, but the strain of prolonged uncertainty was telling on her, and her nervous condition did not improve her larynx. Every morning Miles Creedon looked down her throat, only to put her off with evasions, to pronounce improvement that apparently never got her anywhere, to say that tomorrow he might be able to promise something definite.

Her illness, of course, gave rise to rumours—rumours that she had lost her voice, that at some time last summer she must have lost her discretion. Kitty herself was frightened by the way in which this cold hung on. She had had many sharp illnesses in her life, but always, before this, she had rallied quickly. Was she beginning to lose her resiliency? Was she, by any cursed chance, facing a bleak time when she would have to cherish herself? She protested, as she wandered about her sunny, many-windowed rooms on the tenth floor, that if she was going to have to live frugally, she wouldn't live at all. She wouldn't live on any terms but the very generous ones she had always known. She wasn't going to hoard her vitality. It must be there when she wanted it, be ready for any strain she chose to put upon it, let her play fast and loose with it; and then, if necessary, she would be ill for a while and pay the piper. But be systematically prudent and parsimonious she would not.

When she attempted to deliver all this to Doctor Creedon, he merely put his finger on her lips and said they would discuss these things when she could talk without injuring her throat. He allowed her to see no one except the Director of the Opera, who did not shine in conversation and was not apt to set Kitty going. The Director was a glum fellow, indeed, but during this calamitous time he had tried to be soothing, and he agreed with Creedon that she must not risk a premature appearance. Kitty was tormented by a suspicion that he was secretly backing the little Spanish woman who had sung many of her parts since she had been ill. He furthered the girl's interests because his wife had a very special consideration for her, and Madame had that consideration because— But that was too long and too dreary a story to follow out in one's mind. Kitty felt a tonsilitis disgust for opera-house politics, which, when she was in health, she rather enjoyed, being no mean strategist herself. The worst of being ill was that it made so many things and people look base.

She was always afraid of being disillusioned. She wished to believe that everything for sale in Vanity Fair was worth the advertised price. When she ceased to believe in these delights, she told herself, her pulling power would decline and she would go to pieces. In some way the chill of her disillusionment would quiver through the long, black line which reached from the box-office down to Seventh Avenue on nights when she sang. They shivered there in the rain and cold, all those people, because they loved to believe in her inextinguishable zest. She was no prouder of what she drew in the boxes than she was of that long, oscillating tail; little fellows in thin coats, Italians, Frenchmen, South-Americans, Japanese.

When she had been cloistered like a Trappist[1] for six weeks, with nothing from the outside world but notes and flowers and disquieting morning papers, Kitty told Miles Creedon that she could not endure complete isolation any longer.

"I simply cannot live through the evenings. They have become horrors to me. Every night is the last night of a condemned man. I do nothing but cry, and that makes my throat worse."

Miles Creedon, handsomest of his profession, was better looking with some invalids than with others. His athletic figure, his red cheeks, and splendid teeth always had a cheering effect upon this particular patient, who hated anything weak or broken.

"What can I do, my dear? What do you wish? Shall I come and hold your lovely hand from eight to ten? You have only to suggest it."

"Would you do that, even? No, *caro mio*, I take far too much of your time as it is. For an age now you have been the only man in the world to me, and you have been charming! But the world is big, and I am missing it. Let some one come tonight, some one interesting, but not too interesting. Pierce Tevis, for instance. He is just back from Paris. Tell the nurse I may see him for an hour tonight," Kitty finished pleadingly, and put her fingers on the doctor's sleeve. He looked down at them and smiled whimsically.

Like other people, he was weak to Kitty Ayrshire. He would do for her things that he would do for no one else; would break any engagement, desert a dinner-table, leaving an empty place and an offended hostess, to sit all evening in Kitty's dressing-room, spraying her throat and calming her nerves, using every expedient to get her through a performance. He had studied her voice like a singing master; knew all of its idiosyncracies and the emotional and nervous perturbations which affected it. When it was permissible, sometimes when it was not permissible, he indulged her caprices. On this sunny morning her wan, disconsolate face moved him.

"Yes, you may see Tevis this evening if you will assure me that you will not shed one tear for twenty-four hours. I may depend on your word?" He rose, and stood before the deep couch on which his patient reclined. Her arch look seemed to say, "On what could you depend more?" Creedon smiled, and shook his head. "If I find you worse tomorrow—"

He crossed to the writing-table and began to separate a bunch of tiny flame-coloured rosebuds. "May I?" Selecting one, he sat down on the chair from which he had lately risen, and leaned forward while Kitty pinched the thorns from the stem and arranged the flower in his buttonhole.

"Thank you. I like to wear one of yours. Now I must be off to the hospital. I've a nasty little operation to do this morning. I'm glad it's not you. Shall I telephone Tevis about this evening?"

Kitty hesitated. Her eyes ran rapidly about, seeking a likely pretext. Creedon laughed.

"Oh, I see. You've already asked him to come. You were so sure of me! Two hours in bed after lunch, with all the windows open, remember. Read something diverting, but not exciting; some homely British author; nothing *abandonné*. And don't make faces at me. Until tomorrow!"

When her charming doctor had disappeared through the doorway, Kitty fell back on her cushions and closed her eyes. Her mocking-bird, excited by the sunlight, was singing in his big gilt cage, and a white lilac-tree that had come that morning was giving out its faint sweetness in the warm room. But Kitty looked paler and wearier than when the doctor was with her. Even with him she rose to her part just a little; couldn't help it. And he took his share of her vivacity and sparkle, like every one else. He believed that his presence was soothing to her. But he admired; and whoever admired, blew on the flame, however lightly.

The mocking-bird was in great form this morning. He had the best bird-voice she had ever heard, and Kitty wished there were some way to note down his improvisations; but his intervals were not expressible in any scale she knew. Parker White had brought him to her, from Ojo Caliente, in New Mexico, where he had been trained in the pine forests by an old Mexican and an ill-tempered, lame master-bird, half thrush, that taught young birds to sing. This morning, in his song there were flashes of silvery Southern springtime; they opened inviting roads of memory. In half an hour he had sung his disconsolate mistress to sleep.

That evening Kitty sat curled up on the deep couch before the fire, awaiting Pierce Tevis. Her costume was folds upon folds of diaphanous white over equally diaphanous rose, with a line of white fur about her neck. Her beautiful arms were bare. Her tiny Chinese slippers were embroidered so richly that they resembled the painted porcelain of old vases. She looked like a sultan's youngest, newest bride; a beautiful little toy-woman, sitting at one end of the long room which composed about her,—which, in the soft light, seemed happily arranged for her. There were flowers everywhere: rose-trees; camellia-bushes, red and white; the first forced hyacinths of the season; a feathery mimosa-tree, tall enough to stand under.

The long front of Kitty's study was all windows. At one end was the fireplace, before which she sat. At the other end, back in a lighted alcove, hung a big, warm, sympathetic interior by Lucien Simon,—a group of Kitty's friends having tea in the painter's salon in Paris. The room in the picture was flooded with early lamp-light, and one could feel the grey, chill winter twilight in the Paris streets outside. There stood the cavalier-like old composer, who had done much for Kitty, in his most characteristic attitude, before the hearth. Mme. Simon sat at the tea-table. B——, the historian, and H——, the philologist, stood in animated discussion behind the piano, while Mme. H—— was tying on the bonnet of her lovely little daughter. Marcel Durand, the physicist, sat alone in a corner, his startling black-and-white profile lowered broodingly, his cold hands locked over his sharp knee. A genial, red-bearded sculptor stood over him, about to touch him on the shoulder and waken him from his dream.

This painting made, as it were, another room; so that Kitty's study on Central Park West seemed to open into that charming French interior, into one of the most highly harmonized and richly associated rooms in Paris. There her friends sat or stood about, men distinguished, women at once plain and beautiful, with their furs and bonnets, their clothes that were so distinctly not smart—all held together by the warm lamp-light, by an indescribable atmosphere of graceful and gracious human living.

Pierce Tevis, after he had entered noiselessly and greeted Kitty, stood before her fire and looked over her shoulder at this picture.

"It's nice that you have them there together, now that they are scattered, God knows where, fighting to preserve just that. But your own room, too, is charming," he added at last, taking his eyes from the canvas.

Kitty shrugged her shoulders.

"Bah! I can help to feed the lamp, but I can't supply the dear things it shines upon."

"Well, tonight it shines upon you and me, and we aren't so bad." Tevis stepped forward and took her hand affectionately. "You've been over a rough bit of road. I'm so sorry. It's left you looking very lovely, though. Has it been very hard to get on?"

She brushed his hand gratefully against her cheek and nodded.

"Awfully dismal. Everything has been shut out from me but—gossip. That always gets in. Often I don't mind, but this time I have. People do tell such lies about me."

"Of course we do. That's part of our fun, one of the many pleasures you give us. It only shows how hard up we are for interesting public personages; for a royal family, for romantic fiction, if you will. But I never hear any stories that wound me, and I'm very sensitive about you."

"I'm gossiped about rather more than the others, am I not?"

"I believe! Heaven send that the day when you are not gossiped about is far distant! Do you want to bite off your nose to spite your pretty face? You are the sort of person who makes myths. You can't turn around without making one. That's your singular good luck. A whole staff of publicity men, working day and night, couldn't do for you what you do for yourself. There is an affinity between you and the popular imagination."

"I suppose so," said Kitty, and sighed. "All the same, I'm getting almost as tired of the person I'm supposed to be as of the person I really am. I wish you would invent a new Kitty Ayrshire for me, Pierce. Can't I do something revolutionary? Marry, for instance?"

Tevis rose in alarm.

"Whatever you do, don't try to change your legend. You have now the one that gives the greatest satisfaction to the greatest number of people. Don't disappoint your public. The popular imagination, to which you make such a direct appeal, for some reason wished you to have a son, so it has given you one. I've heard a dozen versions of the story, but it is always a son, never by any chance a daughter. Your public gives you what is best for you. Let well enough alone."

Kitty yawned and dropped back on her cushions.

"He still persists, does he, in spite of never being visible?"

"Oh, but he has been seen by ever so many people. Let me think a moment." He sank into an attitude of meditative ease. "The best description I ever had of him was from a friend of my mother, an elderly woman, thoroughly truthful and matter-of-fact. She has seen him often. He is kept in Russia, in St. Petersburg, that was. He is about eight years old and of marvellous beauty. He is always that in every version. My old friend has seen him being driven in his sledge on the Nevskii Prospekt on winter afternoons; black horses with silver bells and a giant in uniform on the seat beside the driver. He is always attended by this giant, who is responsible to the Grand Duke Paul for the boy. This lady can produce no evidence beyond his beauty and his splendid furs and the fact that all the Americans in Petrograd know he is your son."

Kitty laughed mournfully.

"If the Grand Duke Paul had a son, any old rag of a son, the province of Moscow couldn't contain him! He may, for aught I know, actually pretend to have a son. It would be very like him." She looked at her finger-tips and her rings disapprovingly for a moment. "Do you know, I've been thinking that I would rather like to lay hands on that youngster. I believe he'd be interesting. I'm bored with the world."

Tevis looked up and said quickly:

"Would you like him, really?"

"Of course I should," she said indignantly. "But, then, I like other things, too; and one has to choose. When one has only two or three things to choose from, life is hard; when one has many, it is harder still. No, on the whole, I don't mind that story. It's rather pretty, except for the Grand Duke. But not all of them are pretty."

"Well, none of them are very ugly; at least I never heard but one that troubled me, and that was long ago."

She looked interested.

"That is what I want to know; how do the ugly ones get started?

How did that one get going and what was it about? Is it too dreadful to repeat?"

"No, it's not especially dreadful; merely rather shabby. If you really wish to know, and won't be vexed, I can tell you exactly how it got going, for I took the trouble to find out. But it's a long story, and you really had nothing whatever to do with it."

"Then who did have to do with it? Tell me; I should like to know exactly how even one of them originated."

"Will you be comfortable and quiet and not get into a rage, and let me look at you as much as I please?"

Kitty nodded, and Tevis sat watching her indolently while he debated how much of his story he ought not to tell her. Kitty liked being looked at by intelligent persons. She knew exactly how good looking she was; and she knew, too, that, pretty as she was, some of those rather sallow women in the Simon painting had a kind of beauty which she would never have. This knowledge, Tevis was thinking, this important realization, contributed more to her loveliness than any other thing about her; more than her smooth, ivory skin or her changing grey eyes, the delicate forehead above them, or even the dazzling smile, which was gradually becoming too bright and too intentional,—out in the world, at least. Here by her own fire she still had for her friends a smile less electric than the one she flashed from stages. She could still be, in short, *intime*, a quality which few artists keep, which few ever had.

Kitty broke in on her friend's meditations.

"You may smoke. I had rather you did. I hate to deprive people of things they like."

"No, thanks. May I have those chocolates on the tea-table? They are quite as bad for me. May you? No, I suppose not." He settled himself by the fire, with the candy beside him, and began in the agreeable voice which always soothed his listener.

"As I said, it was a long while ago, when you first came back to this country and were singing at the Manhattan. I dropped in at the Metropolitan one evening to hear something new they were trying out. It was an off night, no pullers in the cast, and nobody in the boxes but governesses and poor relations. At the end of the first act two people entered one of the boxes in the second tier. The man was Siegmund Stein, the department-store millionaire, and the girl, so the men about me in the omnibus box began to whisper, was Kitty Ayrshire. I didn't know you then, but I was unwilling to believe that you were with Stein. I could not contradict them at that time, however, for the resemblance, if it was merely a resemblance, was absolute, and all the world knew that you were not singing at the Manhattan that night. The girl's hair was dressed just as you then wore yours. Moreover, her head was small and restless like yours, and she had your colouring, your eyes, your chin. She carried herself with the critical indifference one might expect in an artist who had come for a look at a new production that was clearly doomed to failure. She applauded lightly. She made comments to Stein when comments were natural enough. I thought, as I studied her face with the glass, that her nose was a trifle thinner than yours, a prettier nose, my dear Kitty, but stupider and more inflexible. All the same, I was troubled until I saw her laugh,—and then I knew she was a counterfeit. I had never seen you laugh, but I knew that you would not laugh like that. It was not boisterous; indeed, it was consciously refined,—mirthless, meaningless. In short, it was not the laugh of one whom our friends in there"—pointing to the Simon painting—"would honour with their affection and admiration."

Kitty rose on her elbow and burst out indignantly:

"So you would really have been hood-winked except for that! You may be sure that no woman, no intelligent woman, would have been. Why do we ever take the trouble to look like anything for any of you? I could count on my four fingers"—she held them up and shook them at him—"the men I've known who had the least perception of what any woman really looked like, and they were all dressmakers. Even painters"—glancing back in the direction of the Simon picture—"never get more than one type through their thick heads; they try to make all women look like some wife or mistress. You are all the same; you never see our real faces. What you do see, is some cheap conception of prettiness you got from a coloured supplement when you were adolescents. It's too discouraging. I'd rather take vows and veil my face for ever from such abominable eyes. In the kingdom of the blind any petticoat is a queen." Kitty thumped the cushion with her elbow. "Well, I can't do anything about it. Go on with your story."

"Aren't you furious, Kitty! And I thought I was so shrewd. I've quite forgotten where I was. Anyhow, I was not the only man fooled. After the last curtain I met Villard, the press man of that management, in the lobby, and asked him whether Kitty Ayrshire was in the house. He said he thought so. Stein had telephoned for a box, and said he was bringing one of the artists from the other company. Villard had been too busy about the new production to go to the box, but he was quite sure the woman was Ayrshire, whom he had met in Paris.

"Not long after that I met Dan Leland, a classmate of mine, at the Harvard Club. He's a journalist, and he used to keep such eccentric hours that I had not run across him for a long time. We got to talking about modern French music, and discovered that we both had a very lively interest in Kitty Ayrshire.

" 'Could you tell me,' Dan asked abruptly, 'why, with pretty much all the known world to choose her friends from, this young woman should flit about with Siegmund Stein? It prejudices people against her. He's a most objectionable person.'

" 'Have you,' I asked, 'seen her with him, yourself?'

"Yes, he had seen her driving with Stein, and some of the men on his paper had seen her dining with him at rather queer places down town. Stein was always hanging about the Manhattan on nights when Kitty sang. I told Dan that I suspected a masquerade. That interested him, and he said he thought he would look into the matter. In short, we both agreed to look into it. Finally, we got the story, though Dan could never use it, could never even hint at it, because Stein carries heavy advertising in his paper.

"To make you see the point, I must give you a little history of Siegmund Stein. Any one who has seen him never forgets him. He is one of the most hideous men in New York, but it's not at all the common sort of ugliness that comes from overeating and automobiles. He isn't one of the fat horrors. He has one of those rigid, horselike faces that never tell anything; a long nose, flattened as if it had been tied down; a scornful chin; long, white teeth; flat cheeks, yellow as a Mongolian's; tiny, black eyes, with puffy lids and no lashes; dingy, dead-looking hair—looks as if it were glued on.

"Stein came here a beggar from somewhere in Austria. He began by working on the machines in old Rosenthal's garment factory. He became a speeder, a foreman, a salesman; worked his way ahead steadily until the hour when he rented an old dwelling-house on Seventh Avenue and began to make misses' and juniors' coats. I believe he was the first manufacturer to specialize in those particular articles. Dozens of garment manufacturers have come along the same road, but Stein is like none of the rest of them. He is, and always was, a personality. While he was still at the machine, a hideous, underfed little whipper-snapper, he was already a youth of many-coloured ambitions, deeply concerned about his dress, his associates, his recreations. He haunted the old Astor Library and the Metropolitan Museum, learned something about pictures and porcelains, took singing lessons, though he had a voice like a crow's. When he sat down to his baked apple and doughnut in a basement lunch-room, he would prop a book up before him and address his food with as much leisure and ceremony as if he were dining at his club. He held himself at a distance from his fellow-workmen and somehow always managed to impress them with his superiority. He had inordinate vanity, and there are many stories about his foppishness. After his first promotion in Rosenthal's factory, he bought a new overcoat. A few days later, one of the men at the machines, which Stein had just quitted, appeared in a coat exactly like it. Stein could not discharge him, but he gave his own coat to a newly arrived Russian boy and got another. He was already magnificent.

"After he began to make headway with misses' and juniors' cloaks, he became a collector—etchings, china, old musical instruments. He had a dancing master, and engaged a beautiful Brazilian widow—she was said to be a secret agent for some South American republic—to teach him Spanish. He cultivated the society of the unknown great; poets, actors, musicians. He entertained them sumptuously, and they regarded him as a deep, mysterious Jew who had the secret of gold, which they had not. His business associates thought him a man of taste and culture, a patron of the arts, a credit to the garment trade.

"One of Stein's many ambitions was to be thought a success with women. He got considerable notoriety in the garment world by his attentions to an emotional actress who is now quite forgotten, but who had her little hour of expectation. Then there was a dancer; then, just after Gorky's visit here,[2] a Russian anarchist woman. After that the coat-makers and shirtwaist-makers began to whisper that Stein's great success was with Kitty Ayrshire.

"It is the hardest thing in the world to disprove such a story, as Dan Leland and I discovered. We managed to worry down[3] the girl's address through a taxi-cab driver who got next to Stein's chauffeur. She had an apartment in a decent-enough house on Waverly Place.[4] Nobody ever came to see her but Stein, her sisters, and a little Italian girl from whom we got the story.

"The counterfeit's name was Ruby Mohr. She worked in a shirtwaist factory, and this Italian girl, Margarita, was her chum. Stein came to the factory when he was hunting for living models for his new department store. He looked the girls over, and picked Ruby out from several hundred. He had her call at his office after business hours, tried her out in cloaks and evening gowns, and offered her a position. She never, however, appeared as a model in the Sixth Avenue store. Her likeness to the newly arrived prima donna suggested to Stein another act in the play he was always putting on. He gave two of her sisters positions as saleswomen, but Ruby he established in an apartment on Waverly Place.

"To the outside world Stein became more mysterious in his behaviour than ever. He dropped his Bohemian friends. No more suppers and theatre-parties. Whenever Kitty sang, he was in his box at the Manhattan, usually alone, but not always. Sometimes he took two or three good customers, large buyers from St. Louis or Kansas City. His coat factory is still the biggest earner of his properties. I've seen him there with these buyers, and they carried themselves as if they were being let in on something; took possession of the box with a proprietory air, smiled and applauded and looked wise as if each and every one of them were friends of Kitty Ayrshire.

While they buzzed and trained their field-glasses on the prima donna, Stein was impassive and silent. I don't imagine he even told many lies. He is the most insinuating cuss, anyhow. He probably dropped his voice or lifted his eyebrows when he invited them, and let their own eager imaginations do the rest. But what tales they took back to their provincial capitals!

"Sometimes, before they left New York, they were lucky enough to see Kitty dining with their clever garment man at some restaurant, her back to the curious crowd, her face half concealed by a veil or a fur collar. Those people are like children; nothing that is true or probable interests them. They want the old, gaudy lies, told always in the same way. Siegmund Stein and Kitty Ayrshire—a story like that, once launched, is repeated unchallenged for years among New York factory sports. In St. Paul, St. Jo, Sioux City, Council Bluffs, there used to be clothing stores where a photograph of Kitty Ayrshire hung in the fitting-room or over the proprietor's desk.

"This girl impersonated you successfully to the lower manufacturing world of New York for two seasons. I doubt if it could have been put across anywhere else in the world except in this city, which pays you so magnificently and believes of you what it likes. Then you went over to the Metropolitan, stopped living in hotels, took this apartment, and began to know people. Stein discontinued his pantomime at the right moment, withdrew his patronage. Ruby, of course, did not go back to shirtwaists. A business friend of Stein's took her over, and she dropped out of sight. Last winter, one cold, snowy night, I saw her once again. She was going into a saloon hotel with a tough-looking young fellow. She had been drinking, she was shabby, and her blue shoes left stains in the slush. But she still looked amazingly, convincingly like a battered, hardened Kitty Ayrshire. As I saw her going up the brass-edged stairs, I said to myself—"

"Never mind that." Kitty rose quickly, took an impatient step to the hearth, and thrust one shining porcelain slipper out to the fire. "The girl doesn't interest me. There is nothing I can do about her, and of course she never looked like me at all. But what did Stein do without me?"

"Stein? Oh, he chose a new rôle. He married with great magnificence—married a Miss Mandelbaum, a California heiress. Her people have a line of department stores along the Pacific Coast. The Steins now inhabit a great house on Fifth Avenue that used to belong to people of a very different sort. To old New-Yorkers, it's an historic house."

Kitty laughed, and sat down on the end of her couch nearest her guest; sat upright, without cushions.

"I imagine I know more about that house than you do. Let me tell you how I made the sequel to your story.

"It has to do with Peppo Amoretti. You may remember that I brought Peppo to this country, and brought him in, too, the year the war broke out, when it wasn't easy to get boys who hadn't done military service out of Italy. I had taken him to Munich to have some singing lessons. After the war came on we had to get from Munich to Naples in order to sail at all. We were told that we could take only hand luggage on the railways, but I took nine trunks and Peppo. I dressed Peppo in knickerbockers, made him brush his curls down over his ears like doughnuts, and carry a little violin-case. It took us eleven days to reach Naples. I got my trunks through purely by personal persuasion. Once at Naples, I had a frightful time getting Peppo on the boat. I declared him as hand luggage; he was so travel-worn and so crushed by his absurd appearance that he did not look like much else. One inspector had a sense of humour, and passed him at that, but the other was inflexible. I had to be very dramatic. Peppo was frightened, and there is no fight in him, anyhow.

" '*Per me tutto e indifferente, Signorina,*' he kept whimpering. 'Why should I go without it? I have lost it.'

" 'Which?' I screamed. '*Not* the hat-trunk?'

" '*No, no; mia voce.* It is gone since Ravenna.'

"He thought he had lost his voice somewhere along the way. At last I told the inspector that I couldn't live without Peppo, and that I would throw myself into the bay. I took him into my confidence. Of course, when I found I had to play on that string, I wished I hadn't made the boy such a spectacle. But ridiculous as he was, I managed to make the inspector believe that I had kidnapped him, and that he was indispensable to my happiness. I found that incorruptible official, like most people, willing to aid one so utterly depraved. I could never have got that boy out for any proper, reasonable purpose, such as giving him a job or sending him to school. Well, it's a queer world! But I must cut all that and get to the Steins.

"That first winter Peppo had no chance at the Opera. There was an iron ring about him, and my interest in him only made it all the more difficult. We've become a nest of intrigues down there; worse than the Scala. Peppo had to scratch along just any way. One evening he came to me and said he could get an engagement to sing for the grand rich Steins, but the condition was that I should sing with him. They would pay, oh, anything! And the fact that I had sung a private engagement with him would give him other engagements of the same sort. As you know, I never sing private engagements; but to help the boy along, I consented.

"On the night of the party, Peppo and I went to the house together in a taxi. My car was ailing. At the hour when the music was about to begin, the host and hostess appeared at my dressing-room, up-stairs. Isn't he wonderful? Your description was most inadequate. I never encountered such restrained, frozen, sculptured vanity. My hostess struck me as extremely good natured and jolly, though somewhat intimate in her manner. Her reassuring pats and smiles puzzled me at the time, I remember, when I didn't know that she had anything in particular to be large-minded and charitable about. Her husband made known his willingness to conduct me to the music-room, and we ceremoniously descended a staircase blooming like the hanging-gardens of Babylon. From there I had my first glimpse of the company. They *were* strange people. The women glittered like Christmas-trees. When we were half-way down the stairs, the buzz of conversation stopped so suddenly that some foolish remark I happened to be making rang out like oratory. Every face was lifted toward us. My host and I completed our descent and went the length of the drawing-room through a silence which somewhat awed me. I couldn't help wishing that one could ever get that kind of attention in a concert-hall. In the music-room Stein insisted upon arranging things for me. I must say that he was enough to send him to me. She did not come back, and I began to fear that I would actually be dragged down to supper. It was as if I had been kidnapped. I felt like *Gulliver* among the giants.[6] These people were all too—well, too much what they were. No chill of manner could hold them off. I was defenceless. I must get away. I ran to the top of the staircase and looked down. There was that fool Peppo, beleaguered by a bevy of fair women. They were simply looting him, and he was grinning like an idiot. I gathered up my train, ran down, and made a dash at him, yanked him out of that circle of rich contours, and dragged him by a limp cuff up the stairs after me. I told him that I must escape from that house at once. If he could get to the telephone, well and good; but if he couldn't get past so many deep-breathing ladies, then he must break out of the front door and hunt me a cab on foot. I felt as if I were about to be immured within a harem.

"He had scarcely dashed off when the host called my name several times outside the door. Then he knocked and walked in, uninvited. I told him that I would be inflexible about supper. He must make my excuses to his charming friends; any pretext he chose. He did not insist. He took up his stand by the fireplace and began to talk; said rather intelligent things. I did not drive him out; it was his own house, and he made himself agreeable. After a time a deputation of his friends came down the hall, somewhat boisterously, to say that supper could not be served until we came down. Stein was still standing by the mantel, I remember. He scattered them, without moving or speaking to them, by a portentous look. There is something hideously forceful about him. He took a very profound leave of me, and said he would order his car at once. In a moment Peppo arrived, splashed to the ankles, and we made our escape together.

"A week later Peppo came to me in a rage, with a paper called *The American Gentleman*, and showed me a page devoted to three photographs: Mr. and Mrs. Siegmund Stein, lately married in New York City, and Kitty Ayrshire, operatic soprano, who sang at their house-warming. Mrs. Stein and I were grinning our best, looked frantic with delight, and Siegmund frowned inscrutably between us. Poor Peppo wasn't mentioned. Stein has a publicity sense."

neither awkward nor stupid, not so wooden as most rich men w rent singers. I was properly affable. One has, under such circun stances, to be either gracious or pouty. Either you have to stanc and sulk, like an old-fashioned German singer who wants the piano moved about for her like a tea-wagon, and the lights turned up and the lights turned down,—or you have to be a trifle forced, like a débutante trying to make good. The fixed attention of my audience affected me. I was aware of unusual interest, of a thoroughly enlisted public. When, however, my host at last left me, I felt the tension relax to such an extent that I wondered whether by any chance he, and not I, was the object of so much curiosity. But, at any rate, their cordiality pleased me so well that after Peppo and I had finished our numbers I sang an encore or two, and I stayed through Peppo's performance because I felt that they liked to look at me.

"I had asked not to be presented to people, but Mrs. Stein, of course, brought up a few friends. The throng began closing in upon me, glowing faces bore down from every direction, and I realized that, among people of such unscrupulous cordiality, I must look out for myself. I ran through the drawing-room and fled up the stairway, which was thronged with Old Testament characters.[5] As I passed them, they all looked at me with delighted, cherishing eyes, as if I had at last come back to my native hamlet. At the top of the stairway a young man, who looked like a camel with its hair parted on the side, stopped me, seized my hands and said he must present himself, as he was such an old friend of Siegmund's bachelor days. I said, 'Yes, how interesting!' The atmosphere was somehow so thick and personal that I felt uncomfortable.

"When I reached my dressing-room Mrs. Stein followed me to say that I would, of course, come down to supper, as a special table had been prepared for me. I replied that it was not my custom.

" 'But here it is different. With us you must feel perfect freedom. Siegmund will never forgive me if you do not stay. After supper our car will take you home.' She was overpowering. She had the manner of an intimate and indulgent friend of long standing. She seemed to have come to make me a visit. I could only get rid of her by telling her that I must see Peppo at once, if she would be good

Tevis rose.

"And you have enormous publicity value and no discretion. It was just like you to fall for such a plot, Kitty. You'd be sure to."

"What's the use of discretion?" she murmured behind her hand. "If the Steins want to adopt you into their family circle, they'll get you in the end. That's why I don't feel compassionate about your Ruby. She and I are in the same boat. We are both the victims of circumstance, and in New York so many of the circumstances are Steins."

Paul's Case

IT WAS Paul's afternoon to appear before the faculty of the Pittsburgh High School to account for his various misdemeanors. He had been suspended a week ago, and his father had called at the Principal's office and confessed his perplexity about his son. Paul entered the faculty room suave and smiling. His clothes were a trifle out-grown, and the tan velvet on the collar of his open overcoat was frayed and worn; but for all that there was something of the dandy about him, and he wore an opal pin in his neatly knotted black four-in-hand, and a red carnation in his button-hole. This latter adornment the faculty somehow felt was not properly significant of the contrite spirit befitting a boy under the ban of suspension.

Paul was tall for his age and very thin, with high, cramped shoulders and a narrow chest. His eyes were remarkable for a certain hysterical brilliancy, and he continually used them in a conscious, theatrical sort of way, peculiarly offensive in a boy. The pupils were abnormally large, as though he were addicted to belladonna,[1] but there was a glassy glitter about them which that drug does not produce.

When questioned by the Principal as to why he was there, Paul stated, politely enough, that he wanted to come back to school. This was a lie, but Paul was quite accustomed to lying; found it, indeed, indispensable for overcoming friction. His teachers were asked to state their respective charges against him, which they did with such a rancour and aggrievedness as evinced that this was not a usual case. Disorder and impertinence were among the offences named, yet each of his instructors felt that it was scarcely possible to put into words the real cause of the trouble, which lay in a sort of hysterically defiant manner of the boy's; in the contempt which they all knew he felt for them, and which he seemingly made not the least effort to conceal. Once, when he had been making a synopsis of a paragraph at the blackboard, his English teacher had stepped to his side and attempted to guide his hand. Paul had started back with a shudder and thrust his hands violently behind him. The astonished woman could scarcely have been more hurt and embarrassed had he struck at her. The insult was so involuntary and definitely personal as to be unforgettable. In one way and another, he had made all his teachers, men and women alike, conscious of the same feeling of physical aversion. In one class he habitually sat with his hand shading his eyes; in another he always looked out of the window during the recitation; in another he made a running commentary on the lecture, with humorous intent.

His teachers felt this afternoon that his whole attitude was symbolized by his shrug and his flippantly red carnation flower, and they fell upon him without mercy, his English teacher leading the pack. He stood through it smiling, his pale lips parted over his white teeth. (His lips were continually twitching, and he had a habit of raising his eyebrows that was contemptuous and irritating to the last degree.) Older boys than Paul had broken down and shed tears under that ordeal, but his set smile did not once desert him, and his only sign of discomfort was the nervous trembling of the fingers that toyed with the buttons of his overcoat, and an occasional jerking of the other hand which held his hat. Paul was always smiling, always glancing about him, seeming to feel that people might be watching him and trying to detect something. This conscious expression, since it was as far as possible from boyish mirthfulness, was usually attributed to insolence or "smartness."

As the inquisition proceeded, one of his instructors repeated an impertinent remark of the boy's, and the Principal asked him whether he thought that a courteous speech to make to a woman. Paul shrugged his shoulders slightly and his eyebrows twitched.

"I don't know," he replied. "I didn't mean to be polite or impolite, either. I guess it's a sort of way I have, of saying things regardless."

The Principal asked him whether he didn't think that a way it would be well to get rid of. Paul grinned and said he guessed so. When he was told that he could go, he bowed gracefully and went out. His bow was like a repetition of the scandalous red carnation.

His teachers were in despair, and his drawing master voiced the feeling of them all when he declared there was something about the boy which none of them understood. He added: "I don't really believe that smile of his comes altogether from insolence; there's something sort of haunted about it. The boy is not strong, for one thing. There is something wrong about the fellow."

The drawing master had come to realize that, in looking at Paul, one saw only his white teeth and the forced animation of his eyes. One warm afternoon the boy had gone to sleep at his drawing-board, and his master had noted with amazement what a white, blue-veined face it was; drawn and wrinkled like an old man's about the eyes, the lips twitching even in his sleep.

His teachers left the building dissatisfied and unhappy; humiliated to have felt so vindictive toward a mere boy, to have uttered this feeling in cutting terms, and to have set each other on, as it were, in the grewsome game of intemperate reproach. One of them remembered having seen a miserable street cat set at bay by a ring of tormentors.

As for Paul, he ran down the hill whistling the Soldiers' Chorus from *Faust*,[2] looking wildly behind him now and then to see whether some of his teachers were not there to witness his light-heartedness. As it was now late in the afternoon and Paul was on duty that evening as usher at Carnegie Hall, he decided that he would not go home to supper.

When he reached the concert hall the doors were not yet open. It was chilly outside, and he decided to go up into the picture gallery—always deserted at this hour—where there were some of Raffaëlli's gay studies[3] of Paris streets and an airy blue Venetian scene or two that always exhilarated him. He was delighted to find no one in the gallery but the old guard, who sat in the corner, a newspaper on his knee, a black patch over one eye and the other closed. Paul possessed himself of the place and walked confidently up and down, whistling under his breath. After a while he sat down before a blue Rico[4] and lost himself. When he bethought him to look at his watch, it was after seven o'clock, and he rose with a start and ran downstairs, making a face at Augustus Cæsar, peering out from the cast-room, and an evil gesture at the Venus of Milo[5] as he passed her on the stairway.

When Paul reached the ushers' dressing-room half-a-dozen boys were there already, and he began excitedly to tumble into his uniform. It was one of the few that at all approached fitting, and Paul thought it very becoming—though he knew the tight, straight coat accentuated his narrow chest, about which he was exceedingly sensitive. He was always excited while he dressed, twanging all over to the tuning of the strings and the preliminary flourishes of the horns in the music-room; but tonight he seemed quite beside himself, and he teased and plagued the boys until, telling him that he was crazy, they put him down on the floor and sat on him.

Somewhat calmed by his suppression, Paul dashed out to the front of the house to seat the early comers. He was a model usher. Gracious and smiling he ran up and down the aisles. Nothing was too much trouble for him; he carried messages and brought programs as though it were his greatest pleasure in life, and all the people in his section thought him a charming boy, feeling that he remembered and admired them. As the house filled, he grew more and more vivacious and animated, and the colour came to his cheeks and lips. It was very much as though this were a great reception and Paul were the host. Just as the musicians came out to take their places, his English teacher arrived with checks for the seats which a prominent manufacturer had taken for the season. She betrayed some embarrassment when she handed Paul the tickets, and a *hauteur*[6] which subsequently made her feel very foolish. Paul was startled for a moment, and had the feeling of wanting to put her out; what business had she here among all these fine people and gay colours? He looked her over and decided that she was not appropriately dressed and must be a fool to sit downstairs in such togs. The tickets had probably been sent her out of kindness, he reflected, as he put down a seat for her, and she had about as much right to sit there as he had.

When the symphony began Paul sank into one of the rear seats with a long sigh of relief, and lost himself as he had done before the Rico. It was not that symphonies, as such, meant anything in particular to Paul, but the first sigh of the instruments seemed to free some hilarious spirit within him; something that struggled there like the Genius in the bottle found by the Arab fisherman.[7] He felt a sudden zest of life; the lights danced before his eyes and the concert hall blazed into unimaginable splendour. When the soprano soloist came on, Paul forgot even the nastiness of his teacher's being there, and gave himself up to the peculiar intoxication such personages always had for him. The soloist chanced to be a German woman, by no means in her first youth, and the mother of many children; but she wore a satin gown and a tiara, and she had that indefinable air of achievement, that world-shine upon her, which always blinded Paul to any possible defects.

After a concert was over, Paul was often irritable and wretched until he got to sleep,—and tonight he was even more than usually restless. He had the feeling of not being able to let down; of its being impossible to give up this delicious excitement which was the only thing that could be called living at all. During the last number he withdrew and, after hastily changing his clothes in the dressing-room, slipped out to the side door where the singer's carriage stood. Here he began pacing rapidly up and down the walk, waiting to see her come out.

Over yonder the Schenley, in its vacant stretch, loomed big and square through the fine rain, the windows of its twelve stories glowing like those of a lighted card-board house under a Christmas tree. All the actors and singers of any importance stayed there when they were in the city, and a number of the big manufacturers of the place lived there in the winter. Paul had often hung about the hotel, watching the people go in and out, longing to enter and leave school-masters and dull care behind him for ever.

At last the singer came out, accompanied by the conductor, who helped her into her carriage and closed the door with a cordial *auf wiedersehen*,—which set Paul to wondering whether she were not an old sweetheart of his. Paul followed the carriage over to the hotel, walking so rapidly as not to be far from the entrance when the singer alighted and disappeared behind the swinging glass doors which were opened by a negro in a tall hat and a long coat. In the moment that the door was ajar, it seemed to Paul that he, too, entered. He seemed to feel himself go after her up the steps, into the warm, lighted building, into an exotic, a tropical world of shiny, glistening surfaces and basking ease. He reflected upon the mysterious dishes that were brought into the dining-room, the green bottles in buckets of ice, as he had seen them in the supper party pictures of the Sunday supplement. A quick gust of wind brought the rain down with sudden vehemence, and Paul was startled to find that he was still outside in the slush of the gravel driveway; that his boots were letting in the water and his scanty overcoat was clinging wet about him; that the lights in front of the concert hall were out, and that the rain was driving in sheets between him and the orange glow of the windows above him. There it was, what he wanted—tangibly before him, like the fairy world of a Christmas pantomime; as the rain beat in his face, Paul wondered whether he were destined always to shiver in the black night outside, looking up at it.

He turned and walked reluctantly toward the car tracks. The end had to come sometime; his father in his night-clothes at the top of the stairs, explanations that did not explain, hastily improvised fictions that were forever tripping him up, his upstairs room and its horrible yellow wall-paper, the creaking bureau with the greasy plush collar-box, and over his painted wooden bed the pictures of George Washington and John Calvin, and the framed motto, "Feed my Lambs," which had been worked in red worsted by his mother, whom Paul could not remember.

Half an hour later, Paul alighted from the Negley Avenue car and went slowly down one of the side streets off the main thoroughfare. It was a highly respectable street, where all the houses were exactly alike, and where business men of moderate means begot and reared large families of children, all of whom went to Sabbath-school and learned the shorter catechism, and were interested in arithmetic; all of whom were as exactly alike as their homes, and of a piece with the monotony in which they lived. Paul never went up Cordelia Street without a shudder of loathing. His home was next the house of the Cumberland minister. He approached it tonight with the nerveless sense of defeat, the hopeless feeling of sinking back forever into ugliness and commonness that he had always had when he came home. The moment he turned into Cordelia Street he felt the waters close above his head. After each of these orgies of living, he experienced all the physical depression which follows a debauch; the loathing of respectable beds, of common food, of a house permeated by kitchen odours; a shuddering repulsion for the flavourless, colourless mass of every-day existence; a morbid desire for cool things and soft lights and fresh flowers.

The nearer he approached the house, the more absolutely unequal Paul felt to the sight of it all; his ugly sleeping chamber; the cold bath-room with the grimy zinc tub, the cracked mirror, the dripping spiggots; his father, at the top of the stairs, his hairy legs sticking out from his nightshirt, his feet thrust into carpet slippers. He was so much later than usual that there would certainly be inquiries and reproaches. Paul stopped short before the door. He felt that he could not be accosted by his father tonight; that he could not toss again on that miserable bed. He would not go in. He would tell his father that he had no car fare, and it was raining so hard he had gone home with one of the boys and stayed all night.

Meanwhile, he was wet and cold. He went around to the back of the house and tried one of the basement windows, found it open, raised it cautiously, and scrambled down the cellar wall to the floor. There he stood, holding his breath, terrified by the noise he had made; but the floor above him was silent, and there was no creak on the stairs. He found a soap-box, and carried it over to the soft ring of light that streamed from the furnace door, and sat down. He was horribly afraid of rats, so he did not try to sleep, but sat looking distrustfully at the dark, still terrified lest he might have awakened his father. In such reactions, after one of the experiences which made days and nights out of the dreary blanks of the calendar, when his senses were deadened, Paul's head was always singularly clear. Suppose his father had heard him getting in at the window and had come down and shot him for a burglar? Then, again, suppose his father had come down, pistol in hand, and he had cried out in time to save himself, and his father had been horrified to think how nearly he had killed him? Then, again, suppose a day should come when his father would remember that night, and wish there had been no warning cry to stay his hand? With this last supposition Paul entertained himself until daybreak.

The following Sunday was fine; the sodden November chill was broken by the last flash of autumnal summer. In the morning Paul had to go to church and Sabbath-school, as always. On seasonable Sunday afternoons the burghers of Cordelia Street usually sat out on their front "stoops," and talked to their neighbours on the next stoop, or called to those across the street in neighbourly fashion. The men sat placidly on gay cushions placed upon the steps that led down to the sidewalk, while the women, in their Sunday "waists," sat in rockers on the cramped porches, pretending to be greatly at their ease. The children played in the streets; there were so many of them that the place resembled the recreation grounds of a kindergarten. The men on the steps—all in their shirt sleeves, their vests unbuttoned—sat with their legs well apart, their stomachs comfortably protruding, and talked of the prices of things, or told anecdotes of the sagacity of their various chiefs and overlords. They occasionally looked over the multitude of squabbling children, listened affectionately to their high-pitched, nasal voices, smiling to see their own proclivities reproduced in their offspring, and interspersed their legends of the iron kings with remarks about their sons' progress at school, their grades in arithmetic, and the amounts they had saved in their toy banks.

On this last Sunday of November, Paul sat all the afternoon on the lowest step of his "stoop," staring into the street, while his sisters, in their rockers, were talking to the minister's daughters next door about how many shirt-waists they had made in the last week, and how many waffles some one had eaten at the last church supper. When the weather was warm, and his father was in a particularly jovial frame of mind, the girls made lemonade, which was always brought out in a red-glass pitcher, ornamented with forget-me-nots in blue enamel. This the girls thought very fine, and the neighbours joked about the suspicious colour of the pitcher.

Today Paul's father, on the top step, was talking to a young man who shifted a restless baby from knee to knee. He happened to be the young man who was daily held up to Paul as a model, and after whom it was his father's dearest hope that he would pattern. This young man was of a ruddy complexion, with a compressed, red mouth, and faded, near-sighted eyes, over which he wore thick spectacles, with gold bows that curved about his ears. He was clerk to one of the magnates of a great steel corporation, and was looked upon in Cordelia Street as a young man with a future. There was a story that, some five years ago—he was now barely twenty-six—he had been a trifle "dissipated," but in order to curb his appetites and save the loss of time and strength that a sowing of wild oats might have entailed, he had taken his chief's advice, oft reiterated to his employés, and at twenty-one had married the first woman whom he could persuade to share his fortunes. She happened to be an angular school-mistress, much older than he, who also wore thick glasses, and who had now borne him four children, all near-sighted, like herself.

The young man was relating how his chief, now cruising in the Mediterranean, kept in touch with all the details of the business, arranging his office hours on his yacht just as though he were at home, and "knocking off work enough to keep two stenographers busy." His father told, in turn, the plan his corporation was considering, of putting in an electric railway plant at Cairo. Paul snapped his teeth; he had an awful apprehension that they might spoil it all before he got there. Yet he rather liked to hear these legends of the iron kings, that were told and retold on Sundays and holidays; these stories of palaces in Venice, yachts on the Mediterranean, and high play at Monte Carlo appealed to his fancy, and he was interested in the triumphs of cash boys[8] who had become famous, though he had no mind for the cash-boy stage.

After supper was over, and he had helped to dry the dishes, Paul nervously asked his father whether he could go to George's to get some help in his geometry, and still more nervously asked for car fare. This latter request he had to repeat, as his father, on principle, did not like to hear requests for money, whether much or little. He asked Paul whether he could not go to some boy who lived nearer, and told him that he ought not to leave his school work until Sunday; but he gave him the dime. He was not a poor man, but he had a worthy ambition to come up in the world. His only reason for allowing Paul to usher was that he thought a boy ought to be earning a little.

Paul bounded upstairs, scrubbed the greasy odour of the dishwater from his hands with the ill-smelling soap he hated, and then shook over his fingers a few drops of violet water from the bottle he kept hidden in his drawer. He left the house with his geometry conspicuously under his arm, and the moment he got out of Cordelia Street and boarded a downtown car, he shook off the lethargy of two deadening days, and began to live again.

The leading juvenile of the permanent stock company which played at one of the downtown theatres was an acquaintance of Paul's, and the boy had been invited to drop in at the Sunday-night rehearsals whenever he could. For more than a year Paul had spent every available moment loitering about Charley Edwards's dressing-room. He had won a place among Edwards's following not only because the young actor, who could not afford to employ a dresser, often found him useful, but because he recognized in Paul something akin to what churchmen term "vocation."

It was at the theatre and at Carnegie Hall that Paul really lived; the rest was but a sleep and a forgetting.[9] This was Paul's fairy tale, and it had for him all the allurement of a secret love. The moment he inhaled the gassy, painty, dusty odour behind the scenes, he breathed like a prisoner set free, and felt within him the possibility of doing or saying splendid, brilliant things. The moment the cracked orchestra beat out the overture from *Martha*,[10] or jerked at the serenade from *Rigoletto*,[11] all stupid and ugly things slid from him, and his senses were deliciously, yet delicately fired.

Perhaps it was because, in Paul's world, the natural nearly always wore the guise of ugliness, that a certain element of artificiality seemed to him necessary in beauty. Perhaps it was because his experience of life elsewhere was so full of Sabbath-school picnics, petty economies, wholesome advice as to how to succeed in life, and the unescapable odours of cooking, that he found this existence so alluring, these smartly-clad men and women so attractive, that he was so moved by these starry apple orchards that bloomed perennially under the lime-light.

It would be difficult to put it strongly enough how convincingly the stage entrance of that theatre was for Paul the actual portal of Romance. Certainly none of the company ever suspected it, least of all Charley Edwards. It was very like the old stories that used to float about London of fabulously rich Jews, who had subterranean halls, with palms, and fountains, and soft lamps and richly apparelled women who never saw the disenchanting light of London day. So, in the midst of that smoke-palled city, enamoured of figures and grimy toil, Paul had his secret temple, his wishing-carpet, his bit of blue-and-white Mediterranean shore bathed in perpetual sunshine.

Several of Paul's teachers had a theory that his imagination had been perverted by garish fiction; but the truth was, he scarcely ever read at all. The books at home were not such as would either tempt or corrupt a youthful mind, and as for reading the novels that some of his friends urged upon him—well, he got what he wanted much more quickly from music; any sort of music, from an orchestra to a barrel organ. He needed only the spark, the indescribable thrill that made his imagination master of his senses, and he could make plots and pictures enough of his own. It was equally true that he was not stage-struck—not, at any rate, in the usual acceptation of that expression. He had no desire to become an actor, any more than he had to become a musician. He felt no necessity to do any of these things; what he wanted was to see, to be in the atmosphere, float on the wave of it, to be carried out, blue league after blue league, away from everything.

After a night behind the scenes, Paul found the school-room more than ever repulsive; the bare floors and naked walls; the prosy men who never wore frock coats, or violets in their button-holes; the women with their dull gowns, shrill voices, and pitiful seriousness about prepositions that govern the dative. He could not bear to have the other pupils think, for a moment, that he took these people seriously; he must convey to them that he considered it all trivial, and was there only by way of a joke, anyway. He had autograph pictures of all the members of the stock company which he showed his classmates, telling them the most incredible stories of his familiarity with these people, of his acquaintance with the soloists who came to Carnegie Hall, his suppers with them and the flowers he sent them. When these stories lost their effect, and his audience grew listless, he would bid all the boys good-bye, announcing that he was going to travel for awhile; going to Naples, to California, to Egypt. Then, next Monday, he would slip back, conscious and nervously smiling; his sister was ill, and he would have to defer his voyage until spring.

Matters went steadily worse with Paul at school. In the itch to let his instructors know how heartily he despised them, and how thoroughly he was appreciated elsewhere, he mentioned once or twice that he had no time to fool with theorems; adding—with a twitch of the eyebrows and a touch of that nervous bravado which so perplexed them—that he was helping the people down at the stock company; they were old friends of his.

The upshot of the matter was, that the Principal went to Paul's father, and Paul was taken out of school and put to work. The manager at Carnegie Hall was told to get another usher in his stead; the doorkeeper at the theatre was warned not to admit him to the house; and Charley Edwards remorsefully promised the boy's father not to see him again.

The members of the stock company were vastly amused when some of Paul's stories reached them—especially the women. They were hard-working women, most of them supporting indolent husbands or brothers, and they laughed rather bitterly at having stirred the boy to such fervid and florid inventions. They agreed with the faculty and with his father, that Paul's was a bad case.

* * *

The east-bound train was ploughing through a January snow-storm; the dull dawn was beginning to show grey when the engine whistled a mile out of Newark. Paul started up from the seat where he had lain curled in uneasy slumber, rubbed the breath-misted window glass with his hand, and peered out. The snow was whirling in curling eddies above the white bottom lands, and the drifts lay already deep in the fields and along the fences, while here and there the long dead grass and dried weed stalks protruded black above it. Lights shone from the scattered houses, and a gang of labourers who stood beside the track waved their lanterns.

Paul had slept very little, and he felt grimy and uncomfortable. He had made the all-night journey in a day coach because he was afraid if he took a Pullman he might be seen by some Pittsburgh business man who had noticed him in Denny & Carson's office. When the whistle woke him, he clutched quickly at his breast pocket, glancing about him with an uncertain smile. But the little, clay-bespattered Italians were still sleeping, the slatternly women across the aisle were in open-mouthed oblivion, and even the crumby, crying babies were for the nonce stilled. Paul settled back to struggle with his impatience as best he could.

When he arrived at the Jersey City station, he hurried through his breakfast, manifestly ill at ease and keeping a sharp eye about him. After he reached the Twenty-third Street station, he consulted a cabman, and had himself driven to a men's furnishing establishment which was just opening for the day. He spent upward of two hours there, buying with endless reconsidering and great care. His new street suit he put on in the fitting-room; the frock coat and dress clothes he had bundled into the cab with his new shirts. Then he drove to a hatter's and a shoe house. His next errand was at Tiffany's, where he selected silver mounted brushes and a scarf-pin. He would not wait to have his silver marked, he said. Lastly, he stopped at a trunk shop on Broadway, and had his purchases packed into various travelling bags.

It was a little after one o'clock when he drove up to the Waldorf, and, after settling with the cabman, went into the office. He registered from Washington; said his mother and father had been abroad, and that he had come down to await the arrival of their steamer. He told his story plausibly and had no trouble, since he offered to pay for them in advance, in engaging his rooms; a sleeping-room, sitting-room and bath.

Not once, but a hundred times Paul had planned this entry into New York. He had gone over every detail of it with Charley Edwards, and in his scrap book at home there were pages of description about New York hotels, cut from the Sunday papers.

When he was shown to his sitting-room on the eighth floor, he saw at a glance that everything was as it should be; there was but one detail in his mental picture that the place did not realize, so he rang for the bell boy and sent him down for flowers. He moved about nervously until the boy returned, putting away his new linen and fingering it delightedly as he did so. When the flowers came, he put them hastily into water, and then tumbled into a hot bath. Presently he came out of his white bath-room, resplendent in his new silk underwear, and playing with the tassels of his red robe. The snow was whirling so fiercely outside his windows that he could scarcely see across the street; but within, the air was deliciously soft and fragrant. He put the violets and jonquils on the tabouret beside the couch, and threw himself down with a long sigh, covering himself with a Roman blanket. He was thoroughly tired; he had been in such haste, he had stood up to such a strain, covered so much ground in the last twenty-four hours, that he wanted to think how it had all come about. Lulled by the sound of the wind, the warm air, and the cool fragrance of the flowers, he sank into deep, drowsy retrospection.

It had been wonderfully simple; when they had shut him out of the theatre and concert hall, when they had taken away his bone, the whole thing was virtually determined. The rest was a mere matter of opportunity. The only thing that at all surprised him was his own courage—for he realized well enough that he had always been tormented by fear, a sort of apprehensive dread that, of late years, as the meshes of the lies he had told closed about him, had been pulling the muscles of his body tighter and tighter. Until now, he could not remember a time when he had not been dreading something. Even when he was a little boy, it was always there—behind him, or before, or on either side. There had always been the shadowed corner, the dark place into which he dared not look, but from which something seemed always to be watching him—and Paul had done things that were not pretty to watch, he knew.

But now he had a curious sense of relief, as though he had at last thrown down the gauntlet to the thing in the corner.

Yet it was but a day since he had been sulking in the traces; but yesterday afternoon that he had been sent to the bank with Denny

& Carson's deposit, as usual—but this time he was instructed to leave the book to be balanced. There was above two thousand dollars in checks, and nearly a thousand in the bank notes which he had taken from the book and quietly transferred to his pocket. At the bank he had made out a new deposit slip. His nerves had been steady enough to permit of his returning to the office, where he had finished his work and asked for a full day's holiday tomorrow, Saturday, giving a perfectly reasonable pretext. The bank book, he knew, would not be returned before Monday or Tuesday, and his father would be out of town for the next week. From the time he slipped the bank notes into his pocket until he boarded the night train for New York, he had not known a moment's hesitation.

How astonishingly easy it had all been; here he was, the thing done; and this time there would be no awakening, no figure at the top of the stairs. He watched the snow flakes whirling by his window until he fell asleep.

When he awoke, it was four o'clock in the afternoon. He bounded up with a start; one of his precious days gone already! He spent nearly an hour in dressing, watching every stage of his toilet carefully in the mirror. Everything was quite perfect; he was exactly the kind of boy he had always wanted to be.

When he went downstairs, Paul took a carriage and drove up Fifth Avenue toward the Park. The snow had somewhat abated; carriages and tradesmen's wagons were hurrying soundlessly to and fro in the winter twilight; boys in woollen mufflers were shovelling off the doorsteps; the avenue stages made fine spots of colour against the white street. Here and there on the corners whole flower gardens blooming behind glass windows, against which the snow flakes stuck and melted; violets, roses, carnations, lilies of the valley—somehow vastly more lovely and alluring that they blossomed thus unnaturally in the snow. The Park itself was a wonderful stage winter-piece.

When he returned, the pause of the twilight had ceased, and the tune of the streets had changed. The snow was falling faster, lights streamed from the hotels that reared their many stories fearlessly up into the storm, defying the raging Atlantic winds. A long, black stream of carriages poured down the avenue, intersected here and there by other streams, tending horizontally. There were a score of cabs about the entrance of his hotel, and his driver had to wait. Boys in livery were running in and out of the awning stretched across the sidewalk, up and down the red velvet carpet laid from the door to the street. Above, about, within it all, was the rumble and roar, the hurry and toss of thousands of human beings as hot for pleasure as himself, and on every side of him towered the glaring affirmation of the omnipotence of wealth.

The boy set his teeth and drew his shoulders together in a spasm of realization; the plot of all dramas, the text of all romances, the nerve-stuff of all sensations was whirling about him like the snow flakes. He burnt like a faggot in a tempest.

When Paul came down to dinner, the music of the orchestra floated up the elevator shaft to greet him. As he stepped into the thronged corridor, he sank back into one of the chairs against the wall to get his breath. The lights, the chatter, the perfumes, the bewildering medley of colour—he had, for a moment, the feeling of not being able to stand it. But only for a moment; these were his own people, he told himself. He went slowly about the corridors, through the writing-rooms, smoking-rooms, reception-rooms, as though he were exploring the chambers of an enchanted palace, built and peopled for him alone.

When he reached the dining-room he sat down at a table near a window. The flowers, the white linen, the many-coloured wine glasses, the gay toilettes of the women, the low popping of corks, the undulating repetitions of the *Blue Danube* from the orchestra, all flooded Paul's dream with bewildering radiance. When the roseate tinge of his champagne was added—that cold, precious, bubbling stuff that creamed and foamed in his glass—Paul wondered that there were honest men in the world at all. This was what all the world was fighting for, he reflected; this was what all the struggle was about. He doubted the reality of his past. Had he ever known a place called Cordelia Street, a place where fagged looking business men boarded the early car? Mere rivets in a machine they seemed to Paul,—sickening men, with combings of children's hair always hanging to their coats, and the smell of cooking in their clothes. Cordelia Street— Ah, that belonged to another time and country! Had he not always been thus, had he not sat here night after night, from as far back as he could remember, looking pensively over just such shimmering textures, and slowly twirling the stem of a glass like this one between his thumb and middle finger? He rather thought he had.

He was not in the least abashed or lonely. He had no especial desire to meet or to know any of these people; all he demanded was the right to look on and conjecture, to watch the pageant. The mere stage properties were all he contended for. Nor was he lonely later in the evening, in his loge at the Opera. He was entirely rid of his nervous misgivings, of his forced aggressiveness, of the imperative desire to show himself different from his surroundings. He felt now that his surroundings explained him. Nobody questioned the purple; he had only to wear it passively. He had only to glance down at his dress coat to reassure himself that here it would be impossible for anyone to humiliate him.

He found it hard to leave his beautiful sitting-room to go to bed that night, and sat long watching the raging storm from his turret window. When he went to sleep, it was with the lights turned on in his bedroom; partly because of his old timidity, and partly so that, if he should wake in the night, there would be no wretched moment of doubt, no horrible suspicion of yellow wall-paper, or of Washington and Calvin above his bed.

On Sunday morning the city was practically snow-bound. Paul breakfasted late, and in the afternoon he fell in with a wild San Francisco boy, a freshman at Yale, who said he had run down for a "little flyer" over Sunday. The young man offered to show Paul the night side of the town, and the two boys went off together after dinner, not returning to the hotel until seven o'clock the next morning. They had started out in the confiding warmth of a champagne friendship, but their parting in the elevator was singularly cool. The freshman pulled himself together to make his train, and Paul went to bed. He awoke at two o'clock in the afternoon, very thirsty and dizzy, and rang for ice-water, coffee, and the Pittsburgh papers.

On the part of the hotel management, Paul excited no suspicion. There was this to be said for him, that he wore his spoils with dignity and in no way made himself conspicuous. His chief greediness lay in his ears and eyes, and his excesses were not offensive ones. His dearest pleasures were the grey winter twilights in his sitting-room; his quiet enjoyment of his flowers, his clothes, his wide divan, his cigarette and his sense of power. He could not remember a time when he had felt so at peace with himself. The mere release from the necessity of petty lying, lying every day and every day, restored his self-respect. He had never lied for pleasure, even at school; but to make himself noticed and admired, to assert his difference from other Cordelia Street boys; and he felt a good deal more manly, more honest, even, now that he had no need for boastful pretensions, now that he could, as his actor friends used to say, "dress the part." It was characteristic that remorse did not occur to him. His golden days went by without a shadow, and he made each as perfect as he could.

On the eighth day after his arrival in New York, he found the whole affair exploited in the Pittsburgh papers, exploited with a wealth of detail which indicated that local news of a sensational nature was at a low ebb. The firm of Denny & Carson announced that the boy's father had refunded the full amount of his theft, and that they had no intention of prosecuting. The Cumberland minister had been interviewed, and expressed his hope of yet reclaiming the motherless lad, and Paul's Sabbath-school teacher declared that she would spare no effort to that end. The rumour had reached Pittsburgh that the boy had been seen in a New York hotel, and his father had gone East to find him and bring him home.

Paul had just come in to dress for dinner; he sank into a chair, weak in the knees, and clasped his head in his hands. It was to be worse than jail, even; the tepid waters of Cordelia Street were to close over him finally and forever. The grey monotony stretched before him in hopeless, unrelieved years; Sabbath-school, Young People's Meeting, the yellow-papered room, the damp dish-towels; it all rushed back upon him with sickening vividness. He had the old feeling that the orchestra had suddenly stopped, the sinking sensation that the play was over. The sweat broke out on his face, and he sprang to his feet, looked about him with his white, conscious smile, and winked at himself in the mirror. With something of the childish belief in miracles with which he had so often gone to class, all his lessons unlearned, Paul dressed and dashed whistling down the corridor to the elevator.

He had no sooner entered the dining-room and caught the measure of the music, than his remembrance was lightened by his old elastic power of claiming the moment, mounting with it, and finding it all sufficient. The glare and glitter about him, the mere scenic accessories had again, and for the last time, their old potency. He would show himself that he was game, he would finish the thing splendidly. He doubted, more than ever, the existence of Cordelia Street, and for the first time he drank his wine recklessly. Was he not, after all, one of these fortunate beings? Was he not still himself, and in his own place? He drummed a nervous accompaniment to the music and looked about him, telling himself over and over that it had paid.

He reflected drowsily, to the swell of the violin and the chill sweetness of his wine, that he might have done it more wisely. He might have caught an outbound steamer and been well out of their clutches before now. But the other side of the world had seemed too far away and too uncertain then; he could not have waited for it; his need had been too sharp. If he had to choose over again, he would do the same thing tomorrow. He looked affectionately about the dining-room, now gilded with a soft mist. Ah, it had paid indeed!

Paul was awakened next morning by a painful throbbing in his head and feet. He had thrown himself across the bed without undressing, and had slept with his shoes on. His limbs and hands were lead heavy, and his tongue and throat were parched. There came upon him one of those fateful attacks of clear-headedness that never occurred except when he was physically exhausted and his nerves hung loose. He lay still and closed his eyes and let the tide of realities wash over him.

His father was in New York; "stopping at some joint or other," he told himself. The memory of successive summers on the front stoop fell upon him like a weight of black water. He had not a hundred dollars left; and he knew now, more than ever, that money was everything, the wall that stood between all he loathed and all he wanted. The thing was winding itself up; he had thought of that on his first glorious day in New York, and had even provided a way to snap the thread. It lay on his dressing-table now; he had got it out last night when he came blindly up from dinner,—but the shiny metal hurt his eyes, and he disliked the look of it, anyway.

He rose and moved about with a painful effort, succumbing now and again to attacks of nausea. It was the old depression exaggerated; all the world had become Cordelia Street. Yet somehow he was not afraid of anything, was absolutely calm; perhaps because he had looked into the dark corner at last, and knew. It was bad enough, what he saw there; but somehow not so bad as his long fear of it had been. He saw everything clearly now. He had a feeling that he had made the best of it, that he had lived the sort of life he was meant to live, and for half an hour he sat staring at the revolver. But he told himself that was not the way, so he went downstairs and took a cab to the ferry.

When Paul arrived at Newark, he got off the train and took another cab, directing the driver to follow the Pennsylvania tracks out of the town. The snow lay heavy on the roadways and had drifted deep in the open fields. Only here and there the dead grass or dried weed stalks projected, singularly black, above it. Once well into the country, Paul dismissed the carriage and walked, floundering along the tracks, his mind a medley of irrelevant things. He seemed to hold in his brain an actual picture of everything he had seen that morning. He remembered every feature of both his drivers, the toothless old woman from whom he had bought the red flowers in his coat, the agent from whom he had got his ticket, and all of his fellow-passengers on the ferry. His mind, unable to cope with vital matters near at hand, worked feverishly and deftly at sorting and grouping these images. They made for him a part of the ugliness of the world, of the ache in his head, and the bitter burning on his tongue. He stooped and put a handful of snow into his mouth as he walked, but that, too, seemed hot. When he reached a little hillside, where the tracks ran through a cut some twenty feet below him, he stopped and sat down.

The carnations in his coat were drooping with the cold, he noticed; all their red glory over. It occurred to him that all the flowers he had seen in the show windows that first night must have gone the same way, long before this. It was only one splendid breath they had, in spite of their brave mockery at the winter outside the glass. It was a losing game in the end, it seemed, this revolt against the homilies by which the world is run. Paul took one of the blossoms carefully from his coat and scooped a little hole in the snow, where he covered it up. Then he dozed a while, from his weak condition, seeming insensible to the cold.

The sound of an approaching train woke him, and he started to his feet, remembering only his resolution, and afraid lest he should be too late. He stood watching the approaching locomotive, his teeth chattering, his lips drawn away from them in a frightened smile; once or twice he glanced nervously sidewise, as though he were being watched. When the right moment came, he jumped. As he fell, the folly of his haste occurred to him with merciless clearness, the vastness of what he had left undone. There flashed through his brain, clearer than ever before, the blue of Adriatic water, the yellow of Algerian sands.

He felt something strike his chest,—his body was being thrown swiftly through the air, on and on, immeasurably far and fast, while his limbs gently relaxed. Then, because the picture making mechanism was crushed, the disturbing visions flashed into black, and Paul dropped back into the immense design of things.[13]

A Wagner Matinée

I RECEIVED one morning a letter, written in pale ink on glassy, blue-lined note-paper, and bearing the postmark of a little Nebraska village. This communication, worn and rubbed, looking as if it had been carried for some days in a coat pocket that was none too clean, was from my uncle Howard, and informed me that his wife had been left a small legacy by a bachelor relative, and that it would be necessary for her to go to Boston to attend to the settling of the estate. He requested me to meet her at the station and render her whatever services might be necessary. On examining the date indicated as that of her arrival, I found it to be no later than tomorrow. He had characteristically delayed writing until, had I been away from home for a day, I must have missed my aunt altogether.

The name of my Aunt Georgiana opened before me a gulf of recollection so wide and deep that, as the letter dropped from my hand, I felt suddenly a stranger to all the present conditions of my existence, wholly ill at ease and out of place amid the familiar surroundings of my study. I became, in short, the gangling farmer-boy my aunt had known, scourged with chilblains and bashfulness, my hands cracked and sore from the corn husking. I sat again before her parlour organ, fumbling the scales with my stiff, red fingers, while she, beside me, made canvas mittens for the huskers.

The next morning, after preparing my landlady for a visitor, I set out for the station. When the train arrived I had some difficulty in finding my aunt. She was the last of the passengers to alight, and it was not until I got her into the carriage that she seemed really to recognize me. She had come all the way in a day coach; her linen duster had become black with soot and her black bonnet grey with dust during the journey. When we arrived at my boarding-house the landlady put her to bed at once and I did not see her again until the next morning.

Whatever shock Mrs. Springer experienced at my aunt's appearance, she considerately concealed. As for myself, I saw my aunt's battered figure with that feeling of awe and respect with which we behold explorers who have left their ears and fingers north of Franz-Joseph-Land,[1] or their health somewhere along the Upper Congo. My Aunt Georgiana had been a music teacher at the Boston Conservatory, somewhere back in the latter sixties. One summer, while visiting in the little village among the Green Mountains[2] where her ancestors had dwelt for generations, she had kindled the callow fancy of my uncle, Howard Carpenter, then an idle, shiftless boy of twenty-one. When she returned to her duties in Boston, Howard followed her, and the upshot of this infatuation was that she eloped with him, eluding the reproaches of her family and the criticism of her friends by going with him to the Nebraska frontier. Carpenter, who, of course, had no money, took up a homestead in Red Willow County, fifty miles from the railroad. There they had measured off their land themselves, driving across the prairie in a wagon, to the wheel of which they had tied a red cotton handkerchief, and counting its revolutions. They built a dug-out[3] in the red hillside, one of those cave dwellings whose inmates so often reverted to primitive conditions. Their water they got from the lagoons where the buffalo drank, and their slender stock of provisions was always at the mercy of bands of roving Indians. For thirty years my aunt had not been farther than fifty miles from the homestead.

I owed to this woman most of the good that ever came my way in my boyhood, and had a reverential affection for her. During the years when I was riding herd for my uncle, my aunt, after cooking the three meals—the first of which was ready at six o'clock in the morning—and putting the six children to bed, would often stand until midnight at her ironing-board, with me at the kitchen table beside her, hearing me recite Latin declensions and conjugations, gently shaking me when my drowsy head sank down over a page of irregular verbs. It was to her, at her ironing or mending, that I read my first Shakspere, and her old text-book on mythology was the first that ever came into my empty hands. She taught me my scales and exercises on the little parlour organ which her husband had bought her after fifteen years during which she had not so much as seen a musical instrument. She would sit beside me by the hour, darning and counting, while I struggled with the "Joyous Farmer." She seldom talked to me about music, and I understood why. Once when I had been doggedly beating out some easy passages from an old score of *Euryanthe*[4] I had found among her music books, she came up to me and, putting her hands over my eyes, gently drew my head back upon her shoulder, saying tremulously, "Don't love it so well, Clark, or it may be taken from you."

When my aunt appeared on the morning after her arrival in Boston, she was still in a semi-somnambulant state. She seemed not to realize that she was in the city where she had spent her youth, the place longed for hungrily half a lifetime. She had been so wretchedly train-sick throughout the journey that she had no recollection of anything but her discomfort, and, to all intents and purposes, there were but a few hours of nightmare between the farm in Red Willow County and my study on Newbury Street. I had planned a little pleasure for her that afternoon, to repay her for some of the glorious moments she had given me when we used to milk together in the straw-thatched cowshed and she, because I was more than usually tired, or because her husband had spoken sharply to me, would tell me of the splendid performance of the *Huguenots*[5] she had seen in Paris, in her youth.

At two o'clock the Symphony Orchestra was to give a Wagner program, and I intended to take my aunt; though, as I conversed with her, I grew doubtful about her enjoyment of it. I suggested our visiting the Conservatory and the Common before lunch, but she seemed altogether too timid to wish to venture out. She questioned me absently about various changes in the city, but she was chiefly concerned that she had forgotten to leave instructions about feeding half-skimmed milk to a certain weakling calf, "old Maggie's calf, you know, Clark," she explained, evidently having forgotten how long I had been away. She was further troubled because she had neglected to tell her daughter about the freshly-opened kit of mackerel in the cellar, which would spoil if it were not used directly.

I asked her whether she had ever heard any of the Wagnerian operas, and found that she had not, though she was perfectly familiar with their respective situations, and had once possessed the piano score of *The Flying Dutchman.*[6] I began to think it would be best to get her back to Red Willow County without waking her, and regretted having suggested the concert.

From the time we entered the concert hall, however, she was a trifle less passive and inert, and for the first time seemed to perceive her surroundings. I had felt some trepidation lest she might become aware of her queer, country clothes, or might experience some painful embarrassment at stepping suddenly into the world to which she had been dead for a quarter of a century. But, again, I found how superficially I had judged her. She sat looking about her with eyes as impersonal, almost as stony, as those with which the granite Rameses in a museum[7] watches the froth and fret that ebbs and flows about his pedestal. I have seen this same aloofness in old miners who drift into the Brown hotel at Denver, their pockets full of bullion, their linen soiled, their haggard faces unshaven; standing in the thronged corridors as solitary as though they were still in a frozen camp on the Yukon.

The matinée audience was made up chiefly of women. One lost the contour of faces and figures, indeed any effect of line whatever, and there was only the colour of bodices past counting, the shimmer of fabrics soft and firm, silky and sheer; red, mauve, pink, blue, lilac, purple, écru, rose, yellow, cream, and white, all the colours that an impressionist finds in a sunlit landscape, with here and there the dead shadow of a frock coat. My Aunt Georgiana regarded them as though they had been so many daubs of tube-paint on a palette.

When the musicians came out and took their places, she gave a little stir of anticipation, and looked with quickening interest down over the rail at that invariable grouping, perhaps the first wholly familiar thing that had greeted her eye since she had left old Maggie and her weakling calf. I could feel how all those details sank into her soul, for I had not forgotten how they had sunk into mine when I came fresh from ploughing forever and forever between green aisles of corn, where, as in a treadmill, one might walk from daybreak to dusk without perceiving a shadow of change. The clean profiles of the musicians, the gloss of their linen, the dull black of their coats, the beloved shapes of the instruments, the patches of yellow light on the smooth, varnished bellies of the 'cellos and the bass viols in the rear, the restless, wind-tossed forest of fiddle necks and bows—I recalled how, in the first orchestra I ever heard, those long bow-strokes seemed to draw the heart out of me, as a conjurer's stick reels out yards of paper ribbon from a hat.

The first number was the *Tannhäuser*[8] overture. When the horns drew out the first strain of the Pilgrim's chorus, Aunt Georgiana clutched my coat sleeve. Then it was I first realized that for her this broke a silence of thirty years. With the battle between the two motives, with the frenzy of the Venusberg theme and its ripping of strings, there came to me an overwhelming sense of the waste and wear we are so powerless to combat; and I saw again the tall, naked house on the prairie, black and grim as a wooden fortress; the black pond where I had learned to swim, its margin pitted with sun-dried cattle tracks; the rain gullied clay banks about the naked house, the four dwarf ash seedlings where the dish-cloths were always hung to dry before the kitchen door. The world there was the flat world of the ancients; to the east, a cornfield that stretched to daybreak; to the west, a corral that reached to sunset; between, the conquests of peace, dearer-bought than those of war.

The overture closed, my aunt released my coat sleeve, but she said nothing. She sat staring dully at the orchestra. What, I wondered, did she get from it? She had been a good pianist in her day, I knew, and her musical education had been broader than that of most music teachers of a quarter of a century ago. She had often told me of Mozart's operas and Meyerbeer's, and I could remember hearing her sing, years ago, certain melodies of Verdi. When I had fallen ill with a fever in her house she used to sit by my cot in the evening—when the cool, night wind blew in through the faded mosquito netting tacked over the window and I lay watching a certain bright star that burned red above the cornfield—and sing "Home to our mountains, O, let us return!" in a way fit to break the heart of a Vermont boy near dead of homesickness already.

I watched her closely through the prelude to *Tristan and Isolde*,[9] trying vainly to conjecture what that seething turmoil of strings and winds might mean to her, but she sat mutely staring at the violin bows that drove obliquely downward, like the pelting streaks of rain in a summer shower. Had this music any message for her? Had she enough left to at all comprehend this power which had kindled the world since she had left it? I was in a fever of curiosity, but Aunt Georgiana sat silent upon her peak in Darien.[10] She preserved this utter immobility throughout the number from *The Flying Dutchman*, though her fingers worked mechanically upon her black dress, as if, of themselves, they were recalling the piano score they had once played. Poor hands! They had been stretched and twisted into mere tentacles to hold and lift and knead with;—on one of them a thin, worn band that had once been a wedding ring. As I pressed and gently quieted one of those groping hands, I remembered with quivering eyelids their services for me in other days.

Soon after the tenor began the "Prize Song,"[11] I heard a quick drawn breath and turned to my aunt. Her eyes were closed, but the tears were glistening on her cheeks, and I think, in a moment more, they were in my eyes as well. It never really died, then—the soul which can suffer so excruciatingly and so interminably; it withers to the outward eye only; like that strange moss which can lie on a dusty shelf half a century and yet, if placed in water, grows green again. She wept so throughout the development and elaboration of the melody.

During the intermission before the second half, I questioned my aunt and found that the "Prize Song" was not new to her. Some years before there had drifted to the farm in Red Willow County a young German, a tramp cow-puncher, who had sung in the chorus at Bayreuth[12] when he was a boy, along with the other peasant boys and girls. Of a Sunday morning he used to sit on his gingham-sheeted bed in the hands' bedroom which opened off the kitchen, cleaning the leather of his boots and saddle, singing the "Prize Song," while my aunt went about her work in the kitchen. She had hovered over him until she had prevailed upon him to join the country church, though his sole fitness for this step, in so far as I could gather, lay in his boyish face and his possession of this divine melody. Shortly afterward, he had gone to town on the Fourth of July, been drunk for several days, lost his money at a faro table, ridden a saddled Texas steer on a bet, and disappeared with a fractured collar-bone. All this my aunt told me huskily, wanderingly, as though she were talking in the weak lapses of illness.

"Well, we have come to better things than the old *Trovatore*[13] at any rate, Aunt Georgie?" I queried, with a well meant effort at jocularity.

Her lip quivered and she hastily put her handkerchief up to her mouth. From behind it she murmured, "And you have been hearing this ever since you left me, Clark?" Her question was the gentlest and saddest of reproaches.

The second half of the program consisted of four numbers from the *Ring*, and closed with Siegfried's funeral march. My aunt wept quietly, but almost continuously, as a shallow vessel overflows in a rain-storm. From time to time her dim eyes looked up at the lights, burning softly under their dull glass globes.

The deluge of sound poured on and on; I never knew what she found in the shining current of it; I never knew how far it bore her, or past what happy islands. From the trembling of her face I could well believe that before the last number she had been carried out where the myriad graves are, into the grey, nameless burying grounds of the sea; or into some world of death vaster yet, where, from the beginning of the world, hope has lain down with hope and dream with dream and, renouncing, slept.

The concert was over; the people filed out of the hall chattering and laughing, glad to relax and find the living level again, but my kinswoman made no effort to rise. The harpist slipped the green felt cover over his instrument; the flute-players shook the water from their mouthpieces; the men of the orchestra went out one by one, leaving the stage to the chairs and music stands, empty as a winter cornfield.

I spoke to my aunt. She burst into tears and sobbed pleadingly. "I don't want to go, Clark, I don't want to go!"

I understood. For her, just outside the concert hall, lay the black pond with the cattle-tracked bluffs; the tall, unpainted house, with weather-curled boards, naked as a tower; the crook-backed ash seedlings where the dish-cloths hung to dry; the gaunt, moulting turkeys picking up refuse about the kitchen door.[14]

The Sculptor's Funeral

A GROUP of the townspeople stood on the station siding of a little Kansas town, awaiting the coming of the night train, which was already twenty minutes overdue. The snow had fallen thick over everything; in the pale starlight the line of bluffs across the wide, white meadows south of the town made soft, smoke-coloured curves against the clear sky. The men on the siding stood first on one foot and then on the other, their hands thrust deep into their trousers pockets, their overcoats open, their shoulders screwed up with the cold; and they glanced from time to time toward the south-east, where the railroad track wound along the river shore. They conversed in low tones and moved about restlessly, seeming uncertain as to what was expected of them. There was but one of the company who looked as if he knew exactly why he was there, and he kept conspicuously apart; walking to the far end of the platform, returning to the station door, then pacing up the track again, his chin sunk in the high collar of his overcoat, his burly shoulders drooping forward, his gait heavy and dogged. Presently he was approached by a tall, spare, grizzled man clad in a faded Grand Army suit, who shuffled out from the group and advanced with a certain deference, craning his neck forward until his back made the angle of a jack-knife three-quarters open.

"I reckon she's a-goin' to be pretty late agin tonight, Jim," he remarked in a squeaky falsetto. "S'pose it's the snow?"

"I don't know," responded the other man with a shade of annoyance, speaking from out an astonishing cataract of red beard that grew fiercely and thickly in all directions.

The spare man shifted the quill toothpick he was chewing to the other side of his mouth. "It ain't likely that anybody from the East will come with the corpse, I s'pose," he went on reflectively.

"I don't know," responded the other, more curtly than before.

"It's too bad he didn't belong to some lodge or other. I like an order funeral myself. They seem more appropriate for people of some repytation," the spare man continued, with an ingratiating concession in his shrill voice, as he carefully placed his toothpick in his vest pocket. He always carried the flag at the G. A. R.[1] funerals in the town.

The heavy man turned on his heel, without replying, and walked up the siding. The spare man rejoined the uneasy group. "Jim's ez full ez a tick, ez ushel," he commented commiseratingly.

Just then a distant whistle sounded, and there was a shuffling of feet on the platform. A number of lanky boys, of all ages, appeared as suddenly and slimily as eels wakened by the crack of thunder; some came from the waiting-room, where they had been warming themselves by the red stove, or half asleep on the slat benches; others uncoiled themselves from baggage trucks or slid out of express wagons. Two clambered down from the driver's seat of a hearse that stood backed up against the siding. They straightened their stooping shoulders and lifted their heads, and a flash of momentary animation kindled their dull eyes at that cold, vibrant scream, the worldwide call for men. It stirred them like the note of a trumpet; just as it had often stirred the man who was coming home tonight, in his boyhood.

The night express shot, red as a rocket, from out the eastward marsh lands and wound along the river shore under the long lines of shivering poplars that sentinelled the meadows, the escaping steam hanging in grey masses against the pale sky and blotting out the Milky Way. In a moment the red glare from the headlight streamed up the snow-covered track before the siding and glittered on the wet, black rails. The burly man with the dishevelled red beard walked swiftly up the platform toward the approaching train, uncovering his head as he went. The group of men behind him hesitated, glanced questioningly at one another, and awkwardly followed his example. The train stopped, and the crowd shuffled up to the express car just as the door was thrown open, the man in the G. A. R. suit thrusting his head forward with curiosity. The express messenger appeared in the doorway, accompanied by a young man in a long ulster and travelling cap.

"Are Mr. Merrick's friends here?" inquired the young man.

The group on the platform swayed uneasily. Philip Phelps, the banker, responded with dignity: "We have come to take charge of the body. Mr. Merrick's father is very feeble and can't be about."

"Send the agent out here," growled the express messenger, "and tell the operator to lend a hand."

The coffin was got out of its rough-box and down on the snowy platform. The townspeople drew back enough to make room for it and then formed a close semicircle about it, looking curiously at the palm leaf[2] which lay across the black cover. No one said anything. The baggage man stood by his truck, waiting to get at the trunks. The engine panted heavily, and the fireman dodged in and out among the wheels with his yellow torch and long oil-can, snapping the spindle boxes. The young Bostonian, one of the dead sculptor's pupils who had come with the body, looked about him helplessly. He turned to the banker, the only one of that black, uneasy, stoop-shouldered group who seemed enough of an individual to be addressed.

"None of Mr. Merrick's brothers are here?" he asked uncertainly.

The man with the red beard for the first time stepped up and joined the others. "No, they have not come yet; the family is scattered. The body will be taken directly to the house." He stooped and took hold of one of the handles of the coffin.

"Take the long hill road up, Thompson, it will be easier on the horses," called the liveryman as the undertaker snapped the door of the hearse and prepared to mount to the driver's seat.

Laird, the red-bearded lawyer, turned again to the stranger: "We didn't know whether there would be any one with him or not," he explained. "It's a long walk, so you'd better go up in the hack." He pointed to a single battered conveyance, but the young man replied stiffly: "Thank you, but I think I will go up with the hearse. If you don't object," turning to the undertaker, "I'll ride with you."

They clambered up over the wheels and drove off in the starlight up the long, white hill toward the town. The lamps in the still village were shining from under the low, snow-burdened roofs; and beyond, on every side, the plains reached out into emptiness, peaceful and wide as the soft sky itself, and wrapped in a tangible, white silence.

When the hearse backed up to a wooden sidewalk before a naked, weather-beaten frame house, the same composite, ill-defined group that had stood upon the station siding was huddled about the gate. The front yard was an icy swamp, and a couple of warped planks, extending from the sidewalk to the door, made a sort of rickety footbridge. The gate hung on one hinge, and was opened wide with difficulty. Steavens, the young stranger, noticed that something black was tied to the knob of the front door.

The grating sound made by the casket, as it was drawn from the hearse, was answered by a scream from the house; the front door was wrenched open, and a tall, corpulent woman rushed out bareheaded into the snow and flung herself upon the coffin, shrieking: "My boy, my boy! And this is how you've come home to me!"

As Steavens turned away and closed his eyes with a shudder of unutterable repulsion, another woman, also tall, but flat and angular, dressed entirely in black, darted out of the house and caught Mrs. Merrick by the shoulders, crying sharply: "Come, come, mother; you mustn't go on like this!" Her tone changed to one of obsequious solemnity as she turned to the banker: "The parlour is ready, Mr. Phelps."

The bearers carried the coffin along the narrow boards, while the undertaker ran ahead with the coffin-rests. They bore it into a large, unheated room that smelled of dampness and disuse and furniture polish, and set it down under a hanging lamp ornamented with jingling glass prisms and before a "Rogers group"[3] of John Alden and Priscilla, wreathed with smilax.[4] Henry Steavens stared about him with the sickening conviction that there had been a mistake, and that he had somehow arrived at the wrong destination. He looked at the clover-green Brussels,[5] the fat plush upholstery, among the hand-painted china placques and panels and vases, for some mark of identification,—for something that might once conceivably have belonged to Harvey Merrick. It was not until he recognized his friend in the crayon portrait of a little boy in kilts and curls, hanging above the piano, that he felt willing to let any of these people approach the coffin.

"Take the lid off, Mr. Thompson; let me see my boy's face," wailed the elder woman between her sobs. This time Steavens looked fearfully, almost beseechingly into her face, red and swollen under its masses of strong, black, shiny hair. He flushed, dropped his eyes, and then, almost incredulously, looked again. There was a kind of power about her face—a kind of brutal handsomeness, even; but it was scarred and furrowed by violence, and so coloured and coarsened by fiercer passions that grief seemed never to have laid a gentle finger there. The long nose was distended and knobbed at the end, and there were deep lines on either side of it; her heavy, black brows almost met across her forehead, her teeth were large and square, and set far apart—teeth that could tear. She filled the room; the men were obliterated, seemed tossed about like twigs in an angry water, and even Steavens felt himself being drawn into the whirlpool.

The daughter—the tall, raw-boned woman in crêpe, with a mourning comb in her hair which curiously lengthened her long face—sat stiffly upon the sofa, her hands, conspicuous for their large knuckles, folded in her lap, her mouth and eyes drawn down, solemnly awaiting the opening of the coffin. Near the door stood a mulatto woman, evidently a servant in the house, with a timid bearing and an emaciated face pitifully sad and gentle. She was weeping silently, the corner of her calico apron lifted to her eyes, occasionally suppressing a long, quivering sob. Steavens walked over and stood beside her.

Feeble steps were heard on the stairs, and an old man, tall and frail, odorous of pipe smoke, with shaggy, unkept grey hair and a dingy beard, tobacco stained about the mouth, entered uncertainly. He went slowly up to the coffin and stood rolling a blue cotton handkerchief between his hands, seeming so pained and embarrassed by his wife's orgy of grief that he had no consciousness of anything else.

"There, there, Annie, dear, don't take on so," he quavered timidly, putting out a shaking hand and awkwardly patting her elbow.

She turned and sank upon his shoulder with such violence that he tottered a little. He did not even glance toward the coffin, but continued to look at her with a dull, frightened, appealing expression, as a spaniel looks at the whip. His sunken cheeks slowly reddened and burned with miserable shame. When his wife rushed from the room, her daughter strode after her with set lips. The servant stole up to the coffin, bent over it for a moment, and then slipped away to the kitchen, leaving Steavens, the lawyer, and the father to themselves. The old man stood looking down at his dead son's face. The sculptor's splendid head seemed even more noble in its rigid stillness than in life. The dark hair had crept down upon the wide forehead; the face seemed strangely long, but in it there was not that repose we expect to find in the faces of the dead. The brows were so drawn that there were two deep lines above the beaked nose, and the chin was thrust forward defiantly. It was as though the strain of life had been so sharp and bitter that death could not at once relax the tension and smooth the countenance into perfect peace—as though he were still guarding something precious, which might even yet be wrested from him.

The old man's lips were working under his stained beard. He turned to the lawyer with timid deference: "Phelps and the rest are comin' back to set up with Harve, ain't they?" he asked. "Thank 'ee, Jim, thank 'ee." He brushed the hair back gently from his son's forehead. "He was a good boy, Jim; always a good boy. He was ez gentle ez a child and the kindest of 'em all—only we didn't none of us ever onderstand him." The tears trickled slowly down his beard and dropped upon the sculptor's coat.

"Martin, Martin! Oh, Martin! come here," his wife wailed from the top of the stairs. The old man started timorously: "Yes, Annie, I'm coming." He turned away, hesitated, stood for a moment in miserable indecision; then reached back and patted the dead man's hair softly, and stumbled from the room.

"Poor old man, I didn't think he had any tears left. Seems as if his eyes would have gone dry long ago. At his age nothing cuts very deep," remarked the lawyer.

Something in his tone made Steavens glance up. While the mother had been in the room, the young man had scarcely seen any one else; but now, from the moment he first glanced into Jim Laird's florid face and blood-shot eyes, he knew that he had found what he had been heartsick at not finding before—the feeling, the understanding, that must exist in some one, even here.

The man was red as his beard, with features swollen and blurred by dissipation, and a hot, blazing blue eye. His face was strained—that of a man who is controlling himself with difficulty—and he kept plucking at his beard with a sort of fierce resentment. Steavens, sitting by the window, watched him turn down the glaring lamp, still its jangling pendants with an angry gesture, and then stand with his hands locked behind him, staring down into the master's face. He could not help wondering what link there had been between the porcelain vessel and so sooty a lump of potter's clay.

From the kitchen an uproar was sounding; when the dining-room door opened, the import of it was clear. The mother was abusing the maid for having forgotten to make the dressing for the chicken salad which had been prepared for the watchers. Steavens had never heard anything in the least like it; it was injured, emotional, dramatic abuse, unique and masterly in its excruciating cruelty, as violent and unrestrained as had been her grief of twenty minutes before. With a shudder of disgust the lawyer went into the dining-room and closed the door into the kitchen.

"Poor Roxy's getting it now," he remarked when he came back. "The Merricks took her out of the poor-house years ago; and if her loyalty would let her, I guess the poor old thing could tell tales that would curdle your blood. She's the mulatto woman who was standing in here a while ago, with her apron to her eyes. The old woman is a fury; there never was anybody like her. She made Harvey's life a hell for him when he lived at home; he was so sick ashamed of it. I never could see how he kept himself sweet."

"He was wonderful," said Steavens slowly, "wonderful; but until tonight I have never known how wonderful."

"That is the eternal wonder of it, anyway; that it can come even from such a dung heap as this," the lawyer cried, with a sweeping gesture which seemed to indicate much more than the four walls within which they stood.

"I think I'll see whether I can get a little air. The room is so close I am beginning to feel rather faint," murmured Steavens, struggling with one of the windows. The sash was stuck, however, and would not yield, so he sat down dejectedly and began pulling at his collar. The lawyer came over, loosened the sash with one blow of his red fist and sent the window up a few inches. Steavens thanked him, but the nausea which had been gradually climbing into his throat for the last half hour left him with but one desire—a desperate feeling that he must get away from this place with what was left of Harvey Merrick. Oh, he comprehended well enough now the quiet bitterness of the smile that he had seen so often on his master's lips!

Once when Merrick returned from a visit home, he brought with him a singularly feeling and suggestive bas-relief of a thin, faded old woman, sitting and sewing something pinned to her knee; while a full-lipped, full-blooded little urchin, his trousers held up by a single gallows,[6] stood beside her, impatiently twitching her gown to call her attention to a butterfly he had caught. Steavens, impressed by the tender and delicate modelling of the thin, tired face, had asked him if it were his mother. He remembered the dull flush that had burned up in the sculptor's face.

The lawyer was sitting in a rocking-chair beside the coffin, his head thrown back and his eyes closed. Steavens looked at him earnestly, puzzled at the line of the chin, and wondering why a man should conceal a feature of such distinction under that disfiguring shock of beard. Suddenly, as though he felt the young sculptor's keen glance, Jim Laird opened his eyes.

"Was he always a good deal of an oyster?" he asked abruptly. "He was terribly shy as a boy."

"Yes, he was an oyster, since you put it so," rejoined Steavens. "Although he could be very fond of people, he always gave one the impression of being detached. He disliked violent emotion; he was reflective, and rather distrustful of himself—except, of course, as regarded his work. He was sure enough there. He distrusted men pretty thoroughly and women even more, yet somehow without believing ill of them. He was determined, indeed, to believe the best; but he seemed afraid to investigate."

"A burnt dog dreads the fire," said the lawyer grimly, and closed his eyes.

Steavens went on and on, reconstructing that whole miserable boyhood. All this raw, biting ugliness had been the portion of the man whose mind was to become an exhaustless gallery of beautiful impressions—so sensitive that the mere shadow of a poplar leaf flickering against a sunny wall would be etched and held there for ever. Surely, if ever a man had the magic word in his finger tips, it was Merrick. Whatever he touched, he revealed its holiest secret; liberated it from enchantment and restored it to its pristine loveliness. Upon whatever he had come in contact with, he had left a beautiful record of the experience—a sort of ethereal signature; a scent, a sound, a colour that was his own.

Steavens understood now the real tragedy of his master's life; neither love nor wine, as many had conjectured; but a blow which had fallen earlier and cut deeper than anything else could have done—a shame not his, and yet so unescapably his, to hide in his heart from his very boyhood. And without—the frontier warfare; the yearning of a boy, cast ashore upon a desert of newness and ugliness and sordidness, for all that is chastened and old, and noble with traditions.

At eleven o'clock the tall, flat woman in black announced that the watchers were arriving, and asked them to "step into the dining-room." As Steavens rose, the lawyer said dryly: "You go on—it'll be a good experience for you. I'm not equal to that crowd tonight; I've had twenty years of them."

As Steavens closed the door after him he glanced back at the lawyer, sitting by the coffin in the dim light, with his chin resting on his hand.

The same misty group that had stood before the door of the express car shuffled into the dining-room. In the light of the kerosene lamp they separated and became individuals. The minister, a pale, feeble-looking man with white hair and blond chin-whiskers, took his seat beside a small side table and placed his Bible upon it. The Grand Army man sat down behind the stove and tilted his chair back comfortably against the wall, fishing his quill toothpick from his waistcoat pocket. The two bankers, Phelps and Elder, sat off in a corner behind the dinner-table, where they could finish their discussion of the new usury law and its effect on chattel security loans. The real-estate agent, an old man with a smiling, hypocritical face, soon joined them. The coal and lumber dealer and the cattle shipper sat on opposite sides of the hard coal-burner, their feet on the nickel-work. Steavens took a book from his pocket and began to read. The talk around him ranged through various topics of local interest while the house was quieting down. When it was clear that the members of the family were in bed, the Grand Army man hitched his shoulders and, untangling his long legs, caught his heels on the rounds of his chair.

"S'pose there'll be a will, Phelps?" he queried in his weak falsetto.

The banker laughed disagreeably, and began trimming his nails with a pearl-handled pocketknife.

"There'll scarcely be any need for one, will there?" he queried in his turn.

The restless Grand Army man shifted his position again, getting his knees still nearer his chin. "Why, the ole man says Harve's done right well lately," he chirped.

The other banker spoke up. "I reckon he means by that Harve ain't asked him to mortgage any more farms lately, so as he could go on with his education."

"Seems like my mind don't reach back to a time when Harve wasn't bein' edycated," tittered the Grand Army man.

There was a general chuckle. The minister took out his handkerchief and blew his nose sonorously. Banker Phelps closed his knife with a snap. "It's too bad the old man's sons didn't turn out better," he remarked with reflective authority. "They never hung together. He spent money enough on Harve to stock a dozen cattle farms, and he might as well have poured it into Sand Creek. If Harve had stayed at home and helped nurse what little they had, and gone into stock on the old man's bottom farm, they might all have been well fixed. But the old man had to trust everything to tenants and was cheated right and left."

"Harve never could have handled stock none," interposed the cattleman. "He hadn't it in him to be sharp. Do you remember when he bought Sander's mules for eight-year olds, when everybody in town knew that Sander's father-in-law give 'em to his wife for a wedding present eighteen years before, an' they was full-grown mules then?"

The company laughed discreetly, and the Grand Army man rubbed his knees with a spasm of childish delight.

"Harve never was much account for anything practical, and he shore was never fond of work," began the coal and lumber dealer. "I mind the last time he was home; the day he left, when the old man was out to the barn helpin' his hand hitch up to take Harve to the train, and Cal Moots was patchin' up the fence; Harve, he come out on the step and sings out, in his ladylike voice: 'Cal Moots, Cal Moots! please come cord my trunk.' "

"That's Harve for you," approved the Grand Army man. "I kin hear him howlin' yet, when he was a big feller in long pants and his mother used to whale him with a rawhide in the barn for lettin' the cows git foundered in the cornfield when he was drivin' 'em home from pasture. He killed a cow of mine that-a-way onct—a pure Jersey and the best milker I had, an' the ole man had to put up for her. Harve, he was watchin' the sun set acrost the marshes when the anamile got away."

"Where the old man made his mistake was in sending the boy East to school," said Phelps, stroking his goatee and speaking in a deliberate, judicial tone. "There was where he got his head full of nonsense. What Harve needed, of all people, was a course in some first-class Kansas City business college."

The letters were swimming before Steavens's eyes. Was it possible that these men did not understand, that the palm on the coffin meant nothing to them? The very name of their town would have remained for ever buried in the postal guide had it not been now and again mentioned in the world in connection with Harvey Merrick's. He remembered what his master had said to him on the day of his death, after the congestion of both lungs had shut off any probability of recovery, and the sculptor had asked his pupil to send his body home. "It's not a pleasant place to be lying while the world is moving and doing and bettering," he had said with a feeble smile, "but it rather seems as though we ought to go back to the place we came from, in the end. The townspeople will come in for a look at me; and after they have had their say, I shan't have much to fear from the judgment of God!"

The cattleman took up the comment. "Forty's young for a Merrick to cash in; they usually hang on pretty well. Probably he helped it along with whisky."

"His mother's people were not long lived, and Harvey never had a robust constitution," said the minister mildly. He would have liked to say more. He had been the boy's Sunday-school teacher, and had been fond of him; but he felt that he was not in a position to speak. His own sons had turned out badly, and it was not a year since one of them had made his last trip home in the express car, shot in a gambling-house in the Black Hills.

"Nevertheless, there is no disputin' that Harve frequently looked upon the wine when it was red,[7] also variegated, and it shore made an oncommon fool of him," moralized the cattleman.

Just then the door leading into the parlour rattled loudly and every one started involuntarily, looking relieved when only Jim Laird came out. The Grand Army man ducked his head when he saw the spark in his blue, blood-shot eye. They were all afraid of Jim; he was a drunkard, but he could twist the law to suit his client's needs as no other man in all western Kansas could do, and there were many who tried. The lawyer closed the door behind him, leaned back against it and folded his arms, cocking his head a little to one side. When he assumed this attitude in the court-room, ears were always pricked up, as it usually foretold a flood of withering sarcasm.

"I've been with you gentlemen before," he began in a dry, even tone, "when you've sat by the coffins of boys born and raised in this town; and, if I remember rightly, you were never any too well satisfied when you checked them up. What's the matter, anyhow? Why is it that reputable young men are as scarce as millionaires in Sand City? It might almost seem to a stranger that there was some way something the matter with your progressive town. Why did Ruben Sayer, the brightest young lawyer you ever turned out, after he had come home from the university as straight as a die, take to drinking and forge a check and shoot himself? Why did Bill Merrit's son die of the shakes in a saloon in Omaha? Why was Mr. Thomas's son, here, shot in a gambling-house? Why did young Adams burn his mill to beat the insurance companies and go to the pen?"

The lawyer paused and unfolded his arms, laying one clenched fist quietly on the table. "I'll tell you why. Because you drummed nothing but money and knavery into their ears from the time they wore knickerbockers; because you carped away at them as you've been carping here tonight, holding our friends Phelps and Elder up to them for their models, as our grandfathers held up George Washington and John Adams. But the boys were young, and raw at the business you put them to, and how could they match coppers with such artists as Phelps and Elder? You wanted them to be successful rascals; they were only unsuccessful ones—that's all the difference. There was only one boy ever raised in this borderland between ruffianism and civilization who didn't come to grief, and you hated Harvey Merrick more for winning out than you hated all the other boys who got under the wheels. Lord, Lord, how you did hate him! Phelps, here, is fond of saying that he could buy and sell us all out any time he's a mind to; but he knew Harve wouldn't have given a tinker's damn for his bank and all his cattle farms put together; and a lack of appreciation, that way, goes hard with Phelps.

"Old Nimrod thinks Harve drank too much; and this from such as Nimrod and me!

"Brother Elder says Harve was too free with the old man's money—fell short in filial consideration, maybe. Well, we can all remember the very tone in which brother Elder swore his own father was a liar, in the county court; and we all know that the old man came out of that partnership with his son as bare as a sheared lamb. But maybe I'm getting personal, and I'd better be driving ahead at what I want to say."

The lawyer paused a moment, squared his heavy shoulders, and went on: "Harvey Merrick and I went to school together, back East. We were dead in earnest, and we wanted you all to be proud of us some day. We meant to be great men. Even I, and I haven't lost my sense of humour, gentlemen, I meant to be a great man. I came back here to practise, and I found you didn't in the least want me to be a great man. You wanted me to be a shrewd lawyer—oh, yes! Our veteran here wanted me to get him an increase of pension, because he had dyspepsia;[8] Phelps wanted a new county survey that would put the widow Wilson's little bottom farm inside his south line; Elder wanted to lend money at 5 per cent. a month, and get it collected; and Stark here wanted to wheedle old women up in Vermont into investing their annuities in real-estate mortgages that are not worth the paper they are written on. Oh, you needed me hard enough, and you'll go on needing me!

"Well, I came back here and became the damned shyster you wanted me to be. You pretend to have some sort of respect for me; and yet you'll stand up and throw mud at Harvey Merrick, whose soul you couldn't dirty and whose hands you couldn't tie. Oh, you're a discriminating lot of Christians! There have been times when the sight of Harvey's name in some Eastern paper has made me hang my head like a whipped dog; and, again, times when I liked to think of him off there in the world, away from all this hog-wallow, climbing the big, clean up-grade he'd set for himself.

"And we? Now that we've fought and lied and sweated and stolen, and hated as only the disappointed strugglers in a bitter, dead little Western town know how to do, what have we got to show for it? Harvey Merrick wouldn't have given one sunset over your marshes for all you've got put together, and you know it. It's not for me to say why, in the inscrutable wisdom of God, a genius should ever have been called from this place of hatred and bitter waters; but I want this Boston man to know that the drivel he's been hearing here tonight is the only tribute any truly great man could have from such a lot of sick, side-tracked, burnt-dog, land-poor sharks as the here-present financiers of Sand City—upon which town may God have mercy!"

The lawyer thrust out his hand to Steavens as he passed him, caught up his overcoat in the hall, and had left the house before the Grand Army man had had time to lift his ducked head and crane his long neck about at his fellows.

Next day Jim Laird was drunk and unable to attend the funeral services. Steavens called twice at his office, but was compelled to start East without seeing him. He had a presentiment that he would hear from him again, and left his address on the lawyer's table; but if Laird found it, he never acknowledged it. The thing in him that Harvey Merrick had loved must have gone under ground with Harvey Merrick's coffin; for it never spoke again, and Jim got the cold he died of driving across the Colorado mountains to defend one of Phelps's sons who had got into trouble out there by cutting government timber.[9]

"A Death in the Desert"[1]

EVERETT HILGARDE was conscious that the man in the seat across the aisle was looking at him intently. He was a large, florid man, wore a conspicuous diamond solitaire upon his third finger, and Everett judged him to be a travelling salesman of some sort. He had the air of an adaptable fellow who had been about the world and who could keep cool and clean under almost any circumstances.

The "High Line Flyer," as this train was derisively called among railroad men, was jerking along through the hot afternoon over the monotonous country between Holdredge and Cheyenne. Besides the blond man and himself the only occupants of the car were two dusty, bedraggled-looking girls who had been to the Exposition at Chicago,[2] and who were earnestly discussing the cost of their first trip out of Colorado. The four uncomfortable passengers were covered with a sediment of fine, yellow dust which clung to their hair and eyebrows like gold powder. It blew up in clouds from the bleak, lifeless country through which they passed, until they were one colour with the sage-brush and sand-hills. The grey and yellow desert was varied only by occasional ruins of deserted towns, and the little red boxes of station-houses, where the spindling trees and sickly vines in the blue-grass yards made little green reserves fenced off in that confusing wilderness of sand.

As the slanting rays of the sun beat in stronger and stronger through the car-windows, the blond gentleman asked the ladies' permission to remove his coat, and sat in his lavender striped shirt-sleeves, with a black silk handkerchief tucked about his collar. He had seemed interested in Everett since they had boarded the train at Holdredge; kept glancing at him curiously and then looking reflectively out of the window, as though he were trying to recall something. But wherever Everett went, some one was almost sure to look at him with that curious interest, and it had ceased to embarrass or annoy him. Presently the stranger, seeming satisfied with his observation, leaned back in his seat, half closed his eyes, and began softly to whistle the Spring Song from *Proserpine*,[3] the cantata that a dozen years before had made its young composer famous in a night. Everett had heard that air on guitars in Old Mexico, on mandolins at college glees, on cottage organs in New England hamlets, and only two weeks ago he had heard it played on sleigh-bells at a variety theatre in Denver. There was literally no way of escaping his brother's precocity. Adriance could live on the other side of the Atlantic, where his youthful indiscretions were forgotten in his mature achievements, but his brother had never been able to outrun *Proserpine*,—and here he found it again, in the Colorado sand-hills. Not that Everett was exactly ashamed of *Proserpine*; only a man of genius could have written it, but it was the sort of thing that a man of genius outgrows as soon as he can.

Everett unbent a trifle, and smiled at his neighbour across the aisle. Immediately the large man rose and coming over dropped into the seat facing Hilgarde, extending his card.

"Dusty ride, isn't it? I don't mind it myself; I'm used to it. Born and bred in de briar patch, like Br'er Rabbit. I've been trying to place you for a long time; I think I must have met you before."

"Thank you," said Everett, taking the card; "my name is Hilgarde. You've probably met my brother, Adriance; people often mistake me for him."

The travelling-man brought his hand down upon his knee with such vehemence that the solitaire blazed.

"So I was right after all, and if you're not Adriance Hilgarde you're his double. I thought I couldn't be mistaken. Seen him? Well, I guess! I never missed one of his recitals at the Auditorium, and he played the piano score of *Proserpine* through to us once at the Chicago Press Club. I used to be on the *Commercial* there before I began to travel for the publishing department of the concern.

So you're Hilgarde's brother, and here I've run into you at the jumping-off place. Sounds like a newspaper yarn, doesn't it?"

The travelling-man laughed and offering Everett a cigar plied him with questions on the only subject that people ever seemed to care to talk to him about. At length the salesman and the two girls alighted at a Colorado way station, and Everett went on to Cheyenne alone.

The train pulled into Cheyenne at nine o'clock, late by a matter of four hours or so; but no one seemed particularly concerned at its tardiness except the station agent, who grumbled at being kept in the office over time on a summer night. When Everett alighted from the train he walked down the platform and stopped at the track crossing, uncertain as to what direction he should take to reach a hotel. A phaeton stood near the crossing and a woman held the reins. She was dressed in white, and her figure was clearly silhouetted against the cushions, though it was too dark to see her face. Everett had scarcely noticed her, when the switch-engine came puffing up from the opposite direction, and the head-light threw a strong glare of light on his face. The woman in the phaeton uttered a low cry and dropped the reins. Everett started forward and caught the horse's head, but the animal only lifted its ears and whisked its tail in impatient surprise. The woman sat perfectly still, her head sunk between her shoulders and her handkerchief pressed to her face. Another woman came out of the depot and hurried toward the phaeton, crying, "Katharine, dear, what is the matter?"

Everett hesitated a moment in painful embarrassment, then lifted his hat and passed on. He was accustomed to sudden recognitions in the most impossible places, especially from women.

While he was breakfasting the next morning, the head waiter leaned over his chair to murmur that there was a gentleman waiting to see him in the parlour. Everett finished his coffee, and went in the direction indicated, where he found his visitor restlessly pacing the floor. His whole manner betrayed a high degree of agitation, though his physique was not that of a man whose nerves lie near the surface. He was something below medium height, square-shouldered and solidly built. His thick, closely cut hair was beginning to show grey about the ears, and his bronzed face was heavily lined. His square brown hands were locked behind him, and he held his shoulders like a man conscious of responsibilities, yet, as he turned to greet Everett, there was an incongruous diffidence in his address.

"Good-morning, Mr. Hilgarde," he said, extending his hand; "I found your name on the hotel register. My name is Gaylord. I'm afraid my sister startled you at the station last night, and I've come around to explain."

"Ah! the young lady in the phaeton? I'm sure I didn't know whether I had anything to do with her alarm or not. If I did, it is I who owe an apology."

The man coloured a little under the dark brown of his face.

"Oh, it's nothing you could help, sir, I fully understand that. You see, my sister used to be a pupil of your brother's, and it seems you favour him; when the switch-engine threw a light on your face, it startled her."

Everett wheeled about in his chair. "Oh! *Katharine* Gaylord! Is it possible! Why, I used to know her when I was a boy. What on earth—"

"Is she doing here?" Gaylord grimly filled out the pause. "You've got at the heart of the matter. You know my sister had been in bad health for a long time?"

"No. The last I knew of her she was singing in London. My brother and I correspond infrequently, and seldom get beyond family matters. I am deeply sorry to hear this."

The lines in Charley Gaylord's brow relaxed a little.

"What I'm trying to say, Mr. Hilgarde, is that she wants to see you. She's set on it. We live several miles out of town, but my rig's below, and I can take you out any time you can go."

"At once, then. I'll get my hat and be with you in a moment."

When he came downstairs Everett found a cart at the door, and Charley Gaylord drew a long sigh of relief as he gathered up the reins and settled back into his own element.

"I think I'd better tell you something about my sister before you see her, and I don't know just where to begin. She travelled in Europe with your brother and his wife, and sang at a lot of his concerts; but I don't know just how much you know about her."

"Very little, except that my brother always thought her the most gifted of his pupils. When I knew her she was very young and very beautiful, and quite turned my head for a while."

Everett saw that Gaylord's mind was entirely taken up by his grief. "That's the whole thing," he went on, flecking his horses with the whip.

"She was a great woman, as you say, and she didn't come of a great family. She had to fight her own way from the first. She got to Chicago, and then to New York, and then to Europe, and got a taste for it all; and now she's dying here like a rat in a hole, out of her own world, and she can't fall back into ours. We've grown apart, some way—miles and miles apart—and I'm afraid she's fearfully unhappy."

"It's a tragic story you're telling me, Gaylord," said Everett. They were well out into the country now, spinning along over the dusty plains of red grass, with the ragged blue outline of the mountains before them.

"Tragic!" cried Gaylord, starting up in his seat, "my God, nobody will ever know how tragic! It's a tragedy I live with and eat with and sleep with, until I've lost my grip on everything. You see she had made a good bit of money, but she spent it all going to health resorts. It's her lungs. I've got money enough to send her anywhere, but the doctors all say it's no use. She hasn't the ghost of a chance. It's just getting through the days now. I had no notion she was half so bad before she came to me. She just wrote that she was run down. Now that she's here, I think she'd be happier anywhere under the sun, but she won't leave. She says it's easier to let go of life here. There was a time when I was a brakeman with a run out of Bird City, Iowa, and she was a little thing I could carry on my shoulder, when I could get her everything on earth she wanted, and she hadn't a wish my $80 a month didn't cover; and now, when I've got a little property together, I can't buy her a night's sleep!"

Everett saw that, whatever Charley Gaylord's present status in the world might be, he had brought the brakeman's heart up the ladder with him.

The reins slackened in Gaylord's hand as they drew up before a showily painted house with many gables and a round tower. "Here we are," he said, turning to Everett, "and I guess we understand each other."

They were met at the door by a thin, colourless woman, whom Gaylord introduced as "My sister, Maggie." She asked her brother to show Mr. Hilgarde into the music-room, where Katharine would join him.

When Everett entered the music-room he gave a little start of surprise, feeling that he had stepped from the glaring Wyoming sunlight into some New York studio that he had always known. He looked incredulously out of the window at the grey plain that ended in the great upheaval of the Rockies.

The haunting air of familiarity perplexed him. Suddenly his eye fell upon a large photograph of his brother above the piano. Then it all became clear enough: this was veritably his brother's room. If it were not an exact copy of one of the many studios that Adriance had fitted up in various parts of the world, wearying of them and leaving almost before the renovator's varnish had dried, it was at least in the same tone. In every detail Adriance's taste was so manifest that the room seemed to exhale his personality.

Among the photographs on the wall there was one of Katharine Gaylord, taken in the days when Everett had known her, and when the flash of her eye or the flutter of her skirt was enough to set his boyish heart in a tumult. Even now, he stood before the portrait with a certain degree of embarrassment. It was the face of a woman already old in her first youth, a trifle hard, and it told of what her brother had called her fight. The *camaraderie* of her frank, confident eyes was qualified by the deep lines about her mouth and the curve of the lips, which was both sad and cynical. Certainly she had more good-will than confidence toward the world. The chief charm of the woman, as Everett had known her, lay in her superb figure and in her eyes, which possessed a warm, life-giving quality like the sunlight; eyes which glowed with a perpetual *salutat* to the world.

Everett was still standing before the picture, his hands behind him and his head inclined, when he heard the door open. A tall woman advanced toward him, holding out her hand. As she started to speak she coughed slightly, then, laughing, said, in a low, rich voice, a trifle husky: "You see I make the traditional Camille entrance.[4] How good of you to come, Mr. Hilgarde."

Everett was acutely conscious that while addressing him she was not looking at him at all, and, as he assured her of his pleasure in coming, he was glad to have an opportunity to collect himself. He had not reckoned upon the ravages of a long illness. The long, loose folds of her white gown had been especially designed to conceal the sharp outlines of her body, but the stamp of her disease was there; simple and ugly and obtrusive, a pitiless fact that could not be disguised or evaded. The splendid shoulders were stooped, there was a swaying unevenness in her gait, her arms seemed disproportionately long, and her hands were transparently white, and cold to the touch. The changes in her face were less obvious; the proud carriage of the head, the warm, clear eyes, even the delicate flush of colour in her cheeks, all defiantly remained, though they were all in a lower key—older, sadder, softer.

She sat down upon the divan and began nervously to arrange the pillows. "Of course I'm ill, and I look it, but you must be quite frank and sensible about that and get used to it at once, for we've no time to lose. And if I'm a trifle irritable you won't mind?—for I'm more than usually nervous."

"Don't bother with me this morning, if you are tired," urged Everett. "I can come quite as well tomorrow."

"Gracious, no!" she protested, with a flash of that quick, keen humour that he remembered as a part of her. "It's solitude that I'm tired to death of—solitude and the wrong kind of people. You see, the minister called on me this morning. He happened to be riding by on his bicycle and felt it his duty to stop. The funniest feature of his conversation is that he is always excusing my own profession to me. But how we are losing time! Do tell me about New York; Charley says you're just on from there. How does it look and taste and smell just now? I think a whiff of the Jersey ferry would be as flagons of cod-liver oil to me. Are the trees still green in Madison Square, or have they grown brown and dusty? Does the chaste Diana still keep her vows through all the exasperating changes of weather? Who has your brother's old studio now, and what misguided aspirants practise their scales in the rookeries about Carnegie Hall? What do people go to see at the theatres, and what do they eat and drink in the world nowadays? Oh, let me die in Harlem!" she was interrupted by a violent attack of coughing, and Everett, embarrassed by her discomfort, plunged into gossip about the professional people he had met in town during the summer, and the musical outlook for the winter. He was diagramming with his pencil some new mechanical device to be used at the Metropolitan in the production of the *Rheingold*, when he became conscious that she was looking at him intently, and that he was talking to the four walls.

Katharine was lying back among the pillows, watching him through half-closed eyes, as a painter looks at a picture. He finished his explanation vaguely enough and put the pencil back in his pocket. As he did so, she said, quietly: "How wonderfully like Adriance you are!"

He laughed, looking up at her with a touch of pride in his eyes that made them seem quite boyish. "Yes, isn't it absurd? It's almost as awkward as looking like Napoleon— But, after all, there are some advantages. It has made some of his friends like me, and I hope it will make you."

Katharine gave him a quick, meaning glance from under her lashes. "Oh, it did that long ago. What a haughty, reserved youth you were then, and how you used to stare at people, and then blush and look cross. Do you remember that night you took me home from a rehearsal, and scarcely spoke a word to me?"

"It was the silence of admiration," protested Everett, "very crude and boyish, but certainly sincere. Perhaps you suspected something of the sort?"

"I believe I suspected a pose; the one that boys often affect with singers. But it rather surprised me in you, for you must have seen a good deal of your brother's pupils." Everett shook his head. "I saw my brother's pupils come and go. Sometimes I was called on to play accompaniments, or to fill out a vacancy at a rehearsal, or to order a carriage for an infuriated soprano who had thrown up her part. But they never spent any time on me, unless it was to notice the resemblance you speak of."

"Yes," observed Katharine, thoughtfully, "I noticed it then, too; but it has grown as you have grown older. That is rather strange, when you have lived such different lives. It's not merely an ordinary family likeness of features, you know, but the suggestion of the other man's personality in your face—like an air transposed to another key. But I'm not attempting to define it; it's beyond me; something altogether unusual and a trifle—well, uncanny," she finished, laughing.

Everett sat looking out under the red window-blind which was raised just a little. As it swung back and forth in the wind it revealed the glaring panorama of the desert—a blinding stretch of yellow, flat as the sea in dead calm, splotched here and there with deep purple shadows; and, beyond, the ragged blue outline of the mountains and the peaks of snow, white as the white clouds. "I remember, when I was a child I used to be very sensitive about it. I don't think it exactly displeased me, or that I would have had it otherwise, but it seemed like a birthmark, or something not to be lightly spoken of. It came into even my relations with my mother. Ad went abroad to study when he was very young, and mother was all broken up over it. She did her whole duty by each of us, but it was generally understood among us that she'd have made burnt-offerings of us all for him any day. I was a little fellow then, and when she sat alone on the porch on summer evenings, she used sometimes to call me to her and turn my face up in the light that streamed out through the shutters and kiss me, and then I always knew she was thinking of Adriance."

"Poor little chap," said Katharine, in her husky voice. "How fond people have always been of Adriance! Tell me the latest news of him. I haven't heard, except through the press, for a year or more. He was in Algiers then, in the valley of the Chelif, riding horseback, and he had quite made up his mind to adopt the Mahometan faith and become an Arab. How many countries and faiths has he adopted, I wonder?"

"Oh, that's Adriance," chuckled Everett. "He is himself barely long enough to write checks and be measured for his clothes. I didn't hear from him while he was an Arab; I missed that."

"He was writing an Algerian *suite* for the piano then; it must be in the publisher's hands by this time. I have been too ill to answer his letter, and have lost touch with him."

Everett drew an envelope from his pocket. "This came a month ago. Read it at your leisure."

"Thanks. I shall keep it as a hostage. Now I want you to play for me. Whatever you like; but if there is anything new in the world, in mercy let me hear it."

He sat down at the piano, and Katharine sat near him, absorbed in his remarkable physical likeness to his brother, and trying to discover in just what it consisted. He was of a larger build than Adriance, and much heavier. His face was of the same oval mould, but it was grey, and darkened about the mouth by continual shaving. His eyes were of the same inconstant April colour, but they were reflective and rather dull; while Adriance's were always points of high light, and always meaning another thing than the thing they meant yesterday. It was hard to see why this earnest man should so continually suggest that lyric, youthful face, as gay as his was grave. For Adriance, though he was ten years the elder, and though his hair was streaked with silver, had the face of a boy of twenty, so mobile that it told his thoughts before he could put them into words. A contralto, famous for the extravagance of her vocal methods and of her affections, once said that the shepherd-boys who sang in the Vale of Tempe must certainly have looked like young Hilgarde.

* * *

Everett sat smoking on the veranda of the Inter-Ocean House that night, the victim of mournful recollections. His infatuation for Katharine Gaylord, visionary as it was, had been the most serious of his boyish love-affairs. The fact that it was all so done and dead and far behind him, and that the woman had lived her life out since then, gave him an oppressive sense of age and loss.

He remembered how bitter and morose he had grown during his stay at his brother's studio when Katharine Gaylord was working there, and how he had wounded Adriance on the night of his last concert in New York. He had sat there in the box—while his brother and Katharine were called back again and again, and the flowers went up over the footlights until they were stacked half as high as the piano—brooding in his sullen boy's heart upon the pride those two felt in each other's work—spurring each other to their best and beautifully contending in song. The footlights had seemed a hard, glittering line drawn sharply between their life and his. He walked back to his hotel alone, and sat in his window staring out on Madison Square until long after midnight, resolved to beat no more at doors that he could never enter.

* * *

Everett's week in Cheyenne stretched to three, and he saw no prospect of release except through the thing he dreaded. The bright, windy days of the Wyoming autumn passed swiftly. Letters and telegrams came urging him to hasten his trip to the coast, but he resolutely postponed his business engagements. The mornings he spent on one of Charley Gaylord's ponies, or fishing in the mountains. In the afternoon he was usually at his post of duty. Destiny, he reflected, seems to have very positive notions about the sort of parts we are fitted to play. The scene changes and the compensation varies, but in the end we usually find that we have played the same class of business from first to last. Everett had been a stop-gap all his life. He remembered going through a looking-glass labyrinth when he was a boy, and trying gallery after gallery, only at every turn to bump his nose against his own face—which, indeed, was not his own, but his brother's. No matter what his mission, east or west, by land or sea, he was sure to find himself employed in his brother's business, one of the tributary lives which helped to swell the shining current of Adriance Hilgarde's. It was not the first time that his duty had been to comfort, as best he could, one of the broken things his brother's imperious speed had cast aside and forgotten. He made no attempt to analyse the situation or to state it in exact terms; but he accepted it as a commission from his brother to help this woman to die. Day by day he felt her need for him grow more acute and positive; and day by day he felt that in his peculiar relation to her, his own individuality played a smaller part. His power to minister to her comfort lay solely in his link with his brother's life. He knew that she sat by him always watching for some trick of gesture, some familiar play of expression, some illusion of light and shadow, in which he should seem wholly Adriance. He knew that she lived upon this, and that in the exhaustion which followed this turmoil of her dying senses, she slept deep and sweet, and dreamed of youth and art and days in a certain old Florentine garden, and not of bitterness and death.

A few days after his first meeting with Katharine Gaylord, he had cabled his brother to write her. He merely said that she was mortally ill; he could depend on Adriance to say the right thing—that was a part of his gift. Adriance always said not only the right thing, but the opportune, graceful, exquisite thing. He caught the lyric essence of the moment, the poetic suggestion of every situation. Moreover, he usually did the right thing,—except, when he did very cruel things—bent upon making people happy when their existence touched his, just as he insisted that his material environment should be beautiful; lavishing upon those near him all the warmth and radiance of his rich nature, all the homage of the poet and troubadour, and, when they were no longer near, forgetting—for that also was a part of Adriance's gift.

Three weeks after Everett had sent his cable, when he made his daily call at the gaily painted ranch-house, he found Katharine laughing like a girl. "Have you ever thought," she said, as he entered the music-room, "how much these séances of ours are like Heine's 'Florentine Nights,'[5] except that I don't give you an opportunity to monopolize the conversation?" She held his hand longer than usual as she greeted him. "You are the kindest man living, the kindest," she added, softly.

Everett's grey face coloured faintly as he drew his hand away, for he felt that this time she was looking at him, and not at a whimsical caricature of his brother.

She drew a letter with a foreign postmark from between the leaves of a book and held it out, smiling. "You got him to write it. Don't say you didn't, for it came direct, you see, and the last address I gave him was a place in Florida. This deed shall be remembered of you when I am with the just in Paradise. But one thing you did not ask him to do, for you didn't know about it. He has sent me his latest work, the new sonata, and you are to play it for me directly. But first for the letter; I think you would better read it aloud to me."

Everett sat down in a low chair facing the window-seat in which she reclined with a barricade of pillows behind her. He opened the letter, his lashes half-veiling his kind eyes, and saw to his satisfaction that it was a long one; wonderfully tactful and tender, even for Adriance, who was tender with his valet and his stable-boy, with his old gondolier and the beggar-women who prayed to the saints for him.

The letter was from Granada, written in the Alhambra, as he sat by the fountain of the Patio di Lindaraxa. The air was heavy with the warm fragrance of the South and full of the sound of splashing, running water, as it had been in a certain old garden in Florence, long ago. The sky was one great turquoise, heated until it glowed. The wonderful Moorish arches threw graceful blue shadows all about him. He had sketched an outline of them on the margin of his note-paper. The letter was full of confidences about his work, and delicate allusions to their old happy days of study and comradeship.

As Everett folded it he felt that Adriance had divined the thing needed and had risen to it in his own wonderful way. The letter was consistently egotistical, and seemed to him even a trifle patronizing, yet it was just what she had wanted. A strong realization of his brother's charm and intensity and power came over him; he felt the breath of that whirlwind of flame in which Adriance passed, consuming all in his path, and himself even more resolutely than he consumed others. Then he looked down at this white, burnt-out brand that lay before him.

"Like him, isn't it?" she said, quietly. "I think I can scarcely answer his letter, but when you see him next you can do that for me. I want you to tell him many things for me, yet they can all be summed up in this: I want him to grow wholly into his best and greatest self, even at the cost of what is half his charm to you and me. Do you understand me?"

"I know perfectly well what you mean," answered Everett, thoughtfully. "And yet it's difficult to prescribe for those fellows; so little makes, so little mars."

Katharine raised herself upon her elbow, and her face flushed with feverish earnestness. "Ah, but it is the waste of himself that I mean; his lashing himself out on stupid and uncomprehending people until they take him at their own estimate."

"Come, come," expostulated Everett, now alarmed at her excitement. "Where is the new sonata? Let him speak for himself."

He sat down at the piano and began playing the first movement, which was indeed the voice of Adriance, his proper speech. The sonata was the most ambitious work he had done up to that time, and marked the transition from his early lyric vein to a deeper and nobler style. Everett played intelligently and with that sympathetic comprehension which seems peculiar to a certain lovable class of men who never accomplish anything in particular. When he had finished he turned to Katharine.

"How he has grown!" she cried. "What the three last years have done for him! He used to write only the tragedies of passion; but this is the tragedy of effort and failure, the thing Keats called hell. This is my tragedy, as I lie here, listening to the feet of the runners as they pass me—ah, God! the swift feet of the runners!"

She turned her face away and covered it with her hands. Everett crossed over to her and knelt beside her. In all the days he had known her she had never before, beyond an occasional ironical jest, given voice to the bitterness of her own defeat. Her courage had become a point of pride with him.

"Don't do it," he gasped. "I can't stand it, I really can't, I feel it too much."

When she turned her face back to him there was a ghost of the old, brave, cynical smile on it, more bitter than the tears she could not shed. "No, I won't; I will save that for the night, when I have no better company. Run over that theme at the beginning again, will you? It was running in his head when we were in Venice years ago, and he used to drum it on his glass at the dinner-table. He had just begun to work it out when the late autumn came on, and he decided to go to Florence for the winter. He lost touch with his idea, I suppose, during his illness. Do you remember those frightful days? All the people who have loved him are not strong enough to save him from himself! When I got word from Florence that he had been ill, I was singing at Monte Carlo. His wife was hurrying to him from Paris, but I reached him first. I arrived at dusk, in a terrific storm. They had taken an old palace there for the winter, and I found him in the library—a long, dark room full of old Latin books and heavy furniture and bronzes. He was sitting by a wood fire at one end of the room, looking, oh, so worn and pale!—as he always does when he is ill, you know. Ah, it is so good that you *do* know! Even his red smoking-jacket lent no colour to his face. His first words were not to tell me how ill he had been, but that that morning he had been well enough to put the last strokes to the score of his *'Souvenirs d' Automne,'* and he was as I most like to remember him; calm and happy, and tired with that heavenly tiredness that comes after a good work done at last. Outside, the rain poured down in torrents, and the wind moaned and sobbed in the garden and about the walls of that desolated old palace. How that night comes back to me! There were no lights in the room, only the wood fire. It glowed on the black walls and floor like the reflection of purgatorial flame. Beyond us it scarcely penetrated the gloom at all. Adriance sat staring at the fire with the weariness of all his life in his eyes, and of all the other lives that must aspire and suffer to make up one such life as his. Somehow the wind with all its world-pain had got into the room, and the cold rain was in our eyes, and the wave came up in both of us at once—that awful vague, universal pain, that cold fear of life and death and God and hope—and we were like two clinging together on a spar in mid-ocean after the shipwreck of everything. Then we heard the front door open with a great gust of wind that shook even the walls, and the servants came running with lights, announcing that Madame had returned, *'and in the book we read no more that night.'* "[6]

She gave the old line with a certain bitter humour, and with the hard, bright smile in which of old she had wrapped her weakness as in a glittering garment. That ironical smile, worn through so many years, had gradually changed the lines of her face, and when she looked in the mirror she saw not herself, but the scathing critic, the amused observer and satirist of herself.

Everett dropped his head upon his hand. "How much you have cared!" he said.

"Ah, yes, I cared," she replied, closing her eyes. "You can't imagine what a comfort it is to have you know how I cared, what a relief it is to be able to tell it to some one."

Everett continued to look helplessly at the floor. "I was not sure how much you wanted me to know," he said.

"Oh, I intended you should know from the first time I looked into your face, when you came that day with Charley. You are so like him, that it is almost like telling him himself. At least, I feel now that he will know some day, and then I will be quite sacred from his compassion."

"And has he never known at all?" asked Everett, in a thick voice.

"Oh! never at all in the way that you mean. Of course, he is accustomed to looking into the eyes of women and finding love there; when he doesn't find it there he thinks he must have been guilty of some discourtesy. He has a genuine fondness for every woman who is not stupid or gloomy, or old or preternaturally ugly. I shared with the rest; shared the smiles and the gallantries and the droll little sermons. It was quite like a Sunday-school picnic; we wore our best clothes and a smile and took our turns. It was his kindness that was hardest."

"Don't; you'll make me hate him," groaned Everett.

Katharine laughed and began to play nervously with her fan. "It wasn't in the slightest degree his fault; that is the most grotesque part of it. Why, it had really begun before I ever met him. I fought my way to him, and I drank my doom greedily enough."

Everett rose and stood hesitating. "I think I must go. You ought to be quiet, and I don't think I can hear any more just now."

She put out her hand and took his playfully. "You've put in three weeks at this sort of thing, haven't you? Well, it ought to square accounts for a much worse life than yours will ever be."

He knelt beside her, saying, brokenly: "I stayed because I wanted to be with you, that's all. I have never cared about other women since I knew you in New York when I was a lad. You are a part of my destiny, and I could not leave you if I would."

She put her hands on his shoulders and shook her head. "No, no; don't tell me that. I have seen enough tragedy. It was only a boy's fancy, and your divine pity and my utter pitiableness have recalled it for a moment. One does not love the dying, dear friend. Now go, and you will come again tomorrow, as long as there are tomorrows." She took his hand with a smile that was both courage and despair, and full of infinite loyalty and tenderness, as she said softly:

> *"For ever and for ever, farewell,*[7] *Cassius;*
> *If we do meet again, why, we shall smile;*
> *If not, why then, this parting was well made."*

The courage in her eyes was like the clear light of a star to him as he went out.

On the night of Adriance Hilgarde's opening concert in Paris, Everett sat by the bed in the ranch-house in Wyoming, watching over the last battle that we have with the flesh before we are done with it and free of it for ever. At times it seemed that the serene soul of her must have left already and found some refuge from the storm, and only the tenacious animal life were left to do battle with death. She laboured under a delusion at once pitiful and merciful, thinking that she was in the Pullman on her way to New York, going back to her life and her work. When she roused from her stupor, it was only to ask the porter to waken her half an hour out of Jersey City, or to remonstrate about the delays and the roughness of the road. At midnight Everett and the nurse were left alone with her. Poor Charley Gaylord had lain down on a couch outside the door. Everett sat looking at the sputtering night-lamp until it made his eyes ache. His head dropped forward, and he sank into heavy, distressful slumber. He was dreaming of Adriance's concert in Paris, and of Adriance, the troubadour. He heard the applause and he saw the flowers going up over the footlights until they were stacked half as high as the piano, and the petals fell and scattered, making crimson splotches on the floor. Down this crimson pathway came Adriance with his youthful step, leading his singer by the hand; a dark woman this time, with Spanish eyes.

The nurse touched him on the shoulder, he started and awoke. She screened the lamp with her hand. Everett saw that Katharine was awake and conscious, and struggling a little. He lifted her gently on his arm and began to fan her. She looked into his face with eyes that seemed never to have wept or doubted. "Ah, dear Adriance, dear, dear!" she whispered.

Everett went to call her brother, but when they came back the madness of art was over for Katharine.

Two days later Everett was pacing the station siding, waiting for the west-bound train. Charley Gaylord walked beside him, but the two men had nothing to say to each other. Everett's bags were piled on the truck, and his step was hurried and his eyes were full of impatience, as he gazed again and again up the track, watching for the train. Gaylord's impatience was not less than his own; these two, who had grown so close, had now become painful and impossible to each other, and longed for the wrench of farewell.

As the train pulled in, Everett wrung Gaylord's hand among the crowd of alighting passengers. The people of a German opera company, *en route* for the coast, rushed by them in frantic haste to snatch their breakfast during the stop. Everett heard an exclamation, and a stout woman rushed up to him, glowing with joyful surprise and caught his coat-sleeve with her tightly gloved hands.

"*Herr Gott*, Adriance, *lieber Freund*," she cried.

Everett lifted his hat, blushing. "Pardon me, madame, I see that you have mistaken me for Adriance Hilgarde. I am his brother." Turning from the crestfallen singer he hurried into the car.

UNCOLLECTED STORIES

Peter[1]

"No, ANTONE, I have told thee many times, no, thou shalt not sell it until I am gone."

"But I need money; what good is that old fiddle to thee? The very crows laugh at thee when thou art trying to play. Thy hand trembles so thou canst scarce hold the bow. Thou shalt go with me to the Blue to cut wood tomorrow. See to it thou art up early."

"What, on the Sabbath, Antone, when it is so cold? I get so very cold, my son, let us not go tomorrow."

"Yes, tomorrow, thou lazy old man. Do not I cut wood upon the Sabbath? Care I how cold it is? Wood thou shalt cut, and haul it too, and as for the fiddle, I tell thee I will sell it yet." Antone pulled his ragged cap down over his low heavy brow, and went out. The old man drew his stool up nearer the fire, and sat stroking his violin with trembling fingers and muttering, "Not while I live, not while I live."

Five years ago they had come here, Peter Sadelack, and his wife, and oldest son Antone, and countless smaller Sadelacks, here to the dreariest part of southwestern Nebraska,[2] and had taken up a homestead. Antone was the acknowledged master of the premises, and people said he was a likely youth, and would do well. That he was mean and untrustworthy every one knew, but that made little difference. His corn was better tended than any in the county, and his wheat always yielded more than other men's.

Of Peter no one knew much, nor had any one a good word to say for him. He drank whenever he could get out of Antone's sight long enough to pawn his hat or coat for whisky. Indeed there were but two things he would not pawn, his pipe and his violin. He was a lazy, absentminded old fellow, who liked to fiddle better than to plow, though Antone surely got work enough out of them all, for that matter. In the house of which Antone was master there was no one, from the little boy three years old, to the old man of sixty, who did not earn his bread. Still people said that Peter was worthless, and was a great drag on Antone, his son, who never drank, and was a much better man than his father had ever been. Peter did not care what people said. He did not like the country, nor the people, least of all he liked the plowing. He was very homesick for Bohemia. Long ago, only eight years ago by the calendar, but it seemed eight centuries to Peter, he had been a second violinist in the great theatre at Prague. He had gone into the theatre very young, and had been there all his life, until he had a stroke of paralysis, which made his arm so weak that his bowing was uncertain. Then they told him he could go. Those were great days at the theatre. He had plenty to drink then, and wore a dress coat every evening, and there were always parties after the play. He could play in those days, ay, that he could! He could never read the notes well, so he did not play first; but his touch, he had a touch indeed, so Herr Mikilsdoff, who led the orchestra, had said. Sometimes now Peter thought he could plow better if he could only bow as he used to. He had seen all the lovely women in the world there, all the great singers and the great players. He was in the orchestra when Rachel played,[3] and he heard Liszt[4] play when the Countess d'Agoult sat in the stage box and threw the master white lilies. Once, a French woman[5] came and played for weeks, he did not remember her name now. He did not remember her face very well either, for it changed so, it was never twice the same. But the beauty of it, and the great hunger men felt at the sight of it, that he remembered. Most of all he remembered her voice. He did not know French, and could not understand a word she said, but it seemed to him that she must be talking the music of Chopin. And her voice, he thought he should know that in the other world. The last night she played a play in which a man touched her arm, and she stabbed him. As Peter sat among the smoking gas jets down below the footlights with his fiddle on his knee, and looked up at her, he thought he would like to die too, if he could touch her arm once, and have her stab him so. Peter went home to his wife very drunk that night. Even in those days he was a foolish fellow, who cared for nothing but music and pretty faces.

It was all different now. He had nothing to drink and little to eat, and here, there was nothing but sun, and grass, and sky. He had forgotten almost everything, but some things he remembered well enough. He loved his violin and the holy Mary, and above all else he feared the Evil One, and his son Antone.

The fire was low, and it grew cold. Still Peter sat by the fire remembering. He dared not throw more cobs on the fire; Antone would be angry. He did not want to cut wood tomorrow, it would be Sunday, and he wanted to go to mass. Antone might let him do that. He held his violin under his wrinkled chin, his white hair fell over it, and he began to play "Ave Maria." His hand shook more than ever before, and at last refused to work the bow at all. He sat stupefied for a while, then arose, and taking his violin with him, stole out into the old sod stable. He took Antone's shotgun down from its peg, and loaded it by the moonlight which streamed in through the door. He sat down on the dirt floor, and leaned back against the dirt wall. He heard the wolves howling in the distance, and the night wind screaming as it swept over the snow. Near him he heard the regular breathing of the horses in the dark. He put his crucifix above his heart, and folding his hands said brokenly all the Latin he had ever known, *"Pater noster, qui in coelum est."*[6] Then he raised his head and sighed, "Not one kreutzer will Antone pay them to pray for my soul, not one kreutzer, he is so careful of his money, is Antone, he does not waste it in drink, he is a better man than I, but hard sometimes. He works the girls too hard, women were not made to work so. But he shall not sell thee, my fiddle, I can play thee no more, but they shall not part us. We have seen it all together, and we will forget it together, the French woman and all." He held his fiddle under his chin a moment, where it had lain so often, then put it across his knee and broke it through the middle. He pulled off his old boot, held the gun between his knees with the muzzle against his forehead, and pressed the trigger with his toe.

In the morning Antone found him stiff, frozen fast in a pool of blood. They could not straighten him out enough to fit a coffin, so they buried him in a pine box. Before the funeral Antone carried to town the fiddle-bow which Peter had forgotten to break. Antone was very thrifty, and a better man than his father had been.

First published in *The Mahogany Tree*, May 31, 1892, pp. 323–24.

The Profile

THE SUBJECT OF DISCUSSION at the Impressionists' Club was a picture, *Circe's Swine*, by a young German painter; a grotesque study showing the enchantress among a herd of bestial things, variously diverging from the human type—furry-eared fauns, shaggy-hipped satyrs, apes with pink palms, snuffing jackals, and thick-jowled swine, all with more or less of human intelligence protesting mutely from their hideous lineaments.

"They are all errors, these freakish excesses," declared an old painter of the Second Empire.[1] "Triboulet, Quasimodo, Gwynplaine,[2] have no proper place in art. Such art belongs to the Huns and Iroquois,[3] who could only be stirred by laceration and dismemberment. The only effects of horror properly within the province of the artist are psychological. Everything else is a mere matter of the abattoir.[4] The body, as Nature has evolved it, is sanctified by her purpose; in any natural function or attitude decent and comely. But lop away so much as a finger, and you have wounded the creature beyond reparation."

Once launched upon this subject, there was no stopping the old lion, and several of his confrères were relieved when Aaron Dunlap quietly rose and left the room. They felt that this was a subject which might well be distasteful to him.

I

Dunlap was a portrait painter—preferably a painter of women. He had the faculty of transferring personalities to his canvas, rather than of putting conceptions there. He was finely sensitive to the merest prettiness, was tender and indulgent of it, careful never to deflower a pretty woman of her little charm, however commonplace.

Nicer critics always discerned, even in his most radiant portraits, a certain quiet element of sympathy, almost of pity, in the treatment. The sharp, flexible profile of Madame R—— of the Française; the worn, but subtle and all-capricious physiognomy of her great Semitic rival;[5] the plump contours of a shopkeeper's pretty wife—Dunlap treated them with equal respect and fidelity. He accepted each as she was, and could touch even obvious prettiness with dignity. Behind the delicate pleasure manifested in his treatment of a beautiful face, one could divine the sadness of knowledge, and one felt that the painter had yearned to arrest what was so fleeting and to hold it back from the cruelty of the years. At an exhibition of Dunlap's pictures, the old painter of the Second Empire had said, with a sigh, that he ought to get together all his portraits of young women and call them "Les Fiançées," so abloom were they with the confidence of their beautiful secret. Then, with that sensitiveness to style, which comes from long and passionate study of form, the old painter had added reflectively, "And, after all, how sad a thing it is to be young."

Dunlap had come from a country where women are hardly used. He had grown up on a farm in the remote mountains of West Virginia, and his mother had died of pneumonia contracted from taking her place at the washtub too soon after the birth of a child. When a boy, he had been apprenticed to his grandfather, a country cobbler, who, in his drunken rages, used to beat his wife with odd strips of shoe leather. The painter's hands still bore the mark of that apprenticeship, and the suffering of the mountain women he had seen about him in his childhood had left him almost morbidly sensitive.

Just how or why Dunlap had come to Paris, none of his fellow-painters had ever learned. When he ran away from his grandfather, he had been sent by a missionary fund to some sectarian college in his own state, after which he had taught a country school for three winters and saved money enough for his passage. He arrived in Paris with something less than a hundred dollars, wholly ignorant of the language, without friends, and, apparently, without especial qualifications for study there.

Perhaps the real reason that he never succumbed to want was, that he was never afraid of it. He felt that he could never be really hungry so long as the poplars flickered along the gray quay behind the Louvre; never friendless while the gay busses rolled home across the bridges through the violet twilight, and the barge lights winked above the water.

Little by little his stripes were healed,[6] his agony of ignorance alleviated. The city herself taught him whatever was needful for him to know. She repeated with him that fanciful romance which she has played at with youth for centuries, in which her spontaneity is ever young. She gave him of her best, quickened in him a sense of the more slight and feminine fairness in things; trained his hand and eye to the subtleties of the thousand types of subtle beauty in which she abounds; made him, after a delicate and chivalrous fashion, the expiator of his mountain race.[7] He lived in a bright atmosphere of clear vision and happy associations, delighted at having to do with what was fair and exquisitely brief.

Life went on so during the first ten years of his residence in Paris—a happiness which, despite its almost timorous modesty, tempted fate. It was after Dunlap's name had become somewhat the fashion, that he chanced one day, in a café on the Boulevard St. Michel, to be of some service to an American who was having trouble about his order. After assisting him, Dunlap had some conversation with the man, a Californian, whose wheatlands comprised acres enough for a principality, and whose enthusiasm was as fresh as a boy's. Several days later, at the Luxembourg, he met him again, standing in a state of abject bewilderment before Manet's *Olympe*.[8] Dunlap again came to his rescue and took him off to lunch, after which they went to the painter's studio. The acquaintance warmed on both sides, and, before they separated, Dunlap was engaged to paint the old gentleman's daughter, agreeing that the sittings should be at the house on the Boulevard de Courcelles, which the family had taken for the winter.

When Dunlap called at the house, he went through one of the most excruciating experiences of his life. He found Mrs. Gilbert and her daughter waiting to receive him. The shock of the introduction over, the strain of desultory conversation began. The only thing that made conversation tolerable—though it added a new element of perplexity—was the girl's seeming unconsciousness, her utter openness and unabashedness. She laughed and spoke, almost with coquetry, of the honor of sitting to him, of having heard that he was fastidious as to his subjects. Dunlap felt that he wanted to rush from the house and escape the situation which confronted him. The conviction kept recurring that it had just happened, had come upon her since last she had passed a mirror; that she would suddenly become conscious of it, and be suffocated with shame. He felt as if some one ought to tell her and lead her away.

"Shall we get to work?" she asked presently, apparently curious and eager to begin. "How do you wish me to sit to you?"

Dunlap murmured something about usually asking his sitters to decide that for themselves.

"Suppose we try a profile, then?" she suggested carelessly, sitting down in a carved wooden chair.

For the first time since he had entered the room, Dunlap felt the pressure about his throat relax. For the first time it was entirely turned from him, and he could not see it at all. What he did see was a girlish profile, unusually firm for a thing so softly colored; oval, flower-tinted, and shadowed by soft, blonde hair that wound about her head and curled and clung about her brow and neck and ears.

Dunlap began setting up his easel, recovering from his first discomfort and grateful to the girl for having solved his difficulty so gracefully. But no sooner was it turned from him than he felt a strong desire to see it again. Perhaps it had been only a delusion, after all; the clear profile before him so absolutely contradicted it. He went behind her chair to experiment with the window shades, and there, as he drew them up and down, he could look unseen. He gazed long and hard, to blunt his curiosity once and for all, and prevent a further temptation to covert glances. It had evidently been caused by a deep burn, as if from a splash of molten metal. It drew the left eye and the corner of the mouth; made of her smile a grinning distortion, like the shameful conception of some despairing medieval imagination. It was as if some grotesque mask, worn for disport, were just slipping sidewise from her face.

When Dunlap crossed to the right again, he found the same clear profile awaiting him, the same curves of twining, silken hair. "What courage," he thought, "what magnificent courage!" His heart ached at the injustice of it; that her very beauty, the alert, girlish figure, the firm, smooth throat and chin, even her delicate hands, should, through an inch or two of seared flesh, seem tainted and false. He felt that in a plain woman it would have been so much less horrible.

Dunlap left the house overcast by a haunting sense of tragedy, and for the rest of the day he was a prey to distressing memories. All that he had tried to forget seemed no longer dim and faraway —like the cruelties of vanished civilizations—but present and painfully near. He thought of his mother and grandmother, of his little sister, who had died from the bite of a copperhead snake, as if they were creatures yet unreleased from suffering.

II

From the first, Virginia's interest in the portrait never wavered; yet, as the sittings progressed, it became evident to Dunlap that her enthusiasm for the picture was but accessory to her interest in him. By her every look and action she asserted her feeling, as a woman, young and handsome and independent, may sometimes do.

As time went on, he was drawn to her by what had once repelled him. Her courageous candor appealed to his chivalry, and he came to love her, not despite the scar, but, in a manner, for its very sake. He had some indefinite feeling that love might heal her; that in time her hurt might disappear, like the deformities imposed by enchantment to test the hardihood of lovers.

He gathered from her attitude, as well as from that of her family, that the thing had never been mentioned to her, never alluded to by word or look. Both her father and mother had made it their first care to shield her. Had she ever, in the streets of some foreign city, heard a brutal allusion to it? He shuddered to think of such a possibility. Was she not living for the moment when she could throw down the mask and point to it and weep, to be comforted for all time? He looked forward to the hour when there would be no lie of unconsciousness between them. The moment must come when she would give him her confidence; perhaps it would be only a whisper, a gesture, a guiding of his hand in the dark; but, however it might come, it was the pledge he awaited.

During the last few weeks before his marriage, the scar, through the mere strength of his anticipation, had ceased to exist for him. He had already entered to the perfect creature which he felt must dwell behind it; the soul of tragic serenity and twofold loveliness.

They went to the South for their honeymoon, through the Midi and along the coast to Italy. Never, by word or sign, did Virginia reveal any consciousness of what he felt must be said once, and only once, between them. She was spirited, adventurous, impassioned; she exacted much, but she gave magnificently. Her interests in the material world were absorbing, and she demanded continual excitement and continual novelty. Granted these, her good spirits were unfailing.

It was during their wedding journey that he discovered her two all-absorbing interests, which were to become intensified as years went on: her passion for dress and her feverish admiration of physical beauty, whether in men or women or children. This touched Dunlap deeply, as it seemed in a manner an admission of a thing she could not speak.

Before their return to Paris Dunlap had, for the time, quite renounced his hope of completely winning her confidence. He tried to believe his exclusion just; he told himself that it was only a part of her splendid self-respect. He thought of how, from her very childhood, she had been fashioning, day by day, that armor of unconsciousness in which she sheathed her scar. After all, so deep a hurt could, perhaps, be bared to any one rather than the man she loved.

Yet, he felt that their life was enmeshed in falsehood; that he could not live year after year with a woman who shut so deep a part of her nature from him; that since he had married a woman outwardly different from others, he must have that within her which other women did not possess. Until this was granted him, he felt there would be a sacredness lacking in their relation which it peculiarly ought to have. He counted upon the birth of her child to bring this about. It would touch deeper than he could hope to do, and with fingers that could not wound. That would be a tenderness more penetrating, more softening than passion; without pride or caprice; a feeling that would dwell most in the one part of her he had failed to reach. The child, certainly, she could not shut out; whatever hardness or defiant shame it was that held him away from her, her maternity would bring enlightenment; would bring that sad wisdom, that admission of the necessity and destiny to suffer, which is, somehow, so essential in a woman.

Virginia's child was a girl, a sickly baby which cried miserably from the day it was born. The listless, wailing, almost unwilling battle for life that daily went on before his eyes saddened Dunlap profoundly. All his painter's sophistries fell away from him, and more than ever his early destiny seemed closing about him. There was, then, no escaping from the cruelty of physical things—no matter how high and bright the sunshine, how gray and poplar-clad the ways of one's life. The more willing the child seemed to relinquish its feeble hold, the more tenderly he loved it, and the more determinedly he fought to save it.

Virginia, on the contrary, had almost from the first exhibited a marked indifference toward her daughter. She showed plainly that the sight of its wan, aged little face was unpleasant to her; she disliked being clutched by its skeleton fingers, and said its wailing made her head ache. She was always taking Madame de Montebello and her handsome children to drive in the Bois, but she was never to be seen with little Eleanor. If her friends asked to see the child, she usually put them off, saying that she was asleep or in her bath.

When Dunlap once impatiently asked her whether she never intended to permit any one to see her daughter, she replied coldly: "Certainly, when she has filled out and begins to look like something."

Little Eleanor grew into a shy, awkward child, who slipped about the house like an unwelcome dependent. She was four years old when a cousin of Virginia's came from California to spend a winter in Paris. Virginia had known her only slightly at home, but, as she proved to be a charming girl, and as she was ill-equipped to bear the hardships of a winter in a *pension*,[9] the Dunlaps insisted upon her staying with them. The cousin's name was also Eleanor —she had been called so after Virginia's mother—and, from the first, the two Eleanors seemed drawn to each other. Miss Vane was studying, and went out to her lectures every day, but whenever she was at home, little Eleanor was with her. The child would sit quietly in her room while she wrote, playing with anything her cousin happened to give her; or would lie for hours on the hearth rug, whispering to her woolly dog. Dunlap felt a weight lifted from his mind. Whenever Eleanor was at home, he knew that the child was happy.

He had long ceased to expect any solicitude for her from Virginia. That had gone with everything else. It was one of so many disappointments that he took it rather as a matter of course, and it seldom occurred to him that it might have been otherwise. For two years he had been living like a man who knows that some reptile has housed itself and hatched its young in his cellar, and who never cautiously puts his foot out of his bed without the dread of touching its coils. The change in his feeling toward his wife kept him in perpetual apprehension; it seemed to threaten everything he held dear, even his self-respect. His life was a continual effort of self-control, and he found it necessary to make frequent trips to London or sketching tours into Brittany to escape from the strain of the repression he put upon himself. Under this state of things, Dunlap aged perceptibly, and his friends made various and usual conjectures. Whether Virginia was conscious of the change in him, he never knew. Her feeling for him had, in its very nature, been as temporary as it was violent; it had abated naturally, and she probably took for granted that the same readjustment had taken place in him. Perhaps she was too much engrossed in other things to notice it at all.

In Dunlap the change seemed never to be finally established, but forever painfully working. Whereas he had once seen the scar on his wife's face not at all, he now saw it continually. Inch by inch it had crept over her whole countenance. Yet the scar itself seemed now a trivial thing; he had known for a long time that the burn had gone deeper than the flesh.

Virginia's extravagant fondness for gaiety seemed to increase, and her mania for lavish display, doubtless common enough in the

Californian wheat empire, was a discordant note in Paris. Dunlap found himself condemned to an existence which daily did violence to his sense of propriety. His wife gave fêtes,[10] the cost of which was noised abroad by the Associated Press and flaunted in American newspapers. Her vanity, the pageantries of her toilet, made them both ridiculous, he felt. She was a woman now, with a husband and child; she had no longer a pretext for keeping up the pitiful bravado under which she had hidden the smarting pride of her girlhood.

He became more and more convinced that she had been shielded from a realization of her disfigurement only to the end of a shocking perversity. Her costumes, her very jewels, blazed defiance. Her confidence became almost insolent, and her laugh was nothing but a frantic denial of a thing so cruelly obvious. The unconsciousness he had once reverenced now continually tempted his brutality, and when he felt himself reduced to the point of actual vituperation, he fled to Normandy or Languedoc to save himself. He had begun, indeed, to feel strangely out of place in Paris. The ancient comfort of the city, never lacking in the days when he had known cold and hunger, failed him now. A certain sordidness had spread itself over ways and places once singularly perfect and pure.

III

One evening when Virginia refused to allow little Eleanor to go down to the music room to see some pantomime performers who were to entertain their guests, Dunlap, to conceal his displeasure, stepped quickly out upon the balcony and closed the window behind him. He stood for some moments in the cold, clear night air.

"God help me," he groaned. "Some day I shall tell her. I shall hold her and tell her."

When he entered the house again, it was by another window, and his anger had cooled. As he stepped into the hallway, he met Eleanor the elder, going upstairs with the little girl in her arms. For the life of him he could not refrain from appealing for sympathy to her kind, grave eyes. He was so hurt, so sick, that he could have put his face down beside the child's and wept.

"Give her to me, little cousin. She is too heavy for you," he said gently, as they went upstairs together.

He remembered with resentment his wife's perfectly candid and careless jests about his fondness for her cousin. After he had put the little girl down in Eleanor's room, as they leaned together above the child's head in the firelight, he became, for the first time, really aware. A sudden tenderness weakened him. He put out his hand and took hers, which was holding the child's, and murmured: "Thank you, thank you, little cousin."

She started violently and caught her hand away from him, trembling all over. Dunlap left the room, thrice more miserable than he had entered it.

After that evening he noticed that Eleanor avoided meeting him alone. Virginia also noticed it, but upon this point she was consistently silent. One morning, as Dunlap was leaving his wife's dressing room, having been to consult her as to whether she intended going to the ball at the Russian Embassy, she called him back. She was carefully arranging her beautiful hair, which she always dressed herself, and said carelessly, without looking up at him:

"Eleanor has a foolish notion of returning home in March. I wish you would speak to her about it. Her family expect her to stay until June, and her going now would be commented upon."

"I scarcely see how I can interfere," he replied coolly. "She doubtless has her reasons."

"Her reasons are not far to seek, I should say," remarked Virginia, carefully slipping the pins into the yellow coils of her hair. "She is pathetically ingenuous about it. I should think you might improve upon the present state of affairs if you were to treat it—well, say a trifle more lightly. That would put her more at ease, at least."

"What nonsense, Virginia," he exclaimed, laughing unnaturally and closing the door behind him with guarded gentleness.

That evening Dunlap joined his wife in her dressing room, his coat on his arm and his hat in his hand. The maid had gone upstairs to hunt for Virginia's last year's fur shoes, as the pair warming before the grate would not fit over her new dancing slippers. Virginia was standing before the mirror, carefully surveying the effect of a new gown, which struck her husband as more than usually conspicuous and defiant. He watched her arranging a pink-and-gold butterfly in her hair and held his peace, but when she put on a pink chiffon collar, with a flaring bow which came directly under her left cheek, in spite of himself he shuddered.

"For heaven's sake, Virginia, take that thing off," he cried. "You ought really to be more careful about such extremes. They only emphasize the scar." He was frightened at the brittleness of his own voice; it seemed to whistle dryly in the air like his grandfather's thong.

She caught her breath and wheeled suddenly about, her face crimson and then gray. She opened her lips twice, but no sound escaped them. He saw the muscles of her throat stiffen, and she began to shudder convulsively, like one who has been plunged into icy water. He started toward her, sick with pity; at last, perhaps—but she pointed him steadily to the door, her eyes as hard as shell, and bright and small, like the sleepless eyes of reptiles.

He went to bed with the sick feeling of a man who has tortured an animal, yet with a certain sense of relief and finality which he had not known in years.

When he came down to breakfast in the morning, the butler told him that Madame and her maid had left for Nice by the early train. Mademoiselle Vane had gone out to her lectures. Madame requested that Monsieur take Mademoiselle to the opera in the evening, where the widowed sister of Madame de Montebello would join them; she would come home with them to remain until Madame's return. Dunlap accepted these instructions as a matter of course, and announced that he would not dine at home.

When he entered the hall upon his return that evening, he heard little Eleanor sobbing, and she flew to meet him, with her dress burned, and her hands black. Dunlap smelled the sickening odor of ointments. The nurse followed with explanations. The doctor was upstairs. Mademoiselle Vane always used a little alcohol lamp in making her toilet; tonight, when she touched a match to it, it exploded. Little Eleanor was leaning against her dressing table at the time, and her dress caught fire; Mademoiselle Vane had wrapped the rug about her and extinguished it. When the nurse arrived,

Mademoiselle Vane was standing in the middle of the floor, plucking at her scorched hair, her face and arms badly burned. She had bent over the lamp in lighting it, and had received the full force of the explosion in her face. The doctor was unable to discover what the explosive had been, as it was entirely consumed. Mademoiselle always filled the little lamp herself; all the servants knew about it, for Madame had sent the nurse to borrow it on several occasions, when little Eleanor had the earache.

The next morning Dunlap received a telegram from his wife, stating that she would go to St. Petersburg for the remainder of the winter. In May he heard that she had sailed for America, and a year later her attorneys wrote that she had begun action for divorce. Immediately after the decree was granted, Dunlap married Eleanor Vane. He never met or directly heard from Virginia again, though when she returned to Russia and took up her residence in St. Petersburg, the fame of her toilets spread even to Paris.

Society, always prone to crude antitheses, knew of Dunlap only that he had painted many of the most beautiful women of his time, that he had been twice married, and that each of his wives had been disfigured by a scar on the face.

First published in *McClure's*, XXIX (June 1907), pp. 135–40.

The Enchanted Bluff

WE HAD OUR SWIM before sundown, and while we were cooking our supper the oblique rays of light made a dazzling glare on the white sand about us. The translucent red ball itself sank behind the brown stretches of corn field as we sat down to eat, and the warm layer of air that had rested over the water and our clean sand bar grew fresher and smelled of the rank ironweed and sunflowers growing on the flatter shore. The river was brown and sluggish, like any other of the half-dozen streams that water the Nebraska corn lands. On one shore was an irregular line of bald clay bluffs where a few scrub oaks with thick trunks and flat, twisted tops threw light shadows on the long grass. The western shore was low and level, with corn fields that stretched to the skyline, and all along the water's edge were little sandy coves and beaches where slim cottonwoods and willow saplings flickered.

The turbulence of the river in springtime discouraged milling, and, beyond keeping the old red bridge in repair, the busy farmers did not concern themselves with the stream; so the Sandtown boys were left in undisputed possession. In the autumn we hunted quail through the miles of stubble and fodder land along the flat shore, and, after the winter skating season was over and the ice had gone out, the spring freshets[1] and flooded bottoms gave us our great excitement of the year. The channel was never the same for two successive seasons. Every spring the swollen stream undermined a bluff to the east, or bit out a few acres of corn field to the west and whirled the soil away to deposit it in spumy mud banks somewhere else. When the water fell low in midsummer, new sand bars were thus exposed to dry and whiten in the August sun. Sometimes these were banked so firmly that the fury of the next freshet failed to unseat them; the little willow seedlings emerged triumphantly from the yellow froth, broke into spring leaf, shot up into summer growth, and with their mesh of roots bound together the moist sand beneath them against the batterings of another April. Here and there a cottonwood soon glittered among them, quivering in the low current of air that, even on breathless days when the dust hung like smoke above the wagon road, trembled along the face of the water.

It was on such an island, in the third summer of its yellow green, that we built our watch fire; not in the thicket of dancing willow wands, but on the level terrace of fine sand which had been added that spring; a little new bit of world, beautifully ridged with ripple marks, and strewn with the tiny skeletons of turtles and fish, all as white and dry as if they had been expertly cured. We had been careful not to mar the freshness of the place, although we often swam to it on summer evenings and lay on the sand to rest.

This was our last watch fire of the year, and there were reasons why I should remember it better than any of the others. Next week the other boys were to file back to their old places in the Sandtown High School, but I was to go up to the Divide to teach my first country school in the Norwegian district. I was already homesick at the thought of quitting the boys with whom I had always played; of leaving the river, and going up into a windy plain that was all windmills and corn fields and big pastures; where there was nothing willful or unmanageable in the landscape, no new islands, and no chance of unfamiliar birds—such as often followed the water-courses.

Other boys came and went and used the river for fishing or skating, but we six were sworn to the spirit of the stream, and we were friends mainly because of the river. There were the two Hassler boys, Fritz and Otto, sons of the little German tailor. They were the youngest of us; ragged boys of ten and twelve, with sunburned hair, weather-stained faces, and pale blue eyes. Otto, the elder, was the best mathematician in school, and clever at his books, but he always dropped out in the spring term as if the river could not get on without him. He and Fritz caught the fat, horned catfish and sold them about the town, and they lived so much in the water that they were as brown and sandy as the river itself.

There was Percy Pound, a fat, freckled boy with chubby cheeks, who took half a dozen boys' story-papers and was always being kept in for reading detective stories behind his desk. There was Tip Smith, destined by his freckles and red hair to be the buffoon in all our games, though he walked like a timid little old man and had a funny, cracked laugh. Tip worked hard in his father's grocery store every afternoon, and swept it out before school in the morning. Even his recreations were laborious. He collected cigarette cards and tin tobacco-tags indefatigably, and would sit for hours humped up over a snarling little scroll-saw which he kept in his attic. His dearest possessions were some little pill bottles that purported to contain grains of wheat from the Holy Land, water from the Jordan and the Dead Sea, and earth from the Mount of Olives. His father had bought these dull things from a Baptist missionary who peddled them, and Tip seemed to derive great satisfaction from their remote origin.

The tall boy was Arthur Adams. He had fine hazel eyes that were almost too reflective and sympathetic for a boy, and such a pleasant voice that we all loved to hear him read aloud. Even when he had to read poetry aloud at school, no one ever thought of laughing. To be sure, he was not at school very much of the time. He was seventeen and should have finished the High School the year before, but he was always off somewhere with his gun. Arthur's mother was dead, and his father, who was feverishly absorbed in promoting schemes, wanted to send the boy away to school and get him off his hands; but Arthur always begged off for another year and promised to study. I remember him as a tall, brown boy with an intelligent face, always lounging among a lot of us little fellows, laughing at us oftener than with us, but such a soft, satisfied laugh that we felt rather flattered when we provoked it. In after-years people said that Arthur had been given to evil ways even as a lad, and it is true that we often saw him with the gambler's sons and with old Spanish Fanny's boy, but if he learned anything ugly in their company he never betrayed it to us. We would have followed Arthur anywhere, and I am bound to say that he led us into no worse places than the cattail marshes and the stubble fields. These, then, were the boys who camped with me that summer night upon the sand bar.

After we finished our supper we beat the willow thicket for driftwood. By the time we had collected enough, night had fallen, and the pungent, weedy smell from the shore increased with the coolness. We threw ourselves down about the fire and made another futile effort to show Percy Pound the Little Dipper. We had tried it often before, but he could never be got past the big one.

"You see those three big stars just below the handle, with the bright one in the middle?" said Otto Hassler; "that's Orion's belt, and the bright one is the clasp." I crawled behind Otto's shoulder and sighted up his arm to the star that seemed perched upon the tip of his steady forefinger. The Hassler boys did seine-fishing[2] at night, and they knew a good many stars.

Percy gave up the Little Dipper and lay back on the sand, his hands clasped under his head. "I can see the North Star," he announced, contentedly, pointing toward it with his big toe. "Anyone might get lost and need to know that."

We all looked up at it.

"How do you suppose Columbus felt when his compass didn't point north any more?" Tip asked.

Otto shook his head. "My father says that there was another North Star once, and that maybe this one won't last always. I wonder what would happen to us down here if anything went wrong with it?"

Arthur chuckled. "I wouldn't worry, Ott. Nothing's apt to happen to it in your time. Look at the Milky Way! There must be lots of good dead Indians."

We lay back and looked, meditating, at the dark cover of the world. The gurgle of the water had become heavier. We had often noticed a mutinous, complaining note in it at night, quite different from its cheerful daytime chuckle, and seeming like the voice of a much deeper and more powerful stream. Our water had always these two moods: the one of sunny complaisance, the other of inconsolable, passionate regret.

"Queer how the stars are all in sort of diagrams," remarked

Otto. "You could do most any proposition in geometry with 'em. They always look as if they meant something. Some folks say everybody's fortune is all written out in the stars, don't they?"

"They believe so in the old country," Fritz affirmed.

But Arthur only laughed at him. "You're thinking of Napoleon, Fritzey. He had a star that went out when he began to lose battles. I guess the stars don't keep any close tally on Sandtown folks."

We were speculating on how many times we could count a hundred before the evening star went down behind the corn fields, when someone cried, "There comes the moon, and it's as big as a cart wheel!"

We all jumped up to greet it as it swam over the bluffs behind us. It came up like a galleon in full sail; an enormous, barbaric thing, red as an angry heathen god.

"When the moon came up red like that, the Aztecs used to sacrifice their prisoners on the temple top," Percy announced.

"Go on, Perce. You got that out of *Golden Days*.[3] Do you believe that, Arthur?" I appealed.

Arthur answered, quite seriously: "Like as not. The moon was one of their gods. When my father was in Mexico City he saw the stone where they used to sacrifice their prisoners."

As we dropped down by the fire again some one asked whether the Mound-Builders were older than the Aztecs. When we once got upon the Mound-Builders we never willingly got away from them, and we were still conjecturing when we heard a loud splash in the water.

"Must have been a big cat jumping," said Fritz. "They do sometimes. They must see bugs in the dark. Look what a track the moon makes!"

There was a long, silvery streak on the water, and where the current fretted over a big log it boiled up like gold pieces.

"Suppose there ever *was* any gold hid away in this old river?" Fritz asked. He lay like a little brown Indian, close to the fire, his chin on his hand and his bare feet in the air. His brother laughed at him, but Arthur took his suggestion seriously.

"Some of the Spaniards thought there was gold up here somewhere. Seven cities chuck full of gold, they had it, and Coronado and his men came up to hunt it. The Spaniards were all over this country once."

Percy looked interested. "Was that before the Mormons went through?"

We all laughed at this.

"Long enough before. Before the Pilgrim Fathers, Perce. Maybe they came along this very river. They always followed the watercourses."

"I wonder where this river really does begin?" Tip mused. That was an old and a favorite mystery which the map did not clearly explain. On the map the little black line stopped somewhere in western Kansas; but since rivers generally rose in mountains, it was only reasonable to suppose that ours came from the Rockies. Its destination, we knew, was the Missouri, and the Hassler boys always maintained that we could embark at Sandtown in floodtime, follow our noses, and eventually arrive at New Orleans. Now they took up their old argument. "If us boys had grit enough to try it, it wouldn't take no time to get to Kansas City and St. Joe."

We began to talk about the places we wanted to go to. The Hassler boys wanted to see the stockyards in Kansas City, and Percy wanted to see a big store in Chicago. Arthur was interlocutor and did not betray himself.

"Now it's your turn, Tip."

Tip rolled over on his elbow and poked the fire, and his eyes looked shyly out of his queer, tight little face. "My place is awful far away. My Uncle Bill told me about it."

Tip's Uncle Bill was a wanderer, bitten with mining fever, who had drifted into Sandtown with a broken arm, and when it was well had drifted out again.

"Where is it?"

"Aw, it's down in New Mexico somewheres. There aren't no railroads or anything. You have to go on mules, and you run out of water before you get there and have to drink canned tomatoes."

"Well, go on, kid. What's it like when you do get there?"

Tip sat up and excitedly began his story.

"There's a big red rock[4] there that goes right up out of the sand for about nine hundred feet. The country's flat all around it, and this here rock goes up all by itself, like a monument. They call it the Enchanted Bluff down there, because no white man has ever been on top of it. The sides are smooth rock, and straight up, like a wall. The Indians say that hundreds of years ago, before the Spaniards came, there was a village away up there in the air. The tribe that lived there had some sort of steps, made out of wood and bark, hung down over the face of the bluff, and the braves went down to hunt and carried water up in big jars swung on their backs. They kept a big supply of water and dried meat up there, and never went down except to hunt. They were a peaceful tribe that made cloth and pottery, and they went up there to get out of the wars. You see, they could pick off any war party that tried to get up their little steps. The Indians say they were a handsome people, and they had some sort of queer religion. Uncle Bill thinks they were Cliff-Dwellers who had got into trouble and left home. They weren't fighters, anyhow.

"One time the braves were down hunting and an awful storm came up—a kind of waterspout—and when they got back to their rock they found their little staircase had been all broken to pieces, and only a few steps were left hanging away up in the air. While they were camped at the foot of the rock, wondering what to do, a war party from the north came along and massacred 'em to a man, with all the old folks and women looking on from the rock. Then the war party went on south and left the village to get down the best way they could. Of course they never got down. They starved to death up there, and when the war party came back on their way north, they could hear the children crying from the edge of the bluff where they had crawled out, but they didn't see a sign of a grown Indian, and nobody has ever been up there since."

We exclaimed at this dolorous legend and sat up.

"There couldn't have been many people up there," Percy demurred. "How big is the top, Tip?"

"Oh, pretty big. Big enough so that the rock doesn't look nearly as tall as it is. The top's bigger than the base. The bluff is sort of worn away for several hundred feet up. That's one reason it's so hard to climb."

I asked how the Indians got up, in the first place.

"Nobody knows how they got up or when. A hunting party came along once and saw that there was a town up there, and that was all."

Otto rubbed his chin and looked thoughtful. "Of course there must be some way to get up there. Couldn't people get a rope over someway and pull a ladder up?"

Tip's little eyes were shining with excitement. "I know a way. Me and Uncle Bill talked it all over. There's a kind of rocket that would take a rope over—life-savers use 'em—and then you could hoist a rope ladder and peg it down at the bottom and make it tight with guy ropes on the other side. I'm going to climb that there bluff, and I've got it all planned out."

Fritz asked what he expected to find when he got up there.

"Bones, maybe, or the ruins of their town, or pottery, or some of their idols. There might be 'most anything up there. Anyhow, I want to see."

"Sure nobody else has been up there, Tip?" Arthur asked.

"Dead sure. Hardly anybody ever goes down there. Some hunters tried to cut steps in the rock once, but they didn't get higher than a man can reach. The Bluff's all red granite, and Uncle Bill thinks it's a boulder the glaciers left. It's a queer place, anyhow. Nothing but cactus and desert for hundreds of miles, and yet right under the Bluff there's good water and plenty of grass. That's why the bison used to go down there."

Suddenly we heard a scream above our fire, and jumped up to see a dark, slim bird floating southward far above us—a whooping crane, we knew by her cry and her long neck. We ran to the edge of the island, hoping we might see her alight, but she wavered southward along the rivercourse until we lost her. The Hassler boys declared that by the look of the heavens it must be after midnight, so we threw more wood on our fire, put on our jackets, and curled down in the warm sand. Several of us pretended to doze, but I fancy we were really thinking about Tip's Bluff and the extinct people. Over in the wood the ring doves were calling mournfully to one another, and once we heard a dog bark, far away. "Somebody getting into old Tommy's melon patch," Fritz murmured sleepily, but nobody answered him. By and by Percy spoke out of the shadows.

"Say, Tip, when you go down there will you take me with you?"

"Maybe."

"Suppose one of us beats you down there, Tip?"

"Whoever gets to the Bluff first has got to promise to tell the rest of us exactly what he finds," remarked one of the Hassler boys, and to this we all readily assented.

Somewhat reassured, I dropped off to sleep. I must have dreamed about a race for the Bluff, for I awoke in a kind of fear that other people were getting ahead of me and that I was losing my chance. I sat up in my damp clothes and looked at the other boys, who lay tumbled in uneasy attitudes about the dead fire. It was still dark, but the sky was blue with the last wonderful azure of night. The stars glistened like crystal globes, and trembled as if they shone through a depth of clear water. Even as I watched, they began to pale and the sky brightened. Day came suddenly, almost instantaneously. I turned for another look at the blue night, and it was gone. Everywhere the birds began to call, and all manner of little insects began to chirp and hop about in the willows. A breeze sprang up from the west and brought the heavy smell of ripened corn. The boys rolled over and shook themselves. We stripped and plunged into the river just as the sun came up over the windy bluffs.

When I came home to Sandtown at Christmas time, we skated out to our island and talked over the whole project of the Enchanted Bluff, renewing our resolution to find it.

* * *

Although that was twenty years ago, none of us have ever climbed the Enchanted Bluff. Percy Pound is a stockbroker in Kansas City and will go nowhere that his red touring car cannot carry him. Otto Hassler went on the railroad and lost his foot braking; after which he and Fritz succeeded their father as the town tailors.

Arthur sat about the sleepy little town all his life—he died before he was twenty-five. The last time I saw him, when I was home on one of my college vacations, he was sitting in a steamer chair under a cottonwood tree in the little yard behind one of the two Sandtown saloons. He was very untidy and his hand was not steady, but when he rose, unabashed, to greet me, his eyes were as clear and warm as ever. When I had talked with him for an hour and heard him laugh again, I wondered how it was that when Nature had taken such pains with a man, from his hands to the arch of his long foot, she had ever lost him in Sandtown. He joked about Tip Smith's Bluff, and declared he was going down there just as soon as the weather got cooler; he thought the Grand Canyon might be worth while, too.

I was perfectly sure when I left him that he would never get beyond the high plank fence and the comfortable shade of the cottonwood. And, indeed, it was under that very tree that he died one summer morning.

Tip Smith still talks about going to New Mexico. He married a slatternly, unthrifty country girl, has been much tied to a perambulator, and has grown stooped and gray from irregular meals and broken sleep. But the worst of his difficulties are now over, and he has, as he says, come into easy water. When I was last in Sandtown I walked home with him late one moonlight night, after he had balanced his cash and shut up his store. We took the long way around and sat down on the schoolhouse steps, and between us we quite revived the romance of the lone red rock and the extinct people. Tip insists that he still means to go down there, but he thinks now he will wait until his boy Bert is old enough to go with him. Bert has been let into the story, and thinks of nothing but the Enchanted Bluff.

First published in *Harper's*, CXVIII (April 1909), pp. 774–78, 780–81.

The Joy of Nelly Deane

NELL AND I WERE almost ready to go on for the last act of *Queen Esther*,[1] and we had for the moment got rid of our three patient dressers,[2] Mrs. Dow, Mrs. Freeze, and Mrs. Spinny. Nell was peering over my shoulder into the little cracked looking glass that Mrs. Dow had taken from its nail on her kitchen wall and brought down to the church under her shawl that morning. When she realized that we were alone, Nell whispered to me in the quick, fierce way she had:

"Say, Peggy, won't you go up and stay with me tonight? Scott Spinny's asked to take me home, and I don't want to walk up with him alone."

"I guess so, if you'll ask my mother."

"Oh, I'll fix her!" Nell laughed, with a toss of her head which meant that she usually got what she wanted, even from people much less tractable than my mother.

In a moment our tiring-women were back again. The three old ladies—at least they seemed old to us—fluttered about us, more agitated than we were ourselves. It seemed as though they would never leave off patting Nell and touching her up. They kept trying things this way and that, never able in the end to decide which way was best. They wouldn't hear to her using rouge, and as they powdered her neck and arms, Mrs. Freeze murmured that she hoped we wouldn't get into the habit of using such things. Mrs. Spinny divided her time between pulling up and tucking down the "illusion" that filled in the square neck of Nelly's dress. She didn't like things much low, she said; but after she had pulled it up, she stood back and looked at Nell thoughtfully through her glasses. While the excited girl was reaching for this and that, buttoning a slipper, pinning down a curl, Mrs. Spinny's smile softened more and more until, just before Esther made her entrance, the old lady tiptoed up to her and softly tucked the illusion down as far as it would go.

"She's so pink; it seems a pity not," she whispered apologetically to Mrs. Dow.

Every one admitted that Nelly was the prettiest girl in Riverbend, and the gayest—oh, the gayest! When she was not singing, she was laughing. When she was not laid up with a broken arm, the outcome of a foolhardy coasting feat, or suspended from school because she ran away at recess to go buggy-riding with Guy Franklin, she was sure to be up to mischief of some sort. Twice she broke through the ice and got soused in the river because she never looked where she skated or cared what happened so long as she went fast enough. After the second of these duckings our three dressers declared that she was trying to be a Baptist despite herself.

Mrs. Spinny and Mrs. Freeze and Mrs. Dow, who were always hovering about Nelly, often whispered to me their hope that she would eventually come into our church and not "go with the Methodists"; her family were Wesleyans. But to me these artless plans of theirs never wholly explained their watchful affection. They had good daughters themselves—except Mrs. Spinny, who had only the sullen Scott—and they loved their plain girls and thanked God for them. But they loved Nelly differently. They were proud of her pretty figure and yellow-brown eyes, which dilated so easily and sparkled with a kind of golden effervescence. They were always making pretty things for her, always coaxing her to come to the sewing circle, where she knotted her thread, and put in the wrong sleeve, and laughed and chattered and said a great many things that she should not have said, and somehow always warmed their hearts. I think they loved her for her unquenchable joy.

All the Baptist ladies liked Nell, even those who criticized her most severely, but the three who were first in fighting the battles of our little church, who held it together by their prayers and the labor of their hands, watched over her as they did over Mrs. Dow's century plant before it blossomed. They looked for her on Sunday morning and smiled at her as she hurried, always a little late, up to the choir. When she rose and stood behind the organ and sang "There Is a Green Hill," one could see Mrs. Dow and Mrs. Freeze settle back in their accustomed seats and look up at her as if she had just come from that hill and had brought them glad tidings.

It was because I sang contralto, or, as we said, alto, in the Baptist choir that Nell and I became friends. She was so gay and grown up, so busy with parties and dances and picnics, that I would scarcely have seen much of her had we not sung together. She liked me better than she did any of the older girls, who tried clumsily to be like her, and I felt almost as solicitous and admiring as did Mrs. Dow and Mrs. Spinny. I think even then I must have loved to see her bloom and glow, and I loved to hear her sing, in "The Ninety and Nine,"[3]

But one was out on the hills away

in her sweet, strong voice. Nell had never had a singing lesson, but she had sung from the time she could talk, and Mrs. Dow used fondly to say that it was singing so much that made her figure so pretty.

After I went into the choir it was found to be easier to get Nelly to choir practice. If I stopped outside her gate on my way to church and coaxed her, she usually laughed, ran in for her hat and jacket, and went along with me. The three old ladies fostered our friendship, and because I was "quiet," they esteemed me a good influence for Nelly. This view was propounded in a sewing-circle discussion and, leaking down to us through our mothers, greatly amused us. Dear old ladies! It was so manifestly for what Nell was that they loved her, and yet they were always looking for "influences" to change her.

The *Queen Esther* performance had cost us three months of hard practice, and it was not easy to keep Nell up to attending the tedious rehearsals. Some of the boys we knew were in the chorus of Assyrian youths, but the solo cast was made up of older people, and Nell found them very poky. We gave the cantata in the Baptist church on Christmas Eve, "to a crowded house," as the Riverbend *Messenger* truly chronicled. The country folk for miles about had come in through a deep snow, and their teams and wagons stood in a long row at the hitch-bars on each side of the church door. It was certainly Nelly's night, for however much the tenor—he was her schoolmaster, and naturally thought poorly of her—might try to eclipse her in his dolorous solos about the rivers of Babylon, there could be no doubt as to whom the people had come to hear —and to see.

After the performance was over, our fathers and mothers came back to the dressing rooms—the little rooms behind the baptistry where the candidates for baptism were robed—to congratulate us, and Nell persuaded my mother to let me go home with her. This arrangement may not have been wholly agreeable to Scott Spinny, who stood glumly waiting at the baptistry door; though I used to think he dogged Nell's steps not so much for any pleasure he got from being with her as for the pleasure of keeping other people away. Dear little Mrs. Spinny was perpetually in a state of humiliation on account of his bad manners, and she tried by a very special tenderness to make up to Nelly for the remissness of her ungracious son.

Scott was a spare, muscular fellow, good-looking, but with a face so set and dark that I used to think it very like the castings he sold. He was taciturn and domineering, and Nell rather liked to provoke him. Her father was so easy with her that she seemed to enjoy being ordered about now and then. That night, when every one was praising her and telling her how well she sang and how pretty she looked, Scott only said, as we came out of the dressing room:

"Have you got your high shoes on?"

"No; but I've got rubbers on over my low ones. Mother doesn't care."

"Well, you just go back and put 'em on as fast as you can."

Nell made a face at him and ran back, laughing. Her mother, fat, comfortable Mrs. Deane, was immensely amused at this.

"That's right, Scott," she chuckled. "You can do enough more with her than I can. She walks right over me an' Jud."

Scott grinned. If he was proud of Nelly, the last thing he wished to do was to show it. When she came back he began to nag again.

"What are you going to do with all those flowers? They'll freeze stiff as pokers."

"Well, there won't none of *your* flowers freeze, Scott Spinny, so there!" Nell snapped. She had the best of him that time, and the Assyrian youths rejoiced. They were most of them high-school boys, and the poorest of them had "chipped in" and sent all the way to Denver for Queen Esther's flowers. There were bouquets from half a dozen townspeople, too, but none from Scott. Scott was a prosperous hardware merchant and notoriously penurious, though he saved his face, as the boys said, by giving liberally to the church.

"There's no use freezing the fool things, anyhow. You get me some newspapers, and I'll wrap 'em up." Scott took from his pocket a folded copy of the Riverbend *Messenger* and began laboriously to wrap up one of the bouquets. When we left the church door he bore three large newspaper bundles, carrying them as carefully as if they had been so many newly frosted wedding cakes, and left Nell and me to shift for ourselves as we floundered along the snow-burdened sidewalk.

Although it was after midnight, lights were shining from many of the little wooden houses, and the roofs and shrubbery were so deep in snow that Riverbend looked as if it had been tucked down into a warm bed. The companies of people, all coming from church, tramping this way and that toward their homes and calling "Good night" and "Merry Christmas" as they parted company, all seemed to us very unusual and exciting.

When we got home, Mrs. Deane had a cold supper ready, and Jud Deane had already taken off his shoes and fallen to on his fried chicken and pie. He was so proud of his pretty daughter that he must give her her Christmas presents then and there, and he went into the sleeping chamber behind the dining room and from the depths of his wife's closet brought out a short sealskin jacket and a round cap and made Nelly put them on.

Mrs. Deane, who sat busy between a plate of spice cake and a tray piled with her famous whipped cream tarts, laughed inordinately at his behavior.

"Ain't he worse than any kid you ever see? He's been running to that closet like a cat shut away from her kittens. I wonder Nell ain't caught on before this. I did think he'd make out now to keep 'em till Christmas morning; but he's never made out to keep anything yet."

That was true enough, and fortunately Jud's inability to keep anything seemed always to present a highly humorous aspect to his wife. Mrs. Deane put her heart into her cooking, and said that so long as a man was a good provider she had no cause to complain. Other people were not so charitable toward Jud's failing. I remember how many strictures were passed upon that little sealskin and how he was censured for his extravagance. But what a public-spirited thing, after all, it was for him to do! How, the winter through, we all enjoyed seeing Nell skating on the river or running about the town with the brown collar turned up about her bright cheeks and her hair blowing out from under the round cap! "No seal," Mrs. Dow said, "would have begrudged it to her. Why should we?" This was at the sewing circle, when the new coat was under grave discussion.

At last Nelly and I got upstairs and undressed, and the pad of Jud's slippered feet about the kitchen premises—where he was carrying up from the cellar things that might freeze—ceased. He called "Good night, daughter," from the foot of the stairs, and the house grew quiet. But one is not a prima donna the first time for nothing, and it seemed as if we could not go to bed. Our light must have burned long after every other in Riverbend was out. The muslin curtains of Nell's bed were drawn back; Mrs. Deane had turned down the white counterpane and taken off the shams and smoothed the pillows for us. But their fair plumpness offered no temptation to two such hot young heads. We could not let go of life even for a little while. We sat and talked in Nell's cozy room, where there was a tiny, white fur rug—the only one in Riverbend—before the bed; and there were white sash curtains, and the prettiest little desk and dressing table I had ever seen. It was a warm, gay little room, flooded all day long with sunlight from east and south windows that had climbing roses all about them in summer. About the dresser were photographs of adoring high-school boys; and one of Guy Franklin, much groomed and barbered, in a dress coat and a boutonnière. I never liked to see that photograph there. The home boys looked properly modest and bashful on the dresser, but he seemed to be staring impudently all the time.

I knew nothing definite against Guy, but in Riverbend all "traveling men" were considered worldly and wicked. He traveled for a Chicago dry-goods firm, and our fathers didn't like him because he put extravagant ideas into our mothers' heads. He had very smooth and flattering ways, and he introduced into our simple community a great variety of perfumes and scented soaps, and he always reminded me of the merchants in Caesar, who brought into Gaul "those things which effeminate the mind," as we translated that delightfully easy passage.

Nell was sitting before the dressing table in her nightgown, holding the new fur coat and rubbing her cheek against it, when I saw a sudden gleam of tears in her eyes. "You know, Peggy," she said in her quick, impetuous way, "this makes me feel bad. I've got a secret from my daddy."

I can see her now, so pink and eager, her brown hair in two springy braids down her back, and her eyes shining with tears and with something even softer and more tremulous.

"I'm engaged, Peggy," she whispered, "really and truly."

She leaned forward, unbuttoning her nightgown, and there on her breast, hung by a little gold chain about her neck, was a diamond ring—Guy Franklin's solitaire; every one in Riverbend knew it well.

"I'm going to live in Chicago, and take singing lessons, and go to operas, and do all those nice things—oh, everything! I know you don't like him, Peggy, but you know you *are* a kid. You'll see how it is yourself when you grow up. He's so *different* from our boys, and he's just terribly in love with me. And then, Peggy,"—flushing all down over her soft shoulders,—"I'm awfully fond of him, too. Awfully."

"Are you, Nell, truly?" I whispered. She seemed so changed to me by the warm light in her eyes and that delicate suffusion of color. I felt as I did when I got up early on picnic mornings in summer, and saw the dawn come up in the breathless sky above the river meadows and make all the corn fields golden.

"Sure I do, Peggy; don't look so solemn. It's nothing to look that way about, kid. It's nice." She threw her arms about me suddenly and hugged me.

"I hate to think about your going so far away from us all, Nell."

"Oh, you'll love to come and visit me. Just you wait."

She began breathlessly to go over things Guy Franklin had told her about Chicago, until I seemed to see it all looming up out there under the stars that kept watch over our little sleeping town. We had neither of us ever been to a city, but we knew what it would be like. We heard it throbbing like great engines, and calling to us, that faraway world. Even after we had opened the windows and scurried into bed, we seemed to feel a pulsation across all the miles of snow. The winter silence trembled with it, and the air was full of something new that seemed to break over us in soft waves. In that snug, warm little bed I had a sense of imminent change and danger. I was somehow afraid for Nelly when I heard her breathing so quickly beside me, and I put my arm about her protectingly as we drifted toward sleep.

* * *

In the following spring we were both graduated from the Riverbend high school, and I went away to college. My family moved to Denver, and during the next four years I heard very little of Nelly Deane. My life was crowded with new people and new experiences, and I am afraid I held her little in mind. I heard indirectly that Jud Deane had lost what little property he owned in a luckless venture in Cripple Creek, and that he had been able to keep his house in Riverbend only through the clemency of his creditors. Guy Franklin had his route changed and did not go to Riverbend any more. He married the daughter of a rich cattleman out near Long Pine, and ran a dry-goods store of his own. Mrs. Dow wrote me a long letter about once a year, and in one of these she told me that Nelly was teaching in the sixth grade in the Riverbend school.

> Dear Nelly does not like teaching very well. The children try her, and she is so pretty it seems a pity for her to be tied down to uncongenial employment. Scott is still very attentive,

and I have noticed him look up at the window of Nelly's room in a very determined way as he goes home to dinner. Scott continues prosperous; he has made money during these hard times and now owns both our hardware stores. He is close, but a very honorable fellow. Nelly seems to hold off, but I think Mrs. Spinny has hopes. Nothing would please her more. If Scott were more careful about his appearance, it would help. He of course gets black about his business, and Nelly, you know, is very dainty. People do say his mother does his courting for him, she is so eager. If only Scott does not turn out hard and penurious like his father! We must all have our schooling in this life, but I don't want Nelly's to be too severe. She is a dear girl, and keeps her color.

Mrs. Dow's own schooling had been none too easy. Her husband had long been crippled with rheumatism, and was bitter and faultfinding. Her daughters had married poorly, and one of her sons had fallen into evil ways. But her letters were always cheerful, and in one of them she gently remonstrated with me because I "seemed inclined to take a sad view of life."

In the winter vacation of my senior year I stopped on my way home to visit Mrs. Dow. The first thing she told me when I got into her old buckboard at the station was that "Scott had at last prevailed," and that Nelly was to marry him in the spring. As a preliminary step, Nelly was about to join the Baptist church. "Just think, you will be here for her baptizing! How that will please Nelly! She is to be immersed tomorrow night."

I met Scott Spinny in the post office that morning and he gave me a hard grip with one black hand. There was something grim and saturnine about his powerful body and bearded face and his strong, cold hands. I wondered what perverse fate had driven him for eight years to dog the footsteps of a girl whose charm was due to qualities naturally distasteful to him. It still seems strange to me that in easygoing Riverbend, where there were so many boys who could have lived contentedly enough with my little grasshopper, it was the pushing ant who must have her and all her careless ways.

By a kind of unformulated etiquette one did not call upon candidates for baptism on the day of the ceremony, so I had my first glimpse of Nelly that evening. The baptistry was a cemented pit directly under the pulpit rostrum, over which we had our stage when we sang *Queen Esther*. I sat through the sermon somewhat nervously. After the minister, in his long, black gown, had gone down into the water and the choir had finished singing, the door from the dressing room opened, and, led by one of the deacons, Nelly came down the steps into the pool. Oh, she looked so little and meek and chastened! Her white cashmere robe clung about her, and her brown hair was brushed straight back and hung in two soft braids from a little head bent humbly. As she stepped down into the water I shivered with the cold of it, and I remembered sharply how much I had loved her. She went down until the water was well above her waist, and stood white and small, with her hands crossed on her breast, while the minister said the words about being buried with Christ in baptism. Then, lying in his arm, she disappeared under the dark water. "It will be like that when she dies," I thought, and a quick pain caught my heart. The choir began to sing "Washed in the Blood of the Lamb" as she rose again, the door behind the baptistry opened, revealing those three dear guardians, Mrs. Dow, Mrs. Freeze, and Mrs. Spinny, and she went up into their arms.

I went to see Nell next day, up in the little room of many memories. Such a sad, sad visit! She seemed changed—a little embarrassed and quietly despairing. We talked of many of the old Riverbend girls and boys, but she did not mention Guy Franklin or Scott Spinny, except to say that her father had got work in Scott's hardware store. She begged me, putting her hands on my shoulders with something of her old impulsiveness, to come and stay a few days with her. But I was afraid—afraid of what she might tell me and of what I might say. When I sat in that room with all her trinkets, the foolish harvest of her girlhood, lying about, and the white curtains and the little white rug, I thought of Scott Spinny with positive terror and could feel his hard grip on my hand again. I made the best excuse I could about having to hurry on to Denver; but she gave me one quick look, and her eyes ceased to plead. I saw that she understood me perfectly. We had known each other so well. Just once, when I got up to go and had trouble with my veil, she laughed her old merry laugh and told me there were some things I would never learn, for all my schooling.

The next day, when Mrs. Dow drove me down to the station to catch the morning train for Denver, I saw Nelly hurrying to school with several books under her arm. She had been working up her lessons at home, I thought. She was never quick at her books, dear Nell.

* * *

It was ten years before I again visited Riverbend. I had been in Rome for a long time, and had fallen into bitter homesickness. One morning, sitting among the dahlias and asters that bloom so bravely upon those gigantic heaps of earth-red ruins that were once the palaces of the Caesars, I broke the seal of one of Mrs. Dow's long yearly letters. It brought so much sad news that I resolved then and there to go home to Riverbend, the only place that had ever really been home to me. Mrs. Dow wrote me that her husband, after years of illness, had died in the cold spell last March. "So good and patient toward the last," she wrote, "and so afraid of giving extra trouble." There was another thing she saved until the last. She wrote on and on, dear woman, about new babies and village improvements, as if she could not bear to tell me; and then it came:

> You will be sad to hear that two months ago our dear Nelly left us. It was a terrible blow to us all. I cannot write about it yet, I fear. I wake up every morning feeling that I ought to go to her. She went three days after her little boy was born. The baby is a fine child and will live, I think, in spite of everything. He and her little girl, now eight years old, whom she named Margaret, after you, have gone to Mrs. Spinny's. She loves them more than if they were her own. It seems as if already they had made her quite young again. I wish you could see Nelly's children.

Ah, that was what I wanted, to see Nelly's children! The wish came aching from my heart along with the bitter homesick tears; along with a quick, torturing recollection that flashed upon me, as

I looked about and tried to collect myself, of how we two had sat in our sunny seat in the corner of the old bare schoolroom one September afternoon and learned the names of the seven hills together. In that place, at that moment, after so many years, how it all came back to me—the warm sun on my back, the chattering girl beside me, the curly hair, the laughing yellow eyes, the stubby little finger on the page! I felt as if even then, when we sat in the sun with our heads together, it was all arranged, written out like a story, that at this moment I should be sitting among the crumbling bricks and drying grass, and she should be lying in the place I knew so well, on that green hill far away.

* * *

Mrs. Dow sat with her Christmas sewing in the familiar sitting room, where the carpet and the wallpaper and the tablecover had all faded into soft, dull colors, and even the chromo of Hagar and Ishmael[4] had been toned to the sobriety of age. In the bay window the tall wire flowerstand still bore its little terraces of potted plants, and the big fuchsia and the Martha Washington geranium had blossomed for Christmastide. Mrs. Dow herself did not look greatly changed to me. Her hair, thin ever since I could remember it, was now quite white, but her spare, wiry little person had all its old activity, and her eyes gleamed with the old friendliness behind her silver-bowed glasses. Her gray house dress seemed just like those she used to wear when I ran in after school to take her angelfood cake down to the church supper.

The house sat on a hill, and from behind the geraniums I could see pretty much all of Riverbend, tucked down in the soft snow, and the air above was full of big, loose flakes, falling from a gray sky which betokened settled weather. Indoors the hard-coal burner made a tropical temperature, and glowed a warm orange from its isinglass[5] sides. We sat and visited, the two of us, with a great sense of comfort and completeness. I had reached Riverbend only that morning, and Mrs. Dow, who had been haunted by thoughts of shipwreck and suffering upon wintry seas, kept urging me to draw nearer to the fire and suggesting incidental refreshment. We had chattered all through the winter morning and most of the afternoon, taking up one after another of the Riverbend girls and boys, and agreeing that we had reason to be well satisfied with most of them. Finally, after a long pause in which I had listened to the contented ticking of the clock and the crackle of the coal, I put the question I had until then held back:

"And now, Mrs. Dow, tell me about the one we loved best of all. Since I got your letter I've thought of her every day. Tell me all about Scott and Nelly."

The tears flashed behind her glasses, and she smoothed the little pink bag on her knee.

"Well, dear, I'm afraid Scott proved to be a hard man, like his father. But we must remember that Nelly always had Mrs. Spinny. I never saw anything like the love there was between those two. After Nelly lost her own father and mother, she looked to Mrs. Spinny for everything. When Scott was too unreasonable, his mother could 'most always prevail upon him. She never lifted a hand to fight her own battles with Scott's father, but she was never afraid to speak up for Nelly. And then Nelly took great comfort of her little girl. Such a lovely child!"

"Had she been very ill before the little baby came?"

"No, Margaret; I'm afraid 't was all because they had the wrong doctor. I feel confident that either Doctor Tom or Doctor Jones could have brought her through. But, you see, Scott had offended them both, and they'd stopped trading at his store, so he would have young Doctor Fox, a boy just out of college and a stranger. He got scared and didn't know what to do. Mrs. Spinny felt he wasn't doing right, so she sent for Mrs. Freeze and me. It seemed like Nelly had got discouraged. Scott would move into their big new house before the plastering was dry, and though 't was summer, she had taken a terrible cold that seemed to have drained her, and she took no interest in fixing the place up. Mrs. Spinny had been down with her back again and wasn't able to help, and things was just anyway. We won't talk about that, Margaret; I think 't would hurt Mrs. Spinny to have you know. She nearly died of mortification when she sent for us, and blamed her poor back. We did get Nelly fixed up nicely before she died. I prevailed upon Doctor Tom to come in at the last, and it 'most broke his heart. 'Why,

Mis' Dow,' he said, 'if you'd only have come and told me how 't was, I'd have come and carried her right off in my arms.' "

"Oh, Mrs. Dow," I cried, "then it needn't have been?"

Mrs. Dow dropped her needle and clasped her hands quickly. "We mustn't look at it that way, dear," she said tremulously and a little sternly; "we mustn't let ourselves. We must just feel that our Lord wanted her *then*, and took her to Himself. When it was all over, she did look so like a child of God, young and trusting, like she did on her baptizing night, you remember?"

I felt that Mrs. Dow did not want to talk any more about Nelly then, and, indeed, I had little heart to listen; so I told her I would go for a walk, and suggested that I might stop at Mrs. Spinny's to see the children.

Mrs. Dow looked up thoughtfully at the clock. "I doubt if you'll find little Margaret there now. It's half-past four, and she'll have been out of school an hour and more. She'll be most likely coasting on Lupton's Hill. She usually makes for it with her sled the minute she is out of the schoolhouse door. You know, it's the old hill where you all used to slide. If you stop in at the church about six o'clock, you'll likely find Mrs. Spinny there with the baby. I promised to go down and help Mrs. Freeze finish up the tree, and Mrs. Spinny said she'd run in with the baby, if 't wasn't too bitter. She won't leave him alone with the Swede girl. She's like a young woman with her first."

Lupton's Hill was at the other end of town, and when I got there the dusk was thickening, drawing blue shadows over the snowy fields. There were perhaps twenty children creeping up the hill or whizzing down the packed sled track. When I had been watching them for some minutes, I heard a lusty shout, and a little red sled shot past me into the deep snowdrift beyond. The child was quite buried for a moment, then she struggled out and stood dusting the snow from her short coat and red woolen comforter. She wore a brown fur cap, which was too big for her and of an old-fashioned shape, such as girls wore long ago, but I would have known her without the cap. Mrs. Dow had said a beautiful child, and there would not be two like this in Riverbend. She was off before I had time to speak to her, going up the hill at a trot, her sturdy little legs plowing through the trampled snow. When she reached the top she never paused to take breath, but threw herself upon her sled and came down with a whoop that was quenched only by the deep drift at the end.

"Are you Margaret Spinny?" I asked as she struggled out in a cloud of snow.

"Yes, 'm." She approached me with frank curiosity, pulling her little sled behind her. "Are you the strange lady staying at Mrs. Dow's?" I nodded, and she began to look my clothes over with respectful interest.

"Your grandmother is to be at the church at six o'clock, isn't she?"

"Yes, 'm."

"Well, suppose we walk up there now. It's nearly six, and all the other children are going home." She hesitated, and looked up at the faintly gleaming track on the hill slope. "Do you want another slide? Is that it?" I asked.

"Do you mind?" she asked shyly.

"No. I'll wait for you. Take your time; don't run."

Two little boys were still hanging about the slide, and they cheered her as she came down, her comforter streaming in the wind.

"Now," she announced, getting up out of the drift, "I'll show you where the church is."

"Shall I tie your comforter again?"

"No, 'm, thanks. I'm plenty warm." She put her mittened hand confidingly in mine and trudged along beside me.

Mrs. Dow must have heard us tramping up the snowy steps of the church, for she met us at the door. Every one had gone except the old ladies. A kerosene lamp flickered over the Sunday school chart, with the lesson-picture of the Wise Men, and the little barrel stove threw out a deep glow over the three white heads that bent above the baby. There the three friends sat, patting him, and smoothing his dress, and playing with his hands, which made theirs look so brown.

"You ain't seen nothing finer in all your travels," said Mrs. Spinny, and they all laughed.

They showed me his full chest and how strong his back was;

had me feel the golden fuzz on his head, and made him look at me with his round, bright eyes. He laughed and reared himself in my arms as I took him up and held him close to me. He was so warm and tingling with life, and he had the flush of new beginnings, of the new morning and the new rose. He seemed to have come so lately from his mother's heart! It was as if I held her youth and all her young joy. As I put my cheek down against his, he spied a pink flower in my hat, and making a gleeful sound, he lunged at it with both fists.

"Don't let him spoil it," murmured Mrs. Spinny. "He loves color so—like Nelly."

First published in *Century*, LXXXII (October 1911), pp. 859–67.

Behind the Singer Tower

It was a hot, close night in May, the night after the burning of the Mont Blanc Hotel, and some half dozen of us who had been thrown together, more or less, during that terrible day, accepted Fred Hallet's invitation to go for a turn in his launch, which was tied up in the North River. We were all tired and unstrung and heartsick, and the quiet of the night and the coolness on the water relaxed our tense nerves a little. None of us talked much as we slid down the river and out into the bay. We were in a kind of stupor. When the launch ran out into the harbor, we saw an Atlantic liner come steaming up the big sea road. She passed so near to us that we could see her crowded steerage decks.

"It's the *Re di Napoli*," said Johnson of the *Herald*. "She's going to land her first cabin passengers tonight, evidently. Those people are terribly proud of their new docks in the North River; feel they've come up in the world."

We ruffled easily along through the bay, looking behind us at the wide circle of lights that rim the horizon from east to west and from west to east, all the way round except for that narrow, much-traveled highway, the road to the open sea. Running a launch about the harbor at night is a good deal like bicycling among the motors on Fifth Avenue. That night there was probably no less activity than usual; the turtle-backed ferry boats swung to and fro, the tugs screamed and panted beside the freight cars they were towing on barges, the Coney Island boats threw out their streams of light and faded away. Boats of every shape and purpose went about their business and made noise enough as they did it, doubtless. But to us, after what we had been seeing and hearing all day long, the place seemed unnaturally quiet and the night unnaturally black. There was a brooding mournfulness over the harbor, as if the ghost of helplessness and terror were abroad in the darkness. One felt a solemnity in the misty spring sky where only a few stars shone, pale and far apart, and in the sighs of the heavy black water that rolled up into the light. The city itself, as we looked back at it, seemed enveloped in a tragic self-consciousness. Those incredible towers of stone and steel seemed, in the mist, to be grouped confusedly together, as if they were confronting each other with a question. They looked positively lonely, like the great trees left after a forest is cut away. One might fancy that the city was protesting, was asserting its helplessness, its irresponsibility for its physical conformation, for the direction it had taken. It was an irregular parallelogram pressed between two hemispheres, and, like any other solid squeezed in a vise, it shot upward.

There were six of us in the launch: two newspapermen—Johnson and myself; Fred Hallet, the engineer, and one of his draftsmen; a lawyer from the District Attorney's office; and Zablowski, a young Jewish doctor from the Rockefeller Institute. We did not talk; there was only one thing to talk about, and we had had enough of that. Before we left town the death list of the Mont Blanc had gone above three hundred.

The Mont Blanc was the complete expression of the New York idea in architecture; a thirty-five story hotel which made the Plaza look modest. Its prices, like its proportions, as the newspapers had so often asseverated, outscaled everything in the known world. And it was still standing there, massive and brutally unconcerned, only a little blackened about its thousand windows and with the foolish fire escapes in its court melted down. About the fire itself nobody knew much. It had begun on the twelfth story, broken out through the windows, shot up long streamers that had gone in at the windows above, and so on up to the top. A high wind and much upholstery and oiled wood had given it incredible speed.

On the night of the fire the hotel was full of people from everywhere, and by morning half a dozen trusts had lost their presidents, two states had lost their governors, and one of the great

European powers had lost its ambassador. So many businesses had been disorganized that Wall Street had shut down for the day. They had been snuffed out, these important men, as lightly as the casual guests who had come to town to spend money, or as the pampered opera singers who had returned from an overland tour and were waiting to sail on Saturday. The lists were still vague, for whether the victims had jumped or not, identification was difficult, and, in either case, they had met with obliteration, absolute effacement, as when a drop of water falls into the sea.

Out of all I had seen that day, one thing kept recurring to me; perhaps because it was so little in the face of a destruction so vast. In the afternoon, when I was going over the building with the firemen, I found, on the ledge of a window on the fifteenth floor, a man's hand snapped off at the wrist as cleanly as if it had been taken off by a cutlass—he had thrown out his arm in falling.

It had belonged to Graziani, the tenor, who had occupied a suite on the thirty-second floor. We identified it by a little-finger ring, which had been given to him by the German Emperor. Yes, it was the same hand. I had seen it often enough when he placed it so confidently over his chest as he began his "Celeste Aida," or when he lifted—much too often, alas!—his little glasses of white arrack[1] at Martin's. When he toured the world he must have whatever was most costly and most characteristic in every city; in New York he had the thirty-second floor, poor fellow! He had plunged from there toward the cobwebby life nets stretched five hundred feet below on the asphalt. Well, at any rate, he would never drag out an obese old age in the English country house he had built near Naples.

Heretofore fires in fireproof buildings of many stories had occurred only in factory lofts, and the people who perished in them, fur workers and garment workers, were obscure for more reasons than one; most of them bore names unpronounceable to the American tongue; many of them had no kinsmen, no history, no record anywhere.

But we realized that, after the burning of the Mont Blanc, the New York idea would be called to account by every state in the Union, by all the great capitals of the world. Never before, in a single day, had so many of the names that feed and furnish the newspapers appeared in their columns all together, and for the last time.

In New York the matter of height was spoken of jocularly and triumphantly. The very window cleaners always joked about it as they buckled themselves fast outside your office in the forty-fifth story of the Wertheimer tower, though the average for window cleaners, who, for one reason or another, dropped to the pavement was something over one a day. In a city with so many millions of windows that was not perhaps an unreasonable percentage. But we felt that the Mont Blanc disaster would bring our particular type of building into unpleasant prominence, as the cholera used to make Naples and the conditions of life there too much a matter of discussion, or as the earthquake of 1906 gave such undesirable notoriety to the affairs of San Francisco.

For once we were actually afraid of being too much in the public eye, of being overadvertised. As I looked at the great incandescent signs along the Jersey shore, blazing across the night the names of beer and perfumes and corsets, it occurred to me that, after all, that kind of thing could be overdone; a single name, a single question, could be blazed too far. Our whole scheme of life and progress and profit was perpendicular.

There was nothing for us but height. We were whipped up the ladder. We depended upon the ever-growing possibilities of girders and rivets as Holland depends on her dikes.

"Did you ever notice," Johnson remarked when we were about halfway across to Staten Island, "what a Jewy-looking thing the Singer Tower is when it's lit up? The fellow who placed those incandescents must have had a sense of humor. It's exactly like the Jewish high priest in the old Bible dictionaries."

He pointed back, outlining with his forefinger the jeweled miter, the high, sloping shoulders, and the hands pressed together in the traditional posture of prayer.

Zablowski, the young Jewish doctor, smiled and shook his head. He was a very handsome fellow, with sad, thoughtful eyes, and we were all fond of him, especially Hallet, who was always teasing him. "No, it's not Semitic, Johnson," he said. "That high-peaked turban is more apt to be Persian. He's a Magi or a fire-worshiper of some sort, your high priest. When you get nearer he looks like a Buddha, with two bright rings in his ears."

Zablowski pointed with his cigar toward the blurred Babylonian heights crowding each other on the narrow tip of the island. Among them rose the colossal figure of the Singer Tower, watching over the city and the harbor like a presiding Genius. He had come out of Asia quietly in the night, no one knew just when or how, and the Statue of Liberty, holding her feeble taper in the gloom off to our left, was but an archeological survival.

"Who could have foreseen that she, in her high-mindedness, would ever spawn a great heathen idol like that?" Hallet exclaimed. "But that's what idealism comes to in the end, Zablowski."

Zablowski laughed mournfully. "What did you expect, Hallet? You've used us for your ends—waste for your machine, and now you talk about infection. Of course we brought germs from over there," he nodded toward the northeast.

"Well, you're all here at any rate, and I won't argue with you about all that tonight," said Hallet wearily. "The fact is," he went on as he lit a cigar and settled deeper into his chair, "when we met the *Re di Napoli* back there, she set me thinking. She recalled something that happened when I was a boy just out of Tech; when I was working under Merryweather on the Mont Blanc foundation."

We all looked up. Stanley Merryweather was the most successful manipulator of structural steel in New York, and Hallet was the most intelligent; the enmity between them was one of the legends of the Engineers' Society.

Hallet saw our interest and smiled. "I suppose you've heard yarns about why Merryweather and I don't even pretend to get on. People say we went to school together and then had a terrible row of some sort. The fact is, we never did get on, and back there in the foundation work of the Mont Blanc our ways definitely parted. You know how Merryweather happened to get going? He was the only nephew of old Hughie Macfarlane, and Macfarlane was the pioneer in steel construction. He dreamed the dream. When he was a lad working for the Pennsylvania Bridge Company, he saw Manhattan just as it towers there tonight. Well, Macfarlane was aging and he had no children, so he took his sister's son to make an engineer of him. Macfarlane was a thoroughgoing Scotch Presbyterian, sound Pittsburgh stock, but his sister had committed an indiscretion. She had married a professor of languages in a theological seminary out there; a professor who knew too much about some Oriental tongues I needn't name to be altogether safe. It didn't show much in the old professor, who looked like a Baptist preacher except for his short, thick hands, and of course it is very much veiled in Stanley. When he came up to the Massachusetts Tech he was a big, handsome boy, but there was something in his moist, bright blue eye—well, something that you would recognize, Zablowski."

Zablowski chuckled and inclined his head delicately forward.

Hallet continued: "Yes, in Stanley Merryweather there were racial characteristics.[2] He was handsome and jolly and glitteringly frank and almost insultingly cordial, and yet he was never really popular. He was quick and superficial, built for high speed and a light load. He liked to come it over people, but when you had him, he always crawled. Didn't seem to hurt him one bit to back down. If you made a fool of him tonight—well, 'Tomorrow's another day,' he'd say lightly, and tomorrow he'd blossom out in a new suit of clothes and a necktie of some unusual weave and haunting color. He had the feeling for color and texture. The worst of it was that, as truly as I'm sitting here, he never bore a grudge toward the fellow who'd called his bluff and shown him up for a lush growth; no ill feeling at all, Zablowski. He simply didn't know what that meant—"

Hallet's sentence trailed and hung wistfully in the air, while Zablowski put his hand penitently to his forehead.

"Well, Merryweather was quick and he had plenty of spurt and a taking manner, and he didn't know there had ever been such a thing as modesty or reverence in the world. He got all round the old man, and old Mac was perfectly foolish about him. It was always: 'Is it well with the young man Absalom?' Stanley was a year ahead of me in school, and when he came out of Tech the old man took him right into the business. He married a burgeoning Jewish beauty, Fanny Reizenstein, the daughter of the importer, and he hung her with the jewels of the East until she looked like the Song of Solomon done into motion pictures. I will say for Stanley that he never pretended that anything stronger than Botticelli hurt his eyes. He opened like a lotus flower to the sun and made a streak of color, even in New York. Stanley always felt that Boston hadn't done well by him, and he enjoyed throwing jobs to old Tech men. 'Largess, largess, Lord Marmion, all as he lighted down.' When they began breaking ground for the Mont Blanc I applied for a job because I wanted experience in deep foundation work. Stanley beamed at me across his mirror-finish mahogany and offered me something better, but it was foundation work I wanted, so early in the spring I went into the hole with a gang of twenty dagos.[3]

"It was an awful summer, the worst New York can do in the way of heat, and I guess that's the worst in the world, excepting India maybe. We sweated away, I and my twenty dagos, and I learned a good deal—more than I ever meant to. Now there was one of those men I liked, and it's about him I must tell you. His name was Caesaro, but he was so little that the other dagos in the hole called him Caesarino, Little Caesar. He was from the island of Ischia,[4] and I had been there when a young lad with my sister who was ill. I knew the particular goat track Caesarino hailed from, and maybe I had seen him there among all the swarms of eager, panting little animals that roll around in the dust and somehow worry through famine and fever and earthquake, with such a curiously hot spark of life in them and such delight in being allowed to live at all.

"Caesarino's father was dead and his older brother was married and had a little swarm of his own to look out for. Caesarino and the next two boys were coral divers and went out with the fleet twice a year; when they were at home they worked about by the day in the vineyards. He couldn't remember ever having had any clothes on in summer until he was ten; spent all his time swimming and diving and sprawling about among the nets on the beach. I've seen 'em, those wild little water dogs; look like little seals with their round eyes and their hair always dripping. Caesarino thought he could make more money in New York than he made diving for coral, and he was the mainstay of the family. There were ever so many little water dogs after him; his father had done the best he could to insure the perpetuity of his breed before he went under the lava to begin all over again by helping to make the vines grow in that marvelously fruitful volcanic soil. Little Caesar came to New York, and that is where we begin.

"He was one of the twenty crumpled, broken little men who worked with me down in that big hole. I first noticed him because he was so young, and so eager to please, and because he was so especially frightened. Wouldn't you be at all this terrifying, complicated machinery, after sun and happy nakedness and a goat track on a volcanic island? Haven't you ever noticed how, when a dago is hurt on the railroad and they trundle him into the station on a truck, another dago always runs alongside him, holding his hand and looking the more scared of the two? Little Caesar ran about the hole looking like that. He was afraid of everything he touched. He never knew what might go off. Suppose we went to work for some great and powerful nation in Asia that had a civilization built on sciences we knew nothing of, as ours is built on physics and chemistry and higher mathematics; and suppose we knew that to these people we were absolutely meaningless as social beings, were waste to clean their engines, as Zablowski says; that we were there to do the dangerous work, to be poisoned in caissons under rivers, blown up by blasts, drowned in coal mines, and that these masters of ours were as indifferent to us individually as the Carthaginians were to their mercenaries? I'll tell you we'd guard the precious little spark of life with trembling hands."

"But I say—" sputtered the lawyer from the District Attorney's office.

"I know, I know, Chambers." Hallet put out a soothing hand. "*We* don't want 'em, God knows. They come. But why do they come? It's the pressure of their time and ours. It's not rich pickings they've got where I've worked with them, let me tell you. Well, Caesarino, with the others, came. The first morning I went on my job he was there, more scared of a new boss than any of the others; literally quaking. He was only twenty-three and lighter than the other men, and he was afraid I'd notice that. I thought he would pull his shoulder blades loose. After one big heave I stopped beside him and dropped a word: '*Buono soldato.*'[5] In a moment he was grinning with all his teeth, and he squeaked out: '*Buono soldato, da boss he talka dago!*' That was the beginning of our acquaintance."

Hallet paused a moment and smoked thoughtfully. He was a soft man for the iron age, I reflected, and it was easy enough to see why Stanley Merryweather had beaten him in the race. There is a string to every big contract in New York, and Hallet was always tripping over the string.

"From that time on we were friends. I knew just six words of Italian, but that summer I got so I could understand his fool dialect pretty well. I used to feel ashamed of the way he'd look at me, like a girl in love. You see, I was the only thing he wasn't afraid of. On Sundays we used to poke off to a beach somewhere, and he'd lie in the water all day and tell me about the coral divers and the bottom of the Mediterranean. I got very fond of him. It was my first summer in New York and I was lonesome, too. The game down here looked pretty ugly to me. There were plenty of disagreeable things to think about, and it was better fun to see how much soda water Caesarino could drink. He never drank wine. He used to say: 'At home—oh, yes-a! At New York,' making that wise little gesture with the forefinger between his eyes, '*niente*. Sav'-a da mon'.' But even his economy had its weak spots. He was very fond of candy, and he was always buying 'pop-a corn off-a da push-a cart.'

"However, he had sent home a good deal of money, and his mother was ailing and he was so frightened about her and so generally homesick that I urged him to go back to Ischia for the winter. There was a poor prospect for steady work, and if he went home he wouldn't be out much more than if he stayed in New York working on half time. He backed and filled and agonized a good deal, but when I at last got him to the point of engaging his passage he was the happiest dago on Manhattan Island. He told me about it all a hundred times.

"His mother, from the *piccola casa* on the cliff, could see all the boats go by to Naples. She always watched for them. Possibly he would be able to see her from the steamer, or at least the *casa*, or certainly the place where the *casa* stood.

"All this time we were making things move in the hole. Old Macfarlane wasn't around much in those days. He passed on the results, but Stanley had a free hand as to ways and means. He made amazing mistakes, harrowing blunders. His path was strewn with hairbreadth escapes, but they never dampened his courage or took the spurt out of him. After a close shave he'd simply duck his head and smile brightly and say: 'Well, I got *that* across, old Persimmons!' I'm not underestimating the value of dash and intrepidity. He made the wheels go round. One of his maxims was that men are cheaper than machinery. He smashed up a lot of hands, but he always got out under the fellow-servant act. 'Never been caught yet, huh?' he used to say with his pleasant, confiding wink. I'd been complaining to him for a long while about the cabling, but he always put me off; sometimes with a surly insinuation that I was nervous about my own head, but oftener with fine good humor. At last something did happen in the hole.

"It happened one night late in August, after a stretch of heat that broke the thermometers. For a week there hadn't been a dry human being in New York. Your linen went down three minutes after you put it on. We moved about insulated in moisture, like the fishes in the sea. That night I couldn't go down into the hole right away. When you once got down there the heat from the boilers and the steam from the diamond drills made a temperature that was beyond anything the human frame was meant to endure. I stood looking down for a long while, I remember. It was a hole nearly three acres square, and on one side the Savoyard rose up twenty stories, a straight blank, brick wall. You know what a mess such a hole is; great boulders of rock and deep pits of sand and gulleys of water, with drills puffing everywhere and little crumpled men crawling about like tumblebugs under the stream from the searchlight. When you got down into the hole, the wall of the Savoyard seemed to go clear up the sky; that pale blue enamel sky of a midsummer New York night. Six of my men were moving a diamond drill and settling it into a new place, when one of the big clamshells that swung back and forth over the hole fell with its load of sand—the worn cabling, of course. It was directly over my men when it fell. They couldn't hear anything for the noise of the drill; didn't know anything had happened until it struck them. They were bending over, huddled together, and the thing came down on them like a brick dropped on an ant hill. They were all buried, Caesarino among them. When we got them out, two were dead and the others were dying. My boy was the first we reached. The edge of the clam-shell had struck him, and he was all broken to pieces. The moment we got his head out he began chattering like a monkey. I put my ear down to his lips—the other drills were still going—and he was talking about what I had forgotten, that his steamer ticket was in his pocket and that he was to sail next Saturday. *'E necessario, signore, è necessario,'* he kept repeating. He had written his family what boat he was coming on, and his mother would be at the door, watching it when it went by to Naples. *'È necessario, signore, è necessario.'*

"When the ambulances got there the orderlies lifted two of the men and had them carried up to the street, but when they turned to Caesarino they dismissed him with a shrug, glancing at him with the contemptuous expression that ambulance orderlies come to have when they see that a man is too much shattered to pick up. He saw the look, and a boy who doesn't know the language learns to read looks. He broke into sobs and began to beat the rock with his hands. 'Curs-a da hole, curs-a da hole, curs-a da build'!' he screamed, bruising his fists on the shale. I caught his hands and leaned over him. *'Buono soldato, buono soldato,'* I said in his ear. His shrieks stopped, and his sobs quivered down. He looked at me—*'Buono soldato,'* he whispered, *'ma, perchè?'*[6] Then the hem-orrhage from his mouth shut him off, and he began to choke. In a few minutes it was all over with Little Caesar.

"About that time Merryweather showed up. Some one had tele-phoned him, and he had come down in his car. He was a little frightened and pleasurably excited. He has the truly journalistic mind—saving your presence, gentlemen—and he likes anything that bites on the tongue. He looked things over and ducked his head and grinned good-naturedly. 'Well, I guess you've got your new cabling out of me now, huh, Freddy?' he said to me. I went up to the car with him. His hand shook a little as he shielded a match to light his cigarette. 'Don't get shaky, Freddy. That wasn't so worse,' he said, as he stepped into his car.

"For the next few days I was busy seeing that the boy didn't get buried in a trench with a brass tag around his neck. On Saturday night I got his pay envelope, and he was paid for only half of the night he was killed; the accident happened about eleven o'clock. I didn't fool with any paymaster. On Monday morning I went straight to Merryweather's office, stormed his bower of rose and gold, and put that envelope on the mahogany between us. 'Merryweather,' said I, 'this is going to cost you something. I hear the relatives of the other fellows have all signed off for a few hundred, but this little dago hadn't any relatives here, and he's going to have the best lawyers in New York to prosecute his claim for him.'

"Stanley flew into one of his quick tempers. 'What business is it of yours, and what are you out to do us for?'

" 'I'm out to get every cent that's coming to this boy's family.'

" 'How in hell is that any concern of yours?'

" 'Never mind that. But we've got one awfully good case, Stanley. I happen to be the man who reported to you on that cabling again and again. I have a copy of the letter I wrote you about it when you were at Mount Desert, and I have your reply.'

"Stanley whirled around in his swivel chair and reached for his checkbook. 'How much are you gouging for?' he asked with his baronial pout.

" 'Just all the courts will give me. I want it settled there,' I said, and I got up to go.

" 'Well, you've chosen your class, sir,' he broke out, ruffling up red. 'You can stay in a hole with the guineas[7] till the end of time for all of me. That's where you've put yourself.'

"I got my money out of that concern and sent it off to the old woman in Ischia, and that's the end of the story. You all know Merryweather. He's the first man in my business since his uncle died, but we manage to keep clear of each other. The Mont Blanc was a milestone for me; one road ended there and another began. It was only a little accident, such as happens in New York every day in the year, but that one happened near me. There's a lot of waste about building a city. Usually the destruction all goes on in the cellar; it's only when it hits high, as it did last night, that it sets us thinking. Wherever there is the greatest output of energy, wherever the blind human race is exerting itself most furiously, there's bound to be tumult and disaster. Here we are, six men, with our pitiful few years to live and our one little chance for happiness, throwing everything we have into that conflagration on Manhattan Island, helping, with every nerve in us, with everything our brain cells can generate, with our very creature heat, to swell its glare, its noise, its luxury, and its power. Why do we do it? And why, in heaven's name, do *they* do it? *Ma, perchè?* as Caesarino said that night in the hole. Why did he, from that lazy volcanic island, so tiny, so forgotten, where life is simple and pellucid and tranquil, shaping itself to tradition and ancestral manners as water shapes itself to the jar, why did he come so far to cast his little spark in the bonfire? And the thousands like him, from islands even smaller and more remote, why do they come, like iron dust to the magnet, like moths to the flame? There must be something wonderful coming. When the frenzy is over, when the furnace has cooled, what marvel will be left on Manhattan Island?"

"What has been left often enough before," said Zablowski dreamily. "What was left in India, only not half so much."

Hallet disregarded him. "What it will be is a new idea of some sort. That's all that ever comes, really. That's what we are all the slaves of, though we don't know it. It's the whip that cracks over us till we drop. Even Merryweather—and that's where the gods have the laugh on him—every firm he crushes to the wall, every deal he puts through, every cocktail he pours down his throat, he does it in the service of this unborn Idea, that he will never know anything about. Some day it will dawn, serene and clear, and your Moloch[8] on the Singer Tower over there will get down and do it Asian obeisance."

We reflected on this while the launch, returning toward the city, ruffled through the dark furrows of water that kept rolling up into the light. Johnson looked back at the black sea road and said quietly:

"Well, anyhow, we are the people who are doing it, and whatever it is, it will be ours."

Hallet laughed. "Don't call anything ours, Johnson, while Zablowski is around."

"Zablowski," Johnson said irritably, "why don't you *ever* hit back?"

First published in *Collier's*, XLIX (May 1912), pp. 16–17, 41.

FROM *OBSCURE DESTINIES* (1932)

Old Mrs. Harris

I

MRS. DAVID ROSEN, cross-stitch in hand, sat looking out of the window across her own green lawn to the ragged, sunburned back yard of her neighbours on the right. Occasionally she glanced anxiously over her shoulder toward her shining kitchen, with a black and white linoleum floor in big squares, like a marble pavement.

"Will dat woman never go?" she muttered impatiently, just under her breath. She spoke with a slight accent—it affected only her *th*'s, and, occasionally, the letter *v*. But people in Skyline thought this unfortunate, in a woman whose superiority they recognized.

Mrs. Rosen ran out to move the sprinkler to another spot on the lawn, and in doing so she saw what she had been waiting to see. From the house next door a tall, handsome woman emerged, dressed in white broadcloth and a hat with white lilacs; she carried a sunshade and walked with a free, energetic step, as if she were going out on a pleasant errand.

Mrs. Rosen darted quickly back into the house, lest her neighbour should hail her and stop to talk. She herself was in her kitchen housework dress, a crisp blue chambray which fitted smoothly over her tightly corseted figure, and her lustrous black hair was done in two smooth braids, wound flat at the back of her head, like a braided rug. She did not stop for a hat—her dark, ruddy, salmon-tinted skin had little to fear from the sun. She opened the half-closed oven door and took out a symmetrically plaited coffee-cake, beautifully browned, delicately peppered over with poppy seeds, with sugary margins about the twists. On the kitchen table a tray stood ready with cups and saucers. She wrapped the cake in a napkin, snatched up a little French coffee-pot with a black wooden handle, and ran across her green lawn, through the alley-way and the sandy, unkept yard next door, and entered her neighbour's house by the kitchen.

The kitchen was hot and empty, full of the untempered afternoon sun. A door stood open into the next room; a cluttered, hideous room, yet somehow homely. There, beside a goods-box covered with figured oilcloth, stood an old woman in a brown calico dress, washing her hot face and neck at a tin basin. She stood with her feet wide apart, in an attitude of profound weariness. She started guiltily as the visitor entered.

"Don't let me disturb you, Grandma," called Mrs. Rosen. "I always have my coffee at dis hour in the afternoon. I was just about to sit down to it when I thought: 'I will run over and see if Grandma Harris won't take a cup with me.' I hate to drink my coffee alone."

Grandma looked troubled,—at a loss. She folded her towel and concealed it behind a curtain hung across the corner of the room to make a poor sort of closet. The old lady was always composed in manner, but it was clear that she felt embarrassment.

"Thank you, Mrs. Rosen. What a pity Victoria just this minute went down town!"

"But dis time I came to see you yourself, Grandma. Don't let me disturb you. Sit down there in your own rocker, and I will put my tray on this little chair between us, so!"

Mrs. Harris sat down in her black wooden rocking-chair with curved arms and a faded cretonne pillow on the wooden seat. It stood in the corner beside a narrow spindle-frame lounge. She looked on silently while Mrs. Rosen uncovered the cake and delicately broke it with her plump, smooth, dusky-red hands. The old lady did not seem pleased,—seemed uncertain and apprehensive, indeed. But she was not fussy or fidgety. She had the kind of quiet, intensely quiet, dignity that comes from complete resignation to the chances of life. She watched Mrs. Rosen's deft hands out of grave, steady brown eyes.

"Dis is Mr. Rosen's favourite coffee-cake, Grandma, and I want you to try it. You are such a good cook yourself, I would like your opinion of my cake."

"It's very nice, ma'am," said Mrs. Harris politely, but without enthusiasm.

"And you aren't drinking your coffee; do you like more cream in it?"

"No, thank you. I'm letting it cool a little. I generally drink it that way."

"Of course she does," thought Mrs. Rosen, "since she never has her coffee until all the family are done breakfast!"

Mrs. Rosen had brought Grandma Harris coffee-cake time and again, but she knew that Grandma merely tasted it and saved it for her daughter Victoria, who was as fond of sweets as her own children, and jealous about them, moreover,—couldn't bear that special dainties should come into the house for anyone but herself. Mrs. Rosen, vexed at her failures, had determined that just once she would take a cake to "de old lady Harris," and with her own eyes see her eat it. The result was not all she had hoped. Receiving a visitor alone, unsupervised by her daughter, having cake and coffee that should properly be saved for Victoria, was all so irregular that Mrs. Harris could not enjoy it. Mrs. Rosen doubted if she tasted the cake as she swallowed it,—certainly she ate it without relish, as a hollow form. But Mrs. Rosen enjoyed her own cake, at any rate, and she was glad of an opportunity to sit quietly and look at Grandmother, who was more interesting to her than the handsome Victoria.

It was a queer place to be having coffee, when Mrs. Rosen liked order and comeliness so much: a hideous, cluttered room, furnished with a rocking-horse, a sewing-machine, an empty baby-buggy. A walnut table stood against a blind window, piled high with old magazines and tattered books, and children's caps and coats. There was a wash-stand (two wash-stands, if you counted the oilcloth-covered box as one). A corner of the room was curtained off with some black-and-red-striped cotton goods, for a clothes closet. In another corner was the wooden lounge with a thin mattress and a red calico spread which was Grandma's bed. Beside it was her wooden rocking-chair, and the little splint-bottom chair with the legs sawed short on which her darning-basket usually stood, but which Mrs. Rosen was now using for a tea-table.

The old lady was always impressive, Mrs. Rosen was thinking, —one could not say why. Perhaps it was the way she held her head,—so simply, unprotesting and unprotected; or the gravity of her large, deep-set brown eyes, a warm, reddish brown, though their look, always direct, seemed to ask nothing and hope for nothing. They were not cold, but inscrutable, with no kindling gleam of intercourse in them. There was the kind of nobility about her head that there is about an old lion's: an absence of self-consciousness, vanity, preoccupation—something absolute. Her grey hair was parted in the middle, wound in two little horns over her ears, and done in a little flat knot behind. Her mouth was large and composed,—resigned, the corners drooping. Mrs. Rosen had very seldom heard her laugh (and then it was a gentle, polite laugh which meant only politeness). But she had observed that whenever Mrs. Harris's grandchildren were about, tumbling all over her, asking for cookies, teasing her to read to them, the old lady looked happy.

As she drank her coffee, Mrs. Rosen tried one subject after another to engage Mrs. Harris's attention.

"Do you feel this hot weather, Grandma? I am afraid you are over the stove too much. Let those naughty children have a cold lunch occasionally."

"No'm, I don't mind the heat. It's apt to come on like this for a spell in May. I don't feel the stove. I'm accustomed to it."

"Oh, so am I! But I get very impatient with my cooking in hot weather. Do you miss your old home in Tennessee very much, Grandma?"

"No'm, I can't say I do. Mr. Templeton thought Colorado was a better place to bring up the children."

"But you had things much more comfortable down there, I'm sure. These little wooden houses are too hot in summer."

"Yes'm, we were more comfortable. We had more room."

"And a flower-garden, and beautiful old trees, Mrs. Templeton told me."

"Yes'm, we had a great deal of shade."

Mrs. Rosen felt that she was not getting anywhere. She almost believed that Grandma thought she had come on an equivocal errand, to spy out something in Victoria's absence. Well, perhaps she had! Just for once she would like to get past the others to the real grandmother,—and the real grandmother was on her guard, as always. At this moment she heard a faint miaow. Mrs. Harris rose, lifting herself by the wooden arms of her chair, said: "Excuse me," went into the kitchen, and opened the screen door.

In walked a large, handsome, thickly furred Maltese cat, with long whiskers and yellow eyes and a white star on his breast. He preceded Grandmother, waited until she sat down. Then he sprang up into her lap and settled himself comfortably in the folds of her full-gathered calico skirt. He rested his chin in his deep bluish fur and regarded Mrs. Rosen. It struck her that he held his head in just the way Grandmother held hers. And Grandmother now became more alive, as if some missing part of herself were restored.

"This is Blue Boy," she said, stroking him. "In winter, when the screen door ain't on, he lets himself in. He stands up on his hind legs and presses the thumb-latch with his paw, and just walks in like anybody."

"He's your cat, isn't he, Grandma?" Mrs. Rosen couldn't help prying just a little; if she could find but a single thing that was Grandma's own!

"He's our cat," replied Mrs. Harris. "We're all very fond of him. I expect he's Vickie's more'n anybody's."

"Of course!" groaned Mrs. Rosen to herself. "Dat Vickie is her mother over again."

Here Mrs. Harris made her first unsolicited remark. "If you was to be troubled with mice at any time, Mrs. Rosen, ask one of the boys to bring Blue Boy over to you, and he'll clear them out. He's a master mouser." She scratched the thick blue fur at the back of his neck, and he began a deep purring. Mrs. Harris smiled. "We call that spinning, back with us. Our children still say: 'Listen to Blue Boy spin,' though none of 'em is ever heard a spinning-wheel—except maybe Vickie remembers."

"Did you have a spinning-wheel in your own house, Grandma Harris?"

"Yes'm. Miss Sadie Crummer used to come and spin for us. She was left with no home of her own, and it was to give her something to do, as much as anything, that we had her. I spun a good deal myself, in my young days." Grandmother stopped and put her hands on the arms of her chair, as if to rise. "Did you hear a door open? It might be Victoria."

"No, it was the wind shaking the screen door. Mrs. Templeton won't be home yet. She is probably in my husband's store this minute, ordering him about. All the merchants down town will take anything from your daughter. She is very popular wid de gentlemen, Grandma."

Mrs. Harris smiled complacently. "Yes'm. Victoria was always much admired."

At this moment a chorus of laughter broke in upon the warm silence, and a host of children, as it seemed to Mrs. Rosen, ran through the yard. The hand-pump on the back porch, outside the kitchen door, began to scrape and gurgle.

"It's the children, back from school," said Grandma. "They are getting a cool drink."

"But where is the baby, Grandma?"

"Vickie took Hughie in his cart over to Mr. Holliday's yard, where she studies. She's right good about minding him."

Mrs. Rosen was glad to hear that Vickie was good for something.

Three little boys came running in through the kitchen; the twins, aged ten, and Ronald, aged six, who went to kindergarten. They snatched off their caps and threw their jackets and school bags on the table, the sewing-machine, the rocking-horse.

"Howdy do, Mrs. Rosen." They spoke to her nicely. They had nice voices, nice faces, and were always courteous, like their father. "We are going to play in our back yard with some of the boys, Gram'ma," said one of the twins respectfully, and they ran out to join a troop of schoolmates who were already shouting and racing over that poor trampled back yard, strewn with velocipedes[1] and croquet mallets and toy wagons, which was such an eyesore to Mrs. Rosen.

Mrs. Rosen got up and took her tray.

"Can't you stay a little, ma'am? Victoria will be here any minute."

But her tone let Mrs. Rosen know that Grandma really wished her to leave before Victoria returned.

A few moments after Mrs. Rosen had put the tray down in her own kitchen, Victoria Templeton came up the wooden sidewalk, attended by Mr. Rosen, who had quitted his store half an hour earlier than usual for the pleasure of walking home with her. Mrs. Templeton stopped by the picket fence to smile at the children playing in the back yard,—and it was a real smile, she was glad to see them. She called Ronald over to the fence to give him a kiss. He was hot and sticky.

"Was your teacher nice today? Now run in and ask Grandma to wash your face and put a clean waist on you."

II

That night Mrs. Harris got supper with an effort—had to drive herself harder than usual. Mandy, the bound girl[2] they had brought with them from the South, noticed that the old lady was uncertain and short of breath. The hours from two to four, when Mrs. Harris usually rested, had not been at all restful this afternoon. There was an understood rule that Grandmother was not to receive visitors alone. Mrs. Rosen's call, and her cake and coffee, were too much out of the accepted order. Nervousness had prevented the old lady from getting any repose during her visit.

After the rest of the family had left the supper table, she went into the dining-room and took her place, but she ate very little. She put away the food that was left, and then, while Mandy washed the dishes, Grandma sat down in her rocking-chair in the dark and dozed.

The three little boys came in from playing under the electric light (arc lights had been but lately installed in Skyline) and began begging Mrs. Harris to read *Tom Sawyer*[3] to them. Grandmother loved to read, anything at all, the Bible or the continued story in the Chicago weekly paper. She roused herself, lit her brass "safety lamp," and pulled her black rocker out of its corner to the wash-stand (the table was too far away from her corner, and anyhow it was completely covered with coats and school satchels). She put on her old-fashioned silver-rimmed spectacles and began to read. Ronald lay down on Grandmother's lounge bed, and the twins, Albert and Adelbert, called Bert and Del, sat down against the wall, one on a low box covered with felt, and the other on the little sawed-off chair upon which Mrs. Rosen had served coffee. They looked intently at Mrs. Harris, and she looked intently at the book.

Presently Vickie, the oldest grandchild, came in. She was fifteen. Her mother was entertaining callers in the parlour, callers who didn't interest Vickie, so she was on her way up to her own room by the kitchen stairway.

Mrs. Harris looked up over her glasses. "Vickie, maybe you'd take the book awhile, and I can do my darning."

"All right," said Vickie. Reading aloud was one of the things she would always do toward the general comfort. She sat down by the wash-stand and went on with the story. Grandmother got her darning-basket and began to drive her needle across great knee-holes in the boys' stockings. Sometimes she nodded for a moment, and her hands fell into her lap. After a while the little boy on the lounge went to sleep. But the twins sat upright, their hands on their knees, their round brown eyes fastened upon Vickie, and when there was anything funny, they giggled. They were chubby, dark-skinned little boys, with round jolly faces, white teeth, and yellow-brown eyes that were always bubbling with fun unless they were sad,—even then their eyes never got red or weepy. Their tears sparkled and fell; left no trace but a streak on the cheeks, perhaps.

Presently old Mrs. Harris gave out a long snore of utter defeat. She had been overcome at last. Vickie put down the book. "That's enough for tonight. Grandmother's sleepy, and Ronald's fast asleep. What'll we do with him?"

"Bert and me'll get him undressed," said Adelbert. The twins roused the sleepy little boy and prodded him up the back stairway to the bare room without window blinds, where he was put into his cot beside their double bed. Vickie's room was across the narrow hallway; not much bigger than a closet, but, anyway, it was her own. She had a chair and an old dresser, and beside her bed was a high stool which she used as a lamp-table,—she always read in bed.

After Vickie went upstairs, the house was quiet. Hughie, the baby, was asleep in his mother's room, and Victoria herself, who still treated her husband as if he were her "beau," had persuaded him to take her down town to the ice-cream parlour. Grandmother's room, between the kitchen and the dining-room, was rather like a passage-way; but now that the children were upstairs and Victoria was off enjoying herself somewhere, Mrs. Harris could be sure of enough privacy to undress. She took off the calico cover from her lounge bed and folded it up, put on her nightgown and white nightcap.

Mandy, the bound girl, appeared at the kitchen door.

"Miz' Harris," she said in a guarded tone, ducking her head, "you want me to rub your feet for you?"

For the first time in the long day the old woman's low composure broke a little. "Oh, Mandy, I would take it kindly of you!" she breathed gratefully.

That had to be done in the kitchen; Victoria didn't like anybody slopping about. Mrs. Harris put an old checked shawl round her shoulders and followed Mandy. Beside the kitchen stove Mandy had a little wooden tub full of warm water. She knelt down and untied Mrs. Harris's garter strings and took off her flat cloth slippers and stockings.

"Oh, Miz' Harris, your feet an' legs is swelled turrible tonight!"

"I expect they air, Mandy. They feel like it."

"Pore soul!" murmured Mandy. She put Grandma's feet in the tub and, crouching beside it, slowly, slowly rubbed her swollen legs. Mandy was tired, too. Mrs. Harris sat in her nightcap and shawl, her hands crossed in her lap. She never asked for this greatest solace of the day; it was something that Mandy gave, who had nothing else to give. If there could be a comparison in absolutes, Mandy was the needier of the two,—but she was younger. The kitchen was quiet and full of shadow, with only the light from an old lantern. Neither spoke. Mrs. Harris dozed from comfort, and Mandy herself was half asleep as she performed one of the oldest rites of compassion.

Although Mrs. Harris's lounge had no springs, only a thin cotton mattress between her and the wooden slats, she usually went to sleep as soon as she was in bed. To be off her feet, to lie flat, to say over the psalm beginning: *"The Lord is my shepherd,"* was comfort enough. About four o'clock in the morning, however, she would begin to feel the hard slats under her, and the heaviness of the old homemade quilts, with weight but little warmth, on top of her. Then she would reach under her pillow for her little comforter (she called it that to herself) that Mrs. Rosen had given her. It was a tan sweater of very soft brushed wool, with one sleeve torn and ragged. A young nephew from Chicago had spent a fortnight with Mrs. Rosen last summer and had left this behind him. One morning, when Mrs. Harris went out to the stable at the back of the yard to pat Buttercup, the cow, Mrs. Rosen ran across the alley-way.

"Grandma Harris," she said, coming into the shelter of the stable, "I wonder if you could make any use of this sweater Sammy left? The yarn might be good for your darning."

Mrs. Harris felt of the article gravely. Mrs. Rosen thought her face brightened. "Yes'm, indeed I could use it. I thank you kindly."

She slipped it under her apron, carried it into the house with her, and concealed it under her mattress. There she had kept it ever since. She knew Mrs. Rosen understood how it was; that Victoria couldn't bear to have anything come into the house that was not for her to dispose of.

On winter nights, and even on summer nights after the cocks began to crow, Mrs. Harris often felt cold and lonely about the chest. Sometimes her cat, Blue Boy, would creep in beside her and warm that aching spot. But on spring and summer nights he was likely to be abroad skylarking, and this little sweater had become the dearest of Grandmother's few possessions. It was kinder to her, she used to think, as she wrapped it about her middle, than any of her own children had been. She had married at eighteen and had had eight children; but some died, and some were, as she said, scattered.

After she was warm in that tender spot under the ribs, the old woman could lie patiently on the slats, waiting for daybreak; thinking about the comfortable rambling old house in Tennessee, its feather beds and handwoven rag carpets and splint-bottom chairs, the mahogany sideboard, and the marble-top parlour table; all that she had left behind to follow Victoria's fortunes.

She did not regret her decision; indeed, there had been no decision. Victoria had never once thought it possible that Ma should not go wherever she and the children went, and Mrs. Harris had never thought it possible. Of course she regretted Tennessee, though she would never admit it to Mrs. Rosen:—the old neighbours, the yard and garden she had worked in all her life, the apple trees she had planted, the lilac arbour, tall enough to walk in, which she had clipped and shaped so many years. Especially she missed her lemon tree, in a tub on the front porch, which bore little lemons almost every summer, and folks would come for miles to see it.

But the road had led westward, and Mrs. Harris didn't believe that women, especially old women, could say when or where they would stop. They were tied to the chariot of young life, and had to go where it went, because they were needed. Mrs. Harris had gathered from Mrs. Rosen's manner, and from comments she occasionally dropped, that the Jewish people had an altogether different attitude toward their old folks; therefore her friendship with this kind neighbour was almost as disturbing as it was pleasant. She didn't want Mrs. Rosen to think that she was "put upon," that there was anything unusual or pitiful in her lot. To be pitied was the deepest hurt anybody could know. And if Victoria once suspected Mrs. Rosen's indignation, it would be all over. She would freeze her neighbour out, and that friendly voice, that quick pleasant chatter with the little foreign twist, would thenceforth be heard only at a distance, in the alley-way or across the fence. Victoria had a good heart, but she was terribly proud and could not bear the least criticism.

As soon as the grey light began to steal into the room, Mrs. Harris would get up softly and wash at the basin on the oilcloth-covered box. She would wet her hair above her forehead, comb it with a little bone comb set in a tin rim, do it up in two smooth little horns over her ears, wipe the comb dry, and put it away in the pocket of her full-gathered calico skirt. She left nothing lying about. As soon as she was dressed, she made her bed, folding her nightgown and nightcap under the pillow, the sweater under the mattress. She smoothed the heavy quilts, and drew the red calico spread neatly over all. Her towel was hung on its special nail behind the curtain. Her soap she kept in a tin tobacco-box; the children's soap was in a crockery saucer. If her soap or towel got mixed up with the children's, Victoria was always sharp about it. The little rented house was much too small for the family, and Mrs. Harris and her "things" were almost required to be invisible. Two clean calico dresses hung in the curtained corner; another was on her back, and a fourth was in the wash. Behind the curtain there was always a good supply of aprons; Victoria bought them at church fairs, and it was a great satisfaction to Mrs. Harris to put on a clean one whenever she liked. Upstairs, in Mandy's attic room over the kitchen, hung a black cashmere dress and a black bonnet with a long crêpe veil, for the rare occasions when Mr. Templeton hired a double buggy and horses and drove his family to a picnic or to Decoration Day exercises. Mrs. Harris rather dreaded these drives, for Victoria was usually cross afterwards.

When Mrs. Harris went out into the kitchen to get breakfast, Mandy always had the fire started and the water boiling. They enjoyed a quiet half-hour before the little boys came running down the stairs, always in a good humour. In winter the boys had their breakfast in the kitchen, with Vickie. Mrs. Harris made Mandy eat the cakes and fried ham the children left, so that she would not fast so long. Mr. and Mrs. Templeton breakfasted rather late, in the dining-room, and they always had fruit and thick cream,—a small pitcher of the very thickest was for Mrs. Templeton. The children were never fussy about their food. As Grandmother often said feelingly to Mrs. Rosen, they were as little trouble as children could possibly be. They sometimes tore their clothes, of course, or got sick. But even when Albert had an abscess in his ear and was in such pain, he would lie for hours on Grandmother's lounge with his cheek on a bag of hot salt, if only she or Vickie would read aloud to him.

"It's true, too, what de old lady says," remarked Mrs. Rosen to her husband one night at supper, "dey are nice children. No one ever taught them anything, but they have good instincts, even dat Vickie. And think, if you please, of all the self-sacrificing mothers we know,—Fannie and Esther, to come near home; how they have planned for those children from infancy and given them every advantage. And now ingratitude and coldness is what dey meet with."

Mr. Rosen smiled his teasing smile. "Evidently your sister and mine have the wrong method. The way to make your children unselfish is to be comfortably selfish yourself."

"But dat woman takes no more responsibility for her children than a cat takes for her kittens. Nor does poor young Mr. Templeton, for dat matter. How can he expect to get so many children started in life, I ask you? It is not at all fair!"

Mr. Rosen sometimes had to hear altogether too much about the Templetons, but he was patient, because it was a bitter sorrow to Mrs. Rosen that she had no children. There was nothing else in the world she wanted so much.

III

Mrs. Rosen in one of her blue working dresses, the indigo blue that became a dark skin and dusky red cheeks with a tone of salmon colour, was in her shining kitchen, washing her beautiful dishes—her neighbours often wondered why she used her best china and linen every day—when Vickie Templeton came in with a book under her arm.

"Good day, Mrs. Rosen. Can I have the second volume?"

"Certainly. You know where the books are." She spoke coolly, for it always annoyed her that Vickie never suggested wiping the dishes or helping with such household work as happened to be going on when she dropped in. She hated the girl's bringing-up so much that sometimes she almost hated the girl.

Vickie strolled carelessly through the dining-room into the parlour and opened the doors of one of the big bookcases. Mr. Rosen had a large library, and a great many unusual books. There was a complete set of the Waverley Novels[4] in German, for example; thick, dumpy little volumes bound in tooled leather, with very black type and dramatic engravings printed on wrinkled, yellowing pages.

There were many French books, and some of the German classics done into English, such as Coleridge's translation of Schiller's *Wallenstein*.

Of course no other house in Skyline was in the least like Mrs. Rosen's; it was the nearest thing to an art gallery and a museum that the Templetons had ever seen. All the rooms were carpeted alike (that was very unusual), with a soft velvet carpet, little blue and rose flowers scattered on a rose-grey ground. The deep chairs were upholstered in dark blue velvet. The walls were hung with engravings in pale gold frames: some of Raphael's "Hours," a large soft engraving of a castle on the Rhine, and another of cypress trees about a Roman ruin, under a full moon. There were a number of water-colour sketches, made in Italy by Mr. Rosen himself when he was a boy. A rich uncle had taken him abroad as his secretary. Mr. Rosen was a reflective, unambitious man, who didn't mind keeping a clothing-store in a little Western town, so long as he had a great deal of time to read philosophy. He was the only unsuccessful member of a large, rich Jewish family.

Last August, when the heat was terrible in Skyline, and the crops were burned up on all the farms to the north, and the wind from the pink and yellow sand-hills to the south blew so hot that it singed the few green lawns in the town, Vickie had taken to dropping in upon Mrs. Rosen at the very hottest part of the afternoon. Mrs. Rosen knew, of course, that it was probably because the girl had no other cool and quiet place to go—her room at home under the roof would be hot enough! Now, Mrs. Rosen liked to undress and take a nap from three to five,—if only to get out of her tight corsets, for she would have an hourglass figure at any cost. She told Vickie firmly that she was welcome to come if she would read in the parlour with the blind up only a little way, and would be as still as a mouse. Vickie came, meekly enough, but she seldom read. She would take a sofa pillow and lie down on the soft carpet and look up at the pictures in the dusky room, and feel a happy, pleasant excitement from the heat and glare outside and the deep shadow and quiet within. Curiously enough, Mrs. Rosen's house never made her dissatisfied with her own; she thought that very nice, too.

Mrs. Rosen, leaving her kitchen in a state of such perfection as the Templetons were unable to sense or to admire, came into the parlour and found her visitor sitting cross-legged on the floor before one of the bookcases.

"Well, Vickie, and how did you get along with *Wilhelm Meister*?"[5]

"I like it," said Vickie.

Mrs. Rosen shrugged. The Templetons always said that; quite as if a book or a cake were lucky to win their approbation.

"Well, *what* did you like?"

"I guess I liked all that about the theatre and Shakspere best."

"It's rather celebrated," remarked Mrs. Rosen dryly. "And are you studying every day? Do you think you will be able to win that scholarship?"

"I don't know. I'm going to try awful hard."

Mrs. Rosen wondered whether any Templeton knew how to try very hard. She reached for her work-basket and began to do cross-stitch. It made her nervous to sit with folded hands.

Vickie was looking at a German book in her lap, an illustrated edition of *Faust*.[6] She had stopped at a very German picture of Gretchen entering the church, with Faustus gazing at her from behind a rose tree, Mephisto at his shoulder.

"I wish I could read this," she said, frowning at the black Gothic text. "It's splendid, isn't it?"

Mrs. Rosen rolled her eyes upward and sighed. "Oh, my dear, one of de world's masterpieces!"

That meant little to Vickie. She had not been taught to respect masterpieces, she had no scale of that sort in her mind. She cared about a book only because it took hold of her.

She kept turning over the pages. Between the first and second parts, in this edition, there was inserted the *Dies Iræ* hymn in full. She stopped and puzzled over it for a long while.

"Here is something I can read," she said, showing the page to Mrs. Rosen.

Mrs. Rosen looked up from her cross-stitch. "There you have the advantage of me. I do not read Latin. You might translate it for me."

Vickie began:

"Day of wrath, upon that day
The world to ashes melts away,
As David and the Sibyl say.

"But that don't give you the rhyme; every line ought to end in two syllables."

"Never mind if it doesn't give the metre," corrected Mrs. Rosen kindly; "go on, if you can."

Vickie went on stumbling through the Latin verses, and Mrs. Rosen sat watching her. You couldn't tell about Vickie. She wasn't pretty, yet Mrs. Rosen found her attractive. She liked her sturdy build, and the steady vitality that glowed in her rosy skin and dark blue eyes,—even gave a springy quality to her curly reddish-brown hair, which she still wore in a single braid down her back. Mrs. Rosen liked to have Vickie about because she was never listless or dreamy or apathetic. A half-smile nearly always played about her lips and eyes, and it was there because she was pleased with something, not because she wanted to be agreeable. Even a half-smile made her cheeks dimple. She had what her mother called "a happy disposition."

When she finished the verses, Mrs. Rosen nodded approvingly. "Thank you, Vickie. The very next time I go to Chicago, I will try to get an English translation of *Faust* for you."

"But I want to read this one." Vickie's open smile darkened. "What I want is to pick up any of these books and just read them, like you and Mr. Rosen do."

The dusky red of Mrs. Rosen's cheeks grew a trifle deeper. Vickie never paid compliments, absolutely never; but if she really admired anyone, something in her voice betrayed it so convincingly that one felt flattered. When she dropped a remark of this kind, she added another link to the chain of responsibility which Mrs. Rosen unwillingly bore and tried to shake off—the irritating sense of being somehow responsible for Vickie, since, God knew, no one else felt responsible.

Once or twice, when she happened to meet pleasant young Mr. Templeton alone, she had tried to talk to him seriously about his daughter's future. "She has finished de school here, and she should be getting training of some sort; she is growing up," she told him severely.

He laughed and said in his way that was so honest, and so disarmingly sweet and frank: "Oh, don't remind me, Mrs. Rosen! I just pretend to myself she isn't. I want to keep my little daughter as long as I can." And there it ended.

Sometimes Vickie Templeton seemed so dense, so utterly unperceptive, that Mrs. Rosen was ready to wash her hands of her. Then some queer streak of sensibility in the child would make her change her mind. Last winter, when Mrs. Rosen came home from a visit to her sister in Chicago, she brought with her a new cloak of the sleeveless dolman type,[7] black velvet, lined with grey and white squirrel skins, a grey skin next a white. Vickie, so indifferent to clothes, fell in love with that cloak. Her eyes followed it with delight whenever Mrs. Rosen wore it. She found it picturesque, romantic. Mrs. Rosen had been captivated by the same thing in the cloak, and had bought it with a shrug, knowing it would be quite out of place in Skyline; and Mr. Rosen, when she first produced it from her trunk, had laughed and said: "Where did you get that?—out of *Rigoletto*?"[8] It looked like that—but how could Vickie know?

Vickie's whole family puzzled Mrs. Rosen; their feelings were so much finer than their way of living. She bought milk from the Templetons because they kept a cow—which Mandy milked,—and every night one of the twins brought the milk to her in a tin pail. Whichever boy brought it, she always called him Albert—she thought Adelbert a silly, Southern name.

One night when she was fitting the lid on an empty pail, she said severely:

"Now, Albert, I have put some cookies for Grandma in this pail, wrapped in a napkin. And they are for Grandma, remember, not for your mother or Vickie."

"Yes'm."

When she turned to him to give him the pail, she saw two full crystal globes in the little boy's eyes, just ready to break. She watched him go softly down the path and dash those tears away with the back of his hand. She was sorry. She hadn't thought the little boys realized that their household was somehow a queer one.

Queer or not, Mrs. Rosen liked to go there better than to most houses in the town. There was something easy, cordial, and carefree in the parlour that never smelled of being shut up, and the ugly furniture looked hospitable. One felt a pleasantness in the human relationships. These people didn't seem to know there were such things as struggle or exactness or competition in the world. They were always genuinely glad to see you, had time to see you, and were usually gay in mood—all but Grandmother, who had the kind of gravity that people who take thought of human destiny must have. But even she liked light-heartedness in others; she drudged, indeed, to keep it going.

There were houses that were better kept, certainly, but the housekeepers had no charm, no gentleness of manner, were like hard little machines, most of them; and some were grasping and narrow. The Templetons were not selfish or scheming. Anyone could take advantage of them, and many people did. Victoria might eat all the cookies her neighbour sent in, but she would give away anything she had. She was always ready to lend her dresses and hats and bits of jewellery for the school theatricals, and she never worked people for favours.

As for Mr. Templeton (people usually called him "young Mr. Templeton"), he was too delicate to collect his just debts. His boyish, eager-to-please manner, his fair complexion and blue eyes and young face, made him seem very soft to some of the hard old money-grubbers on Main Street, and the fact that he always said "Yes, sir," and "No, sir," to men older than himself furnished a good deal of amusement to by-standers.

* * *

Two years ago, when this Templeton family came to Skyline and moved into the house next door, Mrs. Rosen was inconsolable. The new neighbours had a lot of children, who would always be making a racket. They put a cow and a horse into the empty barn, which would mean dirt and flies. They strewed their back yard with packing-cases and did not pick them up.

She first met Mrs. Templeton at an afternoon card party, in a house at the extreme north end of the town, fully half a mile away, and she had to admit that her new neighbour was an attractive woman, and that there was something warm and genuine about her. She wasn't in the least willowy or languishing, as Mrs. Rosen had usually found Southern ladies to be. She was high-spirited and direct; a trifle imperious, but with a shade of diffidence, too, as if she were trying to adjust herself to a new group of people and to do the right thing.

While they were at the party, a blinding snowstorm came on, with a hard wind. Since they lived next door to each other, Mrs. Rosen and Mrs. Templeton struggled homeward together through the blizzard. Mrs. Templeton seemed delighted with the rough weather; she laughed like a big country girl whenever she made a mis-step off the obliterated sidewalk and sank up to her knees in a snow-drift.

"Take care, Mrs. Rosen," she kept calling, "keep to the right! Don't spoil your nice coat. My, ain't this real winter? We never had it like this back with us."

When they reached the Templetons' gate, Victoria wouldn't hear of Mrs. Rosen's going farther. "No, indeed, Mrs. Rosen, you come right in with me and get dry, and Ma'll make you a hot toddy while I take the baby."

By this time Mrs. Rosen had begun to like her neighbour, so she went in. To her surprise, the parlour was neat and comfortable—the children did not strew things about there, apparently. The hard-coal burner threw out a warm red glow. A faded, respectable Brussels carpet covered the floor, an old-fashioned wooden clock ticked on the walnut bookcase. There were a few easy chairs, and no hideous ornaments about. She rather liked the old oil-chromos on the wall: "Hagar and Ishmael in the Wilderness," and "The Light of the World." While Mrs. Rosen dried her feet on the nickel base of the stove, Mrs. Templeton excused herself and withdrew to the next room,—her bedroom,—took off her silk dress and corsets, and put on a white challis négligée. She reappeared with the baby, who was not crying, exactly, but making eager, passionate, gasping entreaties,—faster and faster, tenser and tenser, as he felt his dinner nearer and nearer and yet not his.

Mrs. Templeton sat down in a low rocker by the stove and began to nurse him, holding him snugly but carelessly, still talking to Mrs. Rosen about the card party, and laughing about their wade home through the snow. Hughie, the baby, fell to work so fiercely that beads of sweat came out all over his flushed forehead. Mrs. Rosen could not help admiring him and his mother. They were so comfortable and complete. When he was changed to the other side, Hughie resented the interruption a little; but after a time he became soft and bland, as smooth as oil, indeed; began looking about him as he drew in his milk. He finally dropped the nipple from his lips altogether, turned on his mother's arm, and looked inquiringly at Mrs. Rosen.

"What a beautiful baby!" she exclaimed from her heart. And he was. A sort of golden baby. His hair was like sunshine, and his long lashes were gold over such gay blue eyes. There seemed to be a gold glow in his soft pink skin, and he had the smile of a cherub.

"We think he's a pretty boy," said Mrs. Templeton. "He's the prettiest of my babies. Though the twins were mighty cunning little fellows. I hated the idea of twins, but the minute I saw them, I couldn't resist them."

Just then old Mrs. Harris came in, walking widely in her full-gathered skirt and felt-soled shoes, bearing a tray with two smoking goblets upon it.

"This is my mother, Mrs. Harris, Mrs. Rosen," said Mrs. Templeton.

"I'm glad to know you, ma'am," said Mrs. Harris. "Victoria, let me take the baby, while you two ladies have your toddy."

"Oh, don't take him away, Mrs. Harris, please!" cried Mrs. Rosen.

The old lady smiled. "I won't. I'll set right here. He never frets with his grandma."

When Mrs. Rosen had finished her excellent drink, she asked if she might hold the baby, and Mrs. Harris placed him on her lap. He made a few rapid boxing motions with his two fists, then braced himself on his heels and the back of his head, and lifted himself up in an arc. When he dropped back, he looked up at Mrs. Rosen with his most intimate smile. "See what a smart boy I am!"

When Mrs. Rosen walked home, feeling her way through the

snow by following the fence, she knew she could never stay away from a house where there was a baby like that one.

IV

Vickie did her studying in a hammock hung between two tall cottonwood trees over in the Roadmaster's green yard. The Roadmaster had the finest yard in Skyline, on the edge of the town, just where the sandy plain and the sage-brush began. His family went back to Ohio every summer, and Bert and Del Templeton were paid to take care of his lawn, to turn the sprinkler on at the right hours and to cut the grass. They were really too little to run the heavy lawn-mower very well, but they were able to manage because they were twins. Each took one end of the handlebar, and they pushed together like a pair of fat Shetland ponies. They were very proud of being able to keep the lawn so nice, and worked hard on it. They cut Mrs. Rosen's grass once a week, too, and did it so well that she wondered why in the world they never did anything about their own yard. They didn't have city water, to be sure (it was expensive), but she thought they might pick up a few velocipedes and iron hoops, and dig up the messy "flower-bed," that was even uglier than the naked gravel spots. She was particularly offended by a deep ragged ditch, a miniature arroyo, which ran across the back yard, serving no purpose and looking very dreary.

One morning she said craftily to the twins, when she was paying them for cutting her grass:

"And, boys, why don't you just shovel the sand-pile by your fence into dat ditch, and make your back yard smooth?"

"Oh, no, ma'am," said Adelbert with feeling. "We like to have the ditch to build bridges over!"

Ever since vacation began, the twins had been busy getting the Roadmaster's yard ready for the Methodist lawn party. When Mrs. Holliday, the Roadmaster's wife, went away for the summer, she always left a key with the Ladies' Aid Society and invited them to give their ice-cream social at her place.

This year the date set for the party was June fifteenth. The day was a particularly fine one, and as Mr. Holliday himself had been called to Cheyenne on railroad business, the twins felt personally responsible for everything. They got out to the Holliday place early in the morning, and stayed on guard all day. Before noon the dray-man brought a wagonload of card-tables and folding chairs, which the boys placed in chosen spots under the cottonwood trees. In the afternoon the Methodist ladies arrived and opened up the kitchen to receive the freezers of homemade ice-cream, and the cakes which the congregation donated. Indeed, all the good cake-bakers in town were expected to send a cake. Grandma Harris baked a white cake, thickly iced and covered with freshly grated coconut, and Vickie took it over in the afternoon.

Mr. and Mrs. Rosen, because they belonged to no church, contributed to the support of all, and usually went to the church suppers in winter and the socials in summer. On this warm June evening they set out early, in order to take a walk first. They strolled along the hard gravelled road that led out through the sage toward the sand-hills; tonight it led toward the moon, just rising over the sweep of dunes. The sky was almost as blue as at midday, and had that look of being very near and very soft which it has in desert countries. The moon, too, looked very near, soft and bland and innocent. Mrs. Rosen admitted that in the Adirondacks, for which she was always secretly homesick in summer, the moon had a much colder brilliance, seemed farther off and made of a harder metal. This moon gave the sage-brush plain and the drifted sand-hills the softness of velvet. All countries were beautiful to Mr. Rosen. He carried a country of his own in his mind, and was able to unfold it like a tent in any wilderness.

When they at last turned back toward the town, they saw groups of people, women in white dresses, walking toward the dark spot where the paper lanterns made a yellow light underneath the cottonwoods. High above, the rustling tree-tops stirred free in the flood of moonlight.

The lighted yard was surrounded by a low board fence, painted the dark red Burlington colour, and as the Rosens drew near, they noticed four children standing close together in the shadow of some tall elder bushes just outside the fence. They were the poor Maude children; their mother was the washwoman, the Rosens' laundress and the Templetons'. People said that every one of those children had a different father. But good laundresses were few, and even the members of the Ladies' Aid were glad to get Mrs. Maude's services at a dollar a day, though they didn't like their children to play with hers. Just as the Rosens approached, Mrs. Templeton came out from the lighted square, leaned over the fence, and addressed the little Maudes.

"I expect you children forgot your dimes, now didn't you? Never mind, here's a dime for each of you, so come along and have your ice-cream."

The Maudes put out small hands and said: "Thank you," but not one of them moved.

"Come along, Francie" (the oldest girl was named Frances). "Climb right over the fence." Mrs. Templeton reached over and gave her a hand, and the little boys quickly scrambled after their sister. Mrs. Templeton took them to a table which Vickie and the twins had just selected as being especially private—they liked to do things together.

"Here, Vickie, let the Maudes sit at your table, and take care they get plenty of cake."

The Rosens had followed close behind Mrs. Templeton, and Mr. Rosen now overtook her and said in his most courteous and friendly manner: "Good evening, Mrs. Templeton. Will you have ice-cream with us?" He always used the local idioms, though his voice and enunciation made them sound altogether different from Skyline speech.

"Indeed I will, Mr. Rosen. Mr. Templeton will be late. He went out to his farm yesterday, and I don't know just when to expect him."

Vickie and the twins were disappointed at not having their table to themselves, when they had come early and found a nice one; but they knew it was right to look out for the dreary little Maudes, so they moved close together and made room for them. The Maudes didn't cramp them long. When the three boys had eaten the last crumb of cake and licked their spoons, Francie got up and led them to a green slope by the fence, just outside the lighted circle. "Now set down, and watch and see how folks do," she told them. The boys looked to Francie for commands and support. She was really Amos Maude's child, born before he ran away to the Klondike, and it had been rubbed into them that this made a difference.

The Templeton children made their ice-cream linger out, and sat watching the crowd. They were glad to see their mother go to Mr. Rosen's table, and noticed how nicely he placed a chair for her and insisted upon putting a scarf about her shoulders. Their mother was wearing her new dotted Swiss, with many ruffles, all edged with black ribbon, and wide ruffly sleeves. As the twins watched her over their spoons, they thought how much prettier their mother was than any of the other women, and how becoming her new dress was. The children got as much satisfaction as Mrs. Harris out of Victoria's good looks.

Mr. Rosen was well pleased with Mrs. Templeton and her new dress, and with her kindness to the little Maudes. He thought her manner with them just right,—warm, spontaneous, without anything patronizing. He always admired her way with her own children, though Mrs. Rosen thought it too casual. Being a good mother, he believed, was much more a matter of physical poise and richness than of sentimentalizing and reading doctor-books. Tonight he was more talkative than usual, and in his quiet way made Mrs. Templeton feel his real friendliness and admiration. Unfortunately, he made other people feel it, too.

Mrs. Jackson, a neighbour who didn't like the Templetons, had been keeping an eye on Mr. Rosen's table. She was a stout square woman of imperturbable calm, effective in regulating the affairs of the community because she never lost her temper, and could say the most cutting things in calm, even kindly, tones. Her face was smooth and placid as a mask, rather good-humoured, and the fact that one eye had a cast and looked askance made it the more difficult to see through her intentions. When she had been lingering about the Rosens' table for some time, studying Mr. Rosen's pleasant attentions to Mrs. Templeton, she brought up a trayful of cake.

"You folks are about ready for another helping," she remarked affably.

Mrs. Rosen spoke. "I want some of Grandma Harris's cake. It's a white coconut, Mrs. Jackson."

"How about you, Mrs. Templeton, would you like some of your own cake?"

"Indeed I would," said Mrs. Templeton heartily. "Ma said she had good luck with it. I didn't see it. Vickie brought it over."

Mrs. Jackson deliberately separated the slices on her tray with two forks. "Well," she remarked with a chuckle that really sounded amiable, "I don't know but I'd like my cakes, if I kept somebody in the kitchen to bake them for me."

Mr. Rosen for once spoke quickly. "If I had a cook like Grandma Harris in my kitchen, I'd live in it!" he declared.

Mrs. Jackson smiled. "I don't know as we feel like that, Mrs. Templeton? I tell Mr. Jackson that my idea of coming up in the world would be to forget I had a cook-stove, like Mrs. Templeton. But we can't all be lucky."

Mr. Rosen could not tell how much was malice and how much was stupidity. What he chiefly detected was self-satisfaction; the craftiness of the coarse-fibred country girl putting catch questions to the teacher. Yes, he decided, the woman was merely showing off,—she regarded it as an accomplishment to make people uncomfortable.

Mrs. Templeton didn't at once take it in. Her training was all to the end that you must give a guest everything you have, even if he happens to be your worst enemy, and that to cause anyone embarrassment is a frightful and humiliating blunder. She felt hurt without knowing just why, but all evening it kept growing clearer to her that this was another of those thrusts from the outside which she couldn't understand. The neighbours were sure to take sides against her, apparently, if they came often to see her mother.

Mr. Rosen tried to distract Mrs. Templeton, but he could feel the poison working. On the way home the children knew something had displeased or hurt their mother. When they went into the house, she told them to go upstairs at once, as she had a headache. She was severe and distant. When Mrs. Harris suggested making her some peppermint tea, Victoria threw up her chin.

"I don't want anybody waiting on me. I just want to be let alone." And she withdrew without saying good-night, or "Are you all right, Ma?" as she usually did.

Left alone, Mrs. Harris sighed and began to turn down her bed. She knew, as well as if she had been at the social, what kind of thing had happened. Some of those prying ladies of the Woman's Relief Corps, or the Woman's Christian Temperance Union, had been intimating to Victoria that her mother was "put upon." Nothing ever made Victoria cross but criticism. She was jealous of small attentions paid to Mrs. Harris, because she felt they were paid "behind her back" or "over her head," in a way that implied reproach to her. Victoria had been a belle in their own town in Tennessee, but here she was not very popular, no matter how many pretty dresses she wore, and she couldn't bear it. She felt as if her mother and Mr. Templeton must be somehow to blame; at least they ought to protect her from whatever was disagreeable—they always had!

V

Mrs. Harris wakened at about four o'clock, as usual, before the house was stirring, and lay thinking about their position in this new town. She didn't know why the neighbours acted so; she was as much in the dark as Victoria. At home, back in Tennessee, her place in the family was not exceptional, but perfectly regular. Mrs. Harris had replied to Mrs. Rosen, when that lady asked why in the world she didn't break Vickie in to help her in the kitchen: "We are only young once, and trouble comes soon enough." Young girls, in the South, were supposed to be carefree and foolish; the fault Grandmother found in Vickie was that she wasn't foolish enough. When the foolish girl married and began to have children, everything else must give way to that. She must be humoured and given the best of everything, because having children was hard on a woman, and it was the most important thing in the world. In Tennessee every young married woman in good circumstances had an older woman in the house, a mother or mother-in-law or an old aunt, who managed the household economies and directed the help.

That was the great difference; in Tennessee there had been plenty of helpers. There was old Miss Sadie Crummer, who came to the house to spin and sew and mend; old Mrs. Smith, who always arrived to help at butchering- and preserving-time; Lizzie, the coloured girl, who did the washing and who ran in every day to help Mandy. There were plenty more, who came whenever one of Lizzie's barefoot boys ran to fetch them. The hills were full of solitary old women, or women but slightly attached to some household, who were glad to come to Miz' Harris's for good food and a warm bed, and the little present that either Mrs. Harris or Victoria slipped into their carpet-sack when they went away.

To be sure, Mrs. Harris, and the other women of her age who managed their daughter's house, kept in the background; but it was their own background, and they ruled it jealously. They left the front porch and the parlour to the young married couple and their young friends; the old women spent most of their lives in the kitchen and pantries and back dining-room. But there they ordered life to their own taste, entertained their friends, dispensed charity, and heard the troubles of the poor. Moreover, back there it was Grandmother's own house they lived in. Mr. Templeton came of a superior family and had what Grandmother called "blood," but no property. He never so much as mended one of the steps to the front porch without consulting Mrs. Harris. Even "back home," in the aristocracy, there were old women who went on living like young ones,—gave parties and drove out in their carriage and "went North" in the summer. But among the middle-class people and the country-folk, when a woman was a widow and had married daughters, she considered herself an old woman and wore full-gathered black dresses and a black bonnet and became a housekeeper. She accepted this estate unprotestingly, almost gratefully.

The Templetons' troubles began when Mr. Templeton's aunt died and left him a few thousand dollars, and he got the idea of bettering himself. The twins were little then, and he told Mrs. Harris his boys would have a better chance in Colorado—everybody was going West. He went alone first, and got a good position with a mining company in the mountains of southern Colorado. He had been book-keeper in the bank in his home town, had "grown up in the bank," as they said. He was industrious and honourable, and the managers of the mining company liked him, even if they laughed at his polite, soft-spoken manners. He could have held his position indefinitely, and maybe got a promotion. But the altitude of that mountain town was too high for his family. All the children were sick there; Mrs. Templeton was ill most of the time and nearly died when Ronald was born. Hillary Templeton lost his courage and came north to the flat, sunny, semi-arid country between Wray and Cheyenne, to work for an irrigation project. So far, things had not gone well with him. The pinch told on everyone, but most on Grandmother. Here, in Skyline, she had all her accustomed responsibilities, and no helper but Mandy. Mrs. Harris was no longer living in a feudal society, where there were plenty of landless people glad to render service to the more fortunate, but in a snappy little Western democracy, where every man was as good as his neighbour and out to prove it.

Neither Mrs. Harris nor Mrs. Templeton understood just what was the matter; they were hurt and dazed, merely. Victoria knew that here she was censured and criticized, she who had always been so admired and envied! Grandmother knew that these meddlesome "Northerners" said things that made Victoria suspicious and unlike herself; made her unwilling that Mrs. Harris should receive visitors alone, or accept marks of attention that seemed offered in compassion for her state.

These women who belonged to clubs and Relief Corps lived differently, Mrs. Harris knew, but she herself didn't like the way they lived. She believed that somebody ought to be in the parlour, and somebody in the kitchen. She wouldn't for the world have had Victoria go about every morning in a short gingham dress, with bare arms, and a dust-cap on her head to hide the curling-kids, as these brisk housekeepers did. To Mrs. Harris that would have meant real poverty, coming down in the world so far that one could no longer keep up appearances. Her life was hard now, to be sure, since the family went on increasing and Mr. Templeton's means went on decreasing; but she certainly valued respectability above personal comfort, and she could go on a good way yet if they always had a cool pleasant parlour, with Victoria properly dressed to receive visitors. To keep Victoria different from these "ordinary" women meant everything to Mrs. Harris. She realized that Mrs. Rosen managed to be mistress of any situation, either in kitchen or parlour, but that was because she was "foreign." Grandmother perfectly understood that their neighbour had a superior cultivation which made everything she did an exercise of skill. She knew well enough that their own ways of cooking and cleaning were primitive beside Mrs. Rosen's.

If only Mr. Templeton's business affairs would look up, they could rent a larger house, and everything would be better. They might even get a German girl to come in and help,—but now there was no place to put her. Grandmother's own lot could improve only with the family fortunes—any comfort for herself, aside from that of the family, was inconceivable to her; and on the other hand she could have no real unhappiness while the children were well, and good, and fond of her and their mother. That was why it was worth while to get up early in the morning and make her bed neat and draw the red spread smooth. The little boys loved to lie on her lounge and her pillows when they were tired. When they were sick, Ronald and Hughie wanted to be in her lap. They had no physical shrinking from her because she was old. And Victoria was never jealous of the children's wanting to be with her so much; that was a mercy!

Sometimes, in the morning, if her feet ached more than usual, Mrs. Harris felt a little low. (Nobody did anything about broken arches in those days, and the common endurance test of old age was to keep going after every step cost something.) She would hang up her towel with a sigh and go into the kitchen, feeling that it was hard to make a start. But the moment she heard the children running down the uncarpeted back stairs, she forgot to be low. Indeed, she ceased to be an individual, an old woman with aching feet; she became part of a group, became a relationship. She was drunk up into their freshness when they burst in upon her, telling her about their dreams, explaining their troubles with buttons and shoe-laces and underwear shrunk too small. The tired, solitary old woman Grandmother had been at daybreak vanished; suddenly the morning seemed as important to her as it did to the children, and the mornings ahead stretched out sunshiny, important.

VI

The day after the Methodist social, Blue Boy didn't come for his morning milk; he always had it in a clean saucer on the covered back porch, under the long bench where the tin wash-tubs stood ready for Mrs. Maude. After the children had finished breakfast, Mrs. Harris sent Mandy out to look for the cat.

The girl came back in a minute, her eyes big.

"Law me, Miz' Harris, he's awful sick. He's a-layin' in the straw in the barn. He's swallered a bone, or havin' a fit or somethin'."

Grandmother threw an apron over her head and went out to see for herself. The children went with her. Blue Boy was retching and choking, and his yellow eyes were filled up with rhume.

"Oh, Gram'ma, what's the matter?" the boys cried.

"It's the distemper. How could he have got it?" Her voice was so harsh that Ronald began to cry. "Take Ronald back to the house, Del. He might get bit. I wish I'd kept my word and never had a cat again!"

"Why, Gram'ma!" Albert looked at her. "Won't Blue Boy get well?"

"Not from the distemper, he won't."

"But Gram'ma, can't I run for the veter'nary?"

"You gether up an armful of hay. We'll take him into the coal-house, where I can watch him."

Mrs. Harris waited until the spasm was over, then picked up the limp cat and carried him to the coal-shed that opened off the back porch. Albert piled the hay in one corner—the coal was low, since it was summer—and they spread a piece of old carpet on the hay and made a bed for Blue Boy. "Now you run along with Adelbert. There'll be a lot of work to do on Mr. Holliday's yard, cleaning up after the sociable. Mandy an' me'll watch Blue Boy. I expect he'll sleep for a while."

Albert went away regretfully, but the drayman and some of the Methodist ladies were in Mr. Holliday's yard, packing chairs and tables and ice-cream freezers into the wagon, and the twins forgot the sick cat in their excitement. By noon they had picked up the last paper napkin, raked over the gravel walks where the salt from the freezers had left white patches, and hung the hammock in which Vickie did her studying back in its place. Mr. Holliday paid the boys a dollar a week for keeping up the yard, and they gave the money to their mother—it didn't come amiss in a family where actual cash was so short. She let them keep half the sum Mrs. Rosen paid for her milk every Saturday, and that was more spending money than most boys had. They often made a few extra quarters by cutting grass for other people, or by distributing handbills. Even the disagreeable Mrs. Jackson next door had remarked over the fence to Mrs. Harris: "I do believe Bert and Del are going to be industrious. They must have got it from you, Grandma."

The day came on very hot, and when the twins got back from the Roadmaster's yard, they both lay down on Grandmother's lounge and went to sleep. After dinner they had a rare opportunity; the Roadmaster himself appeared at the front door and invited them to go up to the next town with him on his railroad velocipede. That was great fun: the velocipede always whizzed along so fast on the bright rails, the gasoline engine puffing; and grasshoppers jumped up out of the sage-brush and hit you in the face like sling-shot bullets. Sometimes the wheels cut in two a lazy snake who was sunning himself on the track, and the twins always hoped it was a rattler and felt they had done a good work.

The boys got back from their trip with Mr. Holliday late in the afternoon. The house was cool and quiet. Their mother had taken Ronald and Hughie down town with her, and Vickie was off somewhere. Grandmother was not in her room, and the kitchen was empty. The boys went out to the back porch to pump a drink. The coal-shed door was open, and inside, on a low stool, sat Mrs. Harris beside her cat. Bert and Del didn't stop to get a drink; they felt ashamed that they had gone off for a gay ride and forgotten Blue Boy. They sat down on a big lump of coal beside Mrs. Harris. They would never have known that this miserable rumpled animal was their proud tom. Presently he went off into a spasm and began to froth at the mouth.

"Oh, Gram'ma, can't you do anything?" cried Albert, struggling with his tears. "Blue Boy was such a good cat,—why has he got to suffer?"

"Everything that's alive has got to suffer," said Mrs. Harris. Albert put out his hand and caught her skirt, looking up at her beseechingly, as if to make her unsay that saying, which he only half understood. She patted his hand. She had forgot she was speaking to a little boy.

"Where's Vickie?" Adelbert asked aggrievedly. "Why don't she do something? He's part her cat."

Mrs. Harris sighed. "Vickie's got her head full of things lately; that makes people kind of heartless."

The boys resolved they would never put anything into their heads, then!

Blue Boy's fit passed, and the three sat watching their pet that no longer knew them. The twins had not seen much suffering; Grandmother had seen a great deal. Back in Tennessee, in her own neighbourhood, she was accounted a famous nurse. When any of the poor mountain people were in great distress, they always sent for Miz' Harris. Many a time she had gone into a house where five or six children were all down with scarlet fever or diphtheria, and done what she could. Many a child and many a woman she had laid out and got ready for the grave. In her primitive community the undertaker made the coffin,—he did nothing more. She had seen so much misery that she wondered herself why it hurt so to see her tom-cat die. She had taken her leave of him, and she got up from her stool. She didn't want the boys to be too much distressed.

"Now you boys must wash and put on clean shirts. Your mother will be home pretty soon. We'll leave Blue Boy; he'll likely be easier in the morning." She knew the cat would die at sundown.

After supper, when Bert looked into the coal-shed and found the cat dead, all the family were sad. Ronald cried miserably, and Hughie cried because Ronald did. Mrs. Templeton herself went out and looked into the shed, and she was sorry, too. Though she didn't like cats, she had been fond of this one.

"Hillary," she told her husband, "when you go down town tonight, tell the Mexican to come and get that cat early in the morning, before the children are up."

The Mexican had a cart and two mules, and he hauled away tin cans and refuse to a gully out in the sage-brush.

Mrs. Harris gave Victoria an indignant glance when she heard this, and turned back to the kitchen. All evening she was gloomy and silent. She refused to read aloud, and the twins took Ronald and went mournfully out to play under the electric light. Later, when they had said good-night to their parents in the parlour and were on their way upstairs, Mrs. Harris followed them into the kitchen, shut the door behind her, and said indignantly:

"Air you two boys going to let that Mexican take Blue Boy and throw him onto some trash-pile?"

The sleepy boys were frightened at the anger and bitterness in her tone. They stood still and looked up at her, while she went on:

"You git up early in the morning, and I'll put him in a sack, and one of you take a spade and go to that crooked old willer tree that grows just where the sand creek turns off the road, and you dig a little grave for Blue Boy, an' bury him right."

They had seldom seen such resentment in their grandmother. Albert's throat choked up, he rubbed the tears away with his fist.

"Yes'm, Gram'ma, we will, we will," he gulped.

VII

Only Mrs. Harris saw the boys go out next morning. She slipped a bread-and-butter sandwich into the hand of each, but she said nothing, and they said nothing.

The boys did not get home until their parents were ready to leave the table. Mrs. Templeton made no fuss, but told them to sit down and eat their breakfast. When they had finished, she said commandingly:

"Now you march into my room." That was where she heard explanations and administered punishment. When she whipped them, she did it thoroughly.

She followed them and shut the door.

"Now, what were you boys doing this morning?"

"We went off to bury Blue Boy."

"Why didn't you tell me you were going?"

They looked down at their toes, but said nothing. Their mother studied their mournful faces, and her overbearing expression softened.

"The next time you get up and go off anywhere, you come and tell me beforehand, do you understand?"

"Yes'm."

She opened the door, motioned them out, and went with them into the parlour. "I'm sorry about your cat, boys," she said. "That's why I don't like to have cats around; they're always getting sick and dying. Now run along and play. Maybe you'd like to have a circus in the back yard this afternoon? And we'll all come."

The twins ran out in a joyful frame of mind. Their grandmother had been mistaken; their mother wasn't indifferent about Blue Boy, she was sorry. Now everything was all right, and they could make a circus ring.

They knew their grandmother got put out about strange things, anyhow. A few months ago it was because their mother hadn't asked one of the visiting preachers who came to the church conference to stay with them. There was no place for the preacher to sleep except on the folding lounge in the parlour, and no place for him to wash—he would have been very uncomfortable, and so would all the household. But Mrs. Harris was terribly upset that there should be a conference in the town, and they not keeping a preacher! She was quite bitter about it.

The twins called in the neighbour boys, and they made a ring in the back yard, around their turning-bar. Their mother came to the show and paid admission, bringing Mrs. Rosen and Grandma Harris. Mrs. Rosen thought if all the children in the neighbourhood were to be howling and running in a circle in the Templetons' back yard, she might as well be there, too, for she would have no peace at home.

After the dog races and the Indian fight were over, Mrs. Templeton took Mrs. Rosen into the house to revive her with cake and lemonade. The parlour was cool and dusky. Mrs. Rosen was glad to get into it after sitting on a wooden bench in the sun. Grandmother stayed in the parlour with them, which was unusual. Mrs. Rosen sat waving a palm-leaf fan,—she felt the heat very much, because she wore her stays so tight—while Victoria went to make the lemonade.

"De circuses are not so good, widout Vickie to manage them, Grandma," she said.

"No'm. The boys complain right smart about losing Vickie from their plays. She's at her books all the time now. I don't know what's got into the child."

"If she wants to go to college, she must prepare herself, Grandma. I am agreeably surprised in her. I didn't think she'd stick to it."

Mrs. Templeton came in with a tray of tumblers and the glass pitcher all frosted over. Mrs. Rosen wistfully admired her neighbour's tall figure and good carriage; she was wearing no corsets at all today under her flowered organdie afternoon dress, Mrs. Rosen had noticed, and yet she could carry herself so smooth and straight,—after having had so many children, too! Mrs. Rosen was envious, but she gave credit where credit was due.

When Mrs. Templeton brought in the cake, Mrs. Rosen was still talking to Grandmother about Vickie's studying. Mrs. Templeton shrugged carelessly.

"There's such a thing as overdoing it, Mrs. Rosen," she observed as she poured the lemonade. "Vickie's very apt to run to extremes."

"But, my dear lady, she can hardly be too extreme in dis matter. If she is to take a competitive examination with girls from much better schools than ours, she will have to do better than the others, or fail; no two ways about it. We must encourage her."

Mrs. Templeton bridled a little. "I'm sure I don't interfere with her studying, Mrs. Rosen. I don't see where she got this notion, but I let her alone."

Mrs. Rosen accepted a second piece of chocolate cake. "And what do you think about it, Grandma?"

Mrs. Harris smiled politely. "None of our people, or Mr. Templeton's either, ever went to college. I expect it is all on account of the young gentleman who was here last summer."

Mrs. Rosen laughed and lifted her eyebrows. "Something very personal in Vickie's admiration for Professor Chalmers we think, Grandma? A very sudden interest in de sciences, I should say!"

Mrs. Templeton shrugged. "You're mistaken, Mrs. Rosen. There ain't a particle of romance in Vickie."

"But there are several kinds of romance, Mrs. Templeton. She may not have your kind."

"Yes'm, that's so," said Mrs. Harris in a low, grateful voice. She thought that a hard word Victoria had said of Vickie.

"I didn't see a thing in that Professor Chalmers, myself," Victoria remarked. "He was a gawky kind of fellow, and never had a thing to say in company. Did you think he amounted to much?"

"Oh, widout doubt Doctor Chalmers is a very scholarly man. A great many brilliant scholars are widout de social graces, you know." When Mrs. Rosen, from a much wider experience, corrected her neighbour, she did so somewhat playfully, as if insisting upon something Victoria capriciously chose to ignore.

At this point old Mrs. Harris put her hands on the arms of the chair in preparation to rise. "If you ladies will excuse me, I think I will go and lie down a little before supper." She rose and went heavily out on her felt soles. She never really lay down in the afternoon, but she dozed in her own black rocker. Mrs. Rosen and Victoria sat chatting about Professor Chalmers and his boys.

Last summer the young professor had come to Skyline with four of his students from the University of Michigan, and had stayed three months, digging for fossils out in the sand-hills. Vickie had spent a great many mornings at their camp. They lived at the town hotel, and drove out to their camp every day in a light spring-wagon. Vickie used to wait for them at the edge of the town, in front of the Roadmaster's house, and when the spring-wagon came rattling along, the boys would call: "There's our girl!" slow the horses, and give her a hand up. They said she was their mascot, and were very jolly with her. They had a splendid summer,—found a great bed of fossil elephant bones, where a whole herd must once have perished. Later on they came upon the bones of a new kind of elephant, scarcely larger than a pig. They were greatly excited about their finds, and so was Vickie. That was why they liked her. It was they who told her about a memorial scholarship at Ann Arbor, which was open to any girl from Colorado.

VIII

In August Vickie went down to Denver to take her examinations. Mr. Holliday, the Roadmaster, got her a pass, and arranged that she should stay with the family of one of his passenger conductors.

For three days she wrote examination papers along with other contestants, in one of the Denver high schools, proctored by a teacher. Her father had given her five dollars for incidental expenses, and she came home with a box of mineral specimens for the twins, a singing top for Ronald, and a toy burro for Hughie.

Then began days of suspense that stretched into weeks. Vickie went to the post-office every morning, opened her father's combination box, and looked over the letters, long before he got down town,—always hoping there might be a letter from Ann Arbor. The night mail came in at six, and after supper she hurried to the post-office and waited about until the shutter at the general-delivery window was drawn back, a signal that the mail had all been "distributed." While the tedious process of distribution was going on, she usually withdrew from the office, full of joking men and cigar smoke, and walked up and down under the big cottonwood trees that overhung the side street. When the crowd of men began to come out, then she knew the mail-bags were empty, and she went in to get whatever letters were in the Templeton box and take them home.

After two weeks went by, she grew downhearted. Her young professor, she knew, was in England for his vacation. There would be no one at the University of Michigan who was interested in her fate. Perhaps the fortunate contestant had already been notified of her success. She never asked herself, as she walked up and down under the cottonwoods on those summer nights, what she would do if she didn't get the scholarship. There was no alternative. If she didn't get it, then everything was over.

During the weeks when she lived only to go to the post-office, she managed to cut her finger and get ink into the cut. As a result, she had a badly infected hand and had to carry it in a sling. When she walked her nightly beat under the cottonwoods, it was a kind of comfort to feel that finger throb; it was companionship, made her case more complete.

The strange thing was that one morning a letter came, addressed to Miss Victoria Templeton; in a long envelope such as her father called "legal size," with *"University of Michigan"* in the upper left-hand corner. When Vickie took it from the box, such a wave of fright and weakness went through her that she could scarcely get out of the post-office. She hid the letter under her striped blazer and went a weak, uncertain trail down the sidewalk under the big trees. Without seeing anything or knowing what road she took, she got to the Roadmaster's green yard and her hammock, where she always felt not on the earth, yet of it.

Three hours later, when Mrs. Rosen was just tasting one of those clear soups upon which the Templetons thought she wasted so much pains and good meat, Vickie walked in at the kitchen door and said in a low but somewhat unnatural voice:

"Mrs. Rosen, I got the scholarship."

Mrs. Rosen looked up at her sharply, then pushed the soup back to a cooler part of the stove.

"What is dis you say, Vickie? You have heard from de University?"

"Yes'm. I got the letter this morning." She produced it from under her blazer.

Mrs. Rosen had been cutting noodles. She took Vickie's face in two hot, plump hands that were still floury, and looked at her intently. "Is dat true, Vickie? No mistake? I am delighted—and surprised! Yes, surprised. Den you will *be* something, you won't just sit on de front porch." She squeezed the girl's round, good-natured cheeks, as if she could mould them into something definite then and there. "Now you must stay for lunch and tell us all about it. Go in and announce yourself to Mr. Rosen."

Mr. Rosen had come home for lunch and was sitting, a book in his hand, in a corner of the darkened front parlour where a flood of yellow sun streamed in under the dark green blind. He smiled his friendly smile at Vickie and waved her to a seat, making her understand that he wanted to finish his paragraph. The dark engraving of the pointed cypresses and the Roman tomb was on the wall just behind him.

Mrs. Rosen came into the back parlour, which was the dining-room, and began taking things out of the silver-drawer to lay a place for their visitor. She spoke to her husband rapidly in German.

He put down his book, came over, and took Vickie's hand.

"Is it true, Vickie? Did you really win the scholarship?"

"Yes, sir."

He stood looking down at her through his kind, remote smile,—a smile in the eyes, that seemed to come up through layers and layers of something—gentle doubts, kindly reservations.

"Why do you want to go to college, Vickie?" he asked playfully.

"To learn," she said with surprise.

"But why do you want to learn? What do you want to do with it?"

"I don't know. Nothing, I guess."

"Then what do you want it for?"

"I don't know. I just want it."

For some reason Vickie's voice broke there. She had been terribly strung up all morning, lying in the hammock with her eyes tight shut. She had not been home at all, she had wanted to take her letter to the Rosens first. And now one of the gentlest men she knew made her choke by something strange and presageful in his voice.

"Then if you want it without any purpose at all, you will not be disappointed." Mr. Rosen wished to distract her and help her to keep back the tears. "Listen: a great man once said: *'Le but n'est rien; le chemin, c'est tout.'* That means: The end is nothing, the road is all.[9] Let me write it down for you and give you your first French lesson."

He went to the desk with its big silver inkwell, where he and his wife wrote so many letters in several languages, and inscribed the sentence on a sheet of purple paper, in his delicately shaded foreign script, signing under it a name: *J. Michelet.*[10] He brought it back and shook it before Vickie's eyes. "There, keep it to remember me by. Slip it into the envelope with your college credentials,—that is a good place for it." From his deliberate smile and the twitch of one eyebrow, Vickie knew he meant her to take it along as an antidote, a corrective for whatever colleges might do to her. But she had always known that Mr. Rosen was wiser than professors.

Mrs. Rosen was frowning, she thought that sentence a bad precept to give any Templeton. Moreover, she always promptly called her husband back to earth when he soared a little; though it was exactly for this transcendental quality of mind that she reverenced him in her heart, and thought him so much finer than any of his successful brothers.

"Luncheon is served," she said in the crisp tone that put people in their places. "And Miss Vickie, you are to eat your tomatoes with an oil dressing, as we do. If you are going off into the world, it is quite time you learn to like things that are everywhere accepted."

Vickie said: "Yes'm," and slipped into the chair Mr. Rosen had placed for her. Today she didn't care what she ate, though ordinarily she thought a French dressing tasted a good deal like castor oil.

IX

Vickie was to discover that nothing comes easily in this world. Next day she got a letter from one of the jolly students of Professor Chalmers's party, who was watching over her case in his chief's absence. He told her the scholarship meant admission to the freshman class without further examinations, and two hundred dollars toward her expenses; she would have to bring along about three hundred more to put her through the year.

She took this letter to her father's office. Seated in his revolving desk-chair, Mr. Templeton read it over several times and looked embarrassed.

"I'm sorry, daughter," he said at last, "but really, just now, I couldn't spare that much. Not this year. I expect next year will be better for us."

"But the scholarship is for this year, Father. It wouldn't count next year. I just have to go in September."

"I really ain't got it, daughter." He spoke, oh so kindly! He had lovely manners with his daughter and his wife. "It's just all I can do to keep the store bills paid up. I'm away behind with Mr. Rosen's bill. Couldn't you study here this winter and get along about as fast? It isn't that I wouldn't like to let you have the money if I had it. And with young children, I can't let my life insurance go."

Vickie didn't say anything more. She took her letter and wandered down Main Street with it, leaving young Mr. Templeton to a very bad half-hour.

At dinner Vickie was silent, but everyone could see she had been crying. Mr. Templeton told *Uncle Remus* stories to keep up the family morale and make the giggly twins laugh. Mrs. Templeton glanced covertly at her daughter from time to time. She was sometimes a little afraid of Vickie, who seemed to her to have a hard streak. If it were a love-affair that the girl was crying about, that would be so much more natural—and more hopeful!

At two o'clock Mrs. Templeton went to the Afternoon Euchre Club, the twins were to have another ride with the Roadmaster on his velocipede, the little boys took their nap on their mother's bed. The house was empty and quiet. Vickie felt an aversion for the hammock under the cottonwoods where she had been betrayed into such bright hopes. She lay down on her grandmother's lounge in the cluttered play-room and turned her face to the wall.

When Mrs. Harris came in for her rest and began to wash her face at the tin basin, Vickie got up. She wanted to be alone. Mrs. Harris came over to her while she was still sitting on the edge of the lounge.

"What's the matter, Vickie child?" She put her hand on her grand-daughter's shoulder, but Vickie shrank away. Young misery is like that, sometimes.

"Nothing. Except that I can't go to college after all. Papa can't let me have the money."

Mrs. Harris settled herself on the faded cushions of her rocker. "How much is it? Tell me about it, Vickie. Nobody's around."

Vickie told her what the conditions were, briefly and dryly, as if she were talking to an enemy. Everyone was an enemy; all society was against her. She told her grandmother the facts and then went upstairs, refusing to be comforted.

Mrs. Harris saw her disappear through the kitchen door, and then sat looking at the door, her face grave, her eyes stern and sad. A poor factory-made piece of joiner's work seldom has to bear a look of such intense, accusing sorrow; as if that flimsy pretence of "grained" yellow pine were the door shut against all young aspiration.

X

Mrs. Harris had decided to speak to Mr. Templeton, but opportunities for seeing him alone were not frequent. She watched out of the kitchen window, and when she next saw him go into the barn to fork down hay for his horse, she threw an apron over her head and followed him. She waylaid him as he came down from the hayloft.

"Hillary, I want to see you about Vickie. I was wondering if you could lay hand on any of the money you got for the sale of my house back home."

Mr. Templeton was nervous. He began brushing his trousers with a little whisk-broom he kept there, hanging on a nail.

"Why, no'm, Mrs. Harris. I couldn't just conveniently call in any of it right now. You know we had to use part of it to get moved up here from the mines."

"I know. But I thought if there was any left you could get at, we could let Vickie have it. A body'd like to help the child."

"I'd like to, powerful well, Mrs. Harris. I would, indeedy. But I'm afraid I can't manage it right now. The fellers I've loaned to can't pay up this year. Maybe next year—" He was like a little boy trying to escape a scolding, though he had never had a nagging word from Mrs. Harris.

She looked downcast, but said nothing.

"It's all right, Mrs. Harris," he took on his brisk business tone and hung up the brush. "The money's perfectly safe. It's well invested."

Invested; that was a word men always held over women, Mrs. Harris thought, and it always meant they could have none of their own money. She sighed deeply.

"Well, if that's the way it is—" She turned away and went back to the house on her flat heelless slippers, just in time; Victoria was at that moment coming out to the kitchen with Hughie.

"Ma," she said, "can the little boy play out here, while I go down town?"

XI

For the next few days Mrs. Harris was very sombre, and she was not well. Several times in the kitchen she was seized with what she called giddy spells, and Mandy had to help her to a chair and give her a little brandy.

"Don't you say nothin', Mandy," she warned the girl. But Mandy knew enough for that.

Mrs. Harris scarcely noticed how her strength was failing, because she had so much on her mind. She was very proud, and she wanted to do something that was hard for her to do. The difficulty was to catch Mrs. Rosen alone.

On the afternoon when Victoria went to her weekly euchre, the old lady beckoned Mandy and told her to run across the alley and fetch Mrs. Rosen for a minute.

Mrs. Rosen was packing her trunk, but she came at once. Grandmother awaited her in her chair in the play-room.

"I take it very kindly of you to come, Mrs. Rosen. I'm afraid it's warm in here. Won't you have a fan?" She extended the palm leaf she was holding.

"Keep it yourself, Grandma. You are not looking very well. Do you feel badly, Grandma Harris?" She took the old lady's hand and looked at her anxiously.

"Oh, no, ma'am! I'm as well as usual. The heat wears on me a little, maybe. Have you seen Vickie lately, Mrs. Rosen?"

"Vickie? No. She hasn't run in for several days. These young people are full of their own affairs, you know."

"I expect she's backward about seeing you, now that she's so discouraged."

"Discouraged? Why, didn't the child get her scholarship after all?"

"Yes'm, she did. But they write her she has to bring more money to help her out; three hundred dollars. Mr. Templeton can't raise it just now. We had so much sickness in that mountain town before we moved up here, he got behind. Pore Vickie's downhearted."

"Oh, that is too bad! I expect you've been fretting over it, and that is why you don't look like yourself. Now what can we do about it?"

Mrs. Harris sighed and shook her head. "Vickie's trying to muster courage to go around to her father's friends and borrow from one and another. But we ain't been here long,—it ain't like we had old friends here. I hate to have the child do it."

Mrs. Rosen looked perplexed. "I'm sure Mr. Rosen would help her. He takes a great interest in Vickie."

"I thought maybe he could see his way to. That's why I sent Mandy to fetch you."

"That was right, Grandma. Now let me think." Mrs. Rosen put up her plump red-brown hand and leaned her chin upon it. "Day after tomorrow I am going to run on to Chicago for my niece's wedding." She saw her old friend's face fall. "Oh, I shan't be gone long; ten days, perhaps. I will speak to Mr. Rosen tonight, and if Vickie goes to him after I am off his hands, I'm sure he will help her."

Mrs. Harris looked up at her with solemn gratitude. "Vickie ain't the kind of girl would forget anything like that, Mrs. Rosen. Nor I wouldn't forget it."

Mrs. Rosen patted her arm. "Grandma Harris," she exclaimed, "I will just ask Mr. Rosen to do it for you! You know I care more about the old folks than the young. If I take this worry off your mind, I shall go away to the wedding with a light heart. Now dismiss it. I am sure Mr. Rosen can arrange this himself for you, and

Vickie won't have to go about to these people here, and our gossipy neighbours will never be the wiser." Mrs. Rosen poured this out in her quick, authoritative tone, converting her *th*'s into *d*'s, as she did when she was excited.

Mrs. Harris's red-brown eyes slowly filled with tears,—Mrs. Rosen had never seen that happen before. But she simply said, with quiet dignity: "Thank you, ma'am. I wouldn't have turned to nobody else."

"That means I am an old friend already, doesn't it, Grandma? And that's what I want to be. I am very jealous where Grandma Harris is concerned!" She lightly kissed the back of the purple-veined hand she had been holding, and ran home to her packing. Grandma sat looking down at her hand. How easy it was for these foreigners to say what they felt!

XII

Mrs. Harris knew she was failing. She was glad to be able to conceal it from Mrs. Rosen when that kind neighbour dashed in to kiss her good-bye on the morning of her departure for Chicago. Mrs. Templeton was, of course, present, and secrets could not be discussed. Mrs. Rosen, in her stiff little brown travelling-hat, her hands tightly gloved in brown kid, could only wink and nod to Grandmother to tell her all was well. Then she went out and climbed into the "hack" bound for the depot, which had stopped for a moment at the Templetons' gate.

Mrs. Harris was thankful that her excitable friend hadn't noticed anything unusual about her looks, and, above all, that she had made no comment. She got through the day, and that evening, thank goodness, Mr. Templeton took his wife to hear a company of strolling players sing *The Chimes of Normandy*[11] at the Opera House. He loved music, and just now he was very eager to distract and amuse Victoria. Grandma sent the twins out to play and went to bed early.

Next morning, when she joined Mandy in the kitchen, Mandy noticed something wrong.

"You set right down, Miz' Harris, an' let me git you some whisky. Deed, ma'am, you look awful poorly. You ought to tell Miss Victoria an' let her send for the doctor."

"No, Mandy, I don't want no doctor. I've seen more sickness than ever he has. Doctors can't do no more than linger you out, an' I've always prayed I wouldn't last to be a burden. You git me some whisky in hot water, and pour it on a piece of toast. I feel real empty."

That afternoon when Mrs. Harris was taking her rest, for once she lay down upon her lounge. Vickie came in, tense and excited, and stopped for a moment.

"It's all right, Grandma. Mr. Rosen is going to lend me the money. I won't have to go to anybody else. He won't ask Father to endorse my note, either. He'll just take my name." Vickie rather shouted this news at Mrs. Harris, as if the old lady were deaf, or slow of understanding. She didn't thank her; she didn't know her grandmother was in any way responsible for Mr. Rosen's offer, though at the close of their interview he had said: "We won't speak of our arrangement to anyone but your father. And I want you to mention it to the old lady Harris. I know she has been worrying about you."

Having brusquely announced her news, Vickie hurried away. There was so much to do about getting ready, she didn't know where to begin. She had no trunk and no clothes. Her winter coat, bought two years ago, was so outgrown that she couldn't get into it. All her shoes were run over at the heel and must go to the cobbler. And she had only two weeks in which to do everything! She dashed off.

Mrs. Harris sighed and closed her eyes happily. She thought with modest pride that with people like the Rosens she had always "got along nicely." It was only with the ill-bred and unclassified, like this Mrs. Jackson next door, that she had disagreeable experiences. Such folks, she told herself, had come out of nothing and knew no better. She was afraid this inquisitive woman might find her ailing and come prying round with unwelcome suggestions.

Mrs. Jackson did, indeed, call that very afternoon, with a miserable contribution of veal-loaf as an excuse (all the Templetons hated veal), but Mandy had been forewarned, and she was resourceful. She met Mrs. Jackson at the kitchen door and blocked the way.

"Sh-h-h, ma'am, Miz' Harris is asleep, havin' her nap. No'm, she ain't poorly, she's as usual. But Hughie had the colic last night when Miss Victoria was at the show, an' kep' Miz' Harris awake."

Mrs. Jackson was loath to turn back. She had really come to find out why Mrs. Rosen drove away in the depot hack yesterday morning. Except at church socials, Mrs. Jackson did not meet people in Mrs. Rosen's set.

The next day, when Mrs. Harris got up and sat on the edge of her bed, her head began to swim, and she lay down again. Mandy peeped into the play-room as soon as she came downstairs, and found the old lady still in bed. She leaned over her and whispered:

"Ain't you feelin' well, Miz' Harris?"

"No, Mandy, I'm right poorly," Mrs. Harris admitted.

"You stay where you air, ma'am. I'll git the breakfast fur the chillun, an' take the other breakfast in fur Miss Victoria an' Mr. Templeton." She hurried back to the kitchen, and Mrs. Harris went to sleep.

Immediately after breakfast Vickie dashed off about her own concerns, and the twins went to cut grass while the dew was still on it. When Mandy was taking the other breakfast into the dining-room, Mrs. Templeton came through the play-room.

"What's the matter, Ma? Are you sick?" she asked in an accusing tone.

"No, Victoria, I ain't sick. I had a little giddy spell, and I thought I'd lay still."

"You ought to be more careful what you eat, Ma. If you're going to have another bilious spell, when everything is so upset anyhow, I don't know what I'll do!" Victoria's voice broke. She hurried back into her bedroom, feeling bitterly that there was no place in that house to cry in, no spot where one could be alone, even with misery; that the house and the people in it were choking her to death.

Mrs. Harris sighed and closed her eyes. Things did seem to be upset, though she didn't know just why. Mandy, however, had her suspicions. While she waited on Mr. and Mrs. Templeton at breakfast, narrowly observing their manner toward each other and Victoria's swollen eyes and desperate expression, her suspicions grew stronger.

Instead of going to his office, Mr. Templeton went to the barn and ran out the buggy. Soon he brought out Cleveland, the black horse, with his harness on. Mandy watched from the back window. After he had hitched the horse to the buggy, he came into the kitchen to wash his hands. While he dried them on the roller towel, he said in his most business-like tone:

"I likely won't be back tonight, Mandy. I have to go out to my farm, and I'll hardly get through my business there in time to come home."

Then Mandy was sure. She had been through these times before, and at such a crisis poor Mr. Templeton was always called away on important business. When he had driven out through the alley and up the street past Mrs. Rosen's, Mandy left her dishes and went in to Mrs. Harris. She bent over and whispered low:

"Miz' Harris, I 'spect Miss Victoria's done found out she's goin' to have another baby! It looks that way. She's gone back to bed."

Mrs. Harris lifted a warning finger. "Sh-h-h!"

"Oh yes'm, I won't say nothin'. I never do."

Mrs. Harris tried to face this possibility, but her mind didn't seem strong enough—she dropped off into another doze.

All that morning Mrs. Templeton lay on her bed alone, the room darkened and a handkerchief soaked in camphor tied around her forehead. The twins had taken Ronald off to watch them cut grass, and Hughie played in the kitchen under Mandy's eye.

Now and then Victoria sat upright on the edge of the bed, beat her hands together softly and looked desperately at the ceiling, then about at those frail, confining walls. If only she could meet the situation with violence, fight it, conquer it! But there was nothing for it but stupid animal patience. She would have to go through all that again, and nobody, not even Hillary, wanted another baby,—poor as they were, and in this overcrowded house. Anyhow, she told herself, she was ashamed to have another baby, when she had a daughter old enough to go to college! She was sick of it all; sick of dragging this chain of life that never let her rest and periodically knotted and overpowered her; made her ill and hideous for months, and then dropped another baby into her arms. She had had babies enough; and there ought to be an end to such apprehensions some time before you were old and ugly.

She wanted to run away, back to Tennessee, and lead a free, gay life, as she had when she was first married. She could do a great deal more with freedom than ever Vickie could. She was still young, and she was still handsome; why must she be for ever shut up in a little cluttered house with children and fresh babies and an old woman and a stupid bound girl and a husband who wasn't very successful? Life hadn't brought her what she expected when she married Hillary Templeton; life hadn't used her right. She had tried to keep up appearances, to dress well with very little to do it on, to keep young for her husband and children. She had tried, she had tried! Mrs. Templeton buried her face in the pillow and smothered the sobs that shook the bed.

* * *

Hillary Templeton, on his drive out through the sage-brush, up into the farming country that was irrigated from the North Platte, did not feel altogether cheerful, though he whistled and sang to himself on the way. He was sorry Victoria would have to go through another time. It was awkward just now, too, when he was so short of money. But he was naturally a cheerful man, modest in his demands upon fortune, and easily diverted from unpleasant thoughts. Before Cleveland had travelled half the eighteen miles to the farm, his master was already looking forward to a visit with his tenants, an old German couple who were fond of him because he never pushed them in a hard year—so far, all the years had been hard—and he sometimes brought them bananas and such delicacies from town.

Mrs. Heyse would open her best preserves for him, he knew, and kill a chicken, and tonight he would have a clean bed in her spare room. She always put a vase of flowers in his room when he stayed overnight with them, and that pleased him very much. He felt like a youth out there, and forgot all the bills he had somehow to meet, and the loans he had made and couldn't collect. The Heyses kept bees and raised turkeys, and had honeysuckle vines running over the front porch. He loved all those things. Mr. Templeton touched Cleveland with the whip, and as they sped along into the grass country, sang softly:

"Old Jesse was a gem'man,
Way down in Tennessee."

XIII

Mandy had to manage the house herself that day, and she was not at all sorry. There wasn't a great deal of variety in her life, and she felt very important taking Mrs. Harris's place, giving the children their dinner, and carrying a plate of milk toast to Mrs. Templeton. She was worried about Mrs. Harris, however, and remarked to the children at noon that she thought somebody ought to "set" with their grandma. Vickie wasn't home for dinner. She had her father's office to herself for the day and was making the most of it, writing a long letter to Professor Chalmers. Mr. Rosen had invited her to have dinner with him at the hotel (he boarded there when his wife was away), and that was a great honour.

When Mandy said someone ought to be with the old lady, Bert and Del offered to take turns. Adelbert went off to rake up the grass they had been cutting all morning, and Albert sat down in the play-room. It seemed to him his grandmother looked pretty sick. He watched her while Mandy gave her toast-water with whisky in it, and thought he would like to make the room look a little nicer. While Mrs. Harris lay with her eyes closed, he hung up the caps and coats lying about, and moved away the big rocking-chair that stood by the head of Grandma's bed. There ought to be a table there, he believed, but the small tables in the house all had something on them. Upstairs, in the room where he and Adelbert and Ronald slept, there was a nice clean wooden cracker-box, on which they sat in the morning to put on their shoes and stockings. He brought this down and stood it on end at the head of Grandma's lounge, and put a clean napkin over the top of it.

She opened her eyes and smiled at him. "Could you git me a tin of fresh water, honey?"

He went to the back porch and pumped till the water ran cold. He gave it to her in a tin cup as she had asked, but he didn't think that was the right way. After she dropped back on the pillow, he fetched a glass tumbler from the cupboard, filled it, and set it on the table he had just manufactured. When Grandmother drew a red cotton handkerchief from under her pillow and wiped the moisture from her face, he ran upstairs again and got one of his Sunday-school handkerchiefs, linen ones, that Mrs. Rosen had given him and Del for Christmas. Having put this in Grandmother's hand and taken away the crumpled red one, he could think of nothing else to do—except to darken the room a little. The windows had no blinds, but flimsy cretonne curtains tied back,—not really tied, but caught back over nails driven into the sill. He loosened them and let them hang down over the bright afternoon sunlight. Then he sat down on the low sawed-off chair and gazed about, thinking that now it looked quite like a sick-room.

It was hard for a little boy to keep still. "Would you like me to read *Joe's Luck*[12] to you, Gram'ma?" he said presently.

"You might, Bertie."

He got the "boy's book" she had been reading aloud to them, and began where she had left off. Mrs. Harris liked to hear his voice, and she liked to look at him when she opened her eyes from time to time. She did not follow the story. In her mind she was repeating a passage from the second part of *Pilgrim's Progress*,[13] which she had read aloud to the children so many times; the passage where Christiana and her band come to the arbor on the Hill of Difficulty: *"Then said Mercy, how sweet is rest to them that labour."*

At about four o'clock Adelbert came home, hot and sweaty from raking. He said he had got in the grass and taken it to their cow, and if Bert was reading, he guessed he'd like to listen. He dragged the wooden rocking-chair up close to Grandma's bed and curled up in it.

Grandmother was perfectly happy. She and the twins were about the same age; they had in common all the realest and truest things.

The years between them and her, it seemed to Mrs. Harris, were full of trouble and unimportant. The twins and Ronald and Hughie were important. She opened her eyes.

"Where is Hughie?" she asked.

"I guess he's asleep. Mother took him into her bed."

"And Ronald?"

"He's upstairs with Mandy. There ain't nobody in the kitchen now."

"Then you might git me a fresh drink, Del."

"Yes'm, Gram'ma." He tiptoed out to the pump in his brown canvas sneakers.

When Vickie came home at five o'clock, she went to her mother's room, but the door was locked—a thing she couldn't remember ever happening before. She went into the play-room,—old Mrs. Harris was asleep, with one of the twins on guard, and he held up a warning finger. She went into the kitchen. Mandy was making biscuits, and Ronald was helping her to cut them out.

"What's the matter, Mandy? Where is everybody?"

"You know your papa's away, Miss Vickie; an' your mama's got a headache, an' Miz' Harris has had a bad spell. Maybe I'll just fix supper for you an' the boys in the kitchen, so you won't all have to be runnin' through her room."

"Oh, very well," said Vickie bitterly, and she went upstairs. Wasn't it just like them all to go and get sick, when she had now only two weeks to get ready for school, and no trunk and no clothes or anything? Nobody but Mr. Rosen seemed to take the least interest, "when my whole life hangs by a thread," she told herself fiercely. What were families for, anyway?

After supper Vickie went to her father's office to read; she told Mandy to leave the kitchen door open, and when she got home she would go to bed without disturbing anybody. The twins ran out to play under the electric light with the neighbour boys for a little while, then slipped softly up the back stairs to their room. Mandy came to Mrs. Harris after the house was still.

"Kin I rub your legs fur you, Miz' Harris?"

"Thank you, Mandy. And you might get me a clean nightcap out of the press."

Mandy returned with it.

"Lawsie me! But your legs is cold, ma'am!"

"I expect it's about time, Mandy," murmured the old lady. Mandy knelt on the floor and set to work with a will. It brought the sweat out on her, and at last she sat up and wiped her face with the back of her hand.

"I can't seem to git no heat into 'em, Miz' Harris. I got a hot flat-iron on the stove; I'll wrap it in a piece of old blanket and put it to your feet. Why didn't you have the boys tell me you was cold, poor soul?"

Mrs. Harris did not answer. She thought it was probably a cold that neither Mandy nor the flat-iron could do much with. She hadn't nursed so many people back in Tennessee without coming to know certain signs.

After Mandy was gone, she fell to thinking of her blessings. Every night for years, when she said her prayers, she had prayed that she might never have a long sickness or be a burden. She dreaded the heartache and humiliation of being helpless on the hands of people who would be impatient under such a care. And now she felt certain that she was going to die tonight, without troubling anybody.

She was glad Mrs. Rosen was in Chicago. Had she been at home, she would certainly have come in, would have seen that her old neighbour was very sick, and bustled about. Her quick eye would have found out all Grandmother's little secrets: how hard her bed was, that she had no proper place to wash, and kept her comb in her pocket; that her nightgowns were patched and darned. Mrs. Rosen would have been indignant, and that would have made Victoria cross. She didn't have to see Mrs. Rosen again to know that Mrs. Rosen thought highly of her and admired her—yes, admired her. Those funny little pats and arch pleasantries had meant a great deal to Mrs. Harris.

It was a blessing that Mr. Templeton was away, too. Appearances had to be kept up when there was a man in the house; and he might have taken it into his head to send for the doctor, and stir everybody up. Now everything would be so peaceful. "*The Lord is my shepherd,*" she whispered gratefully. "Yes, Lord, I always spoiled Victoria. She was so much the prettiest. But nobody won't ever be the worse for it: Mr. Templeton will always humour her, and the children love her more than most. They'll always be good to her; she has that way with her."

Grandma fell to remembering the old place at home: what a dashing, high-spirited girl Victoria was, and how proud she had always been of her; how she used to hear her laughing and teasing out in the lilac arbour when Hillary Templeton was courting her. Toward morning all these pleasant reflections faded out. Mrs. Harris felt that she and her bed were softly sinking, through the darkness to a deeper darkness.

Old Mrs. Harris did not really die that night, but she believed she did. Mandy found her unconscious in the morning. Then there was a great stir and bustle; Victoria, and even Vickie, were startled out of their intense self-absorption. Mrs. Harris was hastily carried out of the play-room and laid in Victoria's bed, put into one of Victoria's best nightgowns. Mr. Templeton was sent for, and the doctor was sent for. The inquisitive Mrs. Jackson from next door got into the house at last,—installed herself as nurse, and no one had the courage to say her nay. But Grandmother was out of it all, never knew that she was the object of so much attention and excitement. She died a little while after Mr. Templeton got home.

Thus Mrs. Harris slipped out of the Templetons' story; but Victoria and Vickie had still to go on, to follow the long road that leads through things unguessed at and unforeseeable. When they are old, they will come closer and closer to Grandma Harris. They will think a great deal about her, and remember things they never noticed; and their lot will be more or less like hers. They will regret that they heeded her so little; but they, too, will look into the eager, unseeing eyes of young people and feel themselves alone. They will say to themselves: "I was heartless, because I was young and strong and wanted things so much. But now I know."

New Brunswick, 1931

EXPLANATORY NOTES

Bibliographical references in the notes are to "Suggestions for Further Reading," pp. xxix–xxxi.

1. The epigraph is from "Goblin Market" (1862), a poem by Christina Rossetti (1830–1894). In Cather's earlier story collection, *The Troll Garden* (1905), the Rossetti epigraph was preceded by another quotation, from Charles Kingsley (quoted in the Introduction, p. xxi).

COMING, APHRODITE!

1. *Coming, Aphrodite!:* The title, for *Smart Set* magazine, was "Coming, Eden Bower!" See Bernice Slote's appendix to *Uncle Valentine and Other Stories*, titled "Variants in 'Coming, Eden Bower!' and 'Coming, Aphrodite!' " (pp. 177–81). Sheryl L. Meyering offers a comprehensive summary of pertinent scholarship on this and all the stories included in this volume in her 1994 *Reader's Guide.*

Aphrodite: The goddess of love in Greek mythology.

2. *stages:* Horse-drawn buses.

3. *Brevoort:* A fashionable hotel in Greenwich Village, New York City.

4. *"Don Quixote":* The novel *Don Quixote* (1605) by Miguel de Cervantes (1547–1616).

5. *"The Golden Legend":* A moralistic poem (1872) based on the Faust story; the second part of a trilogy titled *Christus: A Mystery* by Henry Wadsworth Longfellow (1807–1882).

6. *Remington:* Frederic Remington (1861–1909), a painter and sculptor of Western scenes and figures.

7. *Prologue to Pagliacci: I Pagliacci* (1892), an opera by Ruggiero Leoncavallo (1858–1919).

8. *Puccini:* Giacomo Puccini (1858–1924), an immensely popular composer of operas.

9. *Something . . . both of beauty:* In Greek mythology, Actaeon saw the goddess Artemis bathing. As punishment for this intrusion on her privacy, she turned him into a stag. He was eventually attacked and killed by his own dogs.

10. *Helianthine fire:* Brilliant purifying fire of the sun.

11. *Tammany man:* A member of a corrupt controlling organization of New York City politicians.

12. *Veronese's:* Paolo Veronese (1528–1588), a Venetian painter.

13. *Garibaldi statue:* Giuseppe Garibaldi (1807–1882), an Italian patriot.

14. *C———:* Paul Cézanne (1839–1906), the great master of Post-impressionism, spent his later years in Provence in relative seclusion and could well be the model for Hedger's mentor here. Both painters spurn public success in favour of personal freedom of anonymity to express themselves.

15. *Henner:* Jean-Jacques Henner (1829–1905), a French painter of mythological and religious subjects.

16. *Ouida:* The pseudonym of Marie Louise de la Ramée (1839–1908), a British author of sentimental romance novels.

17. *"Sapho"* and *"Mademoiselle de Maupin":* French novels of illicit romances: *Sapho* (1884) by Alphonse Daudet and *Mademoiselle de Maupin* (1835) by Théophile Gautier.

18. *Coney Island:* An amusement park in Brooklyn, by the ocean, for the general public. See John F. Kasson's *Amusing the Million* for a discussion of this setting's importance in turn-of-the-century America.

19. *Coming, Aphrodite! . . . Paris:* The opera *Aphrodite* by Camille Erlanger (1863–1919) was first produced by the Opéra-Comique in Paris in 1906. Louise Wasserman suggests Eden Bower is loosely modeled on the figure of Mary Garden, the Scottish-American diva who played the title role (p. 38). Mary Garden discusses the controversial role at some length in her autobiography (pp. 97–99).

20. *chef d'orchestre:* Conductor (French).

21. *Cerro de Pasco:* A boomtown in the mining district of central Peru.

22. *"Arrêtez, Alphonse. Attendez moi":* "Stop, Alphonse. Wait for me" (French).

23. Completion place/date added in 1937 edition: New York, 1920.

THE DIAMOND MINE

1. *meerschaum:* White claylike mineral used for making tobacco pipes.

2. *facial neuralgia:* Severe sinus trouble.

3. *auto da fé:* Here the phrase means simply "punishment," but it refers more literally to the brief ceremony following the sentencing of heretics by the Spanish Inquisition (established in the fifteenth century).

4. *la sainte Asie:* Possibly a reference to Jerusalem, which is often referred to in French as *la Jérusalem sainte* as a sign of respect.

5. *He was a vulture of the vulture race, and he had the beak of one:* Such comments persuade us that the narrator, Carrie, is anti-Semitic. The conclusion of the story, however, might complicate such simple judgments.

6. Cressida Garnet lives on Tenth Street in Greenwich Village, New York City, near Willa Cather's Bank Street apartment.

7. *"Trilby":* A novel (1894) by George du Maurier. Like Cressida, Trilby is a performer (a singer) heavily under the influence of her theatrical manager; in Trilby's case, it is Svengali.

8. *Penelope:* The wife of Odysseus; she fends off many would-be suitors during his twenty-year absence in Homer's *Odyssey*.

9. *"Manon":* Jules Massenet (1842–1912) composed his opera *Manon* in 1884.

10. *Šárka:* An opera (1897) in Czech by Zdeněk Fibich (1850–1900) that is set in Bohemia in pagan times.

11. *"Dans les ombres des fôrets tristes":* "In the shadows of the sorrowful forests" (French).

12. *"Mais, certainement!":* "But, of course" (French).

13. *"Des gâteaux . . . New York?":* "Such cakes . . . where can they be found in New York?" (French).

14. *"Austrichienne? Je ne pense pas.":* "An Austrian woman? I think not" (French).

15. Bouchalka has little respect for the immensely successful Italian composer Giacomo Puccini (1858–1924).

16. *à deux:* Intimate conversation, one-on-one (French).

17. *"Couleur de gloire, couleur des reines!":* "Color of glory, queenly colour!" (French).

18. *"de l'eau chaude!":* "hot water!" (French).

19. *"Voilà, voilà, tonnerre!":* A rude expletive in French that loses all meaning in English: "There, there, thunder!"

20. *Donna Anna:* Lead soprano role in Mozart's *Don Giovanni* (1787). Donna Anna is one of the many women betrayed by Don Juan.

21. *oisiveté:* Idleness, laziness (French).

22. *méprise:* Mistake (French).

23. *farouche:* Unapproachable, even rude (French).

24. *"Pour des gâteaux":* "For some cakes" (French).

25. *les colombes:* Doves (French).

26. The luxury ocean liner *Titanic*, referred to later in this paragraph as a "sea monster," sank on the night of April 14–15, 1912.

27. *Traulich und Treu . . . freut!:* The Rhine Maidens, who have been robbed of their gold from the bottom of the Rhine River, sing this lament at the end of *Das Rheingold*, Richard Wagner's opera of 1854 (performed 1869): "That which is of worth lies only in the deep; base and false is what is valued above." Wagner's text reads *treulich* (truly, faithfully), not *traulich* (familiar, intimate). See John March's discussion of this discrepancy (pp. 807–8).

28. Completion place/date added in 1937 edition: New York, 1916.

A GOLD SLIPPER

1. *senescent:* Growing old.

2. *appetent:* Uncontrolled, giving in to appetites or desires.

3. *Mr. Worldly-Wiseman:* One of Christian's temptors on his journey to the Celestial City in the prose allegory *Pilgrim's Progress*, Part I (1678), by John Bunyan (1628–1688).

4. In *What Is Art?* (1898), the Russian novelist Leo Tolstoy (1828–1910) argues that art needs to be directed toward the common man, not created and valued for its effects on the privileged few.

5. Kitty Ayrshire compares herself to the adventuresome Balkis, Queen of Sheba, who visited King Solomon (tenth century B.C.).

6. Completion place/date added in 1937 edition: Red Cloud, Nebraska, 1916.

SCANDAL

1. *Trappist:* A member of a reformed branch of the Roman Catholic Cistercian Order of monks that is noted for its strict rule of silence.

2. *Gorky's visit here:* Maksim Gorky (1868–1936) is the pen name of Aleksey Peshkov, a Russian writer of drama and fiction. Gorky came to the United States soon after the failure of the 1905 revolution but stayed less than a year.

3. *worry down:* Run down, discover, find.

4. *Waverly Place:* In Greenwich Village, an area of New York City.

5. *Old Testament characters:* Jewish guests in the Stein house.

6. Gulliver *among the giants:* In Part II of *Gulliver's Travels* (1726), Jonathan Swift (1667–1745) sends his main character to Brobdingnag, to record his feelings at being dwarfed by everyone around him.

7. Completion place/date added in 1937 edition: Denver, Colorado, 1916.

PAUL'S CASE

1. *belladonna:* A plant of the poisonous nightshade family, with purple or green bell-shaped blossoms, whose roots and leaves yield atropine, used in a drug.

2. *Soldiers' Chorus from Faust:* The opera *Faust* (1859) by Charles Gounod (1818–1893).

3. *Raffaëlli's gay studies:* Jean-François Raffaëlli (1850–1924), a minor French painter (of Italian descent) of the Impressionist school who specialized in cityscapes of Paris.

4. *Rico:* Martin Rico (1835–1908), a Spanish landscape painter heavily influenced by the French Barbizon school of landscape painting, which sought a new directness of observation of nature.

5. *Augustus Caesar* and *Venus of Milo:* Copies of famous sculptures from the Roman and Hellenic periods respectively.

6. *hauteur:* Haughtiness (French).

7. *Genius in the bottle found by the Arab fisherman:* This reference is to Scheherazade's stories of Aladdin, Ali Baba, and Sinbad in *A Thousand and One Nights*; her storytelling for 1,001 nights delayed her death sentence and eventually saved her life.

8. *cash boys:* Office clerks who delivered messages and ran errands for others.

9. *a sleep and a forgetting:* In "Ode: Intimations of Immortality from Recollections of Early Childhood" (1807), Part VII, William Wordsworth (1770–1850) describes birth with this phrase.

10. *Martha:* An opera (1847) by Baron Friedrich von Flotow (1812–1883).

11. *Rigoletto:* An opera (1851) by Giuseppe Verdi (1813–1901).

12. Completion place/date added in 1937 edition: Pittsburgh, 1904.

A WAGNER MATINÉE

1. *Franz-Joseph-Land:* Franz Josef Land, islands north of the Arctic Circle; part of Russia.

2. *Green Mountains:* In Vermont.

3. *dug-out:* Settlers on the Great Plains in the 1860s and 1870s created these cavelike dwellings in the absence of wood for cabins. Built into mounds of soil, these sod dwellings provided good insulation against the harsh winters.

4. *Euryanthe:* A romantic opera (1823) by Carl Maria von Weber (1786–1826) about seduction and betrayal.

5. *Huguenots: Les Huguenots* (1836), an opera by Giacomo Meyerbeer (1791–1864).

6. *The Flying Dutchman:* An opera (1841) by Richard Wagner (1813–1883).

7. *the granite Rameses in a museum:* Ramses (or Rameses) was the name shared by eleven kings of ancient Egypt.

8. *Tannhäuser:* An opera (1845) by Wagner.

9. *Tristan and Isolde:* An opera (1859, performed 1865) by Wagner.

10. *silent upon her peak in Darien:* A recasting of the last line of the sonnet "On First Looking into Chapman's Homer" by John Keats (1795–1821): "Silent, upon a peak in Darien."

11. *"Prize Song":* Part of the finale to Wagner's opera *Die Meistersinger von Nürnberg* (1867).

12. *chorus at Bayreuth:* Wagner and his wife, Cosima, moved to this small Bavarian town in 1870 and opened a theater that produced his most famous works, *Der Ring des Nibelungen.*

13. *Trovatore: Il Trovatore*, an opera (1852) by Giuseppe Verdi (1813–1901).

14. Completion place/date added in 1937 edition: Pittsburgh, 1903.

THE SCULPTOR'S FUNERAL

1. *G.A.R.:* The Grand Army of the Republic—an organization for Union veterans of the Civil War.

2. *palm leaf:* Symbol of honors, particularly bestowed by the French. See James Woodress's note in his edition of *The Troll Garden*, p. 125, as well as John March, p. 564.

3. *"Rogers group":* Plaster cast of a popular sculpture by John Rogers (1829–1904). The very American subject depicts two characters from Henry Wadsworth Longfellow's *The Courtship of Miles Standish* (1858).

4. *smilax*: A prickly vine; greenbrier.

5. *clover-green Brussels*: A carpet.

6. *gallows*: Suspenders.

7. *looked upon the wine when it was red*: The phraseology of the King James Version of the Bible offers a euphemism for alcoholic excess, to be avoided by the godly: "Look not thou upon the wine when it is red, when it giveth his colour in the cup, when it moveth itself aright. At the last it biteth like a serpent, and stingeth like an adder" —Proverbs 23 : 31–32.

8. *dyspepsia*: Indigestion.

9. Completion place/date added in 1937 edition: Pittsburgh, 1903.

"A DEATH IN THE DESERT"

1. "*A Death in the Desert*": Title of a poem by Robert Browning (1812–1889), included in his collection *Dramatis Personae* (1864). The speaker is John of the Book of Revelation, awaiting his death.

2. *Exposition at Chicago*: World Columbian Exposition of 1892–93.

3. *Proserpine*: In Roman mythology, Proserpine is the daughter of Ceres and the wife of Pluto, god of the underworld. In the spring and summer she is on the earth, and the world blossoms in her presence. In fall and winter vegetation fades as she joins her husband in the underworld. Ryder, Thurin, and Meyering offer commentary on Cather's use of the Proserpine (Persephone in Greek mythology) figure throughout her stories.

4. *traditional Camille entrance*: Giuseppe Verdi's opera *La Traviata*

(1853) is a retelling of Alexandre Dumas's (*fils*) 1852 novel *Camille*. In both versions, the frail heroine slowly dies of consumption.

5. *"Florentine Nights"*: A fragment of a novel (1837) by the German Romanticist Heinrich Heine (1797–1856).

6. *"and in the book we read no more that night"*: These words from Dante's *The Divine Comedy* (Inferno, 5.138) are one of several famous literary farewells echoed in this story.

7. *"For ever and for ever, farewell"*: Brutus parts with Cassius with these words in William Shakespeare's *Julius Caesar* (5.1.117–19).

PETER

1. Willa Cather's first published story (1892), this tale is retold as a story-within-a-story in *My Ántonia* (1918).

2. *the dreariest part of southwestern Nebraska*: Cather grew up in Webster County and Red Cloud in this section of Nebraska.

3. *Rachel played*: The celebrated actress Elizabeth Félix (1820–1858) used the name Mademoiselle Rachel in her years with the Comédie-Française.

4. Franz Liszt (1811–1886) was a Hungarian concert pianist as well as a composer. He and his wife, the Comtesse d'Agoult, had three children, one of whom—Cosima—married Richard Wagner.

5. *French woman . . . weeks*: The actress Sarah Bernhardt (1844–1923) toured with Victorien Sardou's play *Tosca* after its great success in Paris in 1887.

6. *"Pater noster, qui in coelum est"*: Peter's version of the Lord's Prayer—"all the Latin he had ever known"—is Willa Cather's own translation, not church Latin. As used in the Roman Catholic Church, the Latin prayer begins *Pater noster, qui es in coelis*. See Donald Sutherland's discussion of this phrasing in his essay "Willa Cather: The Classical Voice."

THE PROFILE

1. *Second Empire*: The reign of Napoleon III in France, 1852–71.

2. *Triboulet, Quasimodo, Gwynplaine*: Fictional characters with physical deformities, all drawn from the works of Victor Hugo (1802–1885).

3. *Huns and Iroquois*: The Huns were a nomadic Central Asian

people who gained control over much of central and Eastern Europe under Attila about A.D. 450. The Iroquois were an American Indian confederacy, originally of New York.

4. *abattoir*: Slaughterhouse (French).

5. *Madame R——* and *her great Semitic rival*: Two figures of the stage in France. The celebrated actress Elizabeth Félix (1820–1858) used the name Mademoiselle Rachel in her years with the Comédie-Française; the second actress is Sarah Bernhardt (1844–1923).

6. *his stripes were healed*: This phrasing echoes the rhythms of the King James Version of Isaiah 53 : 5, which foretells of the trials of the Messiah: "But he was wounded for our transgressions, he was bruised for our iniquities: the chastisement of our peace was upon him; and with his stripes we are healed."

7. *the expiator of his mountain race*: Continuing the allusion to Christ, Aaron Dunlap, the artist from West Virginia, is described as one who atones for the sins of others.

8. *Olympe*: A painting of a reclining nude by the French painter Édouard Manet (1832–1883).

9. *pension*: Inexpensive hotel.

10. *fêtes*: Celebratory parties.

THE ENCHANTED BLUFF

1. *freshets*: New and usually temporary streams formed from a swollen, overflowing river.

2. *seine-fishing*: Fishing with nets.

3. *Golden Days for Boys and Girls* was a magazine published from 1880 to 1907 in Philadelphia.

4. *big red rock*: The Enchanted Mesa of Cather's novel *The Professor's House* (1925) is prefigured in this specific reference.

THE JOY OF NELLY DEANE

1. *Queen Esther* (1689) is a tragic play by Jean Racine, written originally for a production by French schoolgirls. The plot is drawn from the Old Testament story of Esther and Ahasuerus in the Book of Esther. Richard Giannone offers direct points of comparison between the biblical Esther and Nelly (p. 47) and suggests an even more likely

adaptation of the material than Racine's: the American composer William B. Bradbury's 1856 oratorio *Esther, the Beautiful Queen.*

2. *three patient dressers*: Susan Rosowski (p. 147) and Mary Ruth Ryder (pp. 85–88) see Mrs. Dow, Mrs. Freeze, and Mrs. Spinny as clear incarnations of the Greek Fates, the Moirai.

3. "*The Ninety and Nine*": The first words in Elizabeth Cecelia Douglass Clephane's hymn "The Lost Sheep" (1868).

4. *chromo of Hagar and Ishmael*: A chromolithograph is a print made by using inked stones in the lithographic process. The subjects of the print are the bondswoman and the son of Abraham, both cast out into the desert after the birth of Isaac, Abraham's son by Sarah (Genesis 21 : 14).

5. *isinglass*: Semitransparent whitish gel hardened into sheets and used like panes of glass.

BEHIND THE SINGER TOWER

1. *arrack*: An alcoholic beverage, from the Far East, that includes coconut and palm juices.

2. "racial characteristics"—a euphemistic reference to Jewishness.

3. *a gang of twenty dagos*: Hallet prefers to get his training as an architect from the bottom up, beginning with the crew of Italian day labourers who are putting in the foundations of the new hotel.

4. *Ischia*: An island in the Tyrrhenian Sea; near Naples, Italy.

5. *Buono soldato*: Good soldier (Italian).

6. *'È necessario, signore . . . ma, perchè?'* Protesting at first that he must return home, as he has promised his mother, Caesarino is calmed by Hallet's presence, and finally simply questions his own needless death as he asks, "but why?"

7. *guineas*: An insulting term for "Italians."

8. *Moloch*: Title of "king" in the ancient Canaanite kingdom.

OLD MRS. HARRIS

1. *velocipedes*: Early forms of self-propelled cycles, bicycles, and railroad handcars.

2. *the bound girl*: A family servant virtually adopted, rather than hired, for lifelong service. See John March's discussion of the Cather

family's "bound girl" Marjorie Anderson, upon whom the character Mandy is clearly based (pp. 456–58).

3. *Tom Sawyer*: *The Adventures of Tom Sawyer*, a novel (1876) by Mark Twain (1835–1910).

4. *Waverley Novels*: Begun in 1814, this was a series of romantic novels, written in English, by the Scottish novelist and poet Sir Walter Scott (1771–1832).

5. *Wilhelm Meister*: A novel (1796) of character development by Johann Wolfgang von Goethe (1749–1832).

6. *Faust*: A play by Goethe (Part I, 1808; Part II, 1832) of the figure Georg Faust, who risked his soul for the reward of great knowledge.

7. *a new cloak of the sleeveless dolman type*: A Turkish-style cape, with holes for the arms and open in front.

8. *Rigoletto*: An opera (1851) by Giuseppe Verdi (1813–1901), set in Renaissance Italy.

9. *Le but . . . the road is all*: In several works, Cather attributes this phrase to Michelet, but the exact source is uncertain. See the discussion of the quotation in John March (pp. 487–88).

10. Jules Michelet, a French historian (1798–1874).

11. *The Chimes of Normandy*: A very popular light opera by Jean-Robert Planquette (1848–1903), first performed in Paris as *Les Cloches de Corneville* in 1877.

12. *Joe's Luck*: A novel by Horatio Alger, Jr., which was written in 1877, serialized in 1878, and published as part of the Boys' Home Libraries series in 1888.

13. *Pilgrim's Progress*: A Christian allegory (Part I, 1678; Part II, 1684) by John Bunyan. The passage quoted echoes the words of the Book of Revelation (14 : 13).

FOR THE BEST IN PAPERBACKS, LOOK FOR THE 

In every corner of the world, on every subject under the sun, Penguin represents quality and variety—the very best in publishing today.

For complete information about books available from Penguin—including Puffins, Penguin Classics, and Arkana—and how to order them, write to us at the appropriate address below. Please note that for copyright reasons the selection of books varies from country to country.

In the United Kingdom: Please write to *Dept. JC, Penguin Books Ltd, FREEPOST, West Drayton, Middlesex UB7 0BR.*

If you have any difficulty in obtaining a title, please send your order with the correct money, plus ten percent for postage and packaging, to *P.O. Box No. 11, West Drayton, Middlesex UB7 0BR*

In the United States: Please write to *Consumer Sales, Penguin USA, P.O. Box 999, Dept. 17109, Bergenfield, New Jersey 07621-0120.* VISA and MasterCard holders call 1-800-253-6476 to order all Penguin titles

In Canada: Please write to *Penguin Books Canada Ltd, 10 Alcorn Avenue, Suite 300, Toronto, Ontario M4V 3B2*

In Australia: Please write to *Penguin Books Australia Ltd, P.O. Box 257, Ringwood, Victoria 3134*

In New Zealand: Please write to *Penguin Books (NZ) Ltd, Private Bag 102902, North Shore Mail Centre, Auckland 10*

In India: Please write to *Penguin Books India Pvt Ltd, 706 Eros Apartments, 56 Nehru Place, New Delhi 110 019*

In the Netherlands: Please write to *Penguin Books Netherlands bv, Postbus 3507, NL-1001 AH Amsterdam*

In Germany: Please write to *Penguin Books Deutschland GmbH, Metzlerstrasse 26, 60594 Frankfurt am Main*

In Spain: Please write to *Penguin Books S.A., Bravo Murillo 19, 1° B, 28015 Madrid*

In Italy: Please write to *Penguin Italia s.r.l., Via Felice Casati 20, I-20124 Milano*

In France: Please write to *Penguin France S. A., 17 rue Lejeune, F–31000 Toulouse*

In Japan: Please write to *Penguin Books Japan, Ishikiribashi Building, 2–5–4, Suido, Bunkyo-ku, Tokyo 112*

In Greece: Please write to *Penguin Hellas Ltd, Dimocritou 3, GR–106 71 Athens*

In South Africa: Please write to *Longman Penguin Southern Africa (Pty) Ltd, Private Bag X08, Bertsham 2013*